KNOT YOUR VICTIM

Other Books by Ember Blaze:

The Secrect Pack Trilogy

Hide or Die
Fight or Fly
Truth or Lie

The Packverse

All for Knot: Book One
All for Knot: Book Two
Knot for Sale

Knot Playing Fair

Knot Playing Fair: Book One
Knot Playing Fair: Book Two
Knot Your Victim

KNOT YOUR VICTIM

EMBER BLAZE

Author's Note

Knot Your Victim is a human omegaverse romance where the main character doesn't have to pick one person in the end. It features protective alphas and the omegas who love them, but no shifters. The series contains steamy LGBT content, and is intended for a mature audience.

Table of Contents

One 1
Two 15
Three 23
Four. 33
Five. 41
Six 51
Seven 61
Eight 71
Nine 79
Ten 89
Eleven 97
Twelve 107
Thirteen 115
Fourteen 123
Fifteen 133
Sixteen 147
Seventeen 155
Eighteen 163
Nineteen 171
Twenty 181
Twenty-One 189
Twenty-Two 199
Twenty-Three 207
Twenty-Four 217
Twenty-Five 225
Twenty-Six 237
Twenty-Seven 247
Twenty-Eight 255
Twenty-Nine 263
Thirty 273
Thirty-One 281
Thirty-Two 289
Thirty-Three 297
Thirty-Four 309
Thirty-Five 321
Thirty-Six 331
Thirty-Seven 341
Thirty-Eight 351

Thirty-Nine 359
Forty 369
Forty-One 379
Forty-Two 387
Forty-Three 397
Forty-Four 407
Forty-Five 417
Forty-Six 425
Forty-Seven 433
Forty-Eight 441
Forty-Nine 449
Fifty 457
Fifty-One 469
Fifty-Two 479
Fifty-Three 487
Fifty-Four 497
Fifty-Five 509
Fifty-Six 515
Fifty-Seven 527
Fifty-Eight 535
Fifty-Nine 545
Sixty 557
Sixty-One 567
Sixty-Two 575
Sixty-Three 585
Sixty-Four 591
Sixty-Five 599
Epilogue 607
Second Epilogue 617

ONE

Jezebel

MY FIRST THOUGHT after sitting down next to my target at the posh hotel bar was that it would be a whole lot easier to murder this asshole if he didn't smell so damned good.

"Hi," I said, sipping my glass of Coca Cola disguised as something alcoholic. "Is it okay if I sit here?"

Seriously, this was one of the many, many downsides of being an omega. There was no freaking universe where my gut reaction to Mr. Sex Trafficker should have been, *'Holy crap… this six-and-a-half-foot-tall alpha in his slick designer suit smells like home.'*

I didn't mean that in some kind of woo-woo emotional way, either. The cloud of cedar-and-campfire pheromones surrounding my latest mark literally took my mind back to the Ontario forests of my childhood, where I'd spent camping trips with my mother and brothers before everything in my life went so terribly wrong.

The alpha glanced at me, then did a double-take as his nostrils flared, taking in my sweet caramel latte scent. In an instant, his regard sharpened until he was looking at me properly.

"Go right ahead," he said. "Can I get you another drink?"

I smiled my sweetest good-girl smile, taking in the subtle dilation of his pupils in the bar's warm lighting. "Sure, that would be great. Rum and Coke, please. My name's Kit, by the way."

It was for tonight, at least. Jezebel was *way* too memorable for a job like this.

"Nice to meet you. My friends call me Knox." Mr. Sex Trafficker dragged his gaze away from me with what appeared to be some difficulty, flagging down the bartender. "A Rum and Coke for the lady. Put it on my tab."

I berated myself silently when I found I was staring at him as avidly as he'd been staring at me a moment ago. As far as I was concerned, this guy was a walking corpse—nothing more. He might have soulful, deep-set brown eyes and tawny golden skin, with a sharp, well-defined jaw and expressive lips, but he was still going to be worm-food before the night was done.

I pasted on a wider smile. Death was the only fitting punishment for his crimes.

If you asked a random person on the street whether omega assassins existed, they'd probably respond with a nervous laugh and say of course not. Omegas were soft. Physically weak. Frightened of their own shadows. They didn't *kill people for money.*

And, okay—to be fair, I was pretty crap at the 'for money' part. Yes, there was usually some kind of payment involved, simply because transforming from a dirty street rat to someone who wouldn't get thrown out of a nice hotel bar like this one wasn't cheap. Fake IDs weren't free. Nice dresses and makeup and pretty shoes weren't free.

But after all the trappings were paid for, I wasn't exactly pulling in the big bucks. For me, killing alpha assholes—and getting away with it—was a passion project rather than a business.

I finished my non-alcoholic drink and accepted the Rum and Coke with murmured thanks, grasping it with satin-gloved fingers. Fingers that wouldn't leave prints.

"So, what brings you to Chicago?" I asked, playing dumb. I knew perfectly well that Matthew Knockley—Knox to his friends—was a Chi-town native who'd inherited a sprawling trade logistics empire from his old-money family. As far as what he got up to on the side…

"Oh, I was born here," he said, his arresting gaze once more focused on me. "As for why I'm in this hotel… I'm afraid it's for an incredibly boring business convention."

"Oh?" I asked, feigning interest in information I already knew about. "What kind of business convention?"

He gave a short, self-deprecating laugh. "The tedious kind. Imports and exports."

"*'Imports and exports'*? Seriously? Or, is that some kind of code for being in the mafia?" I joked, because I was constitutionally incapable of not pushing boundaries.

"I'm not so sure the mafia would have me." He gestured at himself, indicating the clear influence of his mother—who according to the dossier provided by my client, had been Black. Combined with his very un-Italian last name, he was probably right about his prospects with that particular branch of organized crime.

"Unfortunately," he went on, "I'm stuck with the tiresome parts of business, like paying taxes and not being able to murder your competitors."

Ah. Irony.

That was irony, wasn't it?

"Hmm... too bad," I told him. "That must complicate things terribly for you."

His eyes sparkled with hidden humor. "Oh, you've no idea."

Actually, I had a pretty good idea.

He glanced up at the ornate clock hanging on one wall of the bar area, and frowned. "Look... it's getting late—"

I sat up straight on the barstool, preparing to come up with some excuse for continuing our conversation. He wasn't finished, though.

"—and I don't usually do this kind of thing, but... would you like to come up to my room for a nightcap?"

Oh.

I blinked.

That had certainly been a lot easier than I'd expected.

"Only if you promise to tell me more about import and export taxation," I said, striking a vixen-ish pose and fluttering my eyelashes at him.

He laughed. I hated the fact that it was a really *nice* laugh.

"No promises."

I laughed as well, trying to make it sound as natural and seductive as possible. Grabbing my little black clutch with its incredibly important contents, I let him usher me toward the elevators with a hand hovering a few inches away from my lower back. The fact that the almost-contact didn't make my skin crawl was freaking me out a bit, if I were being honest.

I'm locked in an enclosed metal box with a predator, I thought as the doors shut us both inside. *Why don't I feel like I'm in danger?*

Mr. Sex Trafficker kept up an easy flow of conversation as the elevator went up… and *up.*

"Wow," I said, as the counter went all the way to the top floor and gave a cheerful ding. "Penthouse suite?"

He shrugged. His key card slid smoothly through the slot in the nearest door, and the lock clicked. "After you."

I'd never been in a penthouse suite before, needless to say. Making a concerted effort not to gape openly at the elegant décor and clean, airy surroundings that were so utterly different to what I was used to, I whistled in appreciation.

"Not bad," I said, and then promptly zeroed in on the most useful thing in the room. "Ooh, a mini-bar! What can I get you?"

He loosened his tie and tossed his suit jacket over the back of a velvet-upholstered chair. "A bourbon on the rocks would be good. And help yourself to whatever."

This was perfect. For one thing, it saved me from having to faff around with convincing him to get us room service.

"One bourbon on the rocks, coming up," I replied, keeping a peripheral eye on him to make sure he wasn't watching as I snuck a couple of pills out of my clutch and dropped them into his drink.

Acepromazine in the dosage I'd scored was an industrial-strength horse tranquilizer that wasn't too difficult to get from a veterinarian — if you had horses. Which I obviously didn't. But you could get just about anything on the street if you knew the right people... which I obviously *did*.

The thing about acepromazine was that it packed a kick, but it also cleared out of the bloodstream really fast. And, even more importantly, it wasn't approved for human use. Therefore, it wasn't something that was tested for in a typical tox screening after, for instance, a suspicious death.

It also dissolved really nicely in liquid, which was handy.

"Here you go." I handed the cut-crystal tumbler to him, then turned around again to focus on making myself a Midori sour. When it was ready, I lifted it toward him in a toast. "To boring business conventions, and the things that make them *less* boring."

"I'll drink to that," he said, and suited action to word.

I hid my grim smile and lifted my own glass, taking the tiniest of sips.

———◆———

The first time I'd killed a man, it had been an act of desperation carried out with a dozen of my fellow omega prisoners, when the driver of the semi that had been smuggling us south from Canada into America had stopped for fuel. He'd made the mistake of opening the trailer door to make sure none of us had frozen to death, and we'd jumped him without any sort of a plan beyond survival.

I'd been thirteen at the time.

The second time I'd killed a man, it had been… not an accident, exactly. But not planned, by any stretch. I'd walked in on some middle-aged asshole about to rape my closest friend, grabbed the nearest heavy object, and used it to cave in the fucker's skull.

Then, in a fit of combined panic and PTSD, I'd fled, leaving that friend alone with a dead body that had clearly been murdered. Needless to say, we weren't friends anymore. At least, I was pretty sure we weren't, since that had been more than a year ago, and I'd disappeared from his life without a trace rather than face the shame of having abandoned him to the tender mercies of the police.

God… I really hoped he hadn't ended up in jail.

I'd been too afraid to try and find out.

The problem was, once the panic and dissociation had worn off, I'd *enjoyed* the feeling of having removed a dangerous predator from the world. I'd enjoyed it way too much, in fact.

Living on the streets, you tended to hear about stuff. *Bad* stuff. Even so, it had been pure insanity the first time I'd decided to remove a problem in a way that was, um… *premeditated*.

The asshole in question had been grooming little kids at a local karate class and taking nude photos of them being abused. So, I'd killed him. And I hadn't gotten caught.

A couple of months later, I'd taken out a drug dealer who was whoring out his omega girlfriends—shooting them up with heat stimulants and then auctioning them to the highest bidders.

Word began to spread. People started coming to me directly with their problems. And if those problems felt like something I could fix without getting my stupid ass killed … I fixed them. Permanently.

Matthew Knockley was my sixth target, not counting those early, heat-of-the-moment kills. He was also, by far, the biggest.

When a terrified omega boy called Adrian had tracked me down and handed me Matthew

Knockley's dossier, my gut had urged me to run the other way and not look back. Not only was this asshole the leader of a respected pack with a secret sideline in human trafficking; he was fucking *rich*. Not to mention powerful and well-connected. If he died under mysterious circumstances, the police would give a shit about it. *Lots* of people would give a shit about it.

But… Adrian's story hit me squarely in the unresolved childhood trauma.

His sister had been taken. She was only eleven years old. And she wasn't the first.

I knew what kind of life awaited underage omegas sold into the sex trade. I'd almost been one of them, if not for a careless truck driver and a deserted fuel plaza in the middle of the night.

So, I'd taken the job. And now, here I was.

"Sorry," Mr. Sex Trafficker slurred, rubbing at his face with uncoordinated movements. "I feel… really tired all of the sudden."

The tumbler—mostly empty except for a bit of ice, slipped from his grasp and hit the luxurious carpet with barely a sound.

I smiled, thin and tight. "Then you should sleep," I told him. "Here, let me help you get on the bed."

I grabbed his arm and urged him onto unsteady feet, helping him stagger the few steps to the ridiculous king-sized bed. He flopped back, boneless.

"Mmm," he nearly purred. "You smell like…"

"Caramel latte?" I offered dryly.

"Heaven," he finished.

I rolled my eyes and did a quick inventory. Satin gloves? Still on. Hair? Lacquered into an impenetrable chignon that wouldn't shed any incriminating strands of DNA in the room. I dumped my barely-touched Midori sour down the bathroom sink drain, rinsing and drying the glass thoroughly before returning it to the mini bar.

When I returned to the bed with a few squares of clean toilet paper, Matthew Knockley was snoring deeply, his breathing too loud and too slow.

That much acepromazine might kill him on its own, but I wasn't the type to leave things like this to chance. Opening my clutch purse, I pulled out the empty 10cc syringe hidden there and sat at the foot of the bed.

I removed one designer shoe from my victim's left foot, followed by his sock. Finding a vein between a person's toes was always a total pain in the ass, but this trick only worked if it got directly into the victim's bloodstream. Patiently, I delivered ten syringes' worth of air into Mr. Sex Trafficker's circulatory system, taking care to go in through the same needle hole each time.

When I was done, I wiped the blood from the needle, capped it, and returned it to my clutch. I'd toss it in a dumpster somewhere far from here, where it would disappear among all the other drug paraphernalia. Then I pressed the wad of toilet paper hard to the injection site to staunch the tiny amount of blood seeping there.

The area would still bruise, but so far, no medical examiner had gone looking for toe bruising after what seemed like nothing more sinister than a garden-variety heart attack.

Being a successful business owner in the competitive world of trade logistics was probably a stressful career, right? That kind of shit catches up to a person eventually.

Knockley made an awful choking noise and jerked on the bed. Apparently, the air embolism had reached his lungs or his heart. I checked that his foot had stopped bleeding and wrestled his sock and shoe back on. I'd just flushed the blood-spotted toilet paper and was reaching for my clutch on the bedside table when a knock sounded at the door.

I froze.

"Oi, Knox!" called a voice with a faint Irish lilt, muffled by the thick door. "We just got some juicy gossip about the Mexico deal. You gotta hear this!"

I whirled around, my stupid brain seizing up. Should I try to hide? Open the door, dart past them, and make a run for it?

But I was too slow. The lock clicked. Whoever it was, they had a key card, and like an idiot, I hadn't thought to engage the security latch once my target was down for the count. I was still standing there like a surprised statue when the door swung open to reveal two alphas—one with flaming red hair and a beard, the other an absolute mountain of a man with a black buzzcut and heavy five o'clock shadow.

"Sorry, I know it's late, old man—" Red Hair began, only to cut himself off abruptly as he took in his friend having a violent seizure on the bed, and me standing there like the world's guiltiest hotel hookup. "What the *fuck*?"

"Knox!" shouted the giant, rushing forward.

I raised a hand, as though to fend him off.

"Call an ambulance!" I cried, thinking fast. "I… he just collapsed out of the blue! I think he might be having a heart attack!"

It was at that moment when the scents of whiskey and oakwood combined with baking bread and orange peel slammed into me like a freight train, swirling together with Knockley's woodsy campfire aroma and my own sweet coffee and caramel. The suggestion of *belonging* that had struck me earlier multiplied a hundredfold, blotting out every single thought in my head as a switch as old as time itself flipped in the depths of my hindbrain.

Everyone in the room went as still as though we'd been fossilized in amber.

Coffee laced with whiskey and sweetness, holiday bread toasted over an open flame as the sounds and scents of the forest wove around the four of us.

'Home… home… home…' echoed through my consciousness, tolling like a bell.

Oh, my god.

A scent match. It was a *scent match.*

I was scent-matched to alpha slave traffickers… and I'd just murdered their pack leader.

TWO

Jez

THE RED-HAIRED alpha was the first to break free of his paralysis. "*Fuck!*" he snarled, fumbling a phone from his pocket. "Gage! Check his pulse and start CPR!"

The presence of two angry alphas held me frozen in place under the weight of the distant past. On top of that, the overwhelming miasma of pheromones, soured by adrenaline and fear, was making my head swim.

A *scent match*? It couldn't be! Not here, not now, not like *this*.

I had to get away. Christ, why hadn't I engaged the security latch on the damned door when I had the chance? Of course, then I'd still be trapped... but at least there would be something separating me from Mr. Sex Trafficker's packmates.

I tried to sidle unobtrusively toward the door. Surely, they wouldn't chase me while they were so worried about their pack alpha?

"Oh, no you don't!" snapped Red Hair.

He took two long steps and grabbed me by the wrist, fast as a snake. I yelped in shock, trying to jerk free even as my arm tingled through my long glove at the heat of his touch. It was like jerking against an iron manacle.

"Hello?" he said into the cell phone. "I need police and an ambulance to the penthouse suite at the Aurora Hotel downtown! Male alpha, thirty-two years old, possible heart attack—he's undergoing CPR. *Get here fast.*"

With that, he shoved the phone back in his pocket and rounded on me with his teeth bared. "Now, who the hell are you? What happened— what did you do to him?"

I shrank back. "Let me go! I—I'm just a hookup, all right? We were having a drink and he collapsed!"

I had to get out of here. I started struggling again, aiming a kick at my captor. It bounced off. He didn't even *flinch*. Instead, a low growl rumbled in his chest.

"*Stop.*" It wasn't loud, but the power of an alpha bark behind the single word was unmistakable.

I subsided with a frightened whimper, going still except for the tremor in my arms and legs.

"You're scaring her, Heath." The other alpha sounded out of breath. Had my captor called him Gage earlier?

"Goddamn *right* I'm scaring her." Red Hair—*Heath*—gave me a sharp shake. "Knox does not *do* hookups, Gage. You know that as well as I do!"

"Maybe he does hookups with our scent match!" Gage panted, pumping his hands down rhythmically on Mr. Sex Trafficker's chest with rough, almost violent motions.

"*No.*" Heath grabbed my little clutch purse, not letting go of me as he dumped the contents onto the dresser. "I don't trust her. She smells guilty."

"Maybe she's just scared—" Gage began.

"Yes!" I said quickly, my heart rabbiting. "I don't even know this guy! And now you're keeping me here against my will!"

"No phone," Heath said in a monotone. "This ID's fake, or I'm the fuckin' pope. Bit of cash. And then there's *this*."

He held up the empty syringe.

"I-it's mine," I managed. "I have a drug problem, okay?"

He set it down and shoved one of my long gloves back, baring my forearm. Then he repeated the action with the other, turning my arms up to inspect the unblemished skin even as I tried to twist away.

"No," he said. "You don't. What the hell did you inject him with, woman?"

"Nothing!" I protested.

"*Tell me!*" he barked in my face.

I cringed back. "*Nothing*," I repeated hoarsely, because it was mostly the truth. The syringe had been empty. "We were just having a drink!"

But it was the wrong thing to say. Green eyes the color of the forest in summer scanned the room, fixating on the upended glass next to Knox's chair. The sad remains of a couple of ice cubes sat in the last dregs of watered-down bourbon that hadn't spilled out.

Holy shit. I hadn't cleaned up the tumbler with the acepromazine dissolved in it.

I'd only washed and dried my own glass.

"Having a drink," Heath echoed. He dragged me over and picked up the tumbler, careful not to spill any more of the contents. "So, if this was his glass, where's yours?"

"I... wasn't thirsty," I told him, knowing how lame it sounded.

"Horse shit," he growled. "What would the police find if they tested this?"

"Nothing!" I protested. "Bourbon, that's all!"

He threw me down in the chair and held the glass up threateningly. "Just bourbon, eh? Fine, then—why don't you drink what's left here. Come on, down the hatch."

I couldn't help it. I shrank back, not sure how much of the powerful drug had sunk to the bottom of the tumbler.

"What the hell are you doing, Heath?" Gage puffed, not breaking rhythm as he labored over the twitching body on the bed. "Knock it off!"

"She's guilty as sin," Heath hissed, his forest-colored eyes boring into mine. "If Knox dies, you're going to spend the rest of your miserable life in a prison cell, you murdering bitch."

The panic that had been thrumming through me since the two alphas burst in tightened around my ribs like a steel band. I couldn't go to prison... I couldn't be trapped inside four bare walls with bodies all around me in the dark, like the inside of the semi-trailer that had almost delivered me into a life of sexual slavery.

My breathing rasped and stuttered, a sick counterpoint to the weak wheezing coming from the bed.

"Dude, you can't turn her over to the police," Gage said sharply. "She's our scent match!"

I choked, trying not to think what the alternative might entail.

The callused hand gripping my wrist tightened painfully. "She may have just killed Knox!"

Gage huffed. "I know, but…" He hesitated, then just repeated, *She's our scent match.* His voice was softer this time.

Heath glared down at me with bared teeth. I blinked up at him, mute with fear.

Seconds stretched.

"You want to walk out of here not wearing handcuffs?" he demanded aggressively. "You tell me exactly what happened to Knox. Right the fuck *now.*"

My mouth opened, no sound coming out. What would be worse? To get hauled off by the police, or end up at the mercy of this pack?

The phantom prison cell loomed, cold and claustrophobic. I knew Heath would never let me go free… but if I took my chances with him and Gage, maybe I could escape. It felt like more of a chance than I'd have if I was handcuffed and surrounded by armed cops as a murder suspect.

I licked dry lips, trying to bring some moisture to my mouth.

"Acepromazine," I whispered. "And then I injected air into his veins."

Heath cursed sharply.

"Why?" Gage asked, sounding confused.

"Because he's evil," I croaked. "You're all *evil.*"

Gage exchanged a look with his packmate. His expression was bewildered.

"Maybe she's mentally ill?" he said, after a short pause.

I sneered at him… not because he was necessarily wrong, but because if I was, it was alphas like him who'd made me this way.

"Get her out of here," Heath grated out, dragging me up from the chair. "If you're still dead set on this. I'll take over with Knox until the ambulance gets here." He bent over and dragged me close, until we were eye to eye. "And believe me, lass—If Knox does die, I can make you *wish* you were sitting in a courtroom facing murder charges."

I shuddered, not doubting it. I was just going to have to get away somehow before that happened.

"Oh," he added, his tone deadly. "One more thing." He dragged off one of my gloves and grabbed my hand, forcing my bare fingers around Knox's tumbler—pressing my sweaty fingerprints onto the glass. "Insurance," he said grimly. "In case I change my mind and decide to throw you to the legal system's wolves later on."

My lips peeled back in an involuntary growl. He shoved my hand and arm into the glove. Then he pushed the syringe, cash, and fake ID back in my clutch and thrust it at me. I grabbed it and stumbled as he pulled me over to the bed.

I couldn't help looking down at Knox's face, a waxen blue-gray beneath his tawny skin. Gage slid off the mattress where he'd been pumping his pack leader's heart, smoothly grabbing me as Heath handed me off and took his place.

The smell of orange peel and warm bread wove around me like a drug. Gage herded me over and picked up his discarded jacket from where he'd thrown it. Then my breath caught as he pulled out a little snub-nosed revolver and jammed it against my ribs, using the jacket draped over his arm to cover it from view.

"C'mon," he said. "We're going. I don't wanna hurt you, but I can't let you get away, either." He glanced over his shoulder at the pair on the bed. "Take care of him, yeah? He's tough; I know he's gonna make it."

Heath only grunted, not looking up from his task of keeping Knox's heart pumping.

The gun in my side poked me harder, and I gritted my teeth as I was marched to the door of the suite, and into the hallway beyond.

THREE

Jez

I WOULD WAIT UNTIL we got to the lobby and scream bloody murder, I decided. There was no question that I had to get away from this towering alpha who smelled like my mother's kitchen at Christmas, whether he had a gun pointed at me or not.

I couldn't let him get me into a car. Once I was in a car, everything would be harder.

Yes, it was late at night—but the hotel was hosting a business conference. There had to be some people still wandering around, and I didn't think Gage would be willing to blow a hole through my ribcage in a public venue with witnesses.

The elevator doors dinged shut, closing us in. I'd chastised myself for not being afraid enough, when I'd been riding this elevator up to the penthouse with Matthew Knoxley. This time, I knew better. Yet even now, the rich, heady combination of our combined phero-mones was making my head feel fuzzy and stupid.

Apparently, Gage wasn't having the same problem. The gun never wavered against my side as he pulled out his phone and tapped the screen with his thumb a few times before lifting it to his ear.

"Hey," he said. "It's me. Bring the car around. I'll be there in five, with a passenger."

I couldn't hear the voice on the other end as anything more than an unintelligible murmur, but Gage said, "Thanks," and disconnected the call. The phone disappeared back into his pocket, and then his full attention was on me. With every fiber of my being, I hated the sharp-edged impulse that zinged through my hind-brain—urging me to tip my head away from those deep-set hazel eyes and bare the side of my throat to him.

My jaw clenched. The *fuck* was I going to show throat to this asshole.

As the floor numbers counted down, I silently urged the car to stop, and other people to get on. But it continued to glide smoothly downward. There was only one set of doors on the top floor, and it occurred to me that the penthouse suite might have its own dedicated elevator.

As we approached the ground floor, Gage's brow furrowed.

"You're thinking about making a scene in the lobby," he said. "But unless you've changed your mind about taking your chances with an attempted murder charge, you should know that's not going to go down the way you think it is."

I kept my lips pressed tightly closed, not rising to his bait. The elevator slowed, gravity making our bodies heavier as the floor broke our slow-motion fall. I drew a deep lungful of air, ready to start screaming. *Help! Kidnapping! He's got a gun!*

The doors slid open on a scene of controlled chaos, and the words died in my throat. The lobby was swarming with police and EMTs.

"Call me a kidnapper, and I'll tell 'em what you did upstairs," Gage said, too low to be heard by anyone else but me.

I should do it anyway. I *knew* I should. My gaze fell on a pair of handcuffs hanging from the closest cop's belt. The memory of being shackled... of being manhandled by rough hands, unable to balance or catch myself when I was shoved, flooded through my brain like icy water. My breath stuck in my throat.

Gage's grip on my upper arm steered me through the chaos, moving me effortlessly even though my legs felt like they were attached to a completely different person.

Outside, I thought—more than a little hysterically. *Once we're outside, I'll make a run for it.*

But the glass doors opened onto a sea of flashing lights. Police cars. An ambulance. Even a firetruck. The strobing red and blue hurt my eyes. Gage's grip on me never wavered; it might as well have been shackles, because there was no way I was breaking free.

Afterimages still painted my vision as I was dragged toward a long black sedan. *No,* I thought again. *Don't get in his car —*

I aimed a mule-kick at the alpha's shin, hoping to turn the stiletto heels I was wearing into a weapon. The blow connected, but not as hard as I wanted—the high heel raked over his tailored trousers.

He didn't even flinch.

Then I was sprawled in a spacious back seat, scrabbling against leather upholstery. Gage's bulk followed, penning me in, and before I knew it, he once more had me by the upper arm, with the gun pointed at me openly now.

Confused, I looked at the front seat. It was separated from us by a glass barrier, and a driver wearing an honest-to-god chauffeur's cap sat behind the wheel. We were in a *limo*, for fuck's sake. Not a stretch limo, but definitely not a normal car.

"Help!" I shrieked, confident that the glass barrier couldn't be completely soundproofed. "*Help me*! I'm being kidnapped!"

The glass rolled down, and the beta driver craned around with an expression of confusion. "What the *fuck*, Gage?" he asked, and my heart sank.

The driver wasn't hired from an outside company. He was part of the operation.

"She tried to kill Knox," Gage said grimly. "He's the reason all these lights and sirens are blocking the front doors. I'm taking her back to the house so we can figure out who sent her."

My blood ran cold. They'd try to force my client's name out of me. Would they go after Adrian, and shut him up permanently to cover their tracks?

"He's lying!" I choked out. "Please help me!"

But the look of angry disgust on the driver's plain features was its own answer.

"How bad did she mess him up?" he asked Gage. "He gonna be okay?"

"Bad," Gage said. "And he'd *better* be okay, or I'll kill him myself."

The driver's face closed off, and he gave a tight nod. "Back to the house, then." The glass rolled up, and the car pulled smoothly away from the chaos of the hotel parking lot.

I couldn't afford to panic, even though sick terror was clawing at the inside of my chest. I had to keep my wits about me. Where were we going? I tore my attention away from the alpha holding a gun on me, trying to keep track of directions and street names as we left downtown and merged onto the highway.

God—they could be taking me *anywhere*. I never left my usual haunting grounds except when I had a job like this. If I needed to go somewhere, it was on my own two feet, or sometimes on the L, if I had money. I could only afford cabs when I had a client paying me. Once I left the tiny area of Chicago that I knew like the back of my hand, I might as well have been in Alaska.

There was nothing for it, except to try and remember, step by step, the route we were taking. But my head was muddled with fear and adrenaline, while the massive highway system seemed to merge and twist completely at random. I knew I'd missed a couple of exit signs, and at night, I couldn't even tell if we were headed north, south, east, or west.

The trip felt like it took hours, but I was pretty sure that was just my growing panic distorting the passage of time. When we ended up on a dark road with trees looming on either side in the glare of the headlights, my terror finally overflowed in a choked sob.

Were they taking me to the pack's house like Gage had said, or to someplace dark and remote where a body might not be found for weeks… or ever?

"Where are we?" I asked weakly.

"Almost there," Gage said unhelpfully.

With a pang, it occurred to me that the only person likely to miss me would be Adrian. And let's be real—he'd probably just assume that I'd taken his money and run. Or maybe there would be a news story about Matthew Knockley getting hauled away from the hotel in an ambulance, and he'd at least know I'd tried to do the job before I'd disappeared.

I was absolutely alone. I'd made a grand total of one real friend since I'd washed up in Chicago, and then I'd gone and left that friend alone in his apartment with a murdered corpse. No one was coming to save me, because literally no one on the planet even knew I needed saving.

The limo slowed and pulled onto a long, winding driveway surrounded by trees. I felt like Gretel, disappearing into the dark woods without Hansel at my side… not a single bread-crumb in sight to mark the way home.

The car came to a stop in front of a massive old house that looked like it had sat here for as long as the forest around it had. The glass rolled down again.

"Will you need the car again tonight?" asked the driver, giving me a wary look.

"No, not tonight," Gage said. "I'll let you know in the morning if there's any word from the hospital."

"Sure." The man turned unfriendly eyes on me. "Watch yourself with that one, okay?"

"Yeah," Gage agreed, and took me by the arm again.

Outside of the car, I cast a desperate look around, looking for a direction to run. But even if I managed to shake off the alpha's iron grip, there was only the dark outline of trees all around us. I wouldn't make it fifty yards without tripping and breaking an ankle in the impractical fuck-me heels I was wearing.

I was never going to leave this place alive, was I?

Swallowing hard, I tottered after my captor on the gravel driveway. The house was even bigger than I'd first thought—looming over us as I was dragged up the flagstone walkway to the massive front door.

Gage pocketed the gun and fumbled for a keyring, opening it. "Inside. I'll take you upstairs to the attic room and get you some food."

Great. So, apparently, I was going to be the crazy woman locked in the attic? A completely inappropriate urge to laugh burned up my throat like acid—proof that I was finally losing my shit completely.

"Right," I said, my voice high and wavering. "Sure. The attic."

He gave me an odd, sideways look. "It's converted. Might be kinda dusty, though."

"Dusty?" I echoed, disbelieving. "I am *so* giving this place zero stars on Yell."

His odd look grew odder. "You mean Yelp?"

"I have no idea," I said. "I don't have the internet."

"Okay," he said, like he was humoring me. "Come on. It's been a long day."

"You're telling *me*," I shot back, and let him herd me deeper into the house.

I couldn't keep track of the route to get from downtown to this property, but I could at least pay attention to the way to the front door. Maybe in daylight, I'd find out that the house wasn't in as remote an area as it seemed. At the very least, I wouldn't end up getting lost before I even got outside.

The entryway led into a hall that seemed surprisingly narrow for a house this big. Or maybe it was totally normal. Who was I kidding? It wasn't as though I had extensive experience with hundred-year-old mansions. Or *any* experience, really.

Unlike the outside, the inside looked modern. Wall sconces lit the way, but the hall was light and airy, not dark and creepy. A large room with sofas and the biggest TV I'd ever seen opened up to the right, and there were several closed doors on the left.

I jumped as one of them creaked open.

Gage paused. A young face peered out; a male omega, maybe twelve or thirteen, and so skinny that his collarbones jutted above the neck of his loose T-shirt.

Livid bruises decorated one side of his face.

Behind him, I could make out several other small figures—pressing forward, but not as bold as the child in front.

"Gage?" the kid asked in a sweet voice. It was the kind of voice that should be singing in a choir somewhere, not hidden away in an alpha sex trafficker's mansion with a black eye and a swollen jaw. "What's going on?"

"It's not anything you need to worry about," Gage said. "Promise. Try to get some sleep, okay? The van'll be here in the morning."

My gorge rose as the boy frowned. *The van.* Once again, the memory of metal walls trapping me with other small, helpless bodies washed across the reality of the house around me, blocking it out. My breathing went ragged.

"You… you have to run!" I told the child. "All of you! You have to get out of here! Don't let them put you in the van! Hide in the woods—make for the nearest busy road!"

The burning chill of bare feet in snow made me shudder, the past elbowing its way into the present like a waking nightmare. In the doorway, the boy's unbruised eye went wide and frightened. He took a hasty step back. The door slammed shut, cutting him and the others off from my view.

Leaving me alone with the alpha.

Gage's grip on my arm tightened convulsively. For the first time, real anger sparked in his gaze.

"Don't scare them like that," he growled. "What the fuck is *wrong* with you?"

FOUR

Jez

"WHAT'S WRONG WITH *ME*?" I echoed, disbelieving. "What's wrong with *you*, you sick fucker! Why the hell do you have kids with bruises all over their faces locked up in your creepy mega-mansion?"

But of course, I already knew why. I knew it all too well. It was the reason I was in this mess in the first place, after all. I just really, *really* hadn't wanted to see it in person. Was Adrian's eleven-year-old sister trapped in that room with the rest of them?

Gage's expression closed off, the anger disappearing behind a stony mask. "Nothing to do with you. And they're not locked—" He cut himself off with a sharp shake of the head, as though he'd just realized he was arguing with his prisoner. "Come on, *move*."

We passed what looked like the main staircase, and ended up at the back of the house. A second, much narrower set of stairs hugged the wall there. I had a vague notion from reading Agatha Christie novels when I was a kid that some old houses had servant stairs, presumably so the rich owners didn't have to see all the work being done to keep them pampered and comfortable.

The steep steps looked dangerous as hell, even without stiletto heels. Clenching my jaw, I followed Gage halfway up, his hand around my wrist to keep me from bolting. Then I stopped without warning, braced as best I could, and threw my whole weight backward in an attempt to engineer a hopefully fatal accident for my alpha captor.

Mind you, there was a decent chance that I'd get dragged along for the ride and end up breaking my neck as well. I just wasn't sure that was any worse than the alternative, at this point.

Gage cursed and stumbled down a step before catching himself. The gun clattered from his grip, bouncing off the stairway and falling through the banister railings. It hit the floor below with a loud metallic crash.

We both froze for an instant, but it didn't go off. Jammed onto the narrow step with my kidnapper, I snarled and tried to stomp his foot with my sharp heel. When that didn't work, I tried kicking again.

"Jesus Christ!" Gage snapped, but instead of pushing me away, he hauled me close and bent down, lifting me over his shoulder as though I weighed nothing. "You got a death wish or something, woman?"

I shrieked in frustration, trying to hit and kick. One shoe flew off as my foot hit the staircase railing, the sharp pain jolting through me. Gage carried me upstairs, grumbling—completely unfazed by my struggles. We went up two more flights, terminating in a tiny landing with a single doorway set in the wall.

Gage paused only long enough to open the door; then he squeezed through the doorway with me. Surprisingly, he managed not to knock any part of my body into the frame. On some deep level, I wondered why he'd bothered.

He tossed me down on a soft surface. I bounced, sneezing when a small cloud of dust rose around me, and scrambled upright.

It was a bed.

I tensed, but he'd already backed off, his bulk blocking the doorway. A light clicked on, illuminating the room. I whipped my head around, looking for an escape route… for anything to use as a weapon. There were no windows, but there was a second door to my right. I lunged for it, staggering with one shoe still on and the other foot bare.

The doorknob turned under my touch, opening onto a bathroom.

No windows here, either. A medicine cabinet with a mirror had been mounted over the sink. I grabbed it with both hands, trying to pull the mirror free. The little door came partway open, the hinges creaking and twisting—but the mirror didn't budge.

I let out a choked cry of frustration.

"What are you *doing*?" Gage demanded from the bathroom doorway, in the bark of an alpha who was nearing the end of his tether.

I whirled on him. "Trying to break the glass, so I can slice the biggest shard across your *fucking throat!*" I yelled.

"*Why?*" he shot back, his voice rising. "Why did you try and kill Knox? *Why are you doing this?*"

"Because of the kids downstairs!" I shouted back at him, terrified and enraged in equal measure. "The ones who are '*nothing to do with me*'! Just like I'm '*not something they need to worry about,*' apparently!"

He shook his head slowly. "You're not making any *sense*. How could you even know—" Again, he cut himself off. He dragged a hand over his face and let out a slow sigh. "Never mind. Give me your other shoe."

He held out his hand, palm up.

I knew what he was thinking—take the prisoner's shoes so she couldn't run away, in case she got loose. Slowly, I bent over with a sneer and pulled off my remaining stiletto. I straightened and stepped forward as though to hand it over. At the last moment, I hauled back and swung with all my might, aiming for his face with the pointy end.

A hand closed around my wrist before I could blink; it was like slamming my arm into a brick wall. The stiletto heel came to an abrupt stop, inches from his eye. He wrestled my arm down and twisted the shoe free of my grip without a word.

Gage stepped back, putting space between us as I stood there, barefoot and disheveled, panting hard.

"I'll bring you up some food," he said in a monotone. "And, um, some pillows and blankets and stuff, so you can make a nest."

I stared at him in disbelief.

A harsh, high-pitched bark of laughter tore free of my throat.

A nest? He was going to bring me stuff to make *a nest*? Inside the locked-up crazy-woman attic?

"Are you *shitting me* right now?" I demanded, hearing the hysterical edge return to my voice. I'd never had a nest in my entire fucking *life*. Not unless you counted cardboard and crumpled newspapers in an alley.

His face had gone hard and stony again. "I won't be long."

And then he *turned his back on me*. Feral rage bubbled up from someplace deep in my chest at his utter unconcern, moments after I'd done my best to put a knockoff Louboutin stiletto through his eye socket. I stomped after him.

"I hope your asshole of a pack alpha *dies!*" I yelled at him as he reached the door.

He froze, his broad shoulders stiffening... but he didn't turn around or say a word. Instead, he continued through the door, closing it behind him. A heavy click signified the lock engaging. I stood there, trembling with fear and frustration, until the sound of his heavy footsteps on the stairs faded.

The knob on the inside of the door was completely blank; there wasn't even a keyhole. It turned under my grip, but the door wouldn't open. There must be some kind of lock or latch on the outside, where I couldn't get to it.

I knew I should do a thorough search of the rooms, in case there was something useful hidden away. But as my adrenaline waned in the aftermath of the confrontation, it felt as though my body weighed a thousand pounds. My shaking knees didn't want to keep me upright any longer.

I staggered over to the dusty bed and half-sat, half-fell.

My gaze slid down to my bare feet. Two toes missing on the left foot, and one toe on the right.

When he'd taken my shoes, Gage had no way of knowing that I'd once walked five miles barefoot through the snow. We all had. Some of us had even survived the trek.

I wriggled the toes that hadn't succumbed to frostbite after that nightmarish flight through a winter forest. It wouldn't be a lack of shoes that stopped me from running, if I was able to slip free from my captors.

But the looming size of that '*if*' dwarfed me.

Inside my own head, I was still the badass vigilante I'd come to think of myself as being. A one-woman army, dishing out lethal justice to the evil-doers society didn't care enough to punish.

That badass vigilante would find a way out, escaping heroically with the pack of innocent kids trapped downstairs. She would lead them safely back to civilization, where Adrian would rush forward and throw his arms around his little sister, weeping with gratitude for her return.

Unfortunately, while my head might still believe those things, my heart knew better. Sometime during the course of the night, it had realized that the badass vigilante was a myth… a stupid fabrication. I wasn't an avenging assassin, utilizing my unique skillset to pass undetected while bringing much-needed justice to the oppressed.

I was a terrified twenty-one-year-old omega trapped in a remote mansion, right along with the rest of the starved and beaten omegas downstairs. In the year since I'd killed my friend's would-be rapist with a table lamp to the skull, I'd been skating by on sheer luck, not any kind of real skill.

And now, my luck had run out.

FIVE

Jez

I DIDN'T SLEEP. I didn't *dare*. As promised, Gage brought me up a pile of freshly laundered blankets and pillows, the recovered gun held securely pointed at me as he ordered me to stand where he could see me while he dumped them on the end of the bed. Then he made another trip, this time arriving with a massive double-decker sandwich, a pile of potato chips, and a bottle of orange soda balanced on a large plate.

I ignored all of it, being far too familiar with the head-games alphas played to keep captured omegas compliant... and the ease of slipping drugs into food and drink. God knew, I had plenty of personal experience with drugging people into helplessness, so I could do Very Bad Things to them afterward.

Once I was sure he wasn't going to return a third time, I started a thorough search of my two-room prison. My head swam with a combination of exhaustion and soured adrenaline, and my stomach rumbled distractingly — trying to convince me that eating *just one potato chip* would be *fine*, wouldn't it?

I went to the bathroom sink and drank tepid tap water from my cupped hands until my stomach stopped complaining so loudly. My search didn't turn up much of anything useful.

The bedroom area was large, but there was nothing in it, except the old metal-frame bed and a heavy wooden dresser.

I briefly considered trying to drag the bed frame over and use it to block the door. But that wouldn't really help me at all. There were no windows, and no tools that could be used to break through the walls or roof. That door was the only way I'd be getting out of this place.

What I needed was a weapon.

The bed frame was solidly constructed; I didn't find any metal pieces that I could break off or unscrew without a screwdriver. I briefly considered the merits of a drawer from the old dresser—but even the smallest one was heavy, and I wasn't exactly the Incredible Hulk.

Eventually, I dragged one of the drawers into the bathroom and used it to shatter the mirror that had defied my attempts earlier… only for it to break into tiny shards that were too small to be any use as a shiv.

With a frustrated cry, I hurled the drawer at the bathroom wall. It caught the piece of molding at the corner of the shower area, where the wall jutted out. Wood splintered with a sharp crack. I stared listlessly at the damage, willing my brain to stop spinning uselessly inside my skull.

The thin piece of molding had split where the edge of the drawer had snagged it, the top half of the broken piece pulling slightly away from the wall. I frowned, moving closer to look.

Small nails stuck out of the separated length, looking tiny and delicate.

I reached out and grasped the molding between two of the nails, bending it up and back until a section broke off in my hand with a snap. The split end tapered to a wicked point, following the wood grain. I touched my thumb to it—splinter-sharp.

It was flimsy, but I wasn't going to find a better stabbing weapon in here.

I couldn't get the finishing nails out of the molding, but a few minutes of pressing them hard against the edge of the porcelain sink at least left them bent and flattened against the wood. The pointy end was sharp enough to pierce a hole in one of the pillowcases. I stuck two fingers through the gap and ripped off a wide strip of the luxurious cotton fabric. Wrapping that several times around the blunt end of the wooden spar made a serviceable handle.

Feeling a bit better prepared than I had before, I shoved the plate of food under the bed with the dust bunnies, where I wouldn't have to look at it. Then I had a *'duh'* moment, pulled it back out, and tipped the contents under the bed. It was heavy dining wear, not the disposable paper kind. I could throw it at someone and maybe slow them down, at least.

I propped the pillow with the torn case against the bed's headboard, shoved the makeshift knife and the plate behind it, and settled in to wait, keeping my bleary eyes firmly fixed on the door.

Hours passed. An engine rumbled up to the house. Something big and old, I thought. Not a modern car. It was the van that Gage had mentioned, I was willing to bet. My empty stomach roiled.

Gritting my teeth, I tried not to think about the omega kid with the bruised face being loaded onto it… about Adrian's eleven-year-old sister being shoved in after him. The urge to jump up and try the attic door nagged at me. It was stupid, though. I'd already struggled with that damned door half a dozen times during the night. It hadn't magically unlocked itself during the last hour.

The engine idled outside for maybe ten or fifteen minutes before pulling away. The omegas were gone, and with them, my crazy delusion of somehow engineering a heroic rescue.

My jaw clenched tighter.

More time slid by, slow and sticky like molasses.

I could barely make out the smooth purr of the next vehicle to arrive. Omegas didn't like windows as a rule; we wanted things dark and enclosed. But right now, I could understand what betas saw in them. A window or three would have been super useful, and not just as a potential escape route.

Heavy footsteps approached up the stairs—two people, this time. I tensed, easing the handle of my shiv out from behind the pillow, where it would be hidden from view by my thigh, but I could grab it easily.

I didn't take the plate out, or get off the bed. I doubted I'd be able to overpower two alphas on my best day, much less when I felt like I was about to pass out from lack of sleep. If they came too close to me, though, someone was getting splinters in the most vulnerable area I could reach.

A knock sounded on the door.

"It's me," came Gage's muffled voice. "I've got the gun. Stand where I can see you. You know the drill."

A second voice grumbled something, too low to make out. I ignored the 'stand' part, staying right where I was on the bed. The lock outside clicked. The door swung inward, revealing Gage with the gun pointed at me, and the red-haired alpha—Heath?—standing behind him on the landing.

Gage came in, frowning.

"You didn't use the nesting stuff," he said, sounding almost… disappointed?

"Fuck you," I told him. "How's your precious pack leader?"

Heath stalked inside, radiating crackling anger. I made a subtle move to wrap my fingers around the shiv handle, hating the way my instincts tried to uncurl as the scent of whiskey and baking bread swirled around the room in a cloud.

"None of your goddamned business," Heath snapped. He stretched out a hand toward Gage, palm up. "Now, give me that gun. I'm getting some answers."

My heart thudded into a panicked, uneven rhythm as Gage wordlessly handed over the small pistol. My hand clenched convulsively around my pathetic shiv as he strode forward, stopping out of arm's reach and pointing it at my heart.

There was no way I could spring up and stab him before he pulled the trigger. I froze in place, unable to move.

"Tell me your name," Heath said.

My lips worked soundlessly for a couple of seconds before my brain connected.

"K-Kit," I stammered, frantically trying to remember the name on the fake ID I'd been carrying. "I mean… Katherine, uh, Katherine Christenson."

"Bullshit." Heath thumbed the safety off. The barrel of the gun moved smoothly downward, pointing at my right knee.

My vision swam. I'd seen the aftermath of a kid getting kneecapped, a couple of years ago when I'd stumbled onto the scene of a gang retribution.

"Try again," Heath said, his tone dangerously flat. "What's your *real* name?"

"It really is Katherine Christenson!" I squeaked, fighting my freeze response. The need to sink through the mattress and the floor below was like a living thing, squirming in my stomach.

"Sure," Heath gritted out. "And I'm the fuckin' Keebler Elf. Who sent you after Knox?"

The final words cracked across me like a whip—an alpha bark. The urge to spit out Adrian's name was almost overwhelming. I clamped my teeth around it, only my freeze response keeping the word from slipping free. Trembling, I stared up at the alpha looming over me with what I hoped was defiance, but was probably just abject fear.

Heath snarled and pulled the trigger. I screamed and braced for agony as the explosion of noise deafened me.

None came.

A little puff of smoke rose from a blackened hole in the mattress, a few inches away from my leg. The smell of gunpowder joined the confusing cocktail of pheromones in the room.

"What the *fuck*, Heath?" Gage said, striding forward and grabbing the gun from his packmate's hand.

My ears were still ringing, but the noise of the shot had slammed me back into possession of my body. Knowing it was stupid, I lunged up from the bed, shiv in hand, and darted around Heath. Grabbing one meaty shoulder with my left hand, I jammed the point of splintered wood against the side of his neck with my right.

"Put down the gun and let me out of this house, or I'll stab this straight through his jugular and laugh while he bleeds out!" I yelled, my voice high and wavering.

Heath made an angry noise and reached up, wrapping strong fingers around my wrist and yanking the shiv away from his throat. He whirled and shoved me back onto the bed, where I went sprawling. Somehow, the shiv was now in his hand, rather than mine.

I bared my teeth at him and scrambled upright—ready to go for the plate, even though I knew it wouldn't do any good. If it gave one of them a black eye, maybe it would still be worth it.

"I told you," Gage was saying. "I think she's just mentally ill. Doesn't seem like you're gonna get anything out of her this way."

Heath was breathing hard. His forest-green gaze pinned me like a bug. "Right. Because mental cases spend their spare time making knives out of the room furnishings."

Gage shrugged. "I dunno. Maybe they do, if they're scared enough?"

Heath turned on him. "And what do *you* suggest we do with her?"

Gage hesitated. "I mean… we can't let her go. She saw the omegas downstairs. And she might know how to find this place, I guess."

Spoiler alert—I didn't.

Heath made a noise of pure frustration. "*Wonderful.*"

"I say we keep her here until Knox gets better," Gage went on. "He'll know what to do."

So, Knox wasn't dead, then. Pity.

But Gage was still talking. "Guess we'll need to get some stuff for her, in the meantime. Clothes and things."

"'Clothes and things'?" Heath echoed in disbelief. "Did this scent match eat your fucking *brain*?"

But Gage plowed on. "Look, I know one of us has to go back to the hospital while the other stays here to watch her—but you could call that beta kid you like so much, and have him pick up stuff for her. What's his name? Tony?"

An unexpected pang shot straight through my black and shriveled heart.

Tony, the same first name as my one-time friend. The sweet guy whose life I'd probably ruined by trying to save him from his attacker. Idly, I wondered what *my* Tony would think if he could see me now.

The sad reality was that he probably wouldn't be surprised in the least that I'd ended up like this. And somehow, *that* was the thing that broke me. With a stifled whimper, I slithered off the edge of the bed and onto the floor, burying my face in my hands.

SIX

Tony Scalise

THE INSISTENT BUZZ of my phone felt like someone was stabbing me in the ear with an ice pick. I groaned awake, painfully aware of just how many drinks I'd let the cute guy at the bar last night buy me after I'd finished my guitar set.

Christ.

I hadn't even gotten laid afterward. I'd just told the adorable blond himbo that I needed the restroom, and slunk away in to the night like the coward I was.

And now someone was calling me at... I squinted at the phone screen.

Oh.

Okay, it was actually nine-thirty in the morning, so apparently normal people were actually wide awake and doing... er... *normal people stuff*. Right.

'H.,' read the caller notification under the incoming call. It was Heath Dawson, the latest in my long history of really bad decisions. Okay, so not 'normal person stuff,' after all. The temptation to pretend I'd missed the call and hide my head under my pillow until it stopped pounding out a painful drumbeat of regret was... significant.

I'd been helping out Heath's pack with informant work and various other odd jobs for a little over a year now. Along with busking and a collection of other miscellaneous gigs, it kept the bills paid. More or less.

Then, of course, I'd had to screw everything up by getting a painful schoolboy crush on the pack's flame-haired alpha lieutenant. Though honestly, that part might've been okay on its own, since he'd seemed utterly oblivious.

Until a week ago, anyway. I blamed myself for propositioning him, in a moment of courage and/or stupidity. But he didn't have to say *yes*, damn him. He didn't have to end up being the best fuck of my goddamned *life*.

He'd apparently assumed it was a one-night stand. That it was no big deal.

Now, all I could do was try to pretend that it hadn't been a big deal to me, either.

I groaned and thumbed the 'accept call' button, reminding myself firmly about the current state of my bank account. *Think about the money. Don't think about how it felt when he put his —*

No. Stop.

I cleared my throat. Ugh… why couldn't Heath use his phone for its god-given intended purpose of *texting*, rather than insisting on voice calls?

"Hello?" I greeted, trying not to sound like someone who was hungover at nine-thirty on a… whatever day this was.

"*Tony*," came the Irish drawl, sounding strained. "*I need you to pick up some things and deliver them to the house.*"

I frowned. "Okay. Is everything all right? You sound kind of—"

"*Everything is very much* not *all right.*" Heath cut me off, his tone clipped. "*I'm at Northwestern Memorial Hospital.*"

My heart kicked hard; my headache forgotten as I lunged upright in the rumpled bed. "What? Are you hurt?"

"*No, it's Knox. He's—*" He cut himself off. "*Look, it doesn't matter. I'm on the second floor of the Galter Pavilion. Meet me here, and I'll get you some cash for the purchases.*"

"Okay…" I said, aware that I was wearing yesterday's clothes, and that something small and furry had apparently died in my mouth while I was asleep.

"*Thanks,*" Heath said, and then the call disconnected.

I stared at the phone stupidly for a long moment. Then I rolled out of bed, intent on painkillers, a toothbrush, and the world's fastest shower.

◆

On the positive side, focusing on my headache was a reasonably effective way to keep from speculating on what might have happened to Knox. I'd wasted a couple of minutes on an internet search for 'Matthew Knockley hospital,' and found a handful of headlines about how he'd been rushed away from the Aurora Hotel in an ambulance.

An hour and fifteen minutes after Heath's phone call had come in, I navigated the patient parking areas outside the hospital's main campus and headed for the information desk, a greasy brown paper bag containing a fast-food breakfast sandwich and an apple pastry clutched in one hand.

The receptionist cheerfully tapped at her computer, and directed me to a bank of elevators that would take me where I needed to go. In the second-floor waiting area, I found Heath pacing restlessly at the back of the deserted rows of plastic chairs—looking like an alpha who had A) been up all night, and B) wanted rather badly to rip someone's intestines out so he could use them as a noose.

"Hi," I said cautiously, when he looked up at me with sharp green eyes. "I brought you some breakfast." Approaching, I proffered the grease-stained bag. "Would've got you a coffee, but I figured hospitals usually provide that as part of the service. How's Knox?"

Heath stared at the bag for a beat, before a slow blink dispelled some of the barely leashed rage in his gaze, replacing it with exhaustion. He took it from me with a hand that trembled slightly.

"He's in surgery," said the alpha. His voice lowered to a mutter. "*Again.*"

Fresh alarm coursed through me. I didn't know Knox all that well, since most of my dealings were with Heath. But on those few occasions when I'd interacted with him, he'd always been decent with me. Never made me feel like a stupid kid from the gutter, while he was this rich Chicago business bigwig.

"What's wrong with him?" I asked.

"Pulmonary embolism," Heath said tightly.

I nodded as though the words meant anything to me. 'Pulmonary' was something to do with the lungs, right? Whatever it was, it sounded serious.

"Well," I replied, trying to seem upbeat. "He's a strong alpha, and the doctors here are really good. I bet he'll be fine." Then, because the awkwardness of trying to have this conversation with Heath six days after I'd had his cock in my mouth was starting to get to me, I added, "So, what did you need me to buy for you?"

Heath, too, seemed to drag himself back on track. "Oh. Yes." For some reason, the change of topic brought the anger back to his expression. "Basic wardrobe and toiletries for a female, dress size four. Size six in shoes." His frown deepened. "Nothing in glass bottles — plastic only."

I blinked. "O… kay? And you want me to take it to the house, you said?"

"Yeah." Heath set the bag of food on the nearest chair and pulled out his wallet, peeling off a dozen hundred-dollar bills. "It shouldn't cost more than a thousand; she's not exactly going to the Met Gala. Keep whatever you don't spend."

There were *so many* questions here. They were questions I knew better than to ask, though. More than a year into my dealings with Knox's pack, I'd have had to be blind to miss the fact that omegas in trouble ended up coming and going through the secluded pack house like it was a bus station.

This was just the first time anyone had asked me to buy a full wardrobe for one of them.

I clamped down on any further request for clarification.

"On it," I said. "I assume someone'll be at the house to take delivery? Or should I just drop the stuff at the door?"

"Gage is there," Heath said.

"All right." I hesitated, my awkwardness rearing its head again. "I hope Knox recovers quickly."

Heath gave a single, tight nod. Taking it as dismissal, I turned and headed for the elevator bank, already mentally running down the list of big box stores that might have everything I'd need in one place.

"Tony?" Heath's voice stopped me a few steps before I turned the corner.

I looked back.

"Thanks for the food," he said quietly. "You didn't have to do that."

A stupid, self-destructive little flash of warmth glowed behind my ribcage. I tried to stomp on it, but the embers wouldn't die.

"It's nothing," I said. "Don't mention it."

A few hours later, I pulled into the long, winding driveway of the pack house with a truly alarming number of bags in the back of my old Volvo. It turned out, you could buy a *lot* of women's clothes for a cool grand, if you were bargain conscious.

My love for shopping was one of the things that my late, unlamented stepfather had hated about me. One of *many* things, admittedly… but I was pretty sure it had been near the top of the list.

I'd never had a sister — not that I would have wished my so-called family on anyone else. But I couldn't deny that having a built-in excuse to go to clothing stores and paw through the latest fashions with someone female would have been pretty amazing.

I had a sneaking suspicion that I'd be happier not knowing whatever backstory lay behind the recipient of my shopping spree spoils. But regardless, I'd kind of enjoyed it. It wasn't as though I could afford to spend that kind of money on clothes for *myself* — so this felt like the next best thing.

Whoever she was, I hope she agreed with my taste.

Buried under enough shopping to crush a pack mule, I trudged up the flagstone walkway. On the large porch, I set down the bags in my right hand, freeing it up so I could knock on the door. Less than a minute later, the locks clicked and the door opened, revealing Gage's imposing form.

"Hi," I greeted, a bit intimidated as always by the towering alpha with the dark buzzcut and perpetual scruffy stubble. "Heath sent me here to drop this stuff off? It's mostly clothing, plus some shampoo and toothpaste and things."

"Oh. Yeah. Hi, Tony," Gage said. "Come on in. Let me get some of that for you."

Between us, we dragged all of the bags inside.

"Is all this for one of your omegas?" I asked, curiosity getting the better of me.

Gage hesitated. "It's kind of complicated. Can you help me get this upstairs to the attic room? The staircase is a fuckin' deathtrap."

"Sure, but we need to work on your marketing skills," I quipped. "Try, 'the staircase is vintage—maybe you'd like to see the Victorian craftsmanship firsthand.'"

The alpha gave a derisive snort. "As long as you don't see it at high speed while tumbling down it. Come on, kid."

I let him lead me to the back of the massive old house. It was quiet—no sign of any other 'guests' at the moment. I took in the elegant furnishings, comparing them to the squalid studio apartment I was currently renting. I supposed this kind of thing was what a business empire could buy you. It still sounded like a hell of a lot of work to keep it clean and nice, though.

Gage had… not been exaggerating about the staircase. We struggled up the steep, narrow steps, some unspoken male stubbornness driving us to try and get everything up in one trip. Gage paused at the top, where a small landing faced a locked door. He pulled out a concealed pistol, checking the chamber.

"Whoa!" I took a hasty step back, nearly taking that unplanned, high-speed downward tour of the staircase that Gage had just mentioned.

"Sorry," he said. "Should've warned you. She's dangerous. Let me get her covered, then you can pile the bags inside the door."

"Wait, wait, *wait*," I said. "Who the hell *is* this omega? Why do you have a dangerous woman locked in your attic?"

Because maybe I was naïve—but this was *not* what I'd signed up for with this pack.

"She's the one who tried to kill Knox," Gage said.

I gaped at him. "Tried to… *kill*—?"

Idiot that I was, I'd assumed Knox's emergency was some kind of illness. Like… a heart attack, or something.

But Gage only nodded. "Yeah. Almost succeeded, too. But that's not the complicated part."

"It's… not?" I asked stupidly.

"Turns out, she's also our pack's scent match," Gage said, grim-faced. "Now, stay back while I get her where I can see her."

I continued to gape.

Gage knocked on the door. "It's me again. Still got the gun, so no funny business. We've got you some clothes and shit. I'm coming in."

He unlocked the padlock and swung the door open, leading with his gun. No noise came from the interior as he entered cautiously.

Despite myself, I couldn't help peering in behind him. It took me a couple of seconds to find the slight figure in a short, form-fitting dress slumped against the side of an old bed, curled forward with her face in her hands. An untouched plate of food sat next to her on the floor.

"You gotta eat something eventually, you know," Gage said, in a gentler tone than I might have expected.

The girl raised her head slowly, her hands falling to lie limp in her lap. Wavy, platinum-blond hair framed a sharp face dominated by huge, blue-gray eyes. For a split second, my brain tried to tell me that I couldn't possibly be seeing what I thought I was seeing.

Then Jez, the woman who'd killed my abusive stepfather by caving in his skull with a table lamp—and left me alone afterward to face the resulting music—met my gaze with a shocked gasp.

SEVEN

Tony

I DIDN'T EVEN feel the shopping bags slip from my numb fingers and hit the polished wooden floor. I took a hasty step back as images from the past crowded into the present. My foot slipped on a plastic bag stuffed with clothing, and I nearly tumbled down the steep stairs for the second time in less than two minutes.

"*No,*" I said, a bit desperately — then I turned and half-ran, half-fell down the staircase, clutching the intricately carved banister to keep myself upright.

The stairs seemed to telescope outward, taking me ten times as long to go down as they had to go up, even as I leapt down two and three steps at a time. The elegant, well-lit hallway on the main floor flickered in and out of my vision, the image of a damp and dingy basement bedroom superimposed over it.

My palms slapped against a heavy front door, stopping my forward momentum. I scrabbled clumsily at locks and deadbolts until I could tear it open and stagger outside, sucking in great lungfuls of humid midday air.

Even with the sun shining through patchy gray clouds overhead, I couldn't get the dark afterimages of my childhood out of my senses. Angry footfalls pacing overhead… the floorboards creaking beneath them. A door opening at the top of the stairs… a silhouetted figured stalking down, step by deliberate step. A doubled belt held between two fists, the leather snapping with a threatening *crack*.

I stumbled toward the old Volvo station wagon parked in the circle drive, with the vague plan of getting in it and driving away fast enough to outrun the memories. Maybe my legs were smarter than my brain, because they threw in the towel before I got the door open — saving me from getting behind the wheel and immediately causing an accident.

My knees buckled, and I turned as I fell in slow motion, ending up slumped against the driver's side front tire.

My heart felt like it was trying to pound its way out of the cage of my ribs. I couldn't catch my breath properly. Jez could *not* be here, in this house, more than a year after I'd last seen her.

"She's the one who tried to kill Knox," Gage had said.

Jez can't be a killer, my mind tried to tell me, despite the fact that my last memory of her involved struggling out from under the dead weight of my stepfather's corpse as she backed away, her eyes huge in her bone-white face.

Jez already *was* a killer.

She'd killed to protect me from a monster. The monster who'd followed me out of my youth, tracking me down in a new city, in my new, painstakingly built life. And then she'd run away, leaving me alone to deal with the aftermath.

I still remembered the way my hands had shaken as I unlocked my phone, scrolling down to a number that had only been added a few weeks previously.

"*Yeah?*" Heath's gruff voice had picked up on the other end.

"H-hi," I'd told him in a shaky voice. "It's, um… it's Tony Scalise. Sorry—I know I'm nobody to you. But I've been helping your pack out with some stuff lately, and… I need help. I really, *really* need your help."

By all rights, he should have hung up on me without a word. Instead, there was a long pause.

"*What kind of help?*" he'd asked, and it had been all I could do not to spill out the whole story over the phone like an idiot.

I'd bitten down hard on the torrent of words.

"Trash disposal," I'd managed, past a clenched jaw. "It's too big for me to move myself."

The memory rose up, as fresh and visceral as the day it happened.

———— ◆ ————

Half an hour after I got off the phone, a brisk knock sounded at my apartment door. I gasped, my spine jolting me straight up from my slumped huddle on the couch as fresh adrenaline sloshed through me. My first, irrational thought was that it was my stepfather, despite the fact that his disfigured corpse was cooling on the rug in front of me. Like I'd been sucked into some kind of twisted *Groundhog Day*, doomed to repeat the attack over and over.

My second, equally irrational thought was that the police had found out somehow and were here to arrest me for murder.

That was stupid—even if I'd been the one to smash in David Scalise's skull, it would have been clear self-defense. He was sexually assaulting me… I had a fucking *restraining order* against him, for Christ's sake.

A muffled Irish drawl jerked me out of my paralysis.

"Oi. You're the one who called me out to this shithole! Open the damned door."

I got up on trembling legs, skirted the disgusting sack of meat on my floor, and opened the damned door. Sharp green eyes played over me before focusing past me, inside the room. Heath Dawson's gaze caught on the dead body before I could get my tongue to cooperate well enough to form words.

"Oh," he said. "*That* kind of trash."

I let him inside and shut the door, feeling as though my arms and legs weren't properly connected to my body.

His piercing gaze fell on me again. "Self-defense?"

I debated the merits of protesting that I hadn't even been the one to kill him. Instead, I just nodded.

"My stepfather," I said hoarsely. "He's the reason I got emancipated minor status when I was fifteen. The reason I moved here, to Chicago. I... I have a restraining order."

Heath grunted. "Uh-huh. Fat lot of good *that* did you." He gave the crappy studio apartment a quick once-over before returning his attention to me. "You hurt?"

I had no idea. I thought I remembered blood in my mouth from where my tooth had cut into my cheek after his slap, and there would probably be bruises from the struggle.

"No," I said.

He huffed out a sigh and reached into his pocket, pulling out a roll of bills. "Go to a bar and don't come back until closing time. Do not get drunk. Do not talk to anyone. If someone asks, your girlfriend just dumped you."

"Boyfriend," I muttered—not that I'd ever had one, or likely ever would.

"If someone asks, your boyfriend dumped you," he corrected smoothly, pressing a couple of twenties into my hand. "You haven't seen your stepfather. You had no idea he was even in Chicago. After all, why would he be here when there's a *restraining order* against him?"

Even with my brain spinning circles, the heavy irony on the words came through. And he was right. My stupid piece of paper had done fuck-all to protect me, in the end.

"Okay," I said faintly, clutching the cash in a sweaty hand.

I went out to a bar that I'd never been to before. I bought a beer and nursed it for hours, while completely failing to listen to the succession of local bands crooning on the stage. When the place kicked me out, I went back home with no idea of what I was likely to find there.

What I found was... nothing. No corpse. No dropped pizza congealing on the floor. Just my familiar apartment, cluttered and grubby as ever, except for the new table lamp by the couch and the new rug sitting innocently on the floor, as though it had been there for years.

Several days later, a pair of police detectives showed up at my door, asking if I'd seen or heard from David Scalise recently.

"No," I said. "I haven't had contact with him for years. We're estranged because he abused me as a child. I have a restraining order against him... so, I doubt he'd show up here, if he even knows where I live now. Why do you ask? Is he in trouble or something?"

"He's been reported as a missing person," said the female detective. She handed me a card with her information on it. "If he attempts to make contact, please let us know."

"Okay," I said, and that was the last I ever heard on the matter.

Back in the present, footsteps crunched on gravel. I peered up as a tall figure loomed over me, blocking out the sunlight. A faint shiver trembled down my spine, but then Gage crouched down in front of me, a couple of steps away, his forearms resting on his bent knees.

"You know her, then?" he asked.

I blinked myself back to reality with difficulty.

Knox, in the hospital.

Jez—my former friend who'd apparently decided, after her first taste of it, that murder suited her.

"Yeah," I rasped.

"Who is she?" Gage asked.

I swallowed hard. "I… don't even know her last name. She was living on the streets, I'm pretty sure. But we busked together sometimes. We were friends."

Gage digested that before speaking again. "Kind of a funny reaction to seeing a friend."

"She… killed someone," I said reluctantly, before hurrying to clarify. "But it was self-defense! Or, I mean… it was actually me she was defending."

"Go on," Gage said, when I didn't immediately continue.

I took a centering breath, relieved that my panic seemed to be abating. As much as I hated talking about my past, I owed it to this pack if Knox's attempted murder was involved.

"My stepfather abused me when I was younger. I got out… got some help and moved here from St. Louis to get away from him."

"He came after you?" Gage guessed.

"Yeah. Found out where I lived… showed up one night and shoved his way into my apartment." The words were hard to get out, even now. The memory of hands yanking at my clothing, tearing my jeans and underwear down to expose me, made my skin crawl. "Jez was coming over with a pizza. I thought it was her when I opened the door. But she showed up while he was attacking me. The door was still unlocked. She came in, saw what was happening, and bashed his skull in with a table lamp. He died instantly."

"Huh," Gage said.

"She ran away afterward." The words escaped without my conscious decision to say them aloud. "Panicked, I guess. I never saw her again after that… until just now."

"How long ago was that?" Gage asked.

"A little more than a year," I told him.

"Guess that'd give you a shock, for sure." Gage rose from his nonthreatening crouch, dusting himself off.

"Yeah," I agreed in a whisper.

The alpha's mouth curled unhappily.

"We need answers, after what she did to Knox," he said. "And she ain't giving them. You could talk to her. Maybe find out who the hell she's working for."

The instinctive need to say no bubbled up in my throat. But after everything, I *did* owe them this. Heath had cleaned up Jez's mess for me without even knowing it, and then she'd nearly gone and killed his pack leader. Or, at least… Gage thought she had.

If there was any chance this was a terrible misunderstanding, I needed to find out. And, more selfishly, the urge to ask why she'd abandoned me so completely itched beneath my skin. She had to have known that I wouldn't blame her for what she'd done in my own defense. She had to have known that by running, she was leaving me in the shit, with a dead body on my floor.

Gage wanted answers. So did I.

"Okay," I said, steeling myself to walk back up those stairs and confront the woman who'd turned all of our lives upside down.

EIGHT

Jez

AFTER TONY RAN out, it didn't matter that Gage remembered to lock the door to my attic prison. I was paralyzed, unable to rise... barely able to *breathe*.

Tony Scalise was tied up with Knox's pack. Tony Scalise, the closest thing I'd ever had to a real friend, was connected to a human trafficking ring.

The beta guy who I'd once tried to protect from an assault—who I *had* protected from an assault—was now complicit in sentencing underage omegas to a life of terrible abuse.

This couldn't be happening.

I tried to convince myself that it hadn't really been him. I was a mess. I hadn't eaten anything in god knew how long. Hadn't slept for more than a few minutes, here and there, before remembering where I was and jerking my gritty eyes open. Maybe it had been another slender, dark-haired beta named Tony, and my overstretched brain had superimposed my Tony's face over his real face.

That had to be it. A simple hallucination, brought on by exhaustion and low blood sugar.

I tried to psych myself up to go rummage through the bags lying abandoned inside the door. Maybe there was something useful in there. Something sharp, or something that could be used as a garotte, or—

Footsteps thumped up the stairway outside, muffled by the heavy door. Two sets. I took a deep breath and held it. The beta guy would come in, and it wouldn't be my Tony. It would just be some other random asshole with no morals. A paid lackey, sent to get me clothes and a toothbrush so Gage and his cronies could continue to keep me locked up in here.

"We're comin' in again," Gage called. "Tony says you and him know each other. He wants to talk to you."

My heart froze. Icicles pierced through the bloody flesh, making it flutter and skip. *It's a mistake, it's a mistake, it's a mistake,* I thought desperately.

The door creaked open. Gage entered, the familiar gun barrel leading as he stepped over the threshold. And behind him...

"Jez," Tony said hoarsely.

I swallowed a sob. An ugly, cut-off choking noise emerged instead.

Turning my head away, I refused to do him the courtesy of looking at him. If Tony was mixed up in this, that meant he was dead to me. Whatever connection I'd felt with him had been an illusion, because deep down, he'd been the kind of asshole who would do the same thing to other people that had been done to me when I was thirteen.

The silence stretched as I refused to acknowledge him.

"I..." he began eventually, before hesitating. "Gage, I need to talk to her alone, okay?"

"No," Gage replied instantly.

"She's terrified," Tony said. "Look at her. She's not going to talk to anyone while you're in here waving a gun at her."

"Still no." Gage made a low noise in the back of his throat. "She nearly killed Knox, and she's made two convincing attempts at murder since we brought her to the house."

Frustration cut through Tony's voice. "Look, if you want answers, you'll let me talk to her without you looming over her like a gargoyle! Can't you—I don't know... handcuff her to the bed frame or something? So you know she can't hurt me?"

My breathing grew faster despite my best attempts to control it.

"You think I carry around a pair of handcuffs?" Gage asked, sounding incredulous.

"You're the one who wanted me to come back up here and talk to her!" Tony snapped.

Gage grumbled something under his breath.

After a moment, he said, "Fine. Take the gun. Keep her covered."

My gaze shot up. Gage was unbuckling his braided leather belt one-handed. Both Tony and I cringed back.

"No," Tony said. He was eyeing the belt with a scared-rabbit look that probably mirrored mine. "I'm not holding a gun on someone. You do *not* pay me for that kind of shit, Gage."

"Jesus Christ," Gage muttered. The belt slithered free of its loops, and he handed it to Tony, who took it like it was a live snake. "Then go tie her right wrist to the bed frame. Put a bunch of knots in it. I'll be right outside the door. If she starts untying the knots, get out before she gets loose."

Tony looked like he was going to be sick, but he approached me slowly, taking care not to block Gage's line of fire with the pistol. My awareness slipped outside of my body, hovering a few feet above me as a clammy hand took my wrist in a gentle grip and looped the belt around it, tying it to the sturdy metal frame I was leaning against in a listless slouch.

When he was done, he scurried back like my skin burned him. "Okay, now leave us alone, please."

"Don't fuck around with her, Tony," Gage said. "I'm not kidding when I say she's dangerous."

"Yeah, no. I know that," Tony said.

Gage backed out of the room, closing the door as I watched from my hazy vantage point up near the slanted ceiling.

Once he was gone, Tony let out an explosive breath and crept closer to me again, hands upraised as though to calm a wild animal. He crouched next to me, lifting a finger to his lips for quiet, and quickly undid the tangled knots in the belt, freeing my wrist.

I blinked, abruptly back in my body as he backed away again.

"Jez," he said, "what the *actual fuck*?"

I licked my lips, trying to bring moisture back to my parched mouth and throat.

"Shouldn't I be asking *you* that?" I shot back viciously, cradling my wrist to my chest. The belt still looped around it, dangling free.

"Why—" He cut himself off and shook his head. "I'm not the one going around killing people!"

I bared my teeth, trying to summon righteous anger to blot out the betrayal. "No. You're the one playing gofer for a pack of omega sex traffickers," I snarled.

He stared at me like I'd grown a second head. "What the hell are you *talking* about, Jez?"

"Omega. Sex. Traffickers." I bit out each word viciously. "Or have you conveniently failed to notice the little kids with bruised faces being taken in and out of this house in unmarked vans?"

Tony's head shook slowly back and forth. "What? No… Jez, you've got it all turned around. Sometimes they help out omegas in trouble, that's all."

Pity joined the ugly slurry of hurt, fear, and anger sloshing around in my stomach.

"You can't really be that naïve," I told him. "Wake up and look around, Tony. You're a fucking accessory to kidnapping and child sexual abuse."

He took a step back so abruptly that he nearly tripped on one of the bags still lying beside the doorway.

"Don't you *dare* talk to me about child sexual abuse," he said, his voice wavering.

"Why?" I taunted, still desperate to use anger as a shield against everything else. "Did I touch a nerve?"

He steadied himself against the doorframe, an angry flush replacing his unnatural paleness. "You know that asshole you killed in my apartment? Right before you ran off and left me to deal with a dead body on my own? That was my stepdad. He raped me for years until I finally got away and moved here. Then he tracked me down and nearly started up again, right where he'd left off."

I stiffened.

"So, don't you come at me about that shit," he went on, his tone flat and deadly. "Because *you're* the one who doesn't know what the hell they're talking about."

My anger rose to match his, finally giving me the strength to climb onto shaky feet and point an accusing finger at his chest.

"You think I don't? My father auctioned my first heat to the highest bidders so he could pay off his gambling debts! Then he sold me to traffickers in Canada so no one would find out! Traffickers like *this fucking pack*!"

My voice had risen, high and shrill—loud enough that there was no way the sharp alpha ears outside could fail to hear what I was saying. I was *so angry*, though. Too angry to care what happened to me next.

Tony stood staring at me, his mouth hanging open, breathing hard. And sure enough, a moment later the door creaked open. Gage loomed in the doorway with his ever-present gun. His sharp hazel eyes took in my untied wrist, and he let out a gusty sigh.

"Goddamn it, Tony," he said, sounding more tired than anything. Then his heavy gaze returned to me and settled there, pressing down on my shoulders like a physical force. "Still, I guess we're finally getting somewhere, at least. Sounds like you and me need to get a few things straight, *Jez*."

NINE

Jez

I BARED MY TEETH at the alpha in the doorway and crab-crawled inelegantly backwards into the nearest corner. With jerky movements, I yanked the belt free of my wrists and balled it up in my hand.

It wasn't much of a weapon, but it was the only one I had. Though it would have been a better one if not for the distracting hint of yeast and orange peel that had worked its way into the stronger scent of leather.

"I have nothing to say to you," I snarled at Gage. "Stay the fuck away from me!"

Tony had backed up until he was leaning against the wall opposite the bed. One hand was clasped over his mouth, like he was trying to hold back words or tears or both.

Gage looked between us like we were straining his brain cells to the breaking point.

"Okay," he said. "So, you tried to kill Knox because you thought he was leading a pack of traffickers. As... what? Revenge because your dad sold you?"

I clamped my lips shut and glared at him.

When it became obvious that I wasn't going to answer such a stupid fucking question, he continued, "But *we* figured someone had sent you to get back at Knox for intercepting their latest shipment of omegas and getting them to safety. Because we're not trafficking the kids. We're rescuing them."

"Yeah," I sneered, remembering the gaunt, bruised faces. "*Sure* you are."

"Wait, *what*?" Tony said, his hand falling to hang at his side. "You're doing *what*?"

Gage looked at him, a serious expression digging furrows his big, dumb face. "It's what Knox does with his money. He's got a… personal interest, I guess you'd say."

"Heath just said that you help people in trouble sometimes," Tony said weakly. "He made it sound like no big deal."

I didn't want to listen to this, even if it maybe meant that Tony was gullible rather than evil.

"Well," Gage was saying. "I don't think he really wanted you to get dragged into it, is the thing." His eyes pinned me again. "Gets a bit dangerous sometimes."

I lost the fight to hold that alpha gaze, but I was damned if I'd show throat no matter how my neck muscles twitched and spasmed.

"Funny how the bad guys always try to make out like they're the good guys," I growled. "Face it, Tony—you've been played. What did they have you doing, besides buying toothpaste and underwear for their prisoners?"

But Tony was still gaping at us.

Gage answered instead. "Heath started payin' him for any info he heard on the street about the mob families."

"But… he only ever asked about stuff related to the trade unions and the import-export business," Tony said blankly. "He never asked me to look into sex trafficking."

"Course he didn't," Gage told him severely. "Because that's the kind of shit that'll get you killed." His lips twisted unhappily. "Just ask Knox."

"Or," I grated out, "he didn't ask you because he didn't want you to find out what kind of assholes you were working for."

A horrible, niggling voice in my head whispered, *'Unless Adrian was the one who lied, so you wouldn't find out what kind of assholes you were working for.'*

I quashed it. Adrian was an omega. No way in hell was I taking the word of an alpha over his. Alphas couldn't be trusted. My entire life was a case study of that fact.

But Gage wasn't finished.

"The kids you saw downstairs were intercepted on their way to the Vozzina gang," he said, addressing me directly again. "We've been working on the assumption that they're the ones who sent you. But if we're wrong and there's someone else after us, we need to know that."

Tony looked at me with a tinge of desperation in his face. "Jez, what if they lied to you about who you were going after? What if you're a dupe?"

The way the words echoed that unwanted little voice in the back of my head made my teeth ache.

"*I'm not,*" I said past a clenched jaw.

Because if I was a dupe, that would mean I'd just...

No.

The fact that I was scent-matched to this pack was nothing more than another example of nature's mindless cruelty. No matter how my instincts screamed, it had no bearing on whether they were good people or not. It had no bearing on whether or not they deserved to be *punished.*

Maybe it was the reason I was locked up in the pack's crazy-woman attic instead of in a jail cell. That was all. And the jury was still out on whether my snap decision not to throw myself on the tender mercies of the cops would be a good one or a terrible one.

In fact, right now it was leaning heavily toward *terrible.*

"Where do you send the kids?" Tony asked, out of the blue. "Once you get them away from the gangs, where do they go?"

Where do you think *they go,* I wanted to ask. Instead, I waited, curious to see if Gage had another lie at the ready.

The big alpha hesitated, drawing in breath to speak, only to hold it for a couple of seconds.

"I don't think I should tell you that," he said after a pause. "It's not safe information for you to have."

I scoffed, shoving all of my gathering doubts into a shoebox, and stuffing that box away in a deep hole.

"Convenient," I said, laying on the sarcasm with a trowel.

Gage didn't react. "Not safe for Tony. Definitely not safe for *them*, if the Vozzina pack sent you."

"Oh," I said, playing up innocence. "So, you're going to let me go, then?"

"Fuck, no," Gage said. "Do I *look* stupid?"

Frustration and rage welled up in me.

"You look like a cartoon version of Lennie Small, with your stupid five-o'clock shadow, and your stupid muscles, *and your stupid pheromones*!" I shouted at him, levering myself to my feet on shaking legs to point an accusing finger at his chest.

Unfortunately, that was the moment my body decided to remind me that I hadn't eaten or slept in far too long, by the simple expedient of fainting. The last thing I was aware of was two figures rushing toward me as gray fog swirled in to block out my vision.

***

I awoke on a comfortable mattress in a warm room, with the lingering scent of baking bread teasing the back of my throat.

My head was pounding a staccato rhythm in time with my heartbeat, and my mouth was dry. I groaned, some instinct warning me that I'd be a lot happier if I wasn't awake.

"Jez?"

The familiar voice prodded at my consciousness. Had I fallen asleep at Tony's place? A little jolt of adrenaline nudged me further toward awareness. I'd promised myself I'd never do that... never become a pity case because I was incapable of performing the basic functions of adulthood, like holding down a job and renting an apartment.

I blinked gritty eyes open, staring at the slanted ceiling above me until it came properly into focus.

The slanted ceiling. The slanted *attic* ceiling.

I bolted into a sitting position, wallowing in a messy nest of pillows and blankets.

"Whoa!" Tony said. "It's okay —"

He seemed to catch himself. "Well, it's *not* okay. But you're safe."

Christ. I'd passed out from exhaustion and low blood sugar. But it was all right. I was awake now, and it had probably only been a few minutes, if that.

"You've been asleep for thirteen hours," Tony said.

What?

"You've gotta eat something, Jez," he went on. "Gage says you haven't since he brought you here."

With those words, my stomach reminded me of every single one of those hours.

"Yeah?" I shot back. "Well, excuse me if I'm not in a hurry to be drugged so they can do god-knows-what to me!"

"They're not—" He paused, shaking his head as though bewildered. "They're not *drugging your food*, Jez!" He looked around, and picked up an unopened can of soda from the dresser. "Here, look."

He popped the top and chugged several deep swallows, then thrust it at me.

"Drink it, for god's sake."

I took it hesitantly, my throat convulsing with need for the carbonated, sugary goodness. Was I missing something here? Was it a trick, and I just couldn't see the catch?

But why would Tony let himself be drugged for me? There was no reason he'd do that. And the can had been sealed, right? Even if they'd injected something into it with a needle, the gas would have escaped, leaving it flat, not bubbling.

I cautiously lifted it to my lips. After a couple of sips, my thirst took over and I was swilling it, tipping the can up and up until it was empty. My stomach felt bloated once I was finished, and I let out an inelegant belch.

"That's my girl," Tony said… but the words were a monotone, lacking the teasing lilt they once would have held. "Okay. Chips next. Then the sandwich."

There was a plate of food sitting on the dresser as well, similar to all the other plates of food Gage had delivered and removed later, untouched. Giving in to my growing desperation for nourishment, I accepted the bag of chips after Tony tore it open and ate a few. Same with the sandwich. He tore it in half and took a seemingly random bite out of each part. I took the halves and devoured them, not even tasting whatever was on them.

"Better?" Tony asked when I was finished.

I curled into a ball, hugging my knees to my chest on the bed. Someone had arranged all the nesting materials I'd been ignoring, making a cozy little haven in the mostly bare room.

"My stomach hurts now," I said mulishly — because it did.

"Yeah, no kidding," Tony muttered.

"But I guess if they were going to do something while I was unconscious, they would have done it," I admitted. Then, "Was I really asleep for *thirteen hours*?"

"Yeah," Tony said. "And before you get some grand idea that I was glued to your bedside the whole time, I wasn't. I went home to sleep and came back."

"I didn't think you'd stayed," I said.

He shrugged one shoulder, listless. "I still want to know why you left me to deal with my stepdad's body alone."

God, that had been such a shitty thing to do to him. There was no answer I could give that would make it less shitty. The uncomfortable idea that I was a terrible person had begun circling through my head again, prickling like thorns.

I was silent for too long.

"Never mind," Tony said. Then, after a slight pause. "Are you seriously scent-matched to these guys? Because… well… Heath and I… we… um—"

A sharp knock sounded at the door. It swung open less than a second later, revealing my Grimm's fairytale version of the fucking Scotts Lawn commercial spokesman.

"Right, you," Heath said. "Time for some proper answers."

TEN

Heath

AFTER THE BETTER part of a day spent watching Knox struggle on a ventilator while monitors and alarms beeped and chimed endlessly, I was *fucking done*. Gage was still walking around with his alpha hindbrain hanging out, cosseting this sweet-smelling would-be murderer because her goddamned pheromones matched ours.

And now it looked like Tony was marching right along next to him in the *'be nice to killers'* parade.

"You!" I barked, funneling every ounce of alpha rage into the command. "*Stand up.*"

The omega—whose name was apparently Jez—gasped and stumbled to her feet, trembling. Christ, she looked like a baby deer... all long legs and jutting bones and huge eyes. Her caramel coffee scent soured with fear, and I clenched my jaw against the urge to fall right in line with Gage and Tony.

Fawning over the fawn.

"Heath..." Tony said uncertainly.

"*Shut it,*" I said, aware on some level that Tony hadn't done anything to deserve my ire. I didn't have time for more mollycoddling, though.

This time, both of them flinched.

The muscles of my jaw clenched tighter.

"Tell me the name of the person who hired you to kill Knox," I snapped, crossing to loom over the girl.

She made a soft, whimpering noise in the back of her throat, visibly swallowing the word that had almost escaped.

"*Now!*" I roared, directly in her face.

She staggered back a step, hitting the edge of the bed and collapsing onto it when her knees gave way.

"Adrian!" she choked out, as though the name had drawn blood on its way up.

"Fuck's sake," I muttered, stomping on the ridiculous ache in my chest. "Adrian *who?*"

"I don't know!" she yelled. "I didn't ask, okay!"

Christ on a crutch.

"You didn't fucking ask," I echoed. "Of course you didn't, *Just Jez.*"

She glared at me, her fingers clutching handfuls of the rumpled blankets as though she were desperately trying to think of a way to turn microfleece into a weapon.

"Short for Jezebel, is it?" I guessed. "Appropriate, I guess. While we're at it, what *is* your last name?"

"I don't have one," she ground out through gritted teeth.

"Bull fucking shit," I told her. "*Tell me your goddamned last name.*"

She was shaking visibly under the effect of my bark, but she still managed to glare up at me with her huge blue-gray eyes for half a second before her gaze slid to the side.

"It was my father's name," she said with enough vitriol to dissolve steel. "He lost the right to keep his stamp on me when he sold me into sexual slavery. Excuse me if I don't have a different name to replace it!"

This was fucking useless—all of it.

The temper that had landed me in more than a little trouble over the course of my life yanked hard against its tattered leash. My hands clenched into fists as I leaned close.

"Your sob story doesn't interest me one goddamned bit," I snarled. "Do you know why? Because I can name dozens of omegas with stories just as bad, and not a single one of them randomly decided to attempt the murder of one of the people who's *fucking trying to help them!*"

She made another muffled noise of fear and scrambled backward on the bed until her shoulders hit the headboard, her chest rising and falling in convulsive gasps.

"And if you could have been bothered to do the most basic amount of research and fact checking of some random fucker who *wouldn't even give you his last name*," I went on relentlessly, "you'd have fucking *known that!*"

I realized I was breathing just as hard as she was. Meanwhile, Tony had backed up against the wall farthest from me, and was staring at me like he didn't even recognize me. With a low growl, I turned on my heel and stalked out of the room before I lost control of myself completely. The last thing I heard as I slammed the door behind me was the sound of keening omega sobs.

My footsteps echoed dully on the steep staircase as I jogged down to the ground floor. Knowing I didn't dare leave the house with the attic door unlocked, I fetched up halfway along the main hallway—across from the huge parlor we'd retrofitted as a dorm for the omegas that came through this place.

Jesus.

My heart was pounding like I'd run a marathon, and my instincts were screaming nonstop that I'd left my mate curled up in a terrified ball and sobbing her eyes out. This twisted scent-match had to be a punishment straight from the deepest circle of hell.

I braced a hand against the wall, letting my head hang as I tried to get my breath back and figure out what to do next.

Hesitant footsteps approached along the hallway, and I sighed.

"Tell me you locked the attic door behind you," I said, not looking up.

"No, I did not lock the fucking door!" Tony snapped. His voice was shaking. "What the hell is *wrong* with you, Heath!"

I straightened with reluctance, because yeah, Tony was definitely part of the coddling brigade, too. His aggressive stance surprised me, nonetheless. Normally, he went out of his way to show how completely unaffected he was by everything—whether that meant gathering intel on union-busting or sucking my cock.

Tony was *safe*… or so I'd thought.

"Can I *remind* you," I barked, still not in control of my righteous anger, "that my closest friend is currently *lying in a hospital bed on life support* because of that girl?"

I hadn't made a move toward him, but Tony *cringed*—visibly preventing himself from taking a step backward.

A step away from *me*.

By the way, Gage had said when I'd showed up to relieve him of guard duty. *You should know that Tony's stepdad sexually abused him as a kid. The asshole showed up here in Chicago a year ago to start up again, and Jez bashed in his head with a table lamp.*

And because I was an idiot who hadn't had more than half an hour of sleep at a stretch since Gage and I had found Knox unconscious in his hotel suite, that connection hadn't clicked into place in my brain until just this moment.

"The body I cleaned up for you," I realized. "That was your stepfather."

Tony sucked in a sharp breath, derailed. "…What?"

I blinked, suddenly aware of just how desperately I needed sleep, and how unlikely I was to get it anytime soon.

"Gage… told me," I said, and watched his expression shutter into wariness.

"Yeah," Tony admitted. "Jez showed up in the nick of time and saved me. I was too scared to fight back properly."

And now he was scared of me—the angry alpha snarling at him because I was pissed off at his friend who'd rescued him from being assaulted by his childhood abuser. I closed my eyes and took in a huge breath, holding it for several seconds before letting it out slowly.

Of course Tony wasn't going to throw this omega she-devil under the bus without a second thought.

"Okay," I said. "Okay, look. I'm not angry at you."

"You're angry at her," he said, sounding less like he was fighting the urge to break and run. "And, yeah, okay… I get it. Believe me; I do. But I want you to tell me something truthfully. I'm not ever going to ask for details, but tell me you've never killed anyone before. Because people who know how to make a dead body disappear without a trace in the space of a few hours aren't usually the kind of people passing around the collection plate at church every Sunday."

"You already know I can't tell you that," I said, exhaustion washing through the words.

"I figured," he said. "And I know it doesn't excuse what she did. But whatever made you think those people deserved to be dead? She obviously believed the same thing about Knox. Maybe we should focus more on whoever convinced her that was the case. This Adrian character, for one."

My eyes slid closed. "It's next on my list," I muttered. "Not that a first name — and probably a fake one, at that — is gonna be much help."

"But you still think it's someone connected to the Vozzinas," Tony said. "Because apparently you're intercepting shipments of kidnapped omegas from the gangs, and you never thought to, y'know, *mention that.*"

"I do *not* want you mixed up with the omega business," I growled.

"Uh-huh," he said. "So, how's that working out for you? Because no offense, but I'm feeling pretty involved at the moment."

"Yes," I agreed unhappily. "You are. And it's my job to see that you don't get any *more* involved."

He looked like he wanted to say something else that I wouldn't like, but he visibly swallowed it back. "Look, you're about to pass out. I can tell because I just watched someone else pass out after being awake for about the same amount of time you and Gage have been."

"No time for sleep," I said immediately, thinking of Knox, unconscious in his hospital bed.

"Right." Tony sounded unconvinced. "Okay, how about this? I can go sit with Knox and call you if there's any change. Gage can come back here, and you two can trade off sleeping and watching Jez. Only…"

I peered at him with bleary eyes. "What?"

He sighed. "Maybe don't terrify her any more, because it's really not helping the situation."

"It got me Adrian's name," I told him.

Adrian's probably fake name, I didn't add.

"Sure," Tony said, not looking happy about it. "So, follow up on that first. You can bark at her afterward."

I subsided reluctantly. "Yeah, fine. I'll call Gage and let him know you're coming."

ELEVEN

Jez

THE ATTIC DOOR was unlocked. I needed to get up. I needed to try and escape. Instead, I was still curled in a ball on the stupid bed with its stupid pillows and blankets, sobbing.

Tony had glanced back and forth between me and the place where Heath had been standing a moment earlier, obviously torn.

"I have to go after him," he'd said. "I'm not locking you in, but he's probably still downstairs, okay?"

And then, he'd left—shutting the door softly behind him.

There would be windows in the house. Maybe I could climb out of one, unless they were all barred or nailed shut. There were probably weapons stored somewhere. Real weapons... even if it was just a kitchen knife.

But I couldn't move. I couldn't do anything except hug my knees to my chest and cry. Because no matter what the truth was, I'd done something horrible. Something unforgivable. Maybe unsurvivable.

Either Adrian had been lying, and I'd committed attempted murder against an innocent man... or Gage and Heath were lying, and I'd given them Adrian's name. Knox still might die. If he did, what would the others do to me? Whether they took their own revenge or threw me to the wolves in the legal system, I would never be free again.

If Adrian had been telling the truth about them, would they find him and silence him? But, maybe that part would be okay. It was only a first name. Like Heath had said, it might not even be a *real* name. I hadn't bothered to check, because I'd been staring at a worn photo of a cherub-cheeked little girl grinning at the camera with one front tooth missing, thinking about all the things that might happen to her at the hands of evil alphas.

What if I'd been wrong?

Cedar and woodsmoke. A crooked grin. *If I'm going to be bored out of my mind for three days straight, I might as well do it in nice surroundings,* Knox had said, as I poured him a bourbon and slipped horse sedatives into it.

I had no idea how much time had passed, but I was still crying hysterically when Tony came back up and stuck his head in the room, looking deeply uncomfortable.

"Um," he said. "Look, I'm really sorry, but I need to go to the hospital to stay with Knox."

It was too much.

"*Get out!*" I screamed at him, my voice hoarse from sobbing and high-pitched with hysteria. "Get out, *get out!*"

He swallowed hard, his Adam's apple bobbing. "I will," he said, sounding sick at heart. "Heath is still in the house. Gage will be back after I take over at the hospital. I'm… really sorry all of this happened, Jez."

I clenched my fists tight in the mess of blankets to keep from throwing something at him. The emotions inside me were too big; too out of control with nowhere to go.

Tony retreated, closing the door after himself. There was no telltale click of a lock, but it didn't matter. Heath was still downstairs. He would never let me escape. I sat rocking back and forth, trying to hold everything in... until finally, I couldn't any more.

Angry shrieks tore out of my throat as I grabbed the nearest pillow and ripped open the case, one of my fingernails tearing as it snagged—leaving a crimson smear on the cotton. Incensed, I ripped blankets and shredded cushions, screaming like a banshee as I destroyed every single piece of the nest I hadn't made.

When that wasn't enough, I grabbed the bed's dusty mattress and yanked sideways with my full weight, wrestling with it until it slid off the metal bed frame. I howled out my rage and fear until I was too hoarse to make noise, the cries becoming nearly silent. My muscles burned and ached with exertion. My knees grew wobbly, and I staggered over to a bare corner to collapse on the hard floor.

Like a puppet with its strings cut, I sat crumpled and limp, with several of my torn fingernails bleeding sluggishly. I stared sightlessly at the destruction, my vision blurred and unfocused, and waited for whatever would happen next.

Hours passed. It felt like hours. There was no time up here, though. No clocks. No windows. Maybe it had only been minutes. Maybe it had been days. I told myself I didn't care. What did it matter? I wasn't the person I'd always told myself that I was. My life as I'd known it was as good as over.

A knock sounded at the door.

"It's me," came Gage's voice. "I've got food. I'm coming in."

I didn't move.

My tears had run out at some point, leaving my eyes gritty and dry. My head pounded in sluggish agony, while my stomach flip-flopped between sour nausea and ravenous hunger.

No gun barrel led the way this time. Gage simply opened the door and walked in, a plate balanced in one hand. He stopped abruptly, his free hand still on the doorknob, and took in the carnage of pillow stuffing and shredded cloth.

Then he blinked, crossing carefully through the discarded shopping bags and destroyed soft goods to set the plate on the dresser. I'd thought about tipping that dresser over, too, so I could hear it crash to the ground and splinter... but I'd already been so exhausted I could barely stand up.

"Give me a couple of minutes to get this cleaned up," he said without any detectable judgment in his tone. "Tony told me about you being afraid we'd drugged the food, so I'll eat some like he did to prove it's okay."

I didn't move or make a sound, but I couldn't help the small niggle of guilt that threaded its way through my belly.

Pretending disinterest, I watched from the corner of my eye as the big alpha efficiently piled the contents of the shopping bags onto the other end of the dresser from the food. When that was done, he pulled out the largest remaining hunk of blanket, piling the other destroyed items onto it and bundling it up so he could carry it.

He shoved the bundle onto the landing outside, effortlessly returned the mattress to the bed, and went to retrieve the plate and bottle of water he'd brought.

After uncapping the water and taking a couple of deep swallows, he recapped it and set it on the floor near me. Then he retreated and ate a few bites of the food. It was a huge, double-decker burger and fries—he must have picked it up on his way here from the hospital. The smell, which had initially made my stomach rebel, abruptly flipped the invisible switch in my gut that returned me to being famished.

When he set the plate down next to the bottle and returned to sit on the bed, giving me space, I cautiously took the food and started wolfing it down.

"I'll bring you up some more pillows and blankets," he said, jerking his chin toward the door to indicate the remains of the nest. Then he hesitated before adding, "Do you, um… do you want to talk about it?"

I've done something horrible, and I don't even know what it is yet, I didn't say.

"No," I told him between mouthfuls of French fries. Then it was my turn to hesitate. "Why aren't you being awful to me?" It slipped out before I could stop it. I straightened my shoulders, bluffing my way forward. "Are you the good cop, and Heath's the bad cop? Am I supposed to open up to you because you're the nice one?"

He shrugged a shoulder, looking uncomfortable. "Nah. From what I hear, the bad cop did okay without me."

"Then what's your angle?" I demanded. "Why be nice?"

He huffed out a sigh. "Well, you're our scent match. That's really pretty much it. Do you know how rare that is?"

I kept my lips stubbornly closed and resolutely didn't breathe in his citrusy Christmas-bread scent.

"Can't promise things won't get a lot more complicated if Knox doesn't make it, though," he admitted reluctantly.

I steeled myself, knowing I had to ask. "How is he doing?"

"About the same," he said. "It's touch and go. They haven't had to restart his heart again, at least."

The confession that had tried to escape earlier snuck past my guard.

"If you're lying about not being traffickers, then I just gave up my client's name to Heath." My stomach turned over, rebelling against the food I'd just dumped on it. "And if you're telling the truth, I may have killed an innocent alpha."

"We're telling the truth," Gage said. "He's strong, though. He'll pull through. You'll see."

And then what? I wondered.

The silence stretched. Gage rose from his perch on the edge of the bed.

"You want me to leave that for you?" He indicated the half-finished plate.

I shook my head, unable to face eating the rest of it.

He crouched down and picked it up in one big hand, leaving the water bottle. "Okay. Sorry, but I have to lock you in again. I'll be back with the new blankets and stuff, though."

I looked away and chewed on my lower lip, my guilt at destroying the room returning even stronger than before.

"Okay," I whispered.

Gage was good to his word. He dropped off the new pile of nesting materials without a word, and left again, closing and locking the door.

I had no idea if it was day, night, or something in-between. But I was exhausted from crying and ripping up the room. There was no real reason to stay awake. Wind rattled the eaves as I reluctantly changed out of my stinking night-club dress, and into a set of silky pajamas from the bags of stuff Tony had brought.

They were nicer than anything I'd slept in since I was a child. Part of me hated that I was wearing them—it felt like some kind of weird capitulation… although I wasn't sure to what. To make up for it, I shoved the neatly folded blankets onto the floor and curled up in a tight ball on the bare mattress.

The wind howled louder, and I shivered.

God, I *hated* storms.

But I was so tired I could barely keep my eyelids open. I'd been leaving the lights on, because it made me feel less vulnerable to be able to see what was coming. My head was still pounding like a drum, though. As I tried to sleep, the light felt like it was stabbing into my brain through my eyelids, so I got up and turned it off.

It didn't take long for fatigue to drag me under, now that I'd finally given myself permission to sleep in this makeshift prison of a house. The darkness carried me away, exhaustion overcoming the undercurrent of nervousness at the sound of the wind making the roof creak.

Unfortunately, the dreams came soon afterward.

Sometime later, a deafening crack of thunder jolted me out of a nightmare of sweaty, grasping hands. I lurched upright, because someone was screaming—the pain-filled, uncomprehending cries of a child being hurt while the adults around her laughed and jeered.

It was storming—rain and wind rocking the house, just as it had been on that terrible night after my father auctioned off my first heat to a pack of pedophiles. My skin crawled under the touch of those hot, sticky hands. I flailed, fists meeting only air as I cried out for help that would never come.

Another reverberating crack of thunder shook the floor, weight pinning me down from behind as my body and mind fought themselves.

No-no-no-*no*—

Another thump... not loud enough to be thunder. A door? Was someone coming to help me after all?

"P-please!" I begged. "*Please don't let them!*"

"Jez?" The deep voice was familiar, but it wasn't until the lights flicked on and the scent of yeast and orange peel tickled my nose that some fractured part of my mind recognized Gage.

The confining hands melted away, the weight crushing my ribcage dissolving in the glare of the light fixture. I gasped in a wheezing breath.

I was on the floor, clawing at the floorboards with my ragged nails.

"Hey..." Gage said. "Hey, what is it? Are you okay?"

He knelt next me on the floor, one hand hovering over my shoulder like it didn't know where to land. The scent of my mother's kitchen during the holidays surrounded me like one of the blankets I'd refused to use, wrapping me in comfort and security among the whirling madness of the flashback.

With a desperate sob, I scrambled onto my knees and flung myself against Gage's broad chest, burying my face against his shoulder and clutching handfuls of his shirt in a white-knuckled grip.

TWELVE

Gage

IT TOOK ME a second to process the armful of sweet, coffee-scented omega trying to crawl onto my lap. Or maybe she was trying to burrow inside my ribcage, because she just kept wriggling closer and closer until there wasn't a hairsbreadth of space between us.

If the screams echoing from the attic room hadn't been a dead giveaway that something was wrong, the curdling sourness beneath Jez's addictive perfume would have been. They'd been the screams of a terrified child, and god knew we'd all heard those way too often over the years, in our line of business.

But Jez wasn't a child. Whatever nightmare had invaded her sleep, it had taken her back in time—and I could guess where. She'd practically tackled me in her haste for comfort, sending me backward onto my ass—my arms coming around her mostly in self-defense.

This whole clusterfuck was such a fucking mess. Knox needed to get better fast, so we could all figure out what the hell we were supposed to be feeling. Because right now, Heath saw her as the enemy—and not without reason. Meanwhile, Tony felt like he'd been betrayed from two directions, and I felt like fate was a vicious bitch who apparently had it in for us for some reason.

I could only imagine what Jez was feeling.

Her wracking sobs had transformed into a continuous, high-pitched keening sound, broken only by the occasional gasp that sounded like someone drowning in the ocean whenever she ran out of air. I rocked her a bit, hating the world that had brought her—and us—to this point.

If she hadn't tried to kill Knox, you might never have met her, said a traitorous little whisper. *You might have gone your whole life never knowing you had a scent match.*

And I genuinely didn't know if that would have been more or less tragic than the current situation. I mean, yeah… I'd always had a nagging sense of something being missing in my life, and I was pretty sure the others did, too. But maybe that was normal? Maybe everyone on the planet felt like that.

Did Jez feel like that? Or had that part of her been burned out of her soul when her dad sold her to a pack of monsters? Maybe she didn't dream of finding her alphas, because she was too busy dreaming of whatever had sent her screaming into the darkness.

Hoarseness and lack of oxygen eventually muted her cries into pitiful whimpers that tore at my heart. How was I supposed to remember what she'd done to Knox when her face was pressed against the side of my neck, my skin growing slick with her tears and snot?

"Was it the storm?" I asked, following a hunch.

She went very still, her whimpers going silent. For a second, I was worried she would realize what she'd done and who she was trusting to hold her. But after an endless pause, she gave a small nod, not lifting her head.

"Okay," I said, even though I knew her panic wasn't because she was afraid of wind and thunder. She was afraid of something else that had happened at the *same time* as rain and thunder... and I could guess what it was.

"We're going downstairs," I decided. "It ain't as loud down there."

She made a noise of protest, but she didn't struggle as I got us both on our feet, supporting her around the shoulders with one arm.

Another peal of thunder rattled the house, and the lights flickered for a couple of seconds before steadying. Jez's tear-streaked face turned a sickly shade of green, and she gulped ominously. I'd seen that look often enough that I rushed her into the bathroom and positioned her in front of the toilet, where she threw up every bit of the food I'd gotten into her earlier.

Followed by bile, yet *more* bile... and possibly her toenails.

She moaned, weaving like she might fall over.

"Finished?" I asked gruffly, and helped her up again when she gave an exhausted nod.

"M'sorry," she croaked, like *this* was the thing she had to be sorry for.

"It's fine." I flushed the toilet and guided her over to lean against the sink.

The water bottle from earlier was exactly where I'd left it on the floor, with exactly as much water in it as before. I scooped it up and went back to the bathroom, where she'd rallied enough to splash water on her face.

"Rinse and spit," I instructed. "Then drink some. You're gonna be dehydrated."

She did, bracing herself upright with one hand—all the fight finally gone out of her. Another barrage of rain hit the roof directly above our heads, peppered this time with small hail. She twitched.

"I don't like storms," she whispered.

"Yeah, I got that part," I told her. "It'll probably pass soon. C'mon. Downstairs."

"Why?" she rasped.

"Told you. It'll be quieter. You're right under the roof up here." I tried not to think about what Heath would have to say, if he was awake to see this.

"Okay," she said, still with that defeated air.

But when she tried to step away from the sink, her knees buckled. I caught her before she could hit the ground and swept her up into a bridal carry.

"I got you," I told her, hating the way her entire body trembled with fear, or exhaustion, or both.

The back staircase was still a fuckin' death-trap, but on the positive side, she wasn't actively trying to murder me anymore. I eased her down the narrow steps sideways, not letting any part of her touch the wall or the banister. On the second floor, I turned and headed for the hall bathroom, keeping my footsteps quiet so as not to wake Heath.

"I'm not going to puke again," she said, when I settled her to sit on the closed toilet lid.

"Yeah, I know," I told her, gesturing to her hands. "Your fingernails are all torn to shit, though. Just want to get them cleaned and bandaged."

She looked bewildered, but she held out first one dainty hand, and then the other. I cleaned them with antiseptic, more than a little freaked out at the fact that she didn't so much as flinch. Then I covered the six that were torn to the quick with two Band-Aids each—one doubled over the end of her finger, and the other circled around it to hold it in place.

When I was done, she stared down at them blankly.

"Can you eat? Some broth, maybe?" I asked, but she shook her head no.

She needed to eat something—and keep it down. But at least she'd finished the water bottle upstairs. I was beginning to think that she wasn't so much 'model-thin' as a borderline starvation case. Not that those two things were worlds apart… but the starvation probably hadn't been by choice if she was living mostly on the streets.

"When this mess is over, I'm going to feed you steak and lobster until you pop," I said, my mouth running away before my brain.

Shit. You weren't supposed to say stuff like that out loud, were you. That had been… not good.

"Unless you're, I mean, vegetarian or something like that," I hurried on, probably making it worse. "I just mean, I don't like to see you not eating."

I should stop talking. My jaw snapped shut.

She was giving me the same blank stare as when I'd bandaged her hands.

"I'm just really tired," she said, flinching when a distant crack of thunder broke the silence.

"Yeah," I told her. "Yeah, I know."

She looked a bit steadier, so I didn't immediately pick her up and carry her. She let me lead her to my bedroom and pull the covers back on my bed. I'd thought she might balk, but she climbed in without complaint and curled up in a tight comma shape with her back to me.

I could guess the kind of shit she'd been through, so I smoothed the covers over her and sat down on top of them, swinging my sock-clad feet up and scooting in behind her with the sheets and blankets acting as a barrier between us. In a situation where not a single goddamned thing about it was acceptable, I had no idea what would be okay and what wouldn't.

"Can I hold you?" I asked, my arm hovering.

She was silent for long enough that my triceps started to ache.

"Yes," she said eventually.

My arm settled over her waist, making her the small spoon.

"I want to pretend like I chose this," she said. "Just… just for a bit."

"That sounds nice," I said, not sure why my throat had started to ache all of the sudden.

"Goodnight," she murmured.

"Goodnight," I agreed.

Her breathing was congested from crying, but her body went limp within minutes. Snoring cut through the silence of the house, the storm both within and without now long past.

I want to pretend like I chose this, she'd said… and I got it. I really did.

Because somewhere, there was a world where Jez was our scent match, and the four of us were happily mated, and she'd crawled into my bed for comfort because she was scared of storms. I bet that world was pretty fucking awesome, too.

It might not ever be *this* world, but right now, it could be. Just for a few hours, anyway. So, I kept watch like an alpha was supposed to when they were protecting their omega. And I liked it. A lot.

I like the way she felt curled up against me, and the way her caramel coffee scent mixed with mine. I liked how completely relaxed she was, like she knew she was finally safe because I was here with her.

I didn't like it nearly as much when a door opened and closed down the hall, and Heath's exhausted footsteps trudged closer, punctuated by a brisk knock.

"Gage? What are you doing in there? You know you need to keep watch and make sure that she-devil doesn't try to get out..."

I rolled into a sitting position just as the door swung open, Heath's broad figure silhouetted by the hall lights. Beside me, Jez snored on, oblivious, even as a wedge of illumination fell across the bed.

Heath froze in the doorway.

"Oh, *fuck* no," he said faintly. "You have *got* to be kidding me. Gage—what the ever-loving, cock-sucking *shit*?"

THIRTEEN

Heath

I WAS LOSING MY fucking *mind*.

No. Scratch that. Gage had lost *his* fucking mind. The light from the hallway fell across his face, illuminating a look of resignation that made me want to punch him square in his perfect fucking jawline.

The she-devil was passed out in his bed, tucked snugly beneath the covers, and snoring like a freight train.

"She's scared of storms," Gage said, quietly enough not to wake her. "Well… not scared. Pretty sure it was actually a PTSD flashback. I brought her down here where it was quieter."

My teeth hurt where my molars were clenching together. "She tried. To *kill*. Knox." I forced the words out on the back of a growl.

"Yeah, and she's still our scent match," Gage replied, apparently unconcerned. "We can say it back and forth as many times as you want. None of it will change."

I couldn't deal with this. Not on top of everything else. I could *not* fucking deal.

"I'm not having this conversation," I grated out. "Put her back in the fucking attic."

"That's not happening," Gage said. "Our scent match does *not* get locked alone in a room when she's so scared that she ripped half her fingernails off trying to claw her way free."

Rage boiled in my chest, not so much at Gage, as at the fact that any of us had been put in this goddamned situation in the first place. I knew from bitter experience that my two choices were to lose control of myself… or turn around and walk away.

I turned around and walked away without another word.

"Heath—" My packmate's low voice called after me, and I ignored him.

I had a name and a gender designation to work with.

Adrian.

Male omega.

It was barely one step up from nothing, but if I didn't start pounding pavement and fucking *do* something, my head was going to explode.

I'd slept for maybe an hour-and-a-half before my nerves jolted me awake. I looked like three-day-old dogshit, and someone had thrown a scratchy wool blanket over my brain—leaving it itching and stifled.

The vague idea that I should probably eat something wriggled through my awareness like a silverfish struggling through mud to get back to its pond, and then it was gone. Instead, I grabbed my wallet, keys, and phone, slamming the door behind me as I left.

My BMW was parked around back, its shiny blue paint beaded with rain from the storm. The engine purred to life beneath my touch, accelerating smoothly onto the main road as I pointed it toward the Loop, with its collection of trendy bars.

With Knox's help, I'd left my life as a barely functional alcoholic behind. I still knew people, though. It was time to track those people down and start asking some questions.

<hr />

I was six bars deep, and lugging around a pocketful of blank rejections. *Nope…* no one knew anything about a male omega working for the Vozzina pack, who might or might not be called Adrian.

Chartreuse was the second-to-last stop on my list. I'd met Ames, the bartender, during my card-sharking days—assuming she still worked here. Stalking inside, I scanned the area behind the bar until my gaze fell on a shock of shoulder-length purple hair.

Good.

I shouldered my way past the crowd and got her attention. At six-foot-five, Ames had a couple of inches on me in both height and breadth. I was pretty sure she was trans, although I'd never asked since it wasn't my business. Her bi-colored gaze fell on me—one brown eye and one blue eye. Hetero-chrome-something-or-the-other, it was called.

Purple-dyed eyebrows furrowed as she looked me up and down in all my rumpled and sleep-deprived glory; then she visibly smoothed her expression and pasted on a smile.

"Heath," she said in her familiar husky tone. "Been a long time. Gimme a second, I'll be right with you."

I gave her a curt nod and waited while she slid drinks to a group of laughing betas. Biting down on a sudden craving for alcohol, I tapped my fingers impatiently on the deg of the bar until she came back.

"Ames," I said, forcing myself to exhibit some basic degree of not being an asshole. "How've you been keeping?"

Ames raised an eyebrow and poured me a glass of seltzer water, sticking a lime wedge on the edge of the glass before handing it to me.

"Well enough," she said cautiously. "You here for a social call?"

"No," I said, mindlessly twisting the glass back and forth in my grip on the bar top. Christ, I needed to get an answer and get out of this place before I ended up asking her to dump three fingers of gin into the goddamned seltzer. "Got a question, and I'm wondering if you've heard anything."

Her expression softened into sympathy. "I heard about Knox, if that's what you mean. Has there been any change?"

That wasn't a surprise, since the attempted murder had been all over the news.

"He's stabilized some, but that's not what I meant," I said. "I'm trying to find any information I can about a male omega who works for the Vozzinas. He might be called Adrian."

Ames' face closed off again. "Heath, babes… the Vozzinas buy and sell omegas by the dozen. They don't put them on the *payroll*."

I had more reasons than most to know that already. It wasn't the answer I wanted to hear, though.

"I'm well aware," I told her. "But there hasn't been anything making the rounds about an omega mixed up in their business somehow?"

She blinked, wiping her hands on a rag and leaning both palms on the bar across from me. "Well, I mean… when you put it like *that*."

I scowled. "When I put it like what?"

She tipped her head side to side a couple of times—a 'neither here nor there' gesture. "Nothing to do with putting an omega on the payroll… but Lorenzo Vozzina just *mated* a male omega, and it's big news in the gossip mills."

My heart gave a little kick of excitement. "He's mated? When did this happen?"

"Yesterday," Ames said. "Sounds like it was more of a business transaction than anything else. It's outside of a heat, so there's a big reception going on tonight at the Waldorf Astoria."

"Is there, now," I muttered, my craving for a drink forgotten as I turned this new puzzle piece over in my mind. "What's the omega's name? Do you know?"

"Hang on… let me think," Ames said. "Erm… Paolo, I'm pretty sure it was. I don't remember the last name, but it probably wouldn't be hard to track it down."

"That's okay," I said, adrenaline chasing away some of the fog of exhaustion that had been surrounding me. "You said the reception is at the Waldorf? And it's going on right now?"

"Yeah, I guess it's a pretty big deal among the people who like to be photographed at that sort of event," she said with a shrug. "I wouldn't have thought it was your kind of scene, though."

"Oh, it definitely isn't," I replied. "Thanks, Ames—I owe you one."

She snorted, and picked up a beer glass to wipe. "Right. I'll add it to all the others you owe me, asshole."

A mating reception at the Waldorf Astoria wasn't the kind of party you gatecrashed while wearing rumpled street clothes from two days ago. So, I walked into the gleaming marble reception area and booked a room for an eye-watering sum, ignoring the way the receptionist looked down his nose at me. At least that way, no one would summarily toss me out onto the street.

It took a frustratingly long time to find a waiter who would let me borrow his jacket for a cool grand in cash—and I sure as hell hoped I wouldn't need to bribe anyone else tonight, since that was all the money I'd been carrying with me.

As disguises went, it was paper-thin. Anyone who gave me more than the most cursory of glances would do a double-take...and my flaming red hair and beard tended to get quite a few glances at the best of times.

I grabbed a random tray from a pile in the kitchen and followed the parade of champagne and vol-au-vents to the ball room—where the reception was, as promised, in full swing.

My only saving grace was the fact that most assholes with a certain level of wealth looked at serving staff as scenery rather than as people. It didn't take long to read the room and home in on the center of attention in the echoing space.

Lorenzo Vozzina was nowhere to be seen, which was probably just as well. Instead, a slender male omega was holding court by the buffet tables, surrounded by fawning hangers-on holding champagne flutes as they tittered with polite laughter.

Vozzina's new mate was movie-star pretty in an androgynous sort of way, with jet-black hair artfully tousled over half his forehead, and a pair of cool gray eyes that were striking mostly because of their hardness. As I approached, an unpleasant hint of rosewater and peppermint hit the back of my throat.

I was only going to have one chance at this, and I only had a single piece of ammunition in my arsenal.

"Adrian!" I called, pitching my voice to be heard above the chatter. "I need to talk to you! Jez sent me!"

The fake name had only earned me the most fleeting of perplexed glances. But as soon as the word *Jez* came out of my mouth, the omega's eyes widened in clear alarm.

His gaze darted to first one side, then the other—a classic omega escape response. Then his face turned stony as he purposely returned his attention to me, lifting his chin.

"Security!" he called. "Someone detain that man! He's impersonating a waiter!"

Dozens of eyes snapped to me. Cries of alarm went up from the group of social climbers, even as not-Adrian slipped away toward an inconspicuous side door, casting me a sharp glance over his shoulder as he went.

FOURTEEN

Jez

I WOKE UP WITH an aching head and clogged sinuses. Something was vibrating behind my back—a low, rumbling sound that unwound all the tight muscles in my neck and shoulders.

My mate was purring as he watched over my sleep. *Gage*… was purring.

The stuffy nose left over from my crying jag wasn't enough to keep his homey scent from clinging to the back of my throat. It surrounded me every bit as warmly as the soft comforter I was tucked beneath.

The sound of the storm was gone, already fading into a distant, dreamlike memory. I made a congested humming noise, unable to stop myself from rubbing my cheek against the pillow cover my head was resting on. The cool cotton felt divine, and I had to get my scent all over it so Gage would smell it every time he laid down on the bed.

The purring intensified as I curled sinuously against the bedding, catlike. Then it faded away. The mattress shifted behind me—a large form sitting upright. Rough fingers stroked my sweat-dried hair back from my temple. My skin sang beneath the simple sensation, sending lovely tingles skittering down my spine.

Were we still pretending?

I thought we must be, or Gage wouldn't be petting me like this… the gentle touch waking feelings inside me that threatened to crack me right down the middle.

"Feeling better now, kitten?" he asked. "The storm's over."

A strange, pleasurable squirming feeling took up residence in my stomach in reaction to the unexpected pet name. We *were* still pretending.

Did I dare live in this make-believe world for a little bit longer?

I rolled onto my back, looking up at the square-jawed alpha. A wedge of yellow light from the hallway streamed through the open bedroom door, illuminating his face. His perpetual five-o'clock shadow had graduated into full-blown stubble, and a furrow of concern cut small lines between his heavy brows.

No matter how badly I'd provoked him, Gage hadn't hurt me. He'd fed me and wrapped tiny bandages over my torn fingernails, and held me while I got tears and snot all over his shirt.

That sounds nice, he'd said, when I'd told him I wanted to pretend for a while that all of this was normal.

"Yes," I told him. "I feel better."

"That's good," he said, like it was something he actually meant. "I'm glad. This whole thing really blows. For you, and for us."

But I didn't want to talk about that.

"Can I... have a shower and brush my teeth?" I asked hesitantly.

"Yeah, of course," he said. The hand that had been stroking my hair rested over my forehead for a moment, as though checking for a fever. "You've really gotta eat something afterward, though. And keep it down."

Hunger was an old friend, but there was little question that it was contributing to the swimmy sense of unreality floating around me like a cloud. On cue, my stomach cramped, letting out a gurgling noise that echoed around the quiet bedroom.

"Okay," I said meekly.

I let him show me to the en suite. He rummaged around in a drawer beneath the vanity and came up with a new toothbrush still in its plastic packaging. Then he pulled out towels, and a fresh soap bar, and a clean washcloth—placing them on the counter next to the sink like offerings at an altar.

Once he'd gone, closing the door behind him with a soft click, I stared at my face in the mirror. I looked like a zombie—gaunt and pale and red-eyed. It was worse when I pulled off the silken pajamas Tony had brought me. My bones jutted beneath translucent skin, sharp edged and dangerous.

How could he possibly want something like you? The snide little voice whispered its poisoned words inside my mind. *Broken and bitter and worthless...*

I'd put Gage's pack leader in the hospital. I'd wished Matthew Knockley dead with every fiber of my being. And even now, underneath it all, the scent-match sung its quiet melody of belonging to both of us.

But I didn't have to think about that yet. We were pretending… and it was so much better than any part of reality had been since I was a tiny child.

I brushed the sour taste of vomit out of my mouth with a clean new toothbrush and minty toothpaste. I ignored the brand-new bar of soap still wrapped in its waxy paper, instead turning the shower on as hot as I could stand it and scrubbing my body with Gage's body wash. I lathered Gage's shampoo through my straggling platinum-blond hair and rinsed it out, feeling the hot needles of water pepper my nerves.

He didn't use conditioner on his close-cropped buzz cut, but it wasn't like I did either, most of the time. For me, it was usually a quick shower in a gym locker room, using whatever soap I could afford. This was luxury.

When I eventually got out and dried myself off with a soft, fluffy towel so big it practically swallowed me, there was a white button-down shirt hanging from the doorknob. Steam billowed in the enclosed room—but my sinuses were clear now, and I could smell the yeasty fresh-bread scent coming off it, cut through with that sharp hint of citrus.

I froze, looking at the barely worn pajamas lying in a crumpled pile on the vanity... and back at the shirt. Gage was a towering mountain of an alpha. His shirt would practically be a knee-length dress on my five-foot, three-inch frame. I rolled my lower lip between my teeth, torn.

We're pretending, I reminded myself, and grabbed the shirt.

Gage's scent surrounded me in a comforting haze as I shrugged into it and did up the buttons. It immediately quieted my thoughts, dropping me into a sea of soft serenity that made me feel almost drugged.

He was waiting when I opened the bathroom door and walked out. A pleased expression brightened his heavy features when he saw me wearing his clothing, and a low, possessive rumble rose from his chest.

I shivered, unused to the feeling that was rushing through my veins like warm honey.

With a deep breath, Gage seemed to master himself. "Hungry now?" he asked.

Hunger? Was that what this strange, wanting feeling in my belly was?

"Yes," I said. Outside the window, the sky was pitch black. I gestured vaguely in that direction. "But it's the middle of the night."

Gage shrugged. "Kitchen still works at night. C'mon. You like pancakes and bacon?"

"I like anything," I said, as my stomach gave another loud grumble.

I sat on a stool as Gage heated skillets and poured ingredients into a huge bowl. Food started appearing on a plate set before me—crispy bacon that melted in my mouth when I bit down on it, and fluffy pancakes topped with an obscene amount of syrup and fresh fruit and whipped cream from an aerosol can.

My stomach felt like a black hole, but I slowed down after the second plate. I knew from bitter experience that dumping too much food on it after days of barely eating wouldn't end well.

"Are you full?" Gage asked. "Here, have some more orange juice. You need to replenish your fluids."

I drank most of the glass of tangy juice he pressed on me, trying not to wonder if it tasted like Gage's skin.

"I'm full," I assured him. "*Really* full."

"Good," he said. "There's always plenty of food here, Jez. When you're hungry, I want you to say so, okay?"

The perfect illusion wavered like heat haze.

"After you stick me back in the attic, you mean?" I asked, the words slipping free without my permission.

Abruptly, I saw exhaustion on Gage's face that mirrored my own. His control slipped, and his entire body seemed to sag for a moment before he straightened his shoulders again.

"We need to do this different, Jez," he said. "It can't be like it was before. Heath ain't gonna like it, but he's wrong. But the thing is—if it's going to be different, it's got to be different on your end, too. You understand what I'm saying?"

I did, but it didn't stop the shiver of cold that trickled through me.

"What if Knox dies?" I whispered.

"Knox won't die." Gage said it like he could shape reality to his own desires by force of will alone. "He's gonna get better, and then all of us together can figure out what we're supposed to do."

"Knox won't die," I repeated unsteadily. *"Knox won't die."*

"Damn right he won't," Gage agreed. "Now, like you said—it's the middle of the night. Come back to bed. I looked at the weather radar; there won't be any more storms tonight."

With a sudden, desperate longing, I remembered what it felt like to fall asleep with Gage's arm tucking me close and safe against his big body. We'd stopped pretending for a few minutes, but maybe we could start again. Gage didn't want me to be locked in the attic. He wanted me to stay with them of my own free will.

I wanted to stay with him tonight. I wanted to be safe in my alpha's arms, knowing that I could sleep and nothing would hurt me while my guard was down.

"Okay." My voice was a rasp.

Gage quickly cleaned up the mess in the kitchen, putting pots and pans in the dishwasher and efficiently wiping down the countertop. I let him herd me back to his bedroom, to the soft blankets and the pillow that smelled like both of us together.

This time, he stripped down to a white tank top and climbed beneath the covers with me, still wearing his tailored pants. My stomach was full, and my body was warm and contented. I fell asleep once more with our bodies fitting together like spoons nestled safely in a drawer.

When I woke the next time, it was still dark… but the darkness held that hint of gray that said it was closer to dawn than not. Somehow, I'd wriggled around while I was asleep, and I was now sprawled half across Gage's large body with my leg thrown between his.

My brain felt like slow molasses, with my nose pressed to the juncture of his neck and shoulder where his scent was the strongest. The crease of his trousers pressed between my legs, at the sensitive apex of my thighs. Without a single thought in my head, I rolled my hips to rub myself against that small point of friction, moaning softly as the movement set off fireworks behind my closed eyelids.

Gage, still fully asleep, let out an answering moan as his hips curled, rubbing his huge, hard length against my hip. A longing I'd never felt before trembled through my body, centering low in my belly with heavy, liquid heat. My tongue darted out, licking a stripe up the side of my alpha's neck—tasting that tangy spark of citrus I'd wondered about earlier.

A deeper groan spilled from Gage's lips and he shuddered awake. As though his return to consciousness had somehow rebooted my own brain, I froze abruptly, realizing what I was doing.

He went still as well, his breath catching.

"Jez?" he asked, his voice so low and deep that it sent shivers through me.

FIFTEEN

Jez

CHRIST, WHAT WAS I DOING? And more importantly, why did I want so badly to keep doing it? I pushed away with a gasp, putting space between us.

"S-sorry," I stammered, immediately missing the warmth of Gage's body against mine.

"You don't need to apologize for *that*, kitten," he said, still in that delicious low rumble. "Think I might've rubbed on you while I was still half out of it, though. So, I guess we can both be sorry. Say the word, and none of it every happened."

The sultry miasma of pheromones in the bedroom made it very clear that it *had* happened, though. So did the damp patch between my thighs. I was guessing there was a matching patch on the thigh of his trousers, too. The thought made heat rise to my cheeks.

I shook my head sharply. "It's just… I don't do this kind of thing."

Enough gray light was filtering through the window that I could make out his frown.

"What, never?" he asked.

I scooted back to lean against the headboard, wrapping my arms around my knees.

"Never," I confirmed. "I never wanted to."

The frown deepened. "You mean because of what happened to you when you were young?" He shifted further away from me. "You want me to get off the bed? Give you some space?"

The harsh laugh that escaped me sounded halfway like a sob. "No."

I wanted the opposite. I'd had a single, tiny taste of pretending my life was normal, and I was already turning into an addict.

He settled his weight back on the mattress. "Okay. Really, it's fine, though. Lots of people aren't interested in sex. Or, y'know, sex with other people. And I know this whole thing is really complicated already."

It was complicated because I'd made it complicated. It was complicated because I'd believed another omega's sob story and done something about it. It was complicated because I was walking wounded when it came to mental health.

"What if it wasn't, though?" I asked, before clarifying, "Complicated, I mean."

He paused, his big body very still. "You mean… what if we were living in that other world where we chose this?"

I nodded, not looking at him.

He seemed to think about that for a moment. "Then I'd want to show you how good your body can feel. If… that was what you wanted, I mean."

My pussy gave a needy little throb. More honey slicked the inside of my thighs.

"That world sounds a lot nicer than this one," I managed unsteadily.

Gage let out a heavy breath. Silence settled over the bedroom.

"Maybe they don't have to be so far apart," he said. "There's one part of this that's really simple, at least to my mind. You're my mate. *Our* mate. And our mate should at least know what it feels like to be loved in that way."

My eyes flew to him; my body drawn toward him like iron filings to a magnet.

"So… we could pretend for a bit longer?" My voice was a rasp.

But he shook his head. "No, Jez. You being our mate is reality. Everything that you and I do together is real. The fact that there's some seriously fucked-up shit going on in the background doesn't make it less real."

My mind shied away from the words, not ready to hear them. Before I could merge the real and pretend worlds, I had to know whether Adrian had been lying to me or not. Until then, I was a cat in a box with some German-sounding name that I'd forgotten—neither murderer nor righteous avenger, hanging in limbo.

Unreal.

"I need to know what sex feels like when it's something you want," I said in a rush.

I bit my lip, waiting for Gage's answer.

"Yeah," he said after a pause. "Everyone deserves to have that. But, um… maybe don't mention any of this to Heath."

I couldn't help my choked laughter.

"Right, probably not," I agreed.

"Lie back," he said, turning to face me fully on the bed. "Unbutton that shirt far enough that you can get a hand on your breasts. You don't have to undo it all the way unless you want to. And this is real important—if something feels wrong, you've gotta say so right away." He let out an unhappy breath. "I know that can be hard when no one ever listened before. But I'm gonna listen, okay?"

"Okay," I whispered.

He hitched a leg up, his knee bent and one elbow resting on it casually. "Good. Go on, then."

Defiantly, I undid all eight buttons with fumbling fingers. Gage's shirt fell open, exposing me to his gaze. My nerves sang with anticipation, as though his eyes on me were something physical against my skin.

"You're perfect," Gage said, his tone a low purr.

I forced myself to hold his gaze defiantly. "I thought I was too skinny."

He shook his head slowly. "Being skinny or fat or in between doesn't have a thing to do with being perfect. I just want to make sure you have all the food you want, that's all. I feel like maybe you don't always."

I shivered, breaking eye contact before he could see the wetness gathering on my eyelashes.

"Now, touch yourself," he went on. "Run your hands over your skin. Pinch your nipples if that feels good to you. Look at me while you do it."

My breath stuttered. I forced myself to look back at him, focusing on a point above his left collarbone as I lifted my hands and tentatively stroked them over my upper body.

It wasn't accurate to say that I'd never explored myself. But living on the streets didn't come with a whole lot of privacy... and it could be hard to keep my mind from slipping back to the past. Plus, it had never felt anything like this when I was alone.

I'd never had horny alpha hormones flowing around me like a cloud, smelling like the most perfect bakery in existence. Under Gage's approving gaze, the uninspiring slide of skin on skin transformed into bottled lightning rushing along my nerves. My lips parted as I explored, teasing the tender flesh of my tits and stroking down my stomach.

"That's it," Gage murmured. "Touch between your legs. Get that slick all over your fingers and explore a bit."

I moaned, more slick pulsing out as though he'd called it directly into existence with his words. Tentatively, I stroked my wet folds; the whole area awake now after having been asleep for years. My clit, a sullen and uninterested observer since I'd escaped my captivity eight years ago, lit up with electric pleasure.

"*God,*" I yelped, circling a finger around it faster and faster. "Gage! Please... touch me! I need you to touch me!"

Instinct surged, demanding that my mate stop teasing and get to work on me. Gage let out a low rumble of a growl, and then he was leaning over me, his big hands covering mine where they worked my breast and clit.

"You're close already, kitten," he said, the words heavy with satisfaction. "You want me to fill you up with my fingers while you come?"

My passage gave a warning flutter. I arched, my heart pounding furiously.

"Y-yes!" I cried, even though what I really wanted was the hard cock I'd felt nudging against me earlier.

The hand guiding mine slid away, further back. Blunt fingers teased my entrance, meeting no resistance thanks to the slick I was churning out. For a bare instant, the intrusion felt deeply strange—like there was a sense memory trying to fight its way to the fore.

It sunk beneath the wild waves of pleasure rocking me, though. There was no similarity whatsoever between what was happening now, and the last time I'd been penetrated. Gage's fingers slid along the front wall of my passage, igniting new sparks as he rubbed at some magic spot inside me that made me see stars.

"That's it," he said, sounding faintly breathless. "Let go. Let me feel you, kitten. God, you're so beautiful like this."

Pleasure ricocheted between his fingers and mine, tangling up into a ball that got bigger and hotter and wilder until it burst, washing through my entire body in an explosion of pulsing warmth.

I let out a strangled shriek, nearly levitating off the bed as my pussy clenched convulsively, over and over. I could feel my muscles trying to clamp down on Gage's thick knuckles, but he was already pulling his fingers free.

I whimpered, too far gone to be ashamed of the pitiful noise.

"Shh," he soothed. "Do you want more? I can use my mouth on you. See if I can make you come again, only harder this time."

Harder? Was he *insane*?

Only… I *did* want more. I wanted so much more. If his mouth was the thing on offer, then I would take it because I was a greedy bitch living firmly in denial until the sun came up.

"Yes," I said. "Yes, I want your mouth."

I want all of you.

"Good girl," Gage murmured.

I shivered, gooseflesh breaking out across my arms.

He took me by the ankles and tugged me to the edge of the mattress, kneeling on the floor in his white undershirt and tailored suit trousers. I groaned as he slung my knees over his broad shoulders and hitched my hips right to the edge.

His nose tickled my pubic hair, and I heard him inhale greedily.

"Jesus Christ, you smell like heaven," he muttered, before his broad tongue rasped along the length of my folds, lapping up the mess I was making.

Hard on the heels of my first-ever voluntary orgasm, I was essentially a puddle of goo on the bed. The waves of pleasure as Gage devoured me greedily with lips and tongue were deep, rather than wild. My muscles stayed utterly lax as the now-familiar feeling of a vessel being filled gradually to bursting gathered low in my belly.

Those thick fingers returned, stretching and stroking me open. This time, my climax dragged me down deep instead of blowing me open. All of my focus went internal, until I couldn't have said where I was, or even *who* I was.

When I surfaced this time, it was with the same feeling of clenching emptiness. Gage's fingers were gone. I knew, on some level, that they wouldn't have been enough to fill me, anyway.

He was sitting next to me on the edge of the bed, looking down at me with a combination of satisfaction and naked longing.

"Good?" he asked mildly.

That longing connected directly with my own aching emptiness.

"I need your cock," I slurred.

I need your bite, I didn't say.

His brows knitted. "Are you sure? I didn't think you'd—"

"I *need* it," I insisted. "Gage, please… I'm so empty inside."

There was more than one kind of emptiness, of course. But at least this kind could be filled up by Gage's knot.

"Fuck," he mumbled. "Jesus fuck, Jez."

"*Please*," I repeated, in my most pathetic voice.

"You're going to be the death of me, and you're not even trying to kill me anymore," he said under his breath.

Guilt pricked at me, only to be swallowed whole a moment later by the sea of endorphins sloshing around in my skull.

"Hang on, kitten." He got up and rummaged in a dresser drawer, eventually coming up with a foil packet. "Hope these things don't have a use-by date."

I was pretty sure they did, and in that moment, I couldn't have cared less.

He flopped back on the bed with the packet held between his teeth. I got enough muscles cooperating to roll over so I could watch him undo his fly and pull his underwear down. He tore open the foil and tossed it away, rolling the condom over his massive alpha cock. It jutted up, hot and hard and girthy.

"I want you on top, beautiful," he said, his eyes dark in the predawn light. "I'm all yours — do what feels good. You should know I ain't gonna last long, though."

He very deliberately reached up and clasped his hands behind his head — a silent promise not to grab or hold. I clambered clumsily over to straddle him, not sure if I should feel weird about having no hesitation over this. Gage obviously thought it might trigger some kind of PTSD episode, but it was so different than what had happened to me before that I couldn't get the two things to line up in my head.

They were totally unrelated.

It was a bit tricky getting his length lined up. Huge peg, small hole. And, yeah, it kind of hurt when I shoved downward, forcing his hard cock into the grasping space that was begging for something to squeeze and milk. For, like, half a second.

Then it was maybe the best thing I'd ever felt.

The wavering, high-pitched cry probably came from me. The rough curse definitely came from Gage.

"All right?" he asked.

"Shut up," I said, and started moving.

Gage was good to his word. He was still and passive beneath me, except for the quiver of leashed muscles that trembled beneath my thighs every few seconds.

I felt like a wild thing, slamming myself down on the cock inside me over and over. I threw my head back, panting through my open mouth.

"Touch your clit." The words were choked. Desperate.

Gage was close, but so was I. I braced one hand on his muscular chest and delved between my folds with the other, rubbing roughly over my nub until a third orgasm rose up and swamped me. Gage roared, his hips jerking up in a messy rhythm as he emptied his load into the condom.

Sweat was dripping down my body as I collapsed forward against him, panting hard. His knot swelled, and my passage convulsed, trapping him in place. My heart felt like it was trying to crash through my ribs… but slowly, slowly, everything inside me settled into calm serenity.

Gage freed his hands from behind his head. One arm draped over my back, holding me to him. The other hand stroked over the back of my head soothingly, my scalp tingling beneath the gentle touch. The world beyond our joined bodies faded to insignificance, a distant and dreamlike thing. I closed my eyes and breathed out, feeling years of old pain carried away on the exhale.

⬦

I wasn't sure how long we stayed knotted. The cliches weren't as true as I'd been led to believe, though—because I stayed awake the whole time, while Gage was out like a snuffed candle.

I wondered if he'd slept at all since I'd attacked Knox, beyond the couple of hours he'd caught after he'd made me pancakes and taken me back to bed.

It was fully light out as I sat against the headboard, looking down at his rugged face. He looked younger like this. Maybe everyone did, when they were peacefully asleep.

Unfortunately, my own peace was retreating like a mirage as the haze of sex and sleep wore off. Pretend time was over. It was time to face reality. To face the consequences of my actions, whatever that might mean.

I'd been listening intently, and there wasn't a single sound from elsewhere in the house. Which meant this was probably my chance. I didn't want to be stuck here as a cat locked in a box, not knowing what I was guilty of. I needed answers, and those answers lay outside this remote house.

Cautiously, I stroked a hand over Gage's bristly hair, checking how deeply he was asleep. He didn't even stir.

I took a deep breath and got up.

The clothing Tony had bought was still upstairs. I crept up to the attic room, ignoring the shudder of distaste as I crossed over the threshold. After dressing quickly in practical clothes, I went back downstairs, still listening for any other signs of life in the house. Gage was in exactly the same position as when I'd left him.

Ignoring the misgivings rocketing through me, I did a quick search and found his cell phone and wallet. I pocketed the phone and two hundred dollars, tiptoed to the front door, and let myself out.

The driveway was as long and winding as I remembered. I jogged down to the road and hid in the trees near the mailbox while I figured out how to power up the phone. There wasn't a passcode or face recognition, which even *I* knew was fucking stupid.

The Uber app was already installed. I pulled it up and then fumbled around until I figured out how to call a ride. I had a date in the city with an omega named Adrian, and I wasn't putting it off for a moment longer.

SIXTEEN

Heath

I GROWLED AND SNARLED, instinct taking over as four burly private security guards converged on me like a rugby scrum. I might've gotten my answer about the fictional *Adrian*, but I was also an idiot running on soured adrenaline and no sleep.

Screams and raised voices echoed around the high-end hotel event room. Even if I'd had a gun on me, I wouldn't have dared use it. A meaty hand closed around my wrist and twisted, nearly dislocating my shoulder as the paid muscle wrestled me face-first onto the polished marble tile.

Something cracked in my pocket with a sound like crunching glass. Sharp edges jammed into my hip. *Great.* That was the end of my phone, then.

I craned around, trying to catch a glimpse of Lorenzo Vozzina's omega mate—but all I could see were legs and feet. A heavy blow hit the base of my skull, stunning me. The sea of legs tilted, and the sounds of panicked confusion warped in my ears, ringing like a cathedral bell.

A hand yanked me up by the hair. More hands forced my arms behind me. Something thin and flexible looped around my wrists and tightened until it dug into the skin. A zip tie.

Two of the goons hooked hands beneath my armpits and hauled me upright. My injured shoulder screamed; the room spun around me in dizzy circles. Another fist impacted my cheek, snapping my head sharply to the side. Blood flooded my mouth from a cut cheek. I spat it onto the white floor—an ugly red splash of color.

"Come with us," grunted on of the goons.

I sneered at him, tasting blood on my teeth. "Why? Am I under arrest, *officer*?"

"Bring him," said the goon, ignoring me.

A fist drove into my left kidney, and my knees buckled. I tried to get my feet back under me as the two paid grunts supporting me dragged me forward, but I only succeeded in reeling drunkenly within their grip.

'Drunk' sounded pretty nice right about now, actually.

"What're we supposed to do with him?" one of my captors asked.

"Gotta check with the boss," said the one who seemed to be giving orders. "Get him some cement shoes and dump him in the lake, maybe."

"No one actually does that," muttered another goon. "Takes too long for the cement to dry."

I had a confused glimpse of Head Goon pulling out a phone and raising it to his ear as I was dragged into an elevator car.

"Hey boss?" he asked, as the door slid shut. "We captured some asshole that was bothering your mate at the party. An alpha. Hair and beard like a fire engine. He was pretending to be a waiter. What d'you want us to do with him?"

There was a pause, then unintelligible buzz of the answer came. The elevator slid smoothly downward, threatening to send the meager contents of my stomach on a final farewell tour as we headed for the basement.

Fuck, I was dense. I'd been in such a hurry to get away from Gage's fucking bedroom—and the omega sleeping in it—that I'd delivered myself straight into Lorenzo Vozzina's hands. No one knew I'd come here. No one except Vozzina and his goons would have any clue where I ended up next.

No one was coming after me, and Vozzina had every reason to want me gone. After the way Adrian—or *Paolo*, rather—had reacted to Jez's name, it was pretty obvious that he and Vozzina had orchestrated Knox's attempted murder. Gage and I would be the next obvious targets on the list.

Lead Goon put his phone away. "Take him to the hotel's loading dock. The boss wants us to throw him in a van and take him to that warehouse where they film all the shit with the omegas."

I growled and braced myself, struggling as the doors slid open to reveal the hotel's dark underbelly—utilitarian concrete full of clanking machinery and hissing boilers. The goons dragged me out, cursing under their breath. I was manhandled toward a large overhead door surrounded by carts of laundry and crates of god-knew-what. Head Goon pushed a big yellow button on the wall, and the door began to slide up, revealing the darkness of the city night beyond.

A heavy blow came out of nowhere, impacting my temple, and I crumpled like a ragdoll as my consciousness fled.

———————◆———————

When I woke up, I'd been dumped on a metal table in an unfamiliar room. My wrists were still zip tied behind me, and now my ankles had been bound, too. I groaned, trying to roll sideways to get the strain off my trapped arms, but my muscles wouldn't cooperate.

The voices that had been buzzing meaninglessly around me went silent. I blinked into the glare of an overhead light, trying to bring the dark blobs leaning over me into focus.

"He's awake." Not-Adrian's light tenor came from somewhere on my right.

"Yes, we can see that." The deeper rumble, laced with a permanent sneer of disdain, set off alarm bells in my head. I blinked several more times until one of the blurs resolved into a pockmarked, olive-skinned face topped by greasy, overly coiffed hair fashioned into fussy little finger waves.

Lorenzo Vozzina.

He waved impatiently at someone. "Get the stim shot into him before he starts flopping around too much. Are the cameras set up?"

"Yeah, boss," said another voice. "We got 'em set up on the ceiling so he won't be able to get at 'em."

A big hand grabbed my skull, the thumb digging into my bruised temple. I hissed and bucked as the grip jerked my head to the side, forcing me into a position like a scared omega showing throat. An instant later, a sharp prick in the side of my neck made me go still. Something cold pushed into my vein, only to start burning like acid as it spread.

"What the *fuck*?" I slurred, sounding drugged and stupid to my own ringing ears.

The needle pulled out, and Vozzina leaned over me again.

"Heath Dawson," he said. "Age twenty-nine. Born in Belfast, Northern Ireland. Emigrated to Chicago at the age of three with your parents, now deceased. Former alcoholic; former card-sharp. Now in the employ of one Matthew Knockley, soon to be deceased."

"Go fuck a razor blade," I snarled.

"You know, your pack has caused me no end of trouble, these past few years," Vozzina went on.

"No idea what you mean," I grated out. "Who are you supposed to be, anyway?"

"Don't act stupid," Not-Adrian said, his voice dripping with contempt. "You ruined my reception. Now my mate's going to ruin *you*."

A terrible itchy, jittery sensation was spreading along my nerves, moving outward from my shoulder and jaw in hot waves.

"What did you drug me with?" I demanded, as the urge to scream and thrash against the zip ties rose, growing stronger with every second.

"Oh, that?" Vozzina asked, all innocence. "Just a nice big dose of rut-stim. It should kick in within the next few minutes."

Not-Adrian gave a harsh little laugh, and I was struck by the sudden need to get my hands around his throat and squeeze until his eyeballs popped like overripe grapes. At the same time, blood rushed inexplicably southward, while some sick, deeply buried part of me whispered about all the things that could be done to an omega once I'd subdued him and killed his mate.

I cringed back from him with a gasp, so violently that I nearly slid right off the metal gurney.

"Get him to the cell," Vozzina said, sounding as amused as his hateful little mate. He grinned down at me with teeth. "Oh, and someone go get the kid. Don't worry, Dawson. We'll throw you a bit of fluff to shred into pieces, so you don't lose your marbles completely. And, as you may have heard just now, we've got cameras all set up to record and stream the whole thing, directly to the kind of internet cesspits that enjoy that kind of content. You're going to be *famous*."

Not-Adrian tittered again. "Famous with the deviants and pedos, anyway," he added.

Icy dread replaced the burning acid in my veins.

"Wh-what?" I stammered… but the gurney was already moving, its wheels jarring over the uneven concrete floor.

Strong hands held me down, keeping me from rolling off the juddering thing as we traversed hallways and echoing, open spaces. Eventually, the metal cart was pushed through a cell door. I looked around wildly. The room was completely bare, and maybe twelve feet long by twelve feet wide. The front wall and door were made of heavy iron bars. Other than that, it was a concrete cube without so much as a sink or cot.

The gurney tipped sideways, sending me crashing to the hard floor.

Before I could get my bearings past the conflagration burning through my body and mind, the men retreated through the door, leaving me still bound and wriggling like a hooked fish.

The sound of terrified crying penetrated the rushing sound in my ears. Just as I managed to get my body turned around so I could see the door, a huge goon shoved a small boy into the cell before retreating and slamming the bars shut.

The terrified scent of lemon and smoky paprika exploded across the back of my throat. The kid was a male omega—about twelve, or maybe a bit older if he was malnourished.

"Have fun, now," Not-Adrian sing-songed. "Oh… and *smile*! You're on Candid Camera!"

Laughing, Vozzina, Not-Adrian, and his goons all trooped away, the gurney squeaking and rattling into the distance as they left. The omega, still weeping hysterically, scrambled backwards until he was jammed into the farthest corner from me.

My muscles began to shake with rage as the reality of what was happening truly started to sink in. They'd given me a rut stim, and locked me in this tiny fucking cell with a terrified baby omega. *An omega who was not my mate.*

The out-of-control emotion that had been churning through me like a wind-driven wildfire exploded into an inferno. With a roar, I jerked my arms apart with uncontrolled alpha strength, heedless of the way the zip-tie tore into the flesh of my wrists as it snapped. I grabbed at the strap around my ankles with hands like claws, and snapped that as well.

The omega boy screamed, curling sideways into a ball to hide his face.

The memory of caramel and espresso curled through me like liquid torment. *Mate*, it whispered. *Mate. Mate. Your mate is out there somewhere, and you're trapped in here.*

Another agonized howl ripped free of my chest, and I crab-crawled backward—jamming myself into the opposite corner from the child and hugging my knees to my chest as the rut rose up and swallowed me whole.

SEVENTEEN

Tony

THE PRIVATE ROOM at Northwestern Memorial where Knox lay hooked up to machines and monitors was nicer than most of the apartments where I'd lived. Idly, I wondered how much it cost per day. Although, it wasn't like Knox's pack couldn't afford it — even if they didn't have great insurance, which, let's be fair, they probably did.

Maybe it was an odd time to be reminded of the different worlds we lived in. But I'd been thinking about that a lot lately… ever since I'd fallen into bed with Heath. It was my own damned fault, of course. I'd asked for it, and he'd given it to me, and now here I was, unable to get that night out of my head, even weeks later.

I'd known we inhabited different worlds. I wasn't stupid. I just hadn't known *how* different until all of our truths came pouring out in the grim attic bedroom where they were keeping Jez. Heath was helping Knox and the others rescue omegas, and he hadn't trusted me enough to tell me.

I shook my head, trying to clear it. No, that wasn't true. He'd been trying to protect me. They all had been. For some reason, though, it still stung like a betrayal.

A glance at the clock on the wall showed that it was coming up on dawn. I didn't plan on leaving until mid-morning, so the others could both get a meaningful amount of sleep. Alphas were tough, but they weren't superhuman.

I yawned. I was starting to flag a bit, but I much preferred to see the dawn from this direction. I might not be a morning person, but I could handle them if they were at the tail end of a very long night.

A low grunt came from the bed.

I'd been balancing my chair on its back legs—a habit left over from childhood, now that there was no one left to yell at me about it. At the sound, I nearly overbalanced. The chair clunked hard as the front legs came down. I was up and at Knox's bedside in an instant.

A muscle in his angular jaw was twitching. His left hand was above the covers, hooked up to an I.V. His fingers clenched and unclenched spasmodically.

"Knox?" I asked. "Knox, can you hear me?"

Knox gave a low moan, although I couldn't tell if he was responding specifically to my voice. Still, it was something.

"Nurse! Hey, *nurse!*" I shouted, before remembering that there was a call button on the side of the bed. I grabbed it and shoved my thumb hard against the button.

By the time the nurse came in, Knox's eyes were open, staring blank and bloodshot at the ceiling.

"He's awake!" I said, getting out of the man's way as he hurried over.

"That's good news," he said, peeling Knox's eyelids up one at a time and shining a pen light into them. "Mr. Knockley? Matthew? You're in the hospital. I need to check you over, and the doctor will be here shortly to do some tests. Can you blink once for me?"

I sidled up close enough to see while still hopefully being out of the way. Knox continued to stare unseeingly at the ceiling, and worry tugged at me.

"That's all right." The nurse's voice was re-assuring. "You've been unconscious for a while, Matthew, so it may take some time to adjust."

"He's going to be okay now, right?" I couldn't help asking.

The nurse smiled a professional smile. "Well, it's always better to be awake than in a coma. Vitals look good. Let's get the on-call doctor in here to get you some better answers. Keep talking to him, okay? That can help."

I swallowed hard as the nurse left me alone with Knox. Pulling my chair up to the side of the ICU bed, I debated calling Heath and Gage. But what would I say? *'Hey, sorry to wake you, but Knox opened his eyes and twitched a bit… no, he's not responding to questions and doesn't seem to know where he is… we're just waiting for a doctor to show up and figure out if he's a mental vegetable or not.'*

I decided to wait until I had something more concrete to pass on. And in the meantime, I was supposed to be talking to him. Crap.

"Uh… hi, Knox. It's Tony. You and me don't know each other all that well, but I told the others I'd stay with you tonight so they could get some sleep. Things are, um, a bit crazy at the moment. The others are okay though. Well, I mean, they're super worried about you, obviously."

This was a lot harder than I thought it would be. Especially since I might as well have been talking to a wall. I couldn't exactly start spouting my mouth about betrayal and murder plots and scent matches. God, *that* was a thought. Did he already know Jez was his scent match? She'd clearly gotten close to him on the night of the attack.

Thoughts about the scent match led un-helpfully to thoughts about Heath, and what a goddamned mess *that* whole thing had turned into. By the time a tired-looking doctor came in clutching a clipboard, I was babbling nonsensi-cally about sports scores and the weather.

The gray-haired woman saved me from my own awkwardness, thankfully for all of us.

"Good morning, Matthew!" she greeted, her chirpy tone at odds with the exhausted bags under her eyes. "Your friend here says you've been showing signs of wakefulness, which is great news. Unfortunately, it also means I need to poke and prod you for a bit. Can you blink your eyes for us, please?"

I held my breath, but there was still no response.

"Ah, well—poking and prodding it is!" said the doctor, pulling out a ball point pen.

She proceeded to press the pen-point into various parts of Knox's body, hard enough that it looked painful. Sometimes it elicited a small twitch; other times there was nothing. Finally, she tugged the sheet free at the end of the bed and exposed his feet. At the first press of the point into the arch of his right foot, he jerked hard and let out a hoarse curse.

"There we go!" the doctor said cheerfully, stepping nimbly away from accidental kicking range. "Welcome back to the land of the living."

"What the *hell*?" Knox asked, his voice so raspy it was hardly audible.

"Ah, well, that's a bit of a long story, I'm afraid," said the doctor. "Most of which I don't actually have. Basically, they just pay me to wear a stethoscope and poke people with ball-point pens at the end of a thirty-six-hour shift."

Knox stared at her with bleary incomprehension.

The doctor gave him a kind smile. "Maybe we can start with some ice chips and go from there. Nurse?"

"On it," the nurse said.

The doctor turned to me, with her practiced smile in place. "There are still a bunch of tests to run that don't involve a biro, but this is a major milestone. Don't worry if he goes right back to sleep. His body needs proper rest, which is quite a different thing from being unconscious. We'll be monitoring him carefully over the coming hours."

Alone with Knox once more, I couldn't help the way my whole body slumped with relief. I might not be all that close to Knox myself, but knowing how intensely Heath and Gage loved him, it was hard not to feel connected to his recovery.

Speaking of which...

"Hey, Knox? I'm going to call your packmates and let them know you're awake. They'll definitely want to hear the news."

"'Kay," Knox mumbled weakly. My heart soared at the confirmation that he was aware of what was going on and could understand what I was saying.

I pulled my phone out, ignoring an instinctive flash of anxiety at the low battery charge. It was plenty for a couple of short calls.

I pulled up Heath's contact first, not sure which of them was likely to be sleeping, and which of them would be awake guarding Jez. The call went straight to voicemail without ringing, and I frowned. He wouldn't have turned his phone off, but he'd been running on no sleep and might have forgotten to charge it.

It didn't matter. They were both at the house. I called Gage instead. The phone rang four times and disconnected without picking up.

"C'mon, Gage," I muttered, and called again. This time, it only rang twice. I called a third time and it went straight to voicemail.

What the hell?

I left Gage a stilted message updating him on Knox's condition, and another on Heath's voicemail for good measure.

"Problem?" Knox asked, just as the nurse returned with a plastic cup.

"No," I said immediately, telling myself I'd try them again in a few minutes. "I'm sure everything's fine. They're probably asleep, is all. You just worry about resting and getting your strength back."

EIGHTEEN

Jez

I NEARLY JUMPED out of my own skin when Gage's phone rang while I was waiting for the Uber to show up. I fumbled it, nearly dropping it on the pavement in my haste.

The top of the screen spelled out 'Tony Scalise' in large white letters against a black background. I stabbed at the red 'decline' button. When that didn't seem to do anything, I tried dragging it instead. The phone stopped ringing and the screen went dark.

I'd barely gotten it back in my pocket when it rang again, jangling my nerves. This time, I disconnected the call a bit quicker, but I knew I needed a better solution. I had no idea why Tony was trying to reach Gage, but if he was going to keep calling over and over again, I'd end up screaming.

Trying to remember details from the last time I'd owned a phone, I found the little phone icon and went to recent calls. Tony was at the top, and it didn't take much hunting around to find the 'block number' menu option.

I wished there was a way to block everyone from calling, but I couldn't. There was one person I *definitely* needed to have a conversation with.

The Uber was still a few minutes away. Closing my eyes, I called up the phone number

I'd memorized for Adrian. Now *there* was a lost skill for you. But I didn't have a phone, because every time I managed to get one, someone stole it from me almost immediately. Since it also wasn't a great plan to have your client's phone number scribbled on a napkin when you were planning on committing murder for him, that meant memorizing it.

I hummed the ditty from an old television commercial that I'd paired with the numbers to so they'd be easier to remember, tapping the sequence in rapidly and hitting the call button before I could second-guess myself.

My heart raced almost painfully inside my chest. The next few hours would determine if I deserved to keep breathing air, or if I'd be better off dead in a ditch somewhere.

"*Hello?*" came a wary voice on the other end. "*Who is this?*"

"Adrian? It's Jez," I forced out.

There was a pause. I held my breath, not sure what I expected to happen next. It wasn't as though Adrian was going to suddenly spill his guts to me over the phone if he'd been lying about Knox and the others.

"*Jez? You're all right?*"

My breath exploded from my lungs, leaving me lightheaded.

"Yeah, I'm—" I cut myself off and tried again. "I need to talk to you about what happened."

"*I saw the news report,*" Adrian said. "*When I didn't hear anything from you afterward, I got worried. You're okay, though? I didn't see anything about an arrest…"*

His voice was all earnest concern. He'd worn his heart on his sleeve every single time I'd interacted with him, as though he'd never learned how to hide it.

Had it all been bullshit? Had I fallen for an act?

"I'm okay," I said, with something less than full truthfulness.

"Oh, thank goodness." Relief dripped from the words. *"Yes, we definitely need to talk. I don't think we should do it over the phone, though."*

He was sure as hell right about that part. I needed to be able to look him in the eye, and smell what his pheromones were doing when I confronted him. I needed closure. And if it ended up being the permanent kind, because I'd been an idiot who'd tried to kill her own mate on the strength of a lie I'd wanted to believe?

Well… so be it.

"Yeah," I agreed. "You're right. Can we meet somewhere? I'm just about to get in an Uber."

"Sure. Hang on a second — I need to see if I can get a ride." There was a staticky sound like someone covering the phone's mic, followed by muffled voices, the words indistinguishable.

Then he was back. *"Hey, do you remember that park where we had our first meeting? Can you get there in about forty-five minutes."*

Right. A nice, deserted park. Where no one would be around to see whatever happened. The fictional cat in the box flickered, looking more and more like a dupe. My stomach twisted.

I wasn't sure what traffic would be like this early in the morning, and even after seeing the map in the Uber app, I still only had the vaguest idea where I was.

"Um… make it an hour. I'll meet you there," I said, feeling heaviness settle over me.

"*Fair enough.*" Another slight hesitation. "*Just one more thing, though. My sister… did you learn anything?*"

The cat flickered back, gaining resemblance to a vigilante getting justice for the voiceless victims of the traffickers. The heaviness inside me didn't lift, though.

"No, I'm sorry," I managed. "I didn't."

The silence stretched, even as a red sedan pulled up to the curb by the mailbox.

"*Oh,*" Adrian said. "*Okay. Well, I'll see you soon.*"

"Bye," I told him, and disconnected the call with a shaking finger.

◆

The driver dropped me off at the grimy little park where I'd first agreed to meet with Adrian, after someone in our mutual orbits had told him about me. Or, rather, had told him about my reputation as an omega assassin.

I was a few minutes early, but there was an SUV with darkly tinted windows sitting in the postage-stamp parking lot, waiting. It wasn't the same car Adrian had driven before... but then again, he *had* said something over the phone about arranging for a ride.

"You sure you'll be okay if I drop you here, miss?" asked the middle-aged beta guy who'd driven me here.

The passenger door of the SUV opened, and Adrian stepped out. He waved at me.

"Yeah," I told the Uber driver, knowing that no matter what happened in this park, I wasn't going to be okay ever again. "It's fine. Thanks."

It wasn't that I couldn't see the risk involved in being out here alone. I just didn't care. All I needed in this moment was an end to the uncertainty. The fragile fantasy that I might be scent matched to a pack of honorable alphas was fading like mist in the sun. But so was the fantasy that I might be a decent human being rather than a waste of oxygen.

I'd left Gage sleeping peacefully in his bed after a single night of discovering what it would feel like to be a mated omega who was cherished and protected. I'd known the whole time that it wasn't my life. It couldn't be.

Either I'd let myself be seduced by that sweet dream of belonging, and slept with a monster... or I'd betrayed an innocent pack so badly that I had no hope of redemption.

If it was the latter, I was about to step willingly toward my punishment. If Adrian was working for the real bad guys, it wasn't like they could afford to have me walking around and talking to people. They'd need to get rid of me.

Once I knew who'd been lying to me, I could act as my own judge and jury. And if the Knockley pack turned out to be innocent, I had an executioner ready and waiting.

"Jez," Adrian said as I crossed the little parking lot to face him. "Thank *goodness*."

His hair had the same 'artfully maintained bed-head' look as it had every other time we'd met, but he was dressed like he'd come directly from some kind of rich-people party. Sharp, slim-cut suit in a dove gray color that matched his eyes… polished black loafers. His mint and rosewater scent gave nothing away.

"Hello, Adrian," I greeted, keeping a close watch on his expression as I added, "I'm really sorry I couldn't find out anything about your sister."

His face scrunched up, his aquiline nose wrinkling. "Yeah, well, at least you tried. Here, you look like you could use some breakfast. Hop in the back. We can have this discussion over pancakes."

My stomach flip-flopped as the memory of Gage sliding me a plate of fluffy pancakes topped with whipped cream and fresh fruit overlaid my view of the park. The cat paced restlessly in its box.

Righteous vigilante or cold-blooded killer.
Executioner of the guilty or clueless dupe.

Old survival instinct urged me to take a step back, but Adrian had already turned and was opening the SUV's rear passenger door. His other hand reached out, hooking my upper arm and dragging me forward with unexpected force.

I yelped and stumbled toward the vehicle. At the same instant, a huge man stepped out of the open door and grabbed me by the neck. A scream gathered in my throat.

"Quiet!" the man snarled, in a full-on alpha bark.

My jaw snapped shut under the force of the command, and I was bundled into the back seat like a ragdoll. Just like that, the lid lifted away from the box, revealing a clueless dupe blinking up at the world... with her mate's innocent blood staining her lily-white paws.

NINETEEN

Jez

"NO," I WHIMPERED, the force of my voice still crushed beneath the power of the alpha's bark. My eyes squeezed shut, but all I could see was Knox lying on the bed as I injected him with enough air to cause a pulmonary embolism.

Rough hands grabbed my wrists, dragging them forward and strapping them tight together with a zip tie. Not even my fear of having my arms restrained was enough to bring me back to the present.

I'd been wrong. I'd thought nothing could be worse than the uncertainty. But this was worse. So much worse than not knowing. Tears squeezed from the corners of my eyes as the true weight of what I'd done suffocated me with its crushing force.

"Aw, don't cry, honey." Adrian's hateful voice came from the front seat.

I opened my eyes reluctantly to see his blurry form leaning around to watch me.

"You lied," I said stupidly. "You lied to me, and I believed you."

He gave a careless shrug. "It was easy enough to feed you a story that you wanted to hear. And it got me what *I* wanted, too — so, I'd call that a win-win scenario. Wouldn't you?"

A taunting note entered his voice on the final sentence. I stared at him dully.

"What did it get you?" I asked, my voice as weak and raspy as though I'd managed to scream my lungs out earlier.

He snorted. "A mating to a rich alpha, that's what. No more scrounging to make the rent between acting gigs. No more worrying about my safety every time I leave the apartment."

With a deep ache pulsing in time with my heart, I thought about the pack I might have had. I wondered if Gage was still asleep, dreaming of that same thing.

"What are you going to do to me?" I asked, not really caring. It just... seemed like the sort of thing you should ask, in this situation.

One of the alphas flanking me in the back seat chuckled. His copper and lime scent assaulted me from one side, while diesel and pine hit me from the other.

"Oh," Adrian said, "well... you clearly ratted me out to Knox's gang, so I expect you'll be made to disappear. But Enzo likes to get value out of people before he discards them. He sells, y'know, videos and stuff."

I knew exactly what kind of videos those would be. And it should have horrified me... but my mind had already checked out. I was gone, just like I used to go away inside my own head after my father sold me to the traffickers. If anything, it struck me as kind of appropriate that I'd end up going full circle, finishing exactly where I'd started. I'd escaped the gangs once, but instead of making something of my freedom, I'd slowly turned into a monster.

It was like what the Buddhists believed, wasn't it? If you don't learn from your mistakes, you have to come back and do it all over again. Except this time, I didn't have enough strength left to fight what was about to happen. Strength… will… it was all gone. I was just an empty husk, sitting limply between my captors, staring at nothing.

I made no attempt to keep track of the route we took as we left the park. What would be the point? I'd learned what I needed to know, and now I was just… *done*. Things would happen to me that I couldn't control, and then it would be over—and then I could finally rest.

If Knox died too, I wondered if we'd see each other somehow, afterward. I could try and apologize to him; explain how I'd been fooled and manipulated by someone who knew how to take advantage of my blindness about alphas. Would he forgive me? He'd seemed really nice when I'd talked to him, before—

Before I'd tried to murder him.

The SUV pulled up to an old warehouse. The alphas dragged me out of the back seat, hooking meaty hands under my arms and taking my full weight when my legs refused to do anything except hang there like limp noodles. Adrian pulled out a phone and lifted it to his ear.

"Hey, lover," he said. "I'm just dropping off your present. Are the boys inside ready for her?"

There was a pause; I couldn't hear whoever was on the other end.

Adrian's nose scrunched up in distaste. "No, I'll just drop her here and leave afterward. You know I don't like to watch that kind of stuff, baby."

Another pause. Then Adrian softened, his body adopting the appeasing openness that I'd always hated in omegas.

"I'll come straight there, alpha," he said, his tone growing flirtatious. "My mating bite hurts *ever* so much. I need your tongue on it. And your big, fat knot filling me up..."

I let my mind drift away again, feeling vaguely nauseated.

The call ended, and a finger and thumb gripped my chin harshly, tipping my face up until I was staring at Adrian's cold features.

"You shouldn't have snitched on me to your red-haired Viking," he said. "If you'd just kept quiet, we might've forgotten about you. Goodbye, Jez."

I mustered enough energy to spit in his face. The open-handed slap that rocked me an instant later was stronger than I would have guessed Adrian capable of.

"Drop her inside with the others, and let's get the hell out of here," he ordered, sounding coldly furious.

The alphas grunted acknowledgement and half-dragged, half-carried me inside the old, echoing building. The world swung in slow circles around me.

Almost over, I told myself. *Almost done now.*

They dumped me on a metal table. My nose twitched. The sound of gruff voices conferring wasn't enough to distract me from the faint hint of aged whiskey and oakwood that clung to the room… to the table.

The scent burrowed its way past the heavy layer of wool felt wrapped around my awareness, demanding to be smelled. I inhaled. My brain helpfully coughed up more impressions.

Rage.

Pain.

Fear.

Lust.

A heavy hand grabbed the side of my head, pinning me as something sharp slid into the side of my neck. I whimpered, flopping weakly against the table.

Mate, whispered the stale scent clinging to the room. *Mate in danger.*

A low keening noise struggled free of my chest. "Lemme go…"

The hand clamped around my jaw, forcing me to look up at a craggy face looming over me.

"You're not going anywhere, doll face," said the unfamiliar alpha. "Well, except into a cell with Bruno. The boss owes him a bonus for a job he did last week, and you're it. Don't worry, I just gave you a heat-stim. So, you'll probably enjoy it, right up until he brings out his knife and starts cutting." He turned to one of the alphas who'd dragged me in here. "Did anyone search her yet?"

The other alpha patted me down, pulling out Gage's phone and the cash I'd stolen from him. "Here you go," he said, handing them over. He leered down at me. "Don't forget to smile for the cameras, pretty girl. Oh — hey, that reminds me. Did the red-head go feral yet? I've got some money down on that shit."

"Not yet." The first alpha sounded sour. "I'm right there with you. If he doesn't lose control in the next couple of hours, I'm out a couple of Benjamins."

I lost track of the words as waves of blistering heat washed outward from the pain in the side of my neck. The unbearable sensation twisted together with my awareness of my mate's fading scent, and I groaned in distress.

"Fuckin' lightweight," muttered the alpha leaning over me. "Dump her in the cell. Looks like the heat-stim's already taking effect."

The other alphas' hands were like red-hot brands against my skin as they grabbed me and dragged me upright. I hissed and tried to twist away, but they pulled me to my feet and man-handled me out of the room. We went down hallways that seemed to twist and warp around me. Then I was thrown into a bare cell like a sack of garbage.

I cried out as I hit the unforgiving concrete, unable to catch myself with my wrists still zip-tied in front of me. The scent of oak and whiskey was stronger in this part of the building, shredded through with unimaginable distress.

Heavy bars clanged as the cell door slammed shut. A camera in the corner hummed as it turned to focus on me, its single red light like an accusing eye.

"H-Heath?" I whimpered, my higher brain functions struggling beneath the simmering fever rushing along my veins. "Heath? *Heath!*"

There was no reply. Of course there wasn't.

I staggered to my feet, moaning as my thighs rubbed together. Slick was pulsing from my pussy, but it hurt, it *hurt*. The first cramp wracked my belly, and panic swelled inside me as old, carefully buried memories rattled their chains.

The crack and flash of thunder and lightning. Sweaty, grasping hands pawing at me.

Gasping, I dragged and clawed at my clothing, my bound hands clumsy as I tried and failed to get rid of the sickening feeling. Every seam and stitch felt like sandpaper against my skin. Sweat drenched me; I was burning up.

Another cramp doubled me over.

"*Heath*," I whispered, the word barely audible. "*Gage...*"

I wanted to call out for Knox, for that comforting cedar and campfire scent—but my throat closed around the plea. I didn't deserve to have his name on my tongue. I didn't deserve *any* of them. A pitiful sob hitched my chest.

The door clanged open. I stumbled back, my shoulders thumping against the wall. The biggest alpha I'd ever seen loomed in the doorway. Bigger than Gage. And so much scarier.

The scent of rosemary and greasy leather rolled over me, overpowering the hint of Heath's musk that I'd been clinging to. I froze, trying to melt through the concrete wall.

The alpha closed the barred door behind him. He pulled out a wicked stiletto knife, running a thumb along the edge like someone stroking a lover.

"Well, now," he said, in a voice like gravel. "Aren't you a sweet little morsel? Too bad you're so skinny."

His scent wrapped around me, overpowering and so very *wrong*. I doubled over and puked on the floor, my stomach cramping in time with my womb.

The alpha lunged forward and grabbed me. "Fuckin' *cow*. You think I wanna smell that shit the whole time I'm balls-deep in you?"

I coughed, choking on bile, and he slammed me against a different part of the wall.

Heath, I thought desperately — my eyes focusing with laser intensity on the blade of the stiletto as the alpha raised it threateningly to my face.

All at once, a silvery sheen of clarity settled over my mind. One thing mattered, and one thing only. My mate was somewhere in this building, and this alpha was standing between me and what I needed.

I darted forward, the edge of the blade sliding along my cheek as I grabbed the alpha's forearm and buried my teeth in his wrist. My jaws closed with a strength I'd never realized I had; my teeth piercing through skin and gristle.

The alpha howled, taken completely by surprise as the knife slipped from his grasp and clattered to the floor. I jerked my head, tearing at whatever was in my mouth and spitting it out as my teeth came free. The knife hilt felt like a magnet. It drew me to it unerringly as I dove for the floor, coming up with it held in one of my bound hands.

I sprung upright again and jabbed sideways with savage precision. The blade slid into the alpha's jugular with almost no resistance, slicing through flesh like butter. The man made a wet, choking noise of shock as he scrabbled at the protruding knife handle, one hand flopping uselessly as it dangled from his torn wrist. Then he toppled slowly to the side, his knees folding and sending him crashing to the ground.

I stared down blankly as he flopped like a fish, gouts of red spurting rhythmically from his neck. When he stopped moving, I looked slowly past him to the door. Then I looked back down at the twitching corpse.

A ring of keys hung from his belt. I crouched next to him and pulled them free before walking to the door. He hadn't even bothered to lock it. It was heavy, but it swung open with a creak.

I glanced at the camera. Someone would see what had happened, probably. But I didn't need much time. Outside the cell with its choking miasma of blood, rosemary, and leather, I could smell my mate. I clutched the keys tightly in one hand and ran toward the source of the scent.

TWENTY

Jez

MY MATE WAS CLOSE. I was sure of it. My head swam, thoughts becoming harder to hold onto as the smell of his distress overwhelmed my rational mind.

Keys. I had to keep a grip on the keys. My clothing itched and rubbed like burlap. I wanted nothing more than to stop and tear it all off. But to do that, I'd have to drop the keyring. And I needed the keyring. I needed to keep the keyring because… because…

The sour scent of oak-aged whiskey had been growing stronger with every step, until it was the only thing I could focus on. But now, a weaker scent of lemon and paprika wove in with my mate's pheromones.

Omega. It was an omega's scent.

Another omega was with *my mate*.

For a split second, rage the likes of nothing I'd ever felt before exploded behind my lungs. Then my lagging brain caught up to what I was smelling, as more details filtered in through my nose.

Young. This omega was a child. A *frightened* child.

No… not just frightened. *Terrified.*

I staggered toward the barred cell that was the source of the mingled scents. Behind me, shouts erupted from the way I'd come, as though maybe someone had found the open cell door and the crumpled body inside.

My hands shook, the zip tie biting into my skin as I fumbled with the keyring — trying first one key, then the next, and the next, and the next. I didn't dare look at whatever was inside the locked room. I could smell blood now… and I knew that the instant my eyes fell on my mate, it would be the end of any shred of rationality I might still be clinging to.

More shouted curses and the pounding of footsteps approached — coming toward me far too fast. I tried another key, and another. The heavy lock clanked as I twisted as the sixth key rotated in the tumblers. The barred door swung free.

A small boy darted past me through the gap, his smoky lemon scent hitting me in a wave of *fear-dread-distress*. My head whipped around, following the motion as he bolted like a jackrabbit, running full speed in the opposite direction from the approaching guards.

I just had time to take in my flame-haired mate rising from a crouch in the far corner of the cell. Blood streaked his face and neck, dripping sluggishly from parallel jagged scratches, as though he'd been clawing at his own skin in frustration and rage.

Then a heavy body slammed into me, shoving me against the far wall of the corridor so hard that all the breath whooshed out of my lungs.

"Fuck... *shit!*" snarled the alpha who'd held me down on the metal table and injected me with a heat-stim. "Get that cell door closed and locked before—"

His hot breath wafted past my ear, and it was all I could do not to scream at the utter wrongness of having him so close to me. Instead, I growled and bucked, even as a roar of pure, unbridled rage echoed from inside the cell.

Between one heartbeat and the next, a spitting, clawing tornado erupted into the hallway, his scent rising around him like aged spirits and vengeance. The second guard shrieked; the sound choking down to a nauseating gurgle right before the wet crunch of torn cartilage reached me past the ringing in my ears.

The scream I'd swallowed back earlier finally escaped, tearing its way past my throat like the living embodiment of all the unfairness and pain in my life. The alpha holding me cursed again, the sound cut off as he was dragged off me like he weighed no more than a child's rag doll.

I spun and pounced, clawing at eyeballs while my mate held the hated alpha still in a brutal headlock. His roar of anger subsided to a low, warning growl. The sound resonated through my chest and down to my belly, drawing liquid heat as thick and scorching as lava through my veins.

I continued my mindless attack, relishing my former captor's high-pitched cries of agonized horror. Then the man's head jerked to the side in a violent twisting movement. A sharp, popping crack reached me through the haze of my own berserker rage, and the body in my mate's grip went limp, slumping to the floor as he tossed it aside.

I stood, transfixed—my chest rising and falling in rapid, gasping pants as I lifted my gaze to meet my mate's green eyes. The moment we connected, a flood of warmth and need washed through me in a rushing tidal wave. My head fell back and to the side in blissful surrender—showing throat to the alpha who would always protect me whenever danger threatened.

My mate groaned, pulling my body flush against his and clinging to me as though I was the only thing keeping him from flying apart at the seams. His embrace made me feel like the most important person in the entire universe; like I had singlehandedly made him complete, where he had been torn open and bleeding a moment before.

His groan rumbled into a rough purr. The sound vibrated through me, making every other thing in the world feel distant and unimportant. The scorching lava in my veins pumped faster, collecting at the neck of my womb until I thought I would burst into flames on the spot.

Chapped lips closed on my exposed throat, nibbling down to sniff at my scent gland like someone taking a hit of cocaine. My nerves exploded in tingling ecstasy, sensation zinging along my spine to throb in my clit.

"Need you," I whined. "Please, *please*..."

The purr rumbled louder, and strong arms scooped me up into a secure hold. My mate carried me away from the scent of blood and death and terrified child-omega. The room where we ended up was dusty and bare, but it smelled of age and neglect rather than other people.

My alpha set me down as gently as though I was made of glass. He immediately snapped the zip tie holding my wrists with his teeth, freeing me. Then he started tearing at his already torn clothing. I lunged forward and helped him get everything off—my smaller fingers less clumsy with buttons and zippers.

God, he was so beautiful. Even scratched and bloody, with rings of exhaustion under his eyes, he was completely perfect. I thought of my other mate, with his bulging muscles and brilliant hazel eyes. How had I ended up with such perfect, amazing mates? I wished he was here as well... and my third mate, with his tawny skin and soft, kinky black hair.

But... there was a reason I couldn't have my third mate. Something bad... something terrible. Why couldn't I remember...?

A whimper of distress escaped me, and my red-haired alpha was immediately touching me again. His big hands cradled my face, stroking my lank, sweaty hair as he murmured soothing noises.

I twisted unhappily, once again aware of every stitch in my unwanted clothing. Seeming to sense what I needed, he began stripping it from me, exposing my skin to the glorious coolness of the air. When something didn't come off fast enough, he ripped the seams apart like tissue paper.

My nipples hardened as the air caressed them. I moaned, thrusting my small breasts upward in desperate invitation. The chapped lips that had teased my neck earlier closed around one taut peak, and I cried out as a rough tongue rasped over the pebbled flesh.

But that wasn't what either of us really needed.

My scent rose in waves from the slick soaking my jeans and panties. With a low noise of want, my mate pulled away from my breast with a little pop of suction and went to work on the rest of my clothes. He helped me balance as I stepped out of pants and underwear together. Then he shoved all our discarded clothing into the closest approximation of a nest that was possible under our current circumstances.

With a cry of relief, I dropped to my hands and knees on the pile of clothes, breathing in our combined scents. It was pure instinct to flatten my upper body to the floor, sticking my ass in the air—an unspoken demand. With a feral growl, my alpha lowered himself to kneel behind me. The tongue that had lapped at my nipple delved into my folds, licking up my slick like it was the finest nectar.

Pleasure crashed through me. My belly cramped again, the pain twisting together with the wild sensations ricocheting through my body. I sobbed and rubbed my face in the ripped fabric of my mate's shirt as he nosed and licked at me, diving in like a starving man presented with a ripe peach; its sweet juices leaking down his chin.

Just when I thought I wouldn't be able to stand it for another second, the rough hands spreading my ass cheeks apart gripped my hips instead. I felt him shift position, and the thick, blunt heat of a throbbing cock prodded at my opening, seeking. I wailed and reared back, spearing myself on that perfect, punishing girth as though it was the only thing keeping me alive.

"*Yes!*" I shrieked. "Yes… *yes!*"

Every thought, every memory, every scrap of awareness about who I was or what was happening disappeared beneath the earthquake of raw need rushing back and forth between us, with every brutal thrust in and out of my clenching passage.

"Oh, *god…*" I moaned, jerking my hips back and forth with abandon. "More, please, more—oh god, bite me, bite me, *bite me*—!"

My mate was inside me, pushing me toward a climax that would blot out the world… but it still wasn't *enough*. I needed more of him in me. I needed to make sure that he could never, *ever* leave.

His growl dipped into a lower register, resonating inside my chest with every unforgiving stroke.

"*Mine*," he snarled, his grip on my hip tightening until I could feel the finger-shaped bruises forming. "Mine... mine... *mine!*"

He slammed into me, and the dam inside me shattered. I screamed and clamped down on him, slick squirting between us as my muscles milked his length violently. My awareness whited out, the force of the towering orgasm competing with the ravenous hunger for something *more*. My mating gland throbbed and ached with the need for sharp teeth to pierce it.

"*Please!*" I sobbed. "Oh god, please, I *can't—*"

Strong arms pulled me upright on my knees, my back slapping hard against a muscled chest. One arm wrapped around my torso, a hot hand grabbing my breast possessively. The other hand wrapped around my throat, my pulse pounding crazily against the firm grip.

The hand twisted my head to the side, and I let it fall limply. My choked groan of relief vibrated against the warm constriction against my windpipe as unsteady breath puffed against my aching gland. With a rough groan, my alpha bent his head to the juncture of my shoulder and bit down hard, until the blood flowed.

TWENTY-ONE

Tony

I COULDN'T HELP feeling a little guilty about leaving Knox on his own at the hospital. After all, I'd promised to stay with him until one of the others showed up to take over.

Still, I reminded myself repeatedly that he was going to be tied up with doctors and tests and medical questions for the next little while. More importantly, it wasn't as though my presence was going to, I dunno, bring him *comfort* or anything. I was just some random beta guy that did errands for Heath sometimes. Knox barely knew me.

I hadn't received a call back from either Heath or Gage, almost two hours after I'd left them both voicemails. No matter how hard I tried to convince myself that it wasn't a big deal… I knew that it actually was. It didn't matter how tired they were or how little sleep they'd gotten since the attack. There was no way in hell that one or the other of them hadn't heard their phones ringing and checked for messages.

So, here I was in my old Volvo, driving out to the pack house to find out what the heck was going on. My head was pounding after the long, sleepless night—not helped by the early morning sun that had peeked out from behind the clouds seemingly for the sole purpose of burning out my retinas as I'd negotiated my way from the hospital's visitor parking area toward Lake Shore Drive.

Everything was probably fine, I told myself for the dozenth time. There would be a reasonable explanation for why I couldn't contact either of the alphas. Maybe their phones batteries were dead, and they hadn't noticed. Or… something.

Whatever the case, I'd find out soon enough.

I pulled into the winding driveway leading to the old house and parked by the front door. Nothing seemed out of place. There were no other vehicles out front, but I was pretty sure the others usually parked in the back, where an old carriage house had been renovated into a detached garage.

Heart in throat, I jogged up to the door and rapped my knuckles against it until they ached. "Heath?" I called. "Gage? Wake up and get down here!"

When that didn't immediately bring someone down to let me in, I leaned on the doorbell buzzer. I honestly had no idea if the damn thing was even hooked up—but sure enough, the muffled electronic tone reached me faintly through the heavy door.

I was pacing back and forth on the porch, trying to figure out what I should do next, when the door swung open to reveal Gage standing there in rumpled clothes and bare feet. I whirled to face him, my eyes immediately drawn to his gaping fly before I wrenched my attention up to his face.

"Tony," he said blankly, as though I was the last person he'd expected to find at his door. His scruffy stubble had long ago left the land of five o'clock shadow in the rearview mirror, and his square-jawed face was so pale that he looked like a ghost. His hazel eyes were very wide.

"Gage?" I asked stupidly.

He swallowed hard, his prominent Adam's apple bobbing. "We've… um… we've got a problem. A big one."

I held up a hand, unable to take any new crises on board until I'd delivered my news. "Okay, but I have to tell you. Knox is awake. He seems… mostly okay? The doctors are with him now, running tests and stuff."

Gage blinked, opened his mouth, and blinked again.

"Oh. That's… that's great news. The best, actually." He took a deep breath and let it gust out, although it did nothing to ease the tense line of his shoulders. "See? I knew he'd be all right."

I nodded, feeling like someone standing beneath an overhanging boulder on a narrow mountain trail. "Yeah. It's fantastic news. I'm really happy for you all." I braced myself. "So, what's this 'big problem' you mentioned?"

Gage's look of profound relief twisted back into worry. And… guilt?

"I may have… um… let Jez get away," he said.

The words took a second to penetrate. *"What?"*

I stared at the sheepish alpha, who rubbed a hand restlessly over the back of his neck like a schoolboy dragged in front of the principal. How was I supposed to feel about this? Alarmed? Relieved?

"But she was locked in the attic," I said.

Gage's hand dropped to hang limply at his side. "There was a storm. She was scared. I couldn't leave her up there all alone."

Okay. There was probably a totally rational reason why he was half-dressed and his fly was unzipped. And besides, this was none of my business, even if it involved someone I'd once thought was my closest friend. The important part was that Jez was gone.

"Are you sure she's not hiding somewhere in the house?" I asked.

Gage seemed to shake himself back to the present. "The front door was unlocked when I opened it just now," he said. Then he hesitated. "But you're right, we should search to be sure."

He stepped back, inviting me in. Then he seemed to realize what state he was in, and two high spots of color heated his pale features as he quickly zipped and buttoned his pants closed. I jerked my attention away, staring at the opposite wall as my ears burned.

He cleared his throat awkwardly. "Sorry. Um, don't take this the wrong way, but why didn't you just call me from the hospital instead of driving all the way out here?"

"I did," I told him. "Called you, called Heath... no one answered, so I left voicemails. When no one called me back, I started to worry.""

His face, which had been bloodless before, went positively gray.

"Shit," he said, and went running down the hall toward the main stairs with way more speed than someone that big should have possessed.

Unsure what else to do, I followed him, puffing a bit by the time we reached what I assumed was his bedroom. He rushed over to the bedside table, shoving around books and other miscellaneous odds and ends before coming up with a worn leather wallet. He opened it up and rifled through the contents before straightening.

"She took my phone. Some money, too." He sounded completely shellshocked.

"So, she's probably not hiding in the house, then," I concluded. "Your phone's locked though, right?" When he didn't immediately reply, I asked again. *"Right?"*

Another pause.

"It never reads my face or fingerprint on the first try, and I hate having to enter a code every time." The words were a quiet mumble.

I opened my mouth to read him the riot act, only to catch myself just in time. It hardly mattered at this point. "Please tell me you know your cloud account login," I said instead.

"Yeah, of course." He sounded a bit defensive.

That was something, at least.

"Okay." I pulled out my phone, wincing at the red battery warning. "Here, I need to plug into your charger. There's a phone finder app; I think it'll let me look for yours if you use it to log in to your account."

I didn't stop to second-guess whether I should be helping Gage find Jez, or silently cheering that she'd gotten away. The truth was, she'd nearly killed Knox… even if she'd been tricked into doing it. And I knew all too well how effectively she could disappear, if left to her own devices.

Knox deserved the chance to make his own decision about what to do with her, and that wouldn't happen if she vanished into Chicago's underworld like she had after she'd killed my stepdad.

I plugged in my phone and pulled up the app, scrolling down to the 'help a friend' option and tapping it. Gage crowded close, taking the phone when I handed it to him and painstakingly typing in his account information. I supposed with fingers as big and thick as his, it probably *was* a pain in the ass to type on a phone screen.

I'd never really noticed how comforting the huge man's alpha scent was. Heath's scent had always meant the best kind of forbidden danger, in whatever part of my lizard brain was wired to process that kind of shit. But Gage smelled like a bakery at Christmas, and I had to sternly prevent myself from taking a surreptitious sniff.

The phone pinged success, and a map popped up with a red marker pin in the middle. I didn't immediately recognize the area, but Gage scowled.

"Fuck. Is that the old silos out by McKinley?" he asked, pinching and zooming the screen.

I peered at the map. "I thought those were getting demolished? Wasn't it on the news a while back?"

He shook his head. "It got tied up in red tape or something. How reliable is this app?"

I shrugged. "It's not like it's going to randomly show your phone in some old derelict area miles from here if it's actually hidden under a couch cushion downstairs."

Gage straightened. "Okay. We've gotta go, then. I need to get Jez back here before Heath comes back from wherever the hell he stormed off to."

"Heath's not here?" I asked, although of course if he had been, he would've heard the commotion and come running before now."

Gage huffed out a frustrated breath. "No, he's… well, I don't know where he is. Pretty sure I pissed him off earlier."

I didn't really want to poke at that if I didn't have to. "Right. So, my phone's running on fumes. Have you got a charging port in your car? Because my car's too old to have one." I waited for his nod, and glanced down pointedly at his feet. "And, um, you might also want some shoes."

He followed my gaze. "Oh. Yeah. Shoes would probably be good."

***

Forty-five minutes later we were hurtling down the Stevenson Expressway in Gage's white GMC Yukon, while I babysat the finder app to make sure the phone's location didn't move somewhere else while we were on the way.

"Why would she come all the way out here?" Gage muttered, as he took an exit to cross the river.

And that did seem pretty weird. But…

"After she rescued me by killing my stepfather, I tried to find her," I said. "But it was like she'd disappeared off the face of the earth. Maybe she was here? Could there be, like, a homeless encampment in the silos or something?"

"Maybe," Gage replied, although he didn't sound convinced.

Silence stretched for a couple of minutes as we drove toward 28th Street. Then Gage spoke again.

"Look… this is none of my business, but I been meaning to ask you. It seemed like you shut down pretty quick when I mentioned Heath earlier. Is everything okay there?"

My breath caught, even as my heart did a stupid little stutter. Did Gage know that I'd slept with his packmate?

I tried to play it casual. "What? Yeah, of course everything's okay. Why wouldn't it be?"

Gage didn't answer for long enough that I started to squirm.

"No reason," he said, and jerked his chin at the windshield. "That's the silos over there. I think this is the turnoff."

I pressed my lips together tightly and followed the gesture. The massive derelict structure towered over its landscape of grass and weeds in the middle distance, gray and brown and dingy against the morning sky. As we approached, I could see the tall chain link fence surrounding the property, some of its posts bent with age like drunken sailors.

"Wait. That ain't right," Gage said, as he slowed the Yukon and pulled off the road, coming to a stop next to a pair of massive double gates. Inside, parked next to a bleak rectangular warehouse set next to the cylindrical grain silos, sat a dark van and a couple of high-end SUVs.

Only one kind of person drove expensive black SUVs with aftermarket rims that cost more than my monthly income, and also hung out in places like this abandoned urban hellscape. Would Jez have connections with people like that? And if she did, would she have run straight to those people immediately after escaping the pack house?

Clammy sweat broke out on my chest.

"Gage," I whispered. "I've got a really bad feeling about this."

TWENTY-TWO

Tony

"FUCK," GAGE SAID under his breath. He popped his seatbelt free, before reaching under his jacket and pulling out a gun. My heart skipped and pounded—I still wasn't used to members of this pack waving firearms around.

This wasn't the little snub-nosed conceal-carry pistol that I'd seen him use at the pack house, either. It was a very serious looking semi-automatic, carried in a very serious looking shoulder holster. Against all good sense, I grabbed his bulging bicep, my fingers digging in.

"What the *hell* are you planning to do?" I demanded. "There are three vehicles parked out there, and no way of knowing how many people came here in each one!"

"I'm going in for recon," Gage said, not reacting to my hand on his arm as he checked the magazine on the gun and clicked it back into place. "Stay here. Keep the engine running, and if anyone comes outside that isn't me, burn rubber."

"What?" I yelped. "No! Gage… *no*. That's a fucking moronic plan, and it's *not fucking happening*." Inside the battleground of my own damned head, good sense warred with whatever the opposite of good sense was. "Look… you just want to have a sneak around and try to see what's going on in there? Because I've sneaked into a lot more places than you have, I'm willing to bet. I'll go."

My brain made unintelligible gibbering noises at me, because *seriously*? I gritted my teeth and tried to ignore the burning embers of my dearly departed sense of self-preservation.

Gage ran a beady eye over me. "The fuck you will. You're not even armed, and as scared as you are of guns, I'm guessing you've never shot one in your life."

"I'm armed," I said, hearing the defensiveness creep into my voice. I dug into the pocket of my hoodie and pulled out my trusty pepper spray.

Gage grunted. "Right." He hesitated for a long, fraught moment. "Fine, we'll both go."

He didn't sound happy about it, which was fair. I was the one kicking up a fuss, and *I* wasn't happy about it, either.

"Okay," my mouth said, not waiting for approval from whatever was passing for my IQ these days.

"Okay," Gage echoed, and I took a moment to wonder why we were doing this when we both knew how stupid it was.

"Wait, why are we doing this again?" I asked. "We could just call the police instead. Let them sort it out?"

A low rumble vibrated up from Gage's barrel chest, making me shiver.

"Because my mate is in there, and I'm not a hundred percent sure whose side she's on," he growled.

"Your *phone* is in there," I corrected. "That's all we know for sure."

Gage turned off the engine and cracked open the driver's side door. "Come or don't," he said, all traces of the affable alpha marshmallow gone without a trace.

I swallowed whatever words had been gathering in my throat and got out of the Yukon, clutching my pepper spray in one sweaty hand.

There was no question of hiding as we approached. The chain link gates weren't locked, but the rusty hinges shrieked like a banshee as Gage pushed one open far enough for us to slip through. It was broad daylight, and while the area around the derelict grain warehouse was overgrown, it wasn't a forest. I kept as low to the ground as I could, moving through the tall grasses and weeds — hoping that no one inside happened to be looking through one of the missing windows facing in our direction.

Gage also crouched low, although the fact that he had a good eight inches of height on me certainly wasn't helping him in the 'staying out of sight' department. But there was no sign of any guards posted outside, and no movement from inside as we crossed the final distance. A moment later, we fetched up in front of a massive pair of mildewed wooden sliding doors, like the kind you saw on old barns.

I pulled out my phone to double check that Gage's signal was definitely coming from this building rather than one of the huge, cylindrical silos flanking it—then gave him a nod of confirmation. He nodded back, grabbing a rusted handle in one meaty fist and heaving. The door slid to the side with an awful groaning noise, inch by painful inch.

The instant it was open wide enough to admit a person, a slight form bolted through the gap, shoving past me and sending me staggering. Adrenaline surged through me, even as Gage shouted, "Oy!" and lifted his gun.

"Don't!" I gasped, whirling just in time to see a child dart into the tall grass and disappear from view.

Gage cursed and pointed the gun's muzzle safely skyward.

"Was that an—" I began.

"Omega kid?" Gage finished. "Yeah. Pretty sure it was."

Before I could draw breath to say anything else, a full-throated female scream echoed from somewhere inside the abandoned warehouse... muffled by distance and thick walls, but still utterly unmistakable.

"Shit! Come on!" Gage snapped.

In the next instant he was through the gap in the door, pounding toward the source of the noise. I plunged after him, the smell of dust and decay hitting me like a wall as my eyes struggled to adjust to the sudden dimness. It was all I could do not to descend into a coughing fit as

I followed the darker shadow ahead of me, my pepper spray still clutched in one hand and my phone in the other.

We crossed an echoing, empty space, dotted here and there with the hulking skeletons of old machinery. Shafts of light from gaps in the walls cut through the floating dust, turning it brilliant gold while doing little to illuminate the rest of the warehouse floor. My foot skidded on something soft—a moldering pile of old rags. When I righted myself, it was to find Gage disappearing into a hallway deeper in the sprawling old structure.

I ignored my racing heart and followed, wishing I had enough battery left on my phone to risk turning on the flashlight.

If the goal had been stealth, we'd failed like the St. Louis Cardinals in the 2013 World Series. The fact that there still hadn't been any response from whoever had arrived in those fancy SUVs outside was freaking me out more than a little bit. In fact, it was freaking me out so much that I nearly ran headfirst into Gage, who'd rounded a corner in the hallway and promptly come to a screeching halt.

I made a last-second course correction and caught myself against the concrete wall instead, staring open-mouthed at the scene beyond. This section of the corridor was illuminated in flickering fluorescent light, sharp and institutional. It was lined on one side with what could only be described as prison cells—barred fronts with heavy, locked doors.

Or rather, *most* of the doors were locked. One stood open, and two crumpled shapes lay motionless on the floor nearby. My jaw clicked shut. I swallowed heavily, fighting lightheadedness.

"Stay back." Gage stepped cautiously toward the dark lumps on the floor, leading with his gun. He nudged first one, then the other with the toe of his shoe. There was no response.

I wasn't sure what made me glance down and check my phone screen. The map was still pulled up, but now we were right on top of the little red marker pin representing Gage's phone.

"Check their pockets," I said hoarsely. "Your phone's around here somewhere."

Gage crouched down, transferring the gun to his left hand as he checked for pulses. "They're both dead. Broken neck and... uh... crushed trachea, I think." He patted them down and rummaged around in their clothing, eventually coming up with a phone.

"Is that it?" I asked, in order to avoid thinking about everything else that was going on here.

Gage looked down at it, frowning as he scrolled and swiped. "Yeah. There's an Uber confirmation, two calls from your number, and one outbound call to a number I don't recognize." He pocketed the phone and looked through the open cell door. "Empty. Shit, there's a camera."

I flinched hard as he raised the gun and fired a single shot. Glass crunched, somewhere out of view. "Gage!"

"Don't need a bunch of CCTV footage of us being here," he said.

Somewhere deeper in the building, a low, wailing cry tailed into a moan, and Gage was instantly on his feet again.

"That's her!" he said, and charged toward the sound.

Having no desire to be left alone with a couple of dead bodies, I followed him. The hallway branched, leading to more cells and a few rooms that had normal, solid doors. I shuddered as I ran past what looked like a medical gurney, its shiny metal at odds with the dingy surroundings as it sat slewed and abandoned in the corridor.

Gage turned again, alpha ears following the low sounds of female torment. It was getting closer, even as the signs of recent occupation faded. This part of the building was lit only by light coming through the gaps in the ceiling above, and heavy dust coated everything like a blanket. I looked down, seeing Gage's heavy footprints... along with a second set.

Perversely, *now* my stomach chose to sink with some formless, unnamed dread. I slowed, even as Gage slid to a stop in front of an open door. A low, menacing growl emanated from the room beyond.

I'd heard that growl before, for all that it had been playful rather than threatening. Heart in throat, I walked forward in a daze — both desperate to see what lay inside, and desperate *not* to see it.

I came to a halt next to Gage, who for once seemed to have been struck speechless. In the far corner of the room, curled together on a pile of ripped and bloody clothing, Jez and Heath lay entwined, naked and smeared from head to toe in rusty streaks of drying gore. As I stared at them, feeling a dark hole open up where my heart was supposed to be, Heath's ominous growl of warning modulated into a smug, satisfied purr.

TWENTY-THREE

Gage

BESIDE ME, TONY slapped a hand over his eyes and whirled to face away from the open doorway. "Oh, my *god!*" he yelped, sounding about as appalled as I felt.

In the next instant, the full force of an omega's heat pheromones hit me like a slap in the face. But not just *any* omega's pheromones.

Mate, the scent screamed. *Pack. Belonging. Need.*

I opened my mouth to gasp air like a fish, and of course that only made everything worse. The overwhelming urge to tear off my clothes and dive face-first into Jez's pussy tugged me forward a step. Before I could take a second one, a hand wrapped around my upper arm and yanked me back the way we'd come.

A growl rose up in my chest before I connected the hand to the harmless beta kid standing next to me.

"What the fuck?" Tony was whisper-shouting; his voice an ugly, strangled thing. "Gage, *what the fuck*? What is Heath even *doing* here?"

Right now, he's doing Jez. I managed to keep the words from making it out of my brain and past my lips, at least. The heat scent was still wrapped around my spinal cord like a ravenous anaconda, but as I stumbled after Tony, it faded to the point that I could think again.

"She's in heat," I said hoarsely. "Heath's in rut. They probably couldn't stop themselves."

Tony came to an abrupt halt and let my arm go. "She's in..." He shook his head sharply, as though trying to shake something loose. "If her heat was this close, wouldn't she have said something? And, I mean, wouldn't you have been able to smell it on her before now?"

My mouth opened and closed, but the words were all jumbled up against the wreckage of my higher brain functions. I nodded instead. I'd stake my knot that Jez hadn't been coming into heat when I'd had her in my bed, less than half a day ago.

Tony paced up and down the short stretch of hallway, his hand pressed over his mouth as though he wasn't sure what would come out of it next if he uncovered it. Beta scents were weird, but in my heightened state of awareness, I could sense the distress coming off him in waves.

Once again, he came to a stop without warning. His hand dropped to his side.

"There was a camera in that cell," he said. "And that omega kid who ran past us looked like he was escaping from something terrible. If Jez wasn't in heat before, but now she is..."

"Maybe that's what they do here," I finished, feeling nausea roil in my gut.

Tony looked just as queasy, but he raked me up and down with a worried look. "Jez is your scent match. If she's in heat, are you going to be able to keep it together?"

"Probably not," I admitted, all too aware of the painful ache in my cock—not to mention the way it was making a spirited attempt to split the seams of my trousers.

Tony licked his lips, and I made a valiant effort not to stare at the quick dart of his tongue over the pink flesh—because *what the fuck*, brain? I realized I was openly panting, and took a hasty step back. Tony did the same.

"There was, um… I saw a room with a medical gurney sitting outside as we went past," he said. "If those dead alphas back there by the cells brought on Jez's heat artificially, they probably had dampeners on hand so they wouldn't be too distracted to do their work, right?"

I slogged through the torrent of words, trying to make sense of them past my growing haze of incoherency.

When I didn't respond fast enough, Tony blinked at me.

"Dampeners?" he repeated, with understandable worry. "Would that help?"

I nodded wordlessly again.

"This way," he said.

Resisting the painful pull that insisted I was going in the wrong direction, I followed him. I remembered passing the gurney earlier, but it hadn't been the most important thing at the time. The room next to it was just as dingy and run-down as everywhere else in this place, but it had better lighting and a small fridge plugged into a self-contained battery-powered inverter.

A long counter by the far wall had been wiped off. Several plastic drawers and boxes were scattered across it, along with a couple of laptops. Tony ignored the computers in favor of rummaging through the mini-fridge, taking out little bottles and examining the labels before putting them back.

"There's stuff labeled heat-stim and rut-stim in here," he said, his distracting mouth curling down in disgust. Then he paused. "Wait. Here we go. Alpha scent dampener. Someone's definitely been using it; the bottle's two-thirds empty."

"Yeah," I said, my tongue feeling thick and numb. "That. Give me that."

This far away from Jez and Heath, the effects of her pheromones were already starting to wear off. But I needed to be able to get close to them again without losing my shit.

Tony set the bottle down and started searching through the plastic drawers until he came up with a sealed syringe and needle. "Intramuscular, right? Because if it's intravenous, I don't know what the fuck I'm doing."

"Jus' stick it in my arm," I slurred. "S'good enough."

Tony squinted at the tiny print on the side of the bottle. Apparently satisfied, he squinted at the markings on the syringe and nodded. "Okay. No big deal. Just a little jab."

I peeled off my jacket as I watched him draw up the dose through the little rubber membrane on the bottle lid. He let out a breath and came over to my left side, shoving my shirtsleeve out of his way. I barely felt the needle going in, past the clamoring inside my body for *mate-pack-sex*. The contents of the syringe were cold, but they still burned as they spread outward from the injection site.

Tony backed off and looked around uncertainly before placing the spent needle on the countertop. "Better?" he asked.

"About the same," I told him. "But give it a minute, and I'll be able to get close to them without freaking out."

Tony nodded. "Look... I don't want to be the one to tempt fate. But if there are cameras recording everything in this place, doesn't that mean other people might be watching? And if they know what's been happening, isn't there a pretty good chance of them showing up with a bunch of musclebound guys and guns?"

"Uh-huh," I agreed. "There sure is. Which is why we need to get Jez and Heath, and get the fuck outta here."

Tony blanched. "O-*kay*. And... how are we going to do that, exactly?"

I closed my eyes, trying to force my gray matter to work.

"We need the van," I muttered.

"There's a van outside," Tony pointed out. "We could steal it, I guess?"

But I immediately shook my head. "I don't want anything connecting us to this place, once we leave." Thoughts were coming more easily now. I pulled out my recovered phone. "I'll get our van here."

I texted Bud, the driver who chauffeured Knox's limo in addition to helping us run recovered omegas to safety.

How fast do you need it? came the reply.

Triple your hourly rate if you can get it here in twenty minutes, I replied.

"On its way," I told Tony. "Next order of business—I want to do a search of this warehouse before we leave. That kid who ran off didn't come outta nowhere. Can you keep an eye on the lovebirds while I do that?"

Tony blanched. "Maybe you should watch them while I search."

I patted my shoulder holster. "I'm the one with the gun. You don't have to go in with them or nothing. Just camp out in the hallway where you can yell like crazy if anyone tries to go in or out."

The kid looked like he'd rather pull his own toenails out by the roots, but after a short hesitation, he nodded.

"Don't take too long," he said.

I knew I should probably be more worried about the fact that his panties were in a twist… but whatever his problem was, he was going to have to deal with it until we were safely out of this shithole. Pulling my gun, I gave him a final nod and headed out for the quickest search I could manage.

Dampeners or no, I gave the hallway where Heath was knotting our mate a wide berth, sticking to the areas that seemed to be in use. My first major find was a room set up with tables and a dozen or more CCTV screens. The setup was powered by another one of those big portable battery-powered inverters, with a spaghetti tangle of extension cords and power strips.

It took precious time to sort out the file storage system, and there was some shit on there that seriously made me want to puke. I clenched my jaw and sorted through the folders until I found the footage they'd taken of Heath and Jez.

I had to pause and rewind the part where Jez nearly chewed an alpha asshole's hand off at the wrist, then stabbed him in the neck with his own knife despite the fact that her wrists were bound together.

Jesus H. Christ. That was another corpse for her collection.

When I was pretty confident that I had everything I needed, I wiped my packmate's files and left the rest for the police. Because as unhappy as it made me, the police were about to become involved.

One of the cameras was pointed at a cell full of underage omegas packed in like sardines. And while I might want a perfect world where Tony and I could whisk them away to safety without the additional trauma of getting chewed up and spat out by the legal system, they weren't exactly going to be able to share the back of the van with Heath and Jez.

I trudged back to join Tony, feeling slow-burning hatred for the human race pulse through my veins alongside the dampeners.

"There's a bunch of other kids being held here," I told him, keeping my eyes firmly away from the door to the dusty room. "I'm gonna have to call the police in, once we're safely out of this fucking place."

Tony already looked like he'd aged ten years since we got here; at that, he aged another five before my eyes.

"Can't we just let them go?" he asked. "Like the one who got out earlier?"

It occurred to me that he had more experience than most people, when it came to being an underage victim navigating the court system.

But I shook my head. "Throwing them into the ocean to sink or swim on their own is how you end up with people like Jez."

After a long moment, Tony gave a reluctant nod.

"I'd rather me and Knox and Heath were taking care of things directly," I told him. "But Knox is in the hospital, and Heath is… *well.*" I gestured toward the room where he was still curled up with Jez. "This way, the kids will at least get some kind of support."

The distant sound of a familiar eight-cylinder engine filtered through from outside.

"Van's here," I said. "I'll go meet Bud and give him the keys to the Yukon, so he can get out of here pronto. It'll be up to you and me to get these two loaded into the van. And, um, you're probably gonna have to drive. Sorry."

"Fan-fucking-tastic," Tony mumbled. "Seriously, I can hardly wait."

"Be right back," I told him.

Jez and Heath were at least separated after their knotting, but the less said about getting them out of the warehouse and into the van, the better. Heath insisted on carrying Jez, despite the fact that he was practically reeling with exhaustion and artificial hormones. He also kept trying to sniff Tony's hair, which wasn't helping the situation one goddamned bit.

There was still a pretty big question of what the hell Heath was even doing here in the first place. According to the surveillance video, he'd been hauled in unconscious on that damned gurney, but why? How? Had he followed Jez here somehow, or been brought here separately?

I blew out a frustrated breath and set it aside.

The back of the van had been kitted out like a nest, to make it less stressful for the omega kids we transported. It was deep-cleaned after each run, to minimize the smell of unfamiliar omegas.

Heath seemed happy enough to get inside. It was familiar to him, even in his current fucked-up state. But Jez cringed back in his arms and whimpered in fear as they approached the double doors.

"Hey, sweetheart," I said, bracing myself to come close and run a hand through her sweaty hair, soothing. "Easy, now. You've got to trust us, all right? It's safe. We're gonna take you home so you can fuck each other to your heart's content for the next few days. It's actually real nice inside, see?"

I gestured toward the dimly lit, blanket and cushion-strewn space. Huge gray eyes blinked up at me; then Jez turned her head, craning to follow the movement. And that was when I saw the livid, blood-spattered bite mark decorating the right side of her neck, just above her shoulder.

A fresh mating bite.

Fucking.

Shit.

TWENTY-FOUR

Jez

NEVER, EVER, *EVER* let them put you in a van. That lesson had been hammered into me so long ago that it was basically part of my bones at this point. I couldn't string two thoughts together, thanks to the lava pumping through my veins instead of blood, but the old instinct not to be trapped inside a dark, enclosed space on wheels still managed to shove its way to the fore.

I cringed back in my mate's arms, as though the van's open doors had some kind of an invisible force field around them, pushing me away. My mate hesitated as my distress flooded the brand-new bond. *Protect, protect, protect…* echoed across the raw connection, blotting out everything else.

The animal part of me wanted to trust that promise of protection, but there was some reason I shouldn't. I couldn't think… *I couldn't think.* I wanted so badly to pass out, drifting down into the warm darkness that I knew was waiting for me after my mate had knotted me through my first peak.

I didn't dare.

Then another familiar face loomed over me, blunt fingers sliding through my sweaty hair to soothe me.

"Hey, sweetheart," said the alpha that smelled like Christmas Eve in my mother's kitchen. "Easy, now. You've got to trust us, all right? It's safe. We're gonna take you home so you can fuck each other to your heart's content for the next few days. It's actually real nice inside, see?"

That voice had been kind to me in the past. It had also been cruel, but… not recently? I felt like I should listen to that voice. It was becoming harder and harder to keep my eyes open. I craned my head around to follow the alpha's gesture.

The alpha inhaled sharply. "Oh, *fuck*," he said under his breath, although I wasn't sure why.

Inside the double doors, instead of the bare metal box I expected, there was a padded den full of cushions and fleecy blankets, dimly lit by red-tinged fairy lights tacked up around the edges of the van roof. There should have been bars or a metal grill separating the back from the front, but instead, it was just *open*.

The beta male who'd come with us from inside had the driver's door open and was poking around, fiddling with the mirrors. My instincts said '*friend, but complicated.*' My mate's instincts said, '*scent, mark, protect,*' and I wasn't sure how to feel about that.

But whatever the case, this van wasn't like the other vans I'd known. It screamed *nest*, and I'd never had one of those before. Not properly. I'd also never wanted one as much as I did right now. My awareness was circling the drain, and it would feel so much safer to close my eyes inside this cozy little den than to try to keep them open.

Sensing my capitulation, my mate climbed awkwardly into the nest with me still cradled against his hard body. I didn't try to struggle away this time. Maybe, for now, I didn't have to fight. Maybe I could let all this happen… let my mate, and my other mate, and my beta *friend-but-complicated* watch over me while I rested. I knew on a deep, instinctive level that the lava in my veins would drive me toward another peak soon enough.

The strong arms holding me lowered me onto softness and helped me burrow in until I was comfortable. I was distantly aware of the back doors closing us inside, and the passenger door opening a few seconds later. Christmas Eve climbed into the front, and the last thing I heard was his voice, gruff and low-pitched.

"Hello, police? I need to report a human trafficking operation. There are several under-age omegas being held at the abandoned grain silos near McKinley…"

The growing inferno in my womb dragged me back to consciousness some unknown amount of time later. I was someplace different. Familiar, yet not. The layered patchwork of scents made me think of an attic room with dust coating the surfaces and rattling eaves overhead… but it also made me picture a bedroom that smelled like yeasty bread and sweet orange peel.

This was neither of those places.

Here, the whiskey and oak undertones took on a life of their own. The scent of my mate—who even now was stirring in the back of my awareness like a giant predator coming awake.

My belly cramped, dragging a whimper from me. I curled into a tight comma shape among the blankets, clutching at the pain with clumsy arms. Instantly, a huge shape crouched over me, caging me in with its body. The whiskey-barrel scent rolled over me in a slow wave.

I breathed it in, feeling like a bottomless pit had opened up inside me. The terrible *need*... I'd never felt anything like it before, slamming into me from two different directions. Surely it would crush me into nonexistence.

Another cramp curled me tighter into the fetal position. The figure looming over me leaned down, snuffling softly along the side of my neck. A rough tongue swiped across the raw marks decorating my mating gland, and it felt like someone had jammed a live wire directly into my nervous system.

I cried out, arching into the contact.

"Jez?" The gravelly voice came from elsewhere in the room. "Hey. You're back at the pack house, in Heath's room. You're safe. I, um, gave you a birth control shot while you were out, but since you and Heath already did it once, it's not a guarantee. I'm on dampeners. I'm here if you need anything, but... uh... it sounds like what you need right now is a knot. So, just ignore me." The sound of a throat being cleared. "Anyway… yeah."

It was just a bunch of sounds washing in one ear and out the other. Maybe they meant something, but it was too late to try and decipher them. I twisted my neck, looking around until my eyes landed on a tense body perched in an armchair across the room.

Why was he all the way over there when I needed him *here*, with my mate and me on the bed?

I couldn't waste energy on wondering, though. Not when strong hands rolled me onto my aching belly and pinned me there. A thick cock rubbed between my ass cheeks, the tip smearing wet trails against the small of my back.

I whined and snarled, snapping my teeth in frustration at having what I wanted so close to where I needed it. The large hand wrapped around the nape of my neck fell away, which was also the *fucking opposite* of what I needed. But then the weight on top of me lifted, and hands gripped my hips instead.

My mate dragged me up so I was kneeling on the squishy mattress, my upper body still splayed out flat. Thumbs dragged my cheeks apart, and I shrieked as lips and teeth closed around the sensitive flesh that had been revealed.

My mate bit and licked and sucked and growled, marking me with bites and bruises even as one hand slid around to press thick fingers inside me. I sobbed, needing more, more, *more*. The fingers inside me curled, stretching me until it was *almost* enough. A climax hit me broadside and with no warning, unseen and crushing in its intensity.

My sobs rose into a scream as my cramping passage tried to suck my mate's entire hand in up to the wrist. It was like a knot, but it *wasn't* a knot... *and I needed a motherfucking knot.*

"Fuck me!" I begged. "Oh god, *fuck me*! I need it! *I need it!*"

My mate made a noise I'd never heard before, somewhere between a growl and a roar. The hand inside me pulled out, tugging at my fluttering rim as my body tried to keep it there.

The weight pinning me returned, and this time the heavy cock didn't tease. The thick girth slammed into me with a single, violent thrust, bottoming out with a sharp slap of flesh against flesh. I cried out again, even louder than before.

"*Christ.*" The voice across the room sounded faint and hoarse, but I couldn't focus on it.

The hand that had been curled inside me snaked around and covered my mouth like a gag, stifling my shrieks and whines into a desperate, muffled plea for *more*. His fingers were *soaked* in my own slick. Rough skin slid against my lips... the caramel coffee tang working its way into my mouth as I bucked and struggled.

It was hard to breathe like this, and the swimmy sensation of airlessness added to the dizzying jolts of ecstasy spreading outward from where we were joined. My muscles trembled, shuddered, and finally went lax as I submitted to the pleasure being forced on my helpless body.

My mate was taking what he wanted from me, and I was powerless to resist him; both mentally and physically. The realization was divine.

My lips parted, my tongue darting out to lap shamelessly at my own taste. The fingers that had been gagging my cries curled and slid in deep, pressing against my tongue and gagging me in an altogether different and more satisfying way.

Every inch of my skin radiated heat like a furnace. Now that same heat turned inward as well, gathering and gathering until the tip of the cock ramming into me nudged up against a ball of liquid fire with every deep plunge.

My mate's left hand clenched finger-shaped bruises into my hip. His body shuddered once, hard, and the cock inside me pulsed. His pleasure flooded through the bond, and the sphere of heat throbbing in my womb burst wide open. I bit down hard on the fingers in my mouth, groaning as though I was about to die.

The orgasm was less about pleasure and more about runaway nuclear fission. I was only vaguely aware of my mate's knot swelling hot and hard within me, or my muscles clenching around it with crushing force.

With a moan of utter relief, I let the blackness take me again.

TWENTY-FIVE

Knox

THREE DAYS AFTER I woke up from nearly getting my stupid ass killed, the doctors finally agreed to let me go home. This was simultaneously a relief, because hospitals were hell on earth, and not a relief, because I still felt like two-week-old dog shit.

That was going to be a problem on a few different levels. Because, from what I'd been able to gather, someone had basically set off a nuclear bomb in my pack while I was busy drooling onto a hospital pillow.

I wasn't sure how long it was going to take before the congealed lump of porridge between my ears was working well enough to deal with international trade delivery duties, demurrage, HS code, and all the other things that I'd built a business on. For now, I was struggling to wrap my head around the things Tony and Gage had let slip... and, just as importantly, the things they *hadn't* let slip.

Heath's protégé had been the one at my bedside when I'd finally swum up from the murky depths of my coma. Not Heath himself. Not Gage. Just a sweet beta kid who I'd had maybe half a dozen short conversations with, since Heath had picked him up a couple of years ago.

I barely remembered anything of what Tony had been talking about when I'd first woken up. Just that he'd been babbling, speaking faster and faster while saying less and less. Then he'd said something about calling the others to let them know I was awake, after which he'd disappeared for more than a day, only to return looking like he'd just peered into the mouth of Hell itself.

After twenty-four hours of radio silence — and still not so much as a call or a text from either of my packmates — I laid into the kid pretty hard when he finally slunk back into my private hospital room. And then I felt like a total ass when he physically cringed away from me.

"Look," I said, doing my best to modulate my voice. "Just tell me they're okay, Tony. What the hell's been *happening* the past few days?"

Tony's eyes darted around like he was looking for hidden cameras in the room. And, to be fair, there may have been one. With all the lawsuits in the medical industry, hospitals probably had good reason to use surveillance cameras for recorded evidence. None of which explained what Tony might know that he didn't want the hospital's security staff to hear.

He cleared his throat and stuffed his hands in his jean pockets. His shoulders had been tense before, but now they were practically hunched up around his ears.

He cleared his throat. "The others? Oh, y'know… they're, um, okay. They're at the pack house. It's… a bit complicated?"

I stared at him. "It's complicated that they're at our house? Where they *live*?"

Tony looked like he wanted to sink straight through the floor. "Yeah. Some stuff went down, but we should, uh, maybe not talk about it here? You're supposed to be resting, after all."

I wasn't proud of the fact that my spiking blood pressure triggered a medical alarm and brought two nurses running into the room at that point. Worse, it gave Tony the cover he needed to dart out the door and disappear again.

It was only when I got my phone back later in the day and bribed one of the nurses into buying me a charger from the gift shop, that I finally got some answers. As soon as I had enough battery to power up the cell, I tried texting Heath.

No answer.

So, I tried texting Gage instead, and thank all that was holy, he answered almost immediately.

Knox? God, it's good to hear from you, man. How are you?

I instantly hit the call button.

"How *am I?*" I echoed as soon as he picked up. "What the *fuck*, Gage? *Start talking. Now.*"

I could feel the heavy awkwardness behind the silence that followed.

"*Yeah. So,*" Gage said slowly. "*Before I say anything, are you at all still likely to have a heart attack?*"

I breathed deeply in and out through my nose, shooting the bank of medical readouts an evil side-eye.

"If I was, you would not be helping with that right now," I said with deadly calm. "Don't make me say this a third time. Start. Fucking. *Talking.*"

I heard him blow out a breath over the connection.

"Okay. How much do you remember about what happened at the Aurora Hotel on the night you were attacked?"

That was a sore point, despite the doctors' reassurances that some memory loss was normal. I swallowed and licked my lips.

"There was a woman," I said reluctantly. "I think I wanted to take her up to the penthouse with me. Which I know is out of character."

"Yeah, it is," Gage mumbled.

"Then I woke up yesterday in a hospital bed," I finished, ignoring the interruption. "That's it. Nothing in between."

It was the same thing I'd told the cops when they'd showed up earlier in the morning, except with a vague description of platinum-blond hair and the smell of sweet coffee.

"Fun fact," Gage said, his tone grim. *"You probably wanted to get closer to this woman because she's our pack's scent match."*

"What?" I asked faintly, even as the rightness of it settled into my truncated memory.

"Less fun fact," Gage went on. *"She's also the one who tried to kill you."*

The heart monitor next to the bed beeped ominously. I fumbled around and disconnected the lead before it could start screaming an alarm. Of course, disconnecting it would bring a nurse in as well, but it might give me a bit of extra time.

"Where is this woman now?" I demanded. "Did the police get her?"

The pause on the other end felt like it lasted about a million years.

"Gage!" I half-shouted.

"*I don't think I should say anything else over the phone, Knox. Everyone's safe; just focus on that for now, okay?*"

Did he think our phones were compromised? What the *hell*?

I tried to focus on his reassurance. If he was lying about them both being safe, I'd be able to tell. Wouldn't I?

A nurse bustled in, tutting when she saw the dangling wires. I resisted the urge to yell at her until she left the room. Grasping the shreds of my self-control, I covered the phone mic with one hand and dredged up my best tone of contrition.

I was sadly out of practice at it.

"Sorry, nurse," I said. "I was trying to get more comfortable when the wires came loose. Could I just finish up my phone conversation real quick? Won't be a minute."

The nurse made a disapproving humming noise, which I chose to interpret as a yes.

"Look, Gage," I said. "You already know I'm not happy about this. But before we hang up, are your sister's kids doing okay?"

It was a not-very-subtle code for the group of omegas who'd been staying at the house when I'd been taken out of commission.

"*Oh, yeah,*" Gage said. "*They're safely off to camp, as planned. You focus on getting better so you can come home, okay? We need you here.*"

"I'll do my best," wondering if I was ever going to be able to sleep again after this conversation. "Gotta go."

A heavy thud sounded from his end, followed by feral growling.

"*Yeah, me too,*" he said, which was perhaps the least reassuring sign-off in the history of phone calls.

<hr>

Two days later, an orderly wheeled me out of the hospital in a wheelchair, my wrist aching from the number of release forms that had needed to be signed, dated, and initialed.

Tony was waiting for me under the portico with a battered white Volvo station wagon from the previous century. He'd been my only visitor except for a steady trickle of police detectives and lifestyle reporters. The former had received the same — *completely truthful* — story that I had no memory of the attack itself. The latter were barred at the door, except for one chirpy alpha woman from *The Daily Gab,* who'd managed to force her way in and demand to know if the rumors about the attack being a revenge-for-hire plot by a jilted former mate were true.

Since I didn't have any former mates, jilted or otherwise, that angle seemed like a bit of a non-starter. It would probably sell tabloid copies, though.

Every time he'd stopped by, Tony had acted as nervous as a long-tailed cat in a room full of rocking chairs. I'd eventually decided that if both he and Gage thought it was a bad idea to discuss things in a place where it might be overheard or recorded, they must have a reason.

Tony looked as anxious out here as he had during his visits. So, I waited until I was safely in the passenger seat, and the nurse had disappeared back into the hospital, before I spoke.

"Okay. Spill it," I said, no-nonsense.

Tony gave an audible gulp. "Let me find a parking spot first. I don't think I should be driving for this."

I set my jaw and looked straight ahead. "You know, you and Gage could both use some work on acting reassuring."

Tony pulled out of the pick-up area and into one of the large visitors' lots. "Pretty sure no one offers classes on dealing with shit like this," he muttered.

"Still not helping," I told him.

He found a spot at the back of the lot and parked the car, leaving it running. His chest rose and fell on a deep breath.

"Okay. So… when I first moved here, I had a friend named Jez who lived on the streets and busked with me sometimes," he said in a rush. "When my abusive stepdad tracked me down in Chicago and cornered me in my apartment, Jez showed up and bashed him over the head with a table lamp. Killed him stone dead."

I blinked. "And this is relevant because…?"

He shook his head almost angrily. "I'm getting to that. Afterward, she ran off. I'd been doing odd jobs for your pack, and I didn't know who else to call to clean up the body, so I called Heath."

My eyebrows shot up. I'd had no idea about any of this.

"I didn't see Jez again, until just recently," Tony went on. "Turns out, she liked the feeling of getting revenge on a predator so much that she kept doing it. She got a reputation as the person you went to if you needed to deal with alpha vermin."

"She became a vigilante?" I asked, getting a glimmer of where this might be going, and not liking it one bit.

"That's… one word for it." The words were delivered in a monotone. "Unfortunately, she's also a fucking idiot. Because a few weeks ago, someone sold her a story about *you*. And because that story played into the same things that had been done to her when she was young, she bought the lies hook, line, and sinker."

The glimmer grew into a flashing neon sign.

"So, she came at me," I said. "And nearly succeeded."

Tony nodded. "Except she had no clue she was your pack's scent match. Not that knowing would have necessarily stopped her." He took another centering breath. "Gage and Heath captured her in your hotel suite. Gage brought her back to the pack house while Heath got help for you, because he couldn't bear the thought of turning your scent match over to the cops for attempted murder."

"Gage is also a fucking idiot," I said, without much rancor. This was old news, and fortunately for all of us, he had plenty of attributes that made up for it.

"Yeah," Tony agreed heavily. "Anyway, Jez assumed she'd been captured by omega child sex traffickers, just like the people who abused her when she was a kid. And Gage and Heath assumed they were holding a murderer. Which, um… they were."

"Fuck," I said, because this was a lot to take in when you'd been in a coma seventy-two hours ago.

"Definitely." Tony shot me a concerned glance. "And here's where it gets worse. Your heart's okay now, right?"

"I really wish people would stop asking me that," I told him.

"Sorry." Pink flooded his cheeks, and he looked away again. "From what I gather, Heath went looking for the omega who told Jez this story about you. Then Jez managed to get free and sneak away with Gage's phone, and she did exactly the same thing. I guess she was pretty desperate to figure out who was lying to her, and who was telling the truth."

"Understandable," I said carefully.

"As best as Gage and I can figure out, they both confronted this omega who hired her, and they both got captured for their trouble. Gage and I tracked his stolen phone to the old abandoned grain silos near McKinley, where someone was holding a bunch of underage omegas and using them to film kiddie porn."

I tensed. "Do we know who it was?"

Tony shook his head. "Gage thinks it's the Vozzinas, but he doesn't have proof. Whoever it was, they were holding Heath and Jez there, too, and we were more concerned with getting them out than anything else."

"Are they all right?" I asked sharply. Surely, he and Gage couldn't have been lying to me this whole time about Heath being safe. But Heath hadn't called or texted me—

"They injected Heath with a rut-stim and Jez with a heat-stim before we got there," Tony said. "They must have smelled each other, because they killed the guards and got free of their cells. By the time we showed up, they were already… um… *you know.*"

I could guess.

Immediately, my porridge brain jumped to the practicalities. Birth control… sexually transmitted diseases… not to mention the psychological fallout—

Tony hunched lower in the driver's seat, like he was trying to make himself small. "And… uh… he'd already mated her before we got there."

He sounded like the words had been pulled from him one at a time with needle-nose pliers. My thoughts crashed to a standstill as the sense of what he'd said penetrated.

"He… what?" I asked.

"Gage is staying with them until the heat wears off," Tony added miserably. "But once that happens… well. I actually have no idea. I can't imagine it's going to be good, though."

I slumped back in my seat. "No," I said. "I can't imagine it will."

TWENTY-SIX

Knox

GAGE MUST HAVE heard Tony's car pull up, because he was waiting when we reached the front porch. The door swung inward almost violently, and before I could get a word out, I was enveloped in a rib-cracking hug.

"I knew you'd be okay," Gage said, his voice strangled. "Told everyone you would be—didn't I, Tony?"

He was physically shaking in my arms.

"Yeah," Tony agreed, from behind me somewhere. "Yeah, you were right, big guy."

I patted Gage awkwardly on the back, and thankfully, he pulled away before my need to breathe grew impossible to ignore.

"I've got dampeners," he said, nonsensically—once again cutting me off before I could speak. "Come inside."

"Gage—" I began.

"I know," he cut me off. "Knox, I *know*. And I'm so sorry. But seriously, you're gonna want this dampener shot before anything else."

Stymied, I let the pair herd me into the house... where I was immediately slammed in the face by a solid wall of pheromones. All the blood in my battered excuse for a brain fled southward. I wavered, my weakened condition making me lightheaded even as my dick swelled painfully.

Gage steadied me with one meaty hand and shifted me to lean against the entryway wall.

"Shit," he said. "Sorry. Should've brought the shot with me and done it outside. Stay here for a minute, okay? I'll run get it. Tony, watch him for me."

"What?" Tony yelped—but Gage was already disappearing down the long hall.

"I'm okay," I choked out, lying through my teeth.

Only the fact that I could barely stand upright kept me from barging after Gage to find the source of that intoxicating scent... burnt sugar and espresso that promised to wake up my weakened body in the most delicious of ways.

Tony hovered next to me, looking torn between putting his hand on my arm to support me and running for the hills.

"The same thing happened to Gage when we found them at the silos," he said worriedly. "Don't worry, though—a dampener shot fixed him right up."

If I'd dared unclench my teeth long enough to speak, I might've pointed out that Gage was coming apart at the seams, and was very obviously *not* all right. But it was all I could do to stand there leaning against the wall as flashes of memory zapped across my mental movie screen like scenes beneath a strobe light.

Pale hair.

Huge gray eyes.

Long satin gloves, and a little black dress hugging curves and angles in all the right ways.

Tony took a hasty step back, and a second later, I registered the rumbling growl rolling up from the depths of my chest. With an act of willpower, I swallowed the noise. I pushed away from the wall experimentally. Maybe if I took it slow, I'd be able to make it to my mate's side without keeling over—

Heavy footsteps reached my ears. Gage jogged toward me, holding something carefully away from his body in one hand.

"Sorry," he said, breathless. "I expect you're getting' sick of people jabbing you with needles."

He shoved my sleeve up and stuck the needle into my arm, steadily depressing the plunger until it was empty. The cool sting of its contents spread slowly through my veins, distracting me long enough for the drug to start doing its work.

I panted through my nose until the overwhelming scent choking the house faded to manageable levels. My dick throbbed sullenly, but I no longer felt like there was a taut bungee cord physically dragging me toward the source of the pheromones.

"*Jesus Christ*," I said hoarsely.

"Right?" Gage agreed, wide-eyed. "It's fuckin' *mental*, ain't it?" He turned to Tony, who was standing close to the door as though he wanted nothing more than to bolt and never look back. "Hey, Tony—can you keep an eye on the lovebirds while me and Knox have a word? I don't want to leave 'em on their own for too long."

Tony shrank back. "Goddamn it, Gage! No, I will not *'keep an eye on the lovebirds!'* What the fuck do you expect me to do if something goes wrong? They murdered three armed alphas with their bare hands trying to get to each other!"

"Tony, they ain't gonna hurt you," Gage said, sounding surprised by the outburst. "They *like* you."

"No!" Tony said again, louder this time. "Your pack alpha is back; you can deal with this epic shitstorm *without my help!*"

We both stared after him as he yanked the door open and disappeared through it, slamming it so hard behind him that the walls rattled. Outside, the old Volvo's engine roared to life. Gravel sprayed as the car peeled out of the circle drive.

Silence echoed through the house for the space of several heartbeats.

"Gage," I said, already feeling exhausted before we'd even properly begun. "What the hell just happened?"

Gage was still looking fixedly at the closed door. After a moment, he stepped forward and engaged the locks. When he finally turned to meet my eyes, he looked every bit as worn down as I felt.

"With Tony?" he asked. "It's just a guess, and I might be wrong. But I think him and Heath might have a *thing* going."

I filed that information away, along with all the other things I needed to yell at Heath about.

"And Heath just mated someone else," I said, putting two and two together.

"Heath just mated the same girl who ran away and left Tony alone to deal with his murdered stepdad a year ago," Gage clarified. "And who tried to kill *you*."

I took a cautious breath—holding it for a moment to make sure the dampeners had fully kicked in. My shoulders slumped as I let it out.

"Gage." I held his hazel eyes, reading the defeat in them. "Why in the *hell* didn't you let the police take her? Tony said you caught her in the penthouse suite, practically in the act."

The big alpha's expression collapsed, deep lines adding years to his rugged face.

"It was..." He hesitated. "It was complicated, boss. She's our scent match. But she's also a homeless omega wannabe assassin. If the legal system got hold of her, they'd toss her in a dark hole and throw away the key."

"Yes. That tends to happen to people who murder other people for money," I said evenly.

"It wasn't just that, though!" Gage went on quickly. "We needed to find out who hired her. She's not the real threat."

"Isn't she, though?" I couldn't keep the dryness from my tone.

"No, she's *not*." The words were forceful. "She's a hurt, naïve omega who found a way to lash out after her fuckin' dad auctioned off her first heat and sold her to traffickers at the age of thirteen!"

It wasn't like Gage to get this worked up over something—and definitely not with *me*. I made myself take what he was saying on board.

"Okay," I said. "So, she had a rough childhood, and you feel bad for her. And Tony's got a soft spot for her because she offed his abusive stepfather. After which she decided to start offing other people for money. Which is where we've got a bit of a problem."

Gage's jaw clenched stubbornly. "Do we? Because Heath snapped a couple of necks at the silos. And those necks belonged to alpha predators who were abusing kids. You gonna turn him in for that?"

I blew out a frustrated sigh. "No, Gage. I am not going to turn in my packmate for killing the people who kidnapped him and injected him with a rut-stim against his will."

"Well," Gage said doggedly. "That's the same kind of alphas that Jez has been going after. You didn't see her, Knox. When me and Heath caught her at the hotel, she was one-hundred percent convinced that she'd fallen into the hands of the same kind of people who made her childhood a living hell."

"Which we aren't," I reminded him. "And that makes me wonder how many *other* mistakes she's made over her short-lived career in vigilante justice."

That shut Gage up. His jaw snapped closed, and the light of uncertainty flickered behind his gaze before once more being replaced by stubbornness.

"Maybe she did. And maybe she didn't," he said. "But it doesn't change the fact that she's our scent match, and now she's mated to Heath. The past is deeply fucked up, but right now I'm more worried about what happens next."

"A glandectomy, at a guess," I replied, not letting any emotion come through in my voice. Mating bonds were for life... unless you surgically removed the organ responsible for maintaining them.

Gage paled. "That's our *mate* you're talking about maiming."

My temper flared. "For fuck's sake, Gage! I meant *she'll* want the surgery. Not that I plan on holding her down and hacking it out myself! This isn't the goddamned twentieth century!"

He still looked queasy. "Yeah. I guess."

Not for the first time, I was struck by how close my normally unflappable packmate looked to completely breaking down and losing his shit. I wasn't in much better shape after my stint in the hospital, but I *was* his pack leader... and I hadn't spent the last few days cooped up in this house with Jez's pheromones.

"Go get some rest, Gage," I said. "Those dampeners you gave me seem to be doing the trick. I'll watch over Heath and our resident homicidal maniac for now."

I watched him waver.

"You sure?" he asked. "I mean, after everything?"

"I'm sure," I said. If nothing else, I wanted to see for myself that Heath was still in one piece.

"Okay," Gage said reluctantly. Relief and worry warred across his broad features. "But you come get me when you need a break."

"Of course," I told him. "Really, Gage—I'm perfectly fine."

"No, you're not," he said matter-of-factly… but he didn't press the issue.

"Where are they?" I asked.

"Heath's room," he said. "She's between peaks. I'm hoping she's about done, but it just depends on what kind of shit they injected her with."

I nodded my understanding and trudged toward the stairs. Getting to the second floor felt like climbing a mountain, but I managed it. I knocked on Heath's door, but didn't wait before opening it and slipping inside.

My packmate's growl cut off abruptly as soon as he saw and smelled me. The gruff, flame-haired alpha was lounging naked on his bed, the unconscious waif of an omega curled half on his lap. They were both smeared from head to toe with streaks of dirt and dried blood, not to mention covered in bruises and bite marks.

Heath stiffened in place, easing his tiny burden off of his lap and onto the rumpled pile of bedding. In a flash, he was off the bed, stalking toward me and into my personal space. I stood still as he snuffled along the side of my throat. The tension went out of his body, and he rubbed a bearded cheek against mine. A purr vibrated up from his chest.

I couldn't deny the release of tension in my own body in response to the confirmation that he truly was safe. Giving in to the temptation, I lifted a hand and ruffled through his shaggy hair, trying not to think too closely about what kind of bodily fluids had contributed to the tangled mats and tacky patches.

Jez made a little noise of discontent on the bed, and Heath straightened away from me. I shooed him back over to her, setting my misgivings aside for now. They were mated. It was already done. There was nothing more to do about it until they were both in their right mind.

Gage had pulled a comfortable chair into the far corner of the bedroom. I settled myself into it and let my mind drift, trying to ignore the magnetic pull toward the bed. Dampeners or no, I could understand why Gage looked like he was one crack away from shattering after being stuck in here for days.

━━━━◆━━━━

Several hours slid by in a languid haze. The shot Gage had given me filtered out the worst of the involuntary physical reactions to an omega's heat-scent, but I still thought I could detect a gradual change in the tone of Jez's pheromones. For that reason, it wasn't a complete surprise when she groaned and stirred into awareness.

Heath paused in his obsessive stroking of her hair, but he still held the blank-eyed look of the artificial rut. Jez, on the other hand, whimpered and cringed as she tried to roll into a sitting position.

"Ow," she said—a tiny little bleat of a word.

Omegas in heat didn't say '*ow*.' The aches and pains caused by days of often violent sex didn't register until afterward. I watched impassively as she registered my presence and bolted upright, the pain in her overused muscles forgotten. She gasped and scrabbled for a blanket, yanking it over her torso to cover herself.

I smiled—not an ounce of humor in the expression. "Hello, *Kit*," I said, purposely using the fake name she'd given me that night. "Looks like you've had a busy time of things the last few days. And now, you and I need to have a nice little talk."

TWENTY-SEVEN

Jez

I STARED OPEN-MOUTHED at the ghost sitting in the far corner of the unfamiliar room. Everything was wrong, wrong, *wrong*. My body ached. My *brain* ached, flooded with unfamiliar thoughts and feelings that didn't make any sense.

I would *never* think things like this. Things like how amazing I was, and how important it was that I be protected at all costs. What the hell was wrong with me? I wasn't amazing. I wasn't *important*. And why did everything hurt so bad?

I screwed my eyes shut, trying to ignore the hallucination sitting in the corner. There had to be an explanation. I felt a bit like I'd been beaten up… and a bit like when I'd taken drugs early on, before I'd decided properly whether I wanted to live or die after getting free from the omega traffickers.

Could that be it? Had I tried to escape reality with drugs again, and someone had taken advantage of me while I was off my head?

The alien feelings of protectiveness inside my mind sharpened. An alpha purr vibrated next to me, but it had a worried edge. As though it was *bad* that I was freaking out like this.

"You might as well open your eyes," said the ghost in the corner. "This conversation isn't going to get any easier, no matter how long you avoid it."

I reluctantly pried my eyelids open, but I still avoided looking in the direction of the voice. The glance I'd caught before had been bad enough. The innocent alpha I'd killed… now a talking corpse with dark-smudged eyes, gaunt cheeks, and pasty gray skin.

Instead, I looked toward the source of the purr.

Heath Dawson lay naked in bed with me. He was covered in dirt and blood, and… other bodily fluids. Scabby, half-healed wounds like claw marks decorated his face and neck. Some of them looked infected.

My gaze caught and held on his forest-green eyes. In the same instant, the alien feelings in my head spiked. One particular physical ache cut through my body's general clamoring—centered at the top of my right shoulder, over the juncture of my neck.

A horrible, sick realization washed through me. With a gasp, I scrabbled backward across the soft surface I'd been lying on… and promptly fell off the edge of the bed.

I landed with a thud, tangled in the blanket I'd dragged down with me. The presence in my head radiated worry, and Heath crawled to the edge of the mattress as though he might follow me.

"*Don't.*" It wasn't an alpha bark, but Heath paused anyway, looking up. "Leave her be for now," said the ghost of Matthew Knockley, sounding closer than before. "She and I are talking, Heath."

Heath gave a low growl, but he made no further move toward me. The mental presence subsided into watchful silence.

Heart pounding frantically, I looked up at the corpse. Guilt pierced me, and I crab-crawled backward, dragging the blanket with me like a fleecy shield, until my shoulders jammed up in a corner.

The ghost halted a few paces in front of me and sank smoothly into a crouch, his elbows resting loosely on his knees as he brought himself down to my pathetic level. I couldn't keep from looking at him now. I couldn't help scenting him, either, through the cloud of my own filthy stink.

I frowned. Since I killed him, shouldn't he smell like death, instead of a welcoming campfire in a forest of green cedar?

"A few things to start off with," he said, pinning me with soulful brown eyes that hadn't clouded over and faded to gray dullness. "Number one—yes, I'm alive and out of the hospital. Number two—yes, you're back at the pack house. This is Heath's room. And number three—you and he were kidnapped by whoever hired you to murder me. They injected you with heat stim and Heath with rut-stim. Heath had already mated you by the time Gage and Tony showed up to get you out."

My thoughts crashed to a standstill. Heath's worried growl rumbled deeper.

"Wh-what?" I rasped.

"You'll need a pregnancy test as soon as it's feasible," Knox went on.

"But—" I began.

"And I'd like you both to get tested for sexually transmitted diseases," Knox continued.

"But I—"

"There are options for dealing with the mating itself."

The words slid straight past me.

"But I tried—"

"A glandectomy being the most obvious one," he said, as though I hadn't spoken.

"*But I tried to kill you!*" I half-shouted.

He paused for a beat.

"Yes," he agreed steadily. "You did."

I opened my mouth, only for my throat to close up before any words could get out. Air caught and dragged against the constriction, the sound like an ugly, gasping sob. I tried again, with the same result, and before I could get control of my breathing, I collapsed into hysterical tears.

I couldn't be mated.

I couldn't be pregnant.

And I absolutely *could not* be someone who'd tried to murder an innocent man!

Bits and flashes of images—*memories?*—glitched across my hazy vision. My teeth buried in an alpha's wrist, blood blooming across my tongue. A knife in my hand, stabbing into a neck. Red fountaining out, splattering across my cheek. My fingernails scratching at a terrified face… gouging eyeballs…ripping open skin.

I stared down at my hands, blinking past the blur of tears. My nails were crusted with flaky reddish brown. A scream lodged in my throat, stuck behind the thick obstruction that was already strangling my air.

Heath made a noise of distress and jerked toward me, even as I cringed further back into the corner.

"Heath. *Stop.*" It was Knox again. Still not a bark. And again, Heath froze in place, trembling like a hunting dog straining to be let off the leash.

I wheezed, feeling lightheaded.

"Look at me, Jez." The alpha's tone was devoid of anger… of pity.

Unable to help myself, I looked into those brown eyes — trying to focus past the gray swirl of fog gathering at the edges of my vision.

Knox was alive. I hadn't killed him, even if he was pale and hollowed out by days spent in the hospital, fighting to survive. He was keeping Heath away from me, as though he knew that I'd shatter at the first touch from the red-haired alpha who had bitten me while we'd both been out of our minds with lust.

"Where's Gage?" It wasn't even a proper whisper. I didn't have enough air for that.

"Sleeping," Knox said, still without judgment. "He was in here watching over things — making sure you were both safe — for almost three days straight."

The band around my chest snapped, but I could still only breathe in harsh sobs. I curled forward, hugging myself with both arms. I cried… I wasn't sure for how long. My own distress mixed and swirled with Heath's distress at not being able to jump off the bed and magically fix me with the power of his goddamned alpha purr.

But I was also exhausted. And eventually, my body couldn't sustain any more tears. I slumped in the corner, feeling scraped out and empty despite having a second person jammed inside my head with me. Cautiously, I peeked up at Knox through my thick pall of humiliation.

He'd moved to a more comfortable position, sitting propped against the side of the bed. This also allowed him to place a quelling hand on Heath's wrist, wordlessly keeping the other alpha from leaping up and coming to me.

"If you can talk now, then let's talk," Knox said. "Tony said you ran off so you could find out who'd been lying to you, and who was telling the truth. Did you find your answer?"

Why was he acting like this? Like he wasn't furious at me? Like what I had to say mattered?

I nodded wordlessly.

"And what answer was that?" he pressed.

I swallowed. Now my throat and sinuses hurt, along with everything else.

"Adrian lied to me," I rasped. "You don't hurt omegas. You try to help them. And I almost killed you."

Knox rubbed at the back of his neck with his free hand. "Yes. Well. Thankfully, you didn't. At this point, I'm more concerned with this Adrian character, in that regard."

"But—" I stammered, because he couldn't really be *letting it go*, just like that?

"But nothing." He let out a slow breath. "Gage thinks the Vozzina gang is behind the attempted hit. He doesn't have any real proof, though."

The presence in my head jolted.

"I don't know that name," I said. "I'm sorry."

"It's all right," Knox said. "We'll see if Heath learned anything useful before he got himself kidnapped. But until then—"

The mental presence twisted awkwardly, like a newly awakened sleeper trying to get their bearings. I held my breath.

"V'zzina?" Heath slurred, raising a hand to his forehead as though it ached.

On cue, a second headache throbbed in counterpoint to the one I'd already been nursing. A fresh sense of dread settled over me.

"Heath?" Knox asked, still holding his wrist. "Are you coming out of it, finally?"

I bit my lip, wincing as my teeth closed over a spot that had already been bitten repeatedly over the past few days. Heath's silent presence shifted imperceptibly inside me, becoming less animalistic. More human.

Blind protectiveness gave way to confusion... then worry... and then distress.

Against my will, my eyes slid up the length of the alpha's dirty, battered body until I met a wide-eyed green gaze. Shell-shocked and blindsided by the awareness of what the two of us had done under the influence of our captors' drugs, Heath stared at me in utter horror.

TWENTY-EIGHT

Heath

NO. JUST… *NO*. I dragged my gaze away from the small form huddled in the corner, wrapped in a dirty blanket. This couldn't be what it looked like… what it *felt* like.

I was buck-ass naked. My entire body ached like I'd gone ten rounds in the boxing ring with Jack Dempsey. Dried sweat crusted on my skin as though I'd been feverish. The sour scent of old blood and infected wounds turned my stomach.

And the small, alien presence tucked inside my head was—

No.

I wasn't thinking about that yet. I did my best to wall off that soft presence, pushing it away from the rest of me so I could pretend it didn't exist. Because, if it existed, that meant—

I shook my head sharply, even though the movement made my brain slosh around like the last pickled egg in a jar of brine.

Stop.

Instead, I focused on the other impossible thing in the room; doing my best to ignore the little whimper of distress that came from the corner. A familiar hand clasped my forearm. The clean scent of smoky cedarwood pierced through the funk of blood and jizz and sickly-sweet omega stress pheromones.

"Knox?" I asked, hating how small and raw my voice sounded — like my throat had been scraped into sandpaper from screaming.

"I'm here," my pack alpha said. "Everything's going to be okay, you two. Although there's likely to be some rough patches between here and there."

Cautiously, Knox let my arm go. Without that grounding touch, it became harder to block out… *everything else*. Memories clamored for attention.

A metal table.

The wide, terrified eyes of a baby omega jammed against the metal bars of a cage as he tried to get as far away from me as possible.

The feeling of another alpha's vertebrae snapping beneath the force of my grip.

In the corner of the bedroom — and inside my head — soft sobs tore at me like dull knives ripping flesh. I clenched my jaw and built the walls around that presence thicker and higher, until I thought I might collapse under their weight.

"I…" Jez's voice, thick with tears, wavered alarmingly. "I need Gage. Please get Gage."

I squeezed my eyes shut, but that only meant that the images of her in Gage's bed — in *my* bed — grew more vivid. Like an unwanted VR slideshow, pictures of her moaning underneath me alternated with close-ups of Tony Scalise's haggard face as I buried my nose in his dark hair and sniffed along the side of his throat.

Oh, *god*. Tony had been there, while I'd been out of my mind with lust? Please tell me I hadn't—

"All right," Knox said, breaking into my spiraling thoughts. "Stay put. I'll get him for you."

I sat frozen in place, afraid that if I moved, I'd lose the tenuous grip I had on myself. Despite my best efforts, I was hyperaware of the small figure curled into a ball across from me.

"Oy! Gage!" Knox shouted from the open doorway. "Can you come in here, please? Jez is asking for you!"

He stepped back inside, and within seconds, my other packmate arrived. Bare-chested and bleary eyed, Gage stumbled into the room. His shoulder knocked clumsily against the doorframe as though his brain was still half-mired in sleep. His pajama pants hung low around his hips.

His stupid face lit up with relief when he saw me. "Heath! You're both okay now?"

I stared at him. "How the *fuck* do you come to that conclusion?"

Gage's hazel eyes moved to Jez as though drawn there by a magnet. She made another small, stifled noise, and his face fell.

"Aw, kitten," he said softly—because apparently, we were giving Knox's attempted murderer *pet names*, now. "You're a mess after all that. Can I help you clean up and get you some food? Maybe some soup and crackers?"

I ground my teeth together until my jaw creaked, mentally bracing my full weight against the imaginary wall in my head; as though I could prop it up through sheer force of will.

"*Gage*," Jez choked out, reaching up toward him with both hands.

A vein throbbed in my temple as Gage tutted and crouched down, scooping her into his huge arms, blanket and all. She clung to him and buried her face against his neck. I got a glimpse of the red ring of tooth marks decorating the top of her shoulder and quickly dragged my gaze away.

"I'm gonna take her to my bathroom and make sure she doesn't have any injuries we don't know about," he told us. "C'mon, kitten. I've got bubble bath you can use. You'll like it, I promise."

My stomach dipped and rolled as a wave of unwanted jealousy washed through me like acid. My fingers tightened painfully in the mussed bedding as I fought the *fucking psychotic* urge to leap up and wrestle Jez out of my packmate's arms.

I waited until they'd disappeared through the door, Gage's footsteps retreating down the hallway in the direction of his room. My muscles trembled with exhaustion, combined with the irrational need to run after him and take back what was mine.

Knox came and sat on the bed next to me, reclaiming his earlier spot.

I couldn't look at him, even though I knew I should be over the goddamned moon that he was home and safe.

"I need a drink," I whispered hoarsely, knowing there wouldn't be a single drop of alcohol anywhere in the house. My recovering alcoholic ass had seen to that personally.

"Too fucking bad," Knox said, his tone matter-of-fact. "Get up, get in the shower, and slather some antibiotic ointment on those scratches when you're done. We need to talk about what happened."

My grip on the bedding tightened. Four-hundred thread-count Egyptian cotton ripped beneath my ragged fingernails.

"Shower," Knox repeated. "Now. You've got drying spunk in your hair, and I'm not currently equipped to deal with that fact. Not on top of everything else."

As though his words had been the catalyst, I was suddenly overcome with shuddering revulsion at myself. I staggered upright and lunged for the en suite bathroom, slamming the door behind me. I barely made it to the toilet before I was retching up bile.

It's the drugs they gave me, I told myself. I remembered the needle jabbing into my neck… the slow descent into madness while locked in a cell with some poor, innocent kid. *It's just the drugs.*

When the convulsive heaving finally subsided, I straightened. My eyes fell unwillingly on the mirror, revealing something from a low-budget zombie flick. I'd clawed my own face and neck bloody in an attempt to maintain control, during the long hours before Jez had broken into my cell and let the omega kid escape to safety.

I tilted my face from side to side. Some of that shit was going to scar, too. A permanent reminder of the worst fucking day of my life.

She saved you. The internal voice whispered the words like a secret. *If you hadn't scented her while you were trapped in the cell, you wouldn't have been able to hold on as long as you did.*

I whirled away from the mirror before the temptation to put a fist through the glass grew too great to ignore. My balance wavered, and I caught myself on the vanity, breathing deeply. Jez's presence in my mind had quieted, her initial horror receding as Gage fussed over her.

Kitten.

He had a fucking *pet name* for her. Why couldn't I seem to get past that?

Working solely by muscle memory, I turned on the shower as hot as I could stand it and stepped inside. Stinging drops of water pelted me, turning rusty brown as they ran down my body and disappeared into the drain. I stood there for a long time; one arm braced against the wall.

Eventually, I roused myself enough to scrub at my hair and body, trying to physically remove the last few days with the power of shampoo and body wash.

Maybe it worked. At least, I felt marginally more like a human being by the time I emerged. My pale skin had been scrubbed pink and raw. Reluctantly, I swiped a towel across the mirror, clearing the steamy condensation. I still looked worse than Knox, and *he'd* just walked out of the hospital a few hours ago.

On autopilot, I pulled a tube of ointment out of the medicine cabinet and dabbed it over the scratch marks that still looked inflamed. My beard needed a trim. My fingernails were broken and ragged. I couldn't deal with either of those things.

Knox had come in at some point and deposited a pile of clothing next to the sink. I put it on, hating the fact that I could feel Jez calming down under Gage's care.

You should be taking care of her. Not him, said the little voice. My headache started to throb more insistently. I put the ointment away and grabbed three ibuprofen pills from the bottle on the bottom shelf, swallowing them dry.

For a long moment, I leaned against the vanity with my head hanging and my eyes squeezed shut. Then I pushed upright, squared my shoulders, and stepped back into the bedroom.

Knox was waiting for me, sprawled in a chair across from the bed. He looked exhausted.

"That's better," he greeted. "Now, which are we talking about first—Jez, or the kidnapping?"

My mind shied away from the subject of Jez like a nervous horse.

"The kidnapping," I said.

He nodded. "Okay. Tell me everything you remember. I need names, if you have them."

I took a deep breath, opened my mouth, and started from the beginning.

TWENTY-NINE

Tony

AFTER DROPPING KNOX off at the pack house and storming off afterward, I drove aimlessly around the city. I was wasting gas I couldn't afford to waste, and probably risking an accident since only a fraction of my attention was on the road.

Heath and Jez were mated.

Even worse, the fact that Heath and Jez were mated was really none of my goddamned business. Because having a one-night stand with someone didn't exactly give you a say over their future relationships.

Not that Heath and Jez had a *relationship*. That was the most fucked up part of this whole thing. They'd both been captured, drugged, and now they were tied together psychically for the rest of their lives.

From the little I'd seen, they hated each other's guts. And, I mean… they had reason. All of which made my own reaction even stupider.

I spent longer than I'd have liked to admit thinking about how easy it would be to get on Interstate 55 and drive back to St. Louis. Well… except for the fact that I only had a third of a tank of gas, forty bucks in cash, and all of my stuff was back at my apartment.

Also, my mother still lived in St. Louis. As far as I knew, anyway.

That was the thing that finally sent me slinking back to my apartment. I didn't think I was physically capable of looking her in the eye, knowing what had happened to her 'missing' husband.

'Oh, hey Mom! Yeah, it's been a while, hasn't it? By the way, your no-good alcoholic excuse for a man tracked me down in Chicago, barged into my home and tried to rape me again! Yeah, funny how that works, isn't it? Ha, ha. So... a friend of mine bashed his head in and another friend of mine got rid of the body afterward! No, sorry, I don't know where he is now. I guess the cops never found his corpse. Honestly, though? I didn't ask.'

Yeah... no.

I pressed my lips together and let myself into the apartment, trying not to think about that fateful night a couple of weeks ago when Heath and I had fucked on my cramped, sagging mattress.

Had he been thinking about the dead body he'd smuggled out of here while I'd been choking on his cock? I shook my head violently, trying to derail that train of thought. Of course he hadn't been. Hell, he probably had *other people* to do the actual hands-on corpse removal. Knox's pack had people for everything.

I should know. I was one of them.

Angrily, I threw my keys on the side table by the couch. They clattered up against the base of the lamp that had replaced the one Jez used to kill my stepfather.

I winced, hating the fact that he assumed any call from me would be because something was wrong. Hating even more the fact that he was one-hundred percent correct about that assumption. In the background of the call, I could make out the sound of a baby wailing.

"Hey, Byron," I said, forcing my tone to stay casual as I lied through my teeth. "Nah, everything's fine. I just realized I hadn't checked in lately. How are things with you guys?"

Byron's pack had started with two other alphas and a male omega. All four of them worked together at an inner-city youth center founded by the pack leader, Zalen Price. Somehow, they'd picked up a second omega and a male beta along the way—a married couple who'd owned some kind of fancy restaurant in Soulard. Since then, they'd added so many kids—or rather, *pups*—that I was embarrassed to admit I'd lost count.

Another angry shriek pierced the background crackle.

"*Funny you should ask,*" Byron said. "*As it happens, we have pinkeye in the house, and I'm on toddler duty tonight.*" He paused. "*Tell me something truthfully, Tony. Think back to the debonaire, roguishly handsome alpha you met five years ago. Did you ever think you'd find me changing baby diapers and administering antibiotic eyedrops to a squirming three-year-old?*"

I smiled despite myself. "Hmm… not really. You were definitely more on the *'ooh, Daddy'* end of the spectrum than the *'dad'* one."

"Can I record that, so I can play it for the others the next time they ask me to take point on something that involves eyelid crusts?" he grumbled, as the unhappy wailing grew closer to the phone.

"Nope," I told him, feeling unaccountably better after only a few sentences exchanged. "You were clearly born for this. You were just hiding it before." I hesitated, still painfully aware of the emotions roiling inside my chest. "You know, I had *such* a massive crush on you back then."

Silence settled over the connection, broken only by the toddler's cries.

"I know," Byron said, his tone softening. *"I figured it was because not very many people had ever tried to help you, up to that point. And, of course, there was also the 'debonaire and roguishly handsome' thing."*

"Pretty much," I agreed, thinking of Heath. "But you should know that you're by far the nicest person I've ever crushed on."

He snorted. *"Sounds like you need to get out more. Oh, and call Bea one of these days, will you? She'd love to hear from you."*

Byron's adoptive grandmother had let me stay in her house until I was old enough to get emancipated minor status through the courts. I was better at keeping in touch with her than I was with the others, mostly because Bea would blow up my phone if I left it too long without checking in.

"I will," I said. "I should let you get back to your eyelid crusts, though. I just wanted to say hello."

"*Gee, thanks,*" he replied. Then his voice sobered again. "*You know, I can't believe I'm spouting this kind of Hallmark card crap, but... there's a pack out there somewhere for you, Tony — if you want it, I mean. You just have to be open to it when it shows up. Voice of experience speaking here.*"

My throat tightened.

"I'll keep it in mind." I tried my best to keep the words light, and wasn't sure how well I succeeded. "Anyway, tell everyone I said hi. Maybe I'll come down and visit one of these days."

Did my voice waver on the last word? Shit.

If it did, Byron was too engrossed in fussy toddlers to catch it. "*Yeah, you should do that. I'll pass it on to the others. Night, Tony.*"

"G'night, Byron," I rasped, and ended the call.

———◆———

Eventually, I managed to get to sleep even without the edibles, because it had been a hell of a few days, and I was exhausted. That lasted until four thirty-five a.m., according to my phone screen, when a call jangled me out of a hazy nightmare involving my stepfather chasing me through an endless corridor full of omegas trapped inside barred prison cells.

"Whu' the fuck?" I gasped, flailing upright.

The phone continued ringing. I didn't recognize the number. With questionable judgment of the newly awakened, I fumbled for it and accepted the call.

"Who's this?" I demanded. "Why are you calling in the middle of the fucking night?"

"*Tony?*" Heath's voice sounded scraped raw.

My breath caught.

"*Sorry.*" The alpha's Irish accent was broader than usual; like he was drunk… or wrung out from several days of drug-induced, nonstop fucking. "*I had to find out — you were with Gage at the silos. When I was —*" He cut himself off. "*Did I hurt you? Did I… do anything to you?*"

The phantom sensation of an alpha sniffing up the side of my neck and burying his nose in my hair made me shiver.

"No," I said shortly. "No, you didn't do anything." A sick laugh, devoid of humor, choked its way past my control. "Well, I mean… you didn't do anything to *me*. But you mated Jez."

"*I don't want to talk about that,*" Heath said quickly, and I didn't think I was imagining the hint of desperation behind the words.

My temper snapped, as interrupted sleep stripped away my inhibitions. "You don't want to *talk about that*?" I echoed in disbelief. "Okay, how about we talk about the fact that I had to '*keep an eye on you*' while you were balls-deep in my former friend, despite the fact that you'd been balls deep in *me* not so long ago? How about *that?*"

Heath swallowed audibly.

"*Tony... I didn't choose this,*" he said hoarsely. "*And neither did she. When we were together, you said it was casual... that it didn't need to mean anything—*"

Self-loathing at my own cowardice flooded my chest.

"I can't do this anymore," I choked out. "I'm done. I did *not* sign up for *any* of this crazy shit! Just... leave me alone, Heath. Don't contact me again."

"*Tony—*" Heath began.

I ended the call and powered the phone off, slamming it face-down on the bedside table. A horrible sense of wrongness at what I'd just done crept across me like an illness. Groaning, I flopped back on the mattress and dragged the pillow over my eyes.

There's a pack out there somewhere for you, Tony. Byron's words played back to me, over and over. *You just have to be open to it when it shows up.*

I would not cry.

I would not cry, goddamn it. I was nineteen years old, for fuck's sake.

Maybe I should go back to St. Louis after all. It was a big place. I could avoid my mother if I tried hard enough. Or... there were other cities. Anyplace that wasn't fucking Chicago, where I'd managed to fuck up my life *yet again*.

I was still curled on the bed in the fetal position with the pillow covering my head an hour later, when a knock sounded on the apartment door. I jerked into a sitting position, because after what had happened with my stepdad, an unexpected knock at my door inevitably equaled an automatic adrenaline dump.

Creeping silently across the length of the apartment, I peered through the peephole. I wasn't sure who I expected to see—Heath, or the police, or an empty hallway after a stupid teenage prank.

What I got was Gage, looking like he needed to sleep for approximately a solid week. I unlatched the locks and security chains, opening the door.

"*What?*" I demanded.

"Heath sent me." Gage sounded as tired as he looked. "He said you didn't want to see him."

My shoulders slumped.

"Right," I said, defeated. "I guess you'd better come in. Sit down. I'll make coffee. I think we could both use it."

THIRTY

Tony

COFFEE DIDN'T HELP. I was nearly to the bottom of my second cup, and my life was still in a shambles.

Gage hadn't tried to talk to me while we sipped cheap Colombian instant, at least. Maybe he was trying to be tactful. Or maybe he just really needed the caffeine. When he set his empty mug down on the counter with purpose, though, I knew my time was up.

"I know this ain't any of my business," he began.

"Funny how no one ever stops the sentence right there," I muttered, staring at the brown dregs of my coffee.

He snorted in wry amusement. "Yeah, you got a point about that. Okay. So, I guess it's kind of my business because Heath is my packmate, and Jez is our scent match. And because Heath sent my tired ass over here to talk to you."

I felt my walls snap into place. "Talk to me about what?"

As if I couldn't guess.

"You and him have been sleeping together." The words hit like a hammer. I drew breath to say something angry, but Gage shook his head and forged on. "No—before you say anything, he didn't tell me that. He just asked me to come check on you. That's all."

"Then what the hell makes you think—" I cut myself off, not wanting to say the words aloud.

Gage shot me a sidelong glance. "Uh... because I've got eyes?" he said. "So, I'm gonna assume I'm right. You and him got together, and now he's got an omega scent match who tried to kill Knox, and he mated her against both their wills, because they were drugged. If I was in your position, I'd be asking myself where all of that left me?"

I wanted to yell... to rant... to throw the coffee mug at the wall so I could watch it shatter, splashing hot brown liquid across the ugly wallpaper.

I didn't do any of those things.

"Nowhere," I told the bottom of the mug. "It leaves me nowhere, because it was just a goddamned one-night stand. He's hot, all right? And I have a competence kink. It meant nothing to either of us. I scratched the itch, and the rest of it is nothing to do with me."

Silence fell over us, stifling as the seconds dragged on.

"Bullshit," Gage said.

My gaze flew up to his face as my temper flared again.

"What's *that* supposed to mean?" I snapped.

Gage's neutral expression didn't waver. "It means you're lying through your teeth." He sighed, his voice lowering to a rumbling murmur. "I can see why you an' Jez were friends. You're both stubborn as mules."

I surged up from the barstool I was sitting on. It wobbled, its legs screeching a few inches across the faded linoleum tile. "I'm not lying, goddamn it! It was a one-night stand, and I told him at the time that it didn't mean anything! Hell, I don't think he would have agreed to it otherwise!"

Gage made a considering noise. "Well, yeah. *That* part's probably true."

"All of it's true!" I half-shouted.

The alpha nodded sagely. "Right. So, you're not upset at all about him and Jez. And he's not calling you in the middle of the night because he's terrified that he might've hurt you when he was in rut."

Gage had been there when we were trying to get Heath and Jez away from the silos—when Heath had taken a break from growling over Jez's huddled form, in order to corner me up against the van and snuffle along my throat. A completely unwanted spark of heat kindled in my belly; my cock twitching awake at the most fucking ridiculous possible time in response to the visceral memory.

"He's just..." I began weakly. "He must know I have a rough background when it comes to sex. He was only trying to be decent about it."

... And now I was defending Heath. What the hell just happened?

Gage cocked an eyebrow. "He was in full rut, and his new scent-matched mate was *right there*. Yet he was still plastered all over you like a cheap suit on the way to the van. I'm not sure you really understand how mate bonds are supposed to work, Tony."

I started pacing, wishing desperately for a bigger apartment so I'd have more room.

"You said it yourself," I told Gage. "He was in rut. Doesn't that mean he would have gone after anything with a pulse?"

I would *not* think about Heath in a mating frenzy… pushing me up against a wall and grinding against my ass while his teeth gripped my shoulder…

"You're a male beta," Gage said evenly. "Normally, he might've 'gone after' a beta guy, all right—just not in the way you're thinking."

I came to an abrupt halt, looking at him in disbelief. "Wow, thanks so much for warning me about that possibility at the time!"

Gage rolled his eyes. "He wasn't gonna go after *you*, dumbass. He *likes* you. I just didn't expect him to try and snort your body odor like a line of coke, either. Which, once again, is my point."

I crossed my arms, trying to look intimidating. "Oh… you had a *point*? I must have missed that part."

"The point is that you two aren't fooling anyone." He huffed out a breath. "God, I forget how young you are sometimes. And I'm guessing Jez isn't much older." He shrugged. "Not sure what Heath's excuse is, other than being a dried up, bitter old addict."

"He's not *that* old." The words came out before I'd realized I was going to say them, in all their defensive glory.

"He's got a full decade on you," Gage shot back. "Anyway, I can't make you talk to him directly, and I can't make either of you say what you really mean. But Knox is making noises like Jez is probably going to choose to terminate the mating bond, once she's recovered a bit."

I stared at him. "Omega mating bonds are for life."

"Christ," Gage said under his breath. "Someone really needs to do something about sex-ed in the public schools." His lips pressed together, and then he continued in a more normal tone. "There's a surgery to take out the mating gland. Without a mating gland, there's no DNA match. No DNA match, and the bond fades over the course of a few weeks."

He looked sick as he said it.

I frowned. "You don't like that. Why?"

Gage shook his head. "No, it's good that omegas have a way to get out of unwanted bonds. But... she's our *scent match*."

He seemed really hung up on that part, and I had to accept that maybe it wasn't something that I, as a beta, could understand.

"So... if she decides to get this surgery, she can't mate you either?" I hazarded.

"If she gets the surgery, she can't mate anyone," Gage said. "That's kind of the point."

"And you *want* to mate her," I added.

He fiddled with a napkin, and I realized that I'd actually managed to put him on the back foot for the first time.

"Not like she'd want to mate me anyhow," he said after a slight pause. "It's just a fucked-up situation all around. And it's also not your problem. I'm here because Heath's worried about you. Are you sure you won't talk to him? I mean, it kind of sounds like you two have some shit to talk about, is all I'm sayin'."

Heath and Jez wouldn't have to stay mated. Did that change anything?

I swallowed and licked my lips.

"I don't think that we do," I said. "In fact, I'm thinking it might be best if I went somewhere else. I'm not sure Chicago really suits me anymore."

Saying the words aloud opened up a cold pit in my stomach—one that no amount of cheap instant coffee was going to be able to fill.

Gage's heavy brows drew together. "What is it with people around here jamming a steel bar through the spokes of their own motorcycle wheel, while they're still trying to ride the damn thing?"

"I don't want to talk to Heath," I said obstinately.

I was not going to be *that guy*. The one who dumped feelings all over the man he'd fucked, after swearing up and down that it was casual. *Especially* when the man in question had just been drugged into mating someone he despised, and was dealing with *that* whole crock of shit.

"That's your choice," Gage said, in the tone of someone who thought it was a *stupid* choice. "But before you uproot your whole life over this, will you at least come and talk to Jez?"

"No," I told him immediately.

"Because she's got no one," Gage plowed on. "She found out she tried to kill an innocent man… then she got kidnapped, thrown into an unnatural heat, and mated against her will. All in less than a week."

I wavered.

"I know you two fell out," Gage went on. "But you were close once. She *saved* you once."

That was a low blow.

"Maybe," I amended. "I'll have to think about it."

Gage nodded. "That's all I can ask. If you decide to come to the house, I'll let Heath know that you don't want to talk to him. And no one's gonna ask you to do any more crazy shit like storming a kiddie porn ring armed with a keyring pepper spray cannister. Promise."

"You didn't *ask* me to do that," I pointed out. "I was there, and I just sort of… *did it*."

"Well, regardless—Knox is home now, and he ain't too big on doing crazy shit," Gage said. "So, no more two-man rescues."

My eyebrows shot up. "Is Knox—or is he not—the guy who decided to smuggle rescued omegas through your house?"

Gage waved that away. "Yeah, but he does it all *planned* and *organized*, like. I just kinda jump in with both feet."

"Really?" I asked, deadpan. "I hadn't noticed."

He screwed up his nose at me, and I tried desperately not to find it endearing.

"Just… come to the house and talk to Jez," he said. "If you decide to, I mean. I think it'd be good for both of you."

I wasn't so sure about that. But then I pictured Jez, scared and alone — her whole world lying shattered at her feet.

"Maybe," I said again.

THIRTY-ONE

Jez

I WAS SURE I hadn't *actually* slept for a week straight, even if that's what it felt like. After I'd come back to my senses, Gage had dragged me to his room and made me take a shower, followed by a hot bath. He'd given me soup and crackers, along with an entire bottle of some kind of neon-blue sports drink, and then he'd let me fall asleep in his bed.

I didn't really have a lot of experience with sleeping uninterrupted for long periods of time. Living on the street, sleeping made you vulnerable. And on those rare occasions when I'd crashed on someone's couch, sleeping there too long made it feel like I was overstaying my welcome.

Most of the parts of my body that had been aching before were still aching — but it was a different kind of discomfort. Old and stiff, rather than fresh and raw. It was my brain that felt like someone had packed it in cotton wool, though.

My thoughts were slow and stupid. My eyes felt gritty and swollen. My neck and back felt like they belonged to someone three times my age, which was ridiculous since I'd been passed out on a nice fluffy mattress instead of on a park bench or in a concrete doorway.

As soon as I stirred, my stomach made it clear that tomato soup and saltines hadn't been enough food after days spent in an artificial heat, burning through my body's nonexistent reserves.

I was used to getting by on the bare minimum. But that also meant that I knew what it felt like when I was skirting the edge too closely.

I was skirting it *now*.

I'd refused food after Gage first brought me here and locked me in the attic, afraid it might be drugged. When I'd finally started eating, half of it came right back up after the thunderstorm sent me into a PTSD episode. Later, Gage had made me pancakes the night we'd slept together, but that had been days ago.

Omegas were designed to live off their body's reserves during heat. Unfortunately, I'd barely had an ounce of fat to draw on.

Hunger cramped my stomach. I tried very hard not to be reminded of the other ways my body had cramped—with sexual need and emptiness—when I'd been injected with the heat-stim shot. I tried even harder not to think about what had come afterward.

The mental wall Heath had thrown up between us groaned and shifted with sudden strain. Metaphorical chunks of concrete crumbled from the gaps... but the barrier held. My stupid omega hindbrain whined at the enforced separation from my mate. I silently snarled at it to shut the hell up. I didn't *want* to feel whatever Heath was feeling; just like he didn't want to feel what *I* was feeling.

The bedroom door cracked open.

"Hey, kitten," Gage called through the gap. "You awake? I heard you moving around."

"Yeah," I said reluctantly. "I'm up."

"I want you to eat something," he said, and my stomach gave an enthusiastic gurgle of agreement with the idea. "You can have another bath afterward, okay? But you really need to get some calories in you."

"I don't want to see Heath," I said in a rush.

The door opened a bit wider. "He'll steer clear. Honestly, I think he's still sleeping."

He wasn't, but I didn't say that aloud.

"Okay," I agreed, knowing that if I didn't eat some proper food, I was going to be completely useless.

Gage opened the door all the way. "Great. Come down to the kitchen. Do you like shepherd's pie?"

I had no idea what shepherd's pie was, but it didn't matter. "It's fine. I'll eat anything."

<hr>

Gage's borrowed terrycloth bathrobe was so huge on me that I had to roll up the sleeves and lift the hem so I didn't trip on it. But it was warm, and soft, and it smelled like sweet Christmas bread as I wrapped it around me and padded down to the kitchen.

Shepherd's pie turned out to be—surprise, surprise—a pie. But instead of cherries or apples, it had some kind of spicy ground-up meat and diced vegetables in it, with big poofy waves of browned mashed potatoes on top instead of whipped cream or meringue.

"Good?" Gage asked, as I shoveled down the generous wedge he'd put on my plate.

I nodded, swallowing. "I like it. Doesn't taste like hamburger, though."

He pulled out a chair and sat across from me. "It's ground lamb. That's why they called it *shepherd's* pie. Drink your electrolytes."

I paused, not sure how I felt about eating a fluffy little lamb ground up in a pie. Then I decided I was too hungry to care, and I went back to scarfing it down like a starving coyote—pausing every few bites to drink some of the sports drink, which was red this time.

As promised, Heath didn't make an appearance. But as I was finishing up seconds, Knox did.

My fork clattered to the plate as my shoulders stiffened abruptly in surprise.

He came in and pulled out a third chair, sitting down and making himself comfortable as though he owned the place. Which, in his defense, he *did*.

"Hello again, Jez," he said. "I apologize for interrupting your meal. There are some logistics we need to discuss, though."

The mouthful of shepherd's pie I'd been chewing suddenly tasted like dry cardboard. I had to force myself to swallow it down.

"What... kind of logistics?" I asked cautiously. He still didn't *seem* mad... but he *should* be mad.

"We're all kind of working on the assumption that you'll choose to break the mating," he said, without any detectable judgment in his tone. "Which generally means a glandectomy. That, in turn, means finding a good surgeon and getting sucked into the medical system. For most people, that wouldn't be a problem. But for you…"

He trailed off.

"What about me?" I demanded, unable to keep the defensiveness out of my voice.

"Do you have any sort of legal identification?" he asked. "Birth certificate, social security card, state ID, passport?"

I scoffed. "Of course I don't. As far as the authorities are concerned, my life ended when I was thirteen. And that's the way I like it."

"I'd figured that might be the case," Knox said. "And while that's certainly your choice, it's going to make scheduling a glandectomy challenging, to put it mildly."

I huddled back in the chair, wrapping my arms around myself protectively. "I can find someone to do it."

There were always people for stuff like that… just like you could find someone to stitch up a wound or do a clothes-hanger abortion, if you knew who to talk to.

"You are *not* letting some back-alley butcher hack out your mating gland," Gage said, seeming to grow taller and broader in his chair as he puffed up with alpha indignation.

"*Jez.* What if they miss part of it, or they use dirty tools and you get an infection?"

I didn't want to think about this. I didn't want to think about letting someone cut out my mating gland, *period.* Whether it was in some sterile operating room that cost tens of thousands of dollars, or in a shady back room that cost a couple of grams of cocaine.

The barrier in the back of my head rumbled ominously again.

"I don't want to talk about it," I told Gage tightly.

"That's understandable," Knox said. "Nevertheless, I'd like you to consider letting me get you set up with legal documents and a new identity to ease the way. The fact that you're mated to one of us simplifies things, but I'm afraid it will still take some time to arrange. Even so, I think you'll find using a licensed doctor much safer and less traumatic than the alternative."

An image of the back-alley hack job I would otherwise have to endure wavered in my mind's eye, urging me not to dismiss the offer out of hand.

"I'll... consider it," I said warily.

Knox nodded. "That's all I ask. There's just one other thing. I know you're still recovering physically, but you and Heath need to talk to each other sooner rather than later."

"*No,*" I said immediately.

"Not yet," Gage amended, and I glared at him.

"Soon," Knox said, with the implacable certainty of a pack alpha. "In the meantime, the pack will provide you with anything you need. Just make a list."

Stubbornness made me want to refuse the offer out of hand. How the hell had we gotten from me trying to kill this man, to him offering to buy me stuff?

For now, I bit my tongue.

He seemed to take my silence for agreement.

"Good," he said briskly, pushing away from the table.

He, at least, looked like less of a two-day-old corpse than he had when I'd come out of my heat. Maybe I'd slept longer than I thought? I should probably ask what day it was.

An electronic chiming noise echoed through the house. I tensed for a moment, before identifying the sound as a doorbell.

Knox frowned. "Are we expecting anybody this morning?"

Gage got up. "Yeah, maybe. I'll get it."

I sat in uncomfortable silence with my would-be victim, while Gage's heavy footfalls retreated to the front door. Low voices filtered back to the kitchen, the words unintelligible. A few moments later, Gage reappeared. Behind him, a slender, dark-haired figure hovered in the doorway.

"Hi," Tony said sheepishly. "Um... Jez... would it be okay if we talked for a bit? There's some stuff I should probably tell you. About, uh… me and Heath."

I blinked at him for a moment, trying to switch mental gears. What did he mean, *him and Heath*?

"Sure," I said, painfully aware of the way I'd fucked up the friendship I used to have with this sweet and gentle beta. "We can talk."

THIRTY-TWO

Jez

I FIGURED THAT as long as I was talking to Tony, no one would try to guilt me into talking with Heath. I'd count that as a win, despite the fact that I'd screwed Tony over nearly as badly as I'd tried to screw over Heath's pack.

The only difference was, before I'd run away and left Tony to deal with the corpse in his apartment, I'd saved him. Hopefully, that counted for something, since in my years-long history of fucking things up, the good deeds were relatively few and far between.

Tony glanced at the two alphas in the kitchen. "Can we have some privacy?"

Gage grunted. "Course. I expect you two have got a lot to talk about."

Knox rose from the table. "There's an office at the end of the hall on the left. It's all yours."

"Thanks," Tony said. He seemed really nervous… picking at a seam on his sleeve and shifting his weight from foot to foot. "Jez?"

I tried not to let his nerves transmit themselves to me—and mostly failed. Instead of standing up from my chair like a normal person, I shoved it back with a high-pitched shriek of chair legs on tile, wavering a little as my head protested the change in elevation.

"Okay," I said, steadying myself against the table edge.

Gage took an abortive step toward me, before seeming to catch himself.

Tony frowned. "Are you all right?"

Not even remotely, I thought.

"I'm fine," I said aloud. "Let's go."

I still felt like I'd been flattened by a steamroller, although getting some solid food in me had helped. My stomach sloshed around unpleasantly, but I gathered myself and walked out of the kitchen without stumbling. Tony hovered a step behind, and the two of us made our way to the last door on the left, leaving the alphas behind.

The office had the same understated elegance as most of the rest of the house—not counting that hateful room in the attic. There was a bit more clutter in here, as though it saw regular use. Idly, I wondered if there were any incriminating documents lying around.

Tony closed the door behind us.

Knowing it might send the wrong message—but needing a place to sit down before my precarious balance deserted me again, I pulled out the leather-upholstered rolling chair behind the desk and sank down in it. Rolling it forward, I rested my elbows on the desk blotter and pondered whether this was what being a rich CEO felt like.

I guessed not. If I'd been a rich CEO, my feet would probably have reached the floor.

There were two other chairs in the room, but instead of sitting down, Tony immediately started pacing back and forth across the rich carpet. He ran fingers through his messy black hair, not looking at me as he worked up to saying whatever he wanted to say.

"You know," I told him after a few moments, "whatever it is, it can't possibly be worse than what's already happened… or worse than I deserve. You might as well just say it."

He came to a stop, still not facing me.

"I slept with Heath," he blurted. "A couple of weeks ago. Just once… although I wanted it to be more."

Oh.

A flash of unwanted memory assaulted me. A van with a nest in the back. Tony in the driver's seat, fiddling with the mirrors. Heath's presence through the mate-bond, thinking the same possessive thoughts about both of us.

Scent, mark, protect.

I swallowed hard. Well—that answered one question, anyway.

But I'd let Tony's declaration hang in the air too long. He scurried onward, trying to explain.

"I told him it was just a one-night stand, see?" he said, finally turning to look at me. His hands were out, palm up, like he was trying to physically hand me the explanation. "It seemed safer, and honestly? I didn't think he'd even agree if he thought I was pining after him like some love-struck teenager."

I didn't point out that he was, in fact, nineteen, unless I'd missed a birthday… and pretty obviously love-struck. None of that mattered.

What mattered was that I'd managed to screw up Tony Scalise's life in a whole new way, long after I should have been a speck in his rearview mirror.

"He likes you." The words escaped before I'd fully thought them through.

"What?" Tony asked, momentarily derailed.

I took a slow breath. "We're in each other's minds. And, I mean, he's doing his best to block the bond now—but when you and Gage showed up to rescue us from that terrible place, he wasn't. He responded to you while he was in rut."

"That doesn't count," Tony said, too quickly. "He was drugged."

"Um... I'm pretty sure it *does* count," I shot back. "Trust me, if some random beta dude had walked in off the street while he was in rut and protecting me, it would *not* have gone well."

Tony blinked at me, his expression slack. His face looked like the screen on one of those old computers in the public library while it was rebooting.

Abruptly, the weight of everything that had happened in the last week felt unbearable. I slumped forward, resting my chin on my hands on the desk.

"Tony, I think it's safe to say that Heath likes you a hell of a lot more than he likes *me*," I said. "The scent match thing... it's just chemicals."

With a pang, I remembered the feeling of being tucked in Gage's bed, surrounded by his Christmas bakery smell as he purred me to sleep. I squeezed my eyes shut and tried not to think about it.

The room was quiet for a long moment. Then the shuffle of movement reached me. I forced myself to open my eyes again and meet Tony's gaze as he pulled a chair over and set it down in front of the desk, sinking into it.

"Neither of us wanted that mate bond," I went on. "We didn't ask to be drugged into an artificial lust. There's only one way to break that kind of connection, though. So, I'll be getting my mating gland surgically removed as soon as it can be arranged. And then it'll be like it never happened. You should talk to Heath afterward. Tell him what you told me."

His face crinkled up with worry. I hadn't noticed how many worry lines he had. Too many, for someone as young as we were.

"It *won't* be like nothing happened," he said. "Your mating gland will be gone! Is that really what you want, Jez?"

My visceral, twisting revulsion at the idea of letting anyone take such an important part of me tried to surge up. I grabbed it in both hands, strangling it and shoving it back down where it belonged.

"Of course it's what I want," I said. "You think I'm going to stay mated to a rude-ass alpha that hates my guts because I tried to kill his pack leader? No thanks. You can have him."

Tony's face continued to cycle through too many emotions for me to keep track of. Not for the first time, I wondered how he'd managed to survive everything that had been thrown at him, without learning to project a poker face somewhere along the way.

I pushed my upper body off the desk, straightening in the too-large chair.

"Tell you what I *am* going to do, though. Mister Moneybags wants me to playact at being his pack's omega while he forges me a new identity, so I can get the surgery." I rotated the chair left and right on its swivel, pasting on a devilish expression. "He literally just told me that he'll pay for whatever I want while I'm here."

Tony managed a weak smile. "That sounds like Knox, all right."

I nodded. "Well, I figure he can afford it, you know? So, how about you and me go out to the fanciest stores in Chicago, and find out what it feels like to be rich snobs buying a bunch of posh shit that we don't really need?"

"I already bought you a bunch of clothes!" Tony protested, but I was pretty sure there was a hint of laughter hidden behind the words. "And he didn't say anything about paying for *me* to buy myself stuff."

I waved the words away, already falling into the role of 'spoiled omega.' "Pfft. Like he's even going to notice. We're a *decimal point* to him, Tony. Like, a… whaddya call it? A *rounding error.*"

"I'm not doing that without asking first," he insisted.

"Fine, we'll ask Gage," I said airily. "He'll think it's a *great* idea. You'll see."

The time I'd spent playacting at a normal life with Gage had been the best few hours of my pathetic life. I wasn't above playing that role a little longer, while Knox pulled whatever strings he needed to pull to get me out of his pack's life for good. And if it also meant I could playact at not having ruined my friendship with Tony—even better.

"I… guess?" Tony said uncertainly. "I mean, I've kind of always wanted to do a proper 'gay best friend' shopping spree with someone else's credit card."

"That's the spirit!" I told him, trying to ignore the little flutter in my chest at his slip of the tongue. He hadn't really *meant* to say 'best friend,' had he? "Let's go find Gage and see what he has to say."

I could be the Knockley pack's mysterious new mate, throwing money around the city on my alphas' dime. If nothing else, having some fancy jewelry to pawn when they eventually tossed me back on the street was good planning. And in the meantime, Tony and I would see how the one percent lived. What could possibly go wrong?

296

THIRTY-THREE

Jez

TO NO ONE'S surprise, I'd been right. Gage thought the shopping spree was a *fantastic* plan. His broad face had been pinched with stress and worry pretty much nonstop since he and Heath first found me in the hotel room, standing over Knox's unconscious body. Now, it brightened like the sun coming out.

"Oh, yeah—we are *so* doing this," he said. "Shopping and dinner. Let me go tell the others where we'll be."

Tony, who was apparently still hell-bent on refusing to take money from the rich alpha pack he worked for, cleared his throat. "Gage… I can't ask Knox to pay for me to buy stuff I don't need. I could just tag along for moral support, or—"

"*Tony.*" Gage's deep voice sounded almost sad, despite his enthusiasm only a few moments before. "Knox has the kind of money that doesn't run out just because you buy a friend some nice clothes. He already gives a shit-ton of it away to charity every month, and of course there's the work we do on the down-low with the omegas. That doesn't come cheap—but even so, what's left over could keep someone in luxury for a *dozen* lifetimes, even if his business never made another dime."

"C'mon, Tony. This pack is *rich* rich," I said, hoping to close the deal. "How they think about money isn't the same as how you or I think about money."

We are not the same.

That universal truth had been rattling around in my head since I first walked up to Knox in the hotel bar and tried to seduce him. It wasn't any less true now than it had been back then.

Tony wavered for a moment. "You're sure Knox is okay with this?" he asked Gage.

"Of *course* he's okay with it," Gage said, like it was obvious. "Here. Tell you what. Think of it as the pack's thank-you for staying with Knox at the hospital and bringing him home when we were... um... *otherwise occupied*. Does that help?"

I winced at the reminder of exactly *how* we'd been occupied. But Tony took a deep breath and nodded.

"Okay. But only this once," he said uncertainly.

Gage's face brightened again. "Cool. Get dressed, Jez, and we'll go spend some money."

◆

The clothing Tony had picked up for me after Gage brought me to the pack house was still the nicest I'd had access to since I was a little kid. My 'alpha hunting' outfits had always, by financial necessity, been cheap, low-quality dresses and shoes from dodgy Chinese shopping sites — stuff that looked okay when it was brand new, but wouldn't have lasted a month under regular use.

The wardrobe Tony had gotten me didn't include fancy dresses or shoes, but it was well-made and most of it fit me. At his suggestion, I went with stylish jeans, a classy scoop-neck blouse, and comfortable shoes.

"It says, 'I just mated a pack so rich that I don't have to dress up to impress you,'" he told me, frowning as he fussed with my wayward hair until he was happy with it.

It was strange, having people touch me casually. I wasn't completely sure Tony had even realized what he was doing.

Before everything else that had happened between us, we'd sometimes ended up slumped together on his ratty sofa late at night, leaning against each other as we shared microwave popcorn while watching a movie or TV show on his laptop. I'd cherished those evenings for the sense of safety and belonging they'd given me at the time.

After I set fire to my friendship with him, I'd had to lock those feelings away. Otherwise, I'd have missed them so badly that their absence would've eaten me up inside. My loneliness after I'd run away from Tony was my own damned fault, and no one else's. I couldn't afford to open myself up to that kind of loss and disappointment again.

So, I hadn't.

And now here I was, back at the beginning, sharing space with the boy who'd wormed his way past my defenses with his kind eyes and clever guitar pick. I'd come full circle.

Once I was dressed and groomed to his satisfaction, we rejoined Gage in the kitchen. He was scrolling on his recovered phone, all his attention on the screen. At our entrance, he looked up and smiled.

"Ready to go?" he asked. "Okay, first things first. Dinner plans—something with burgers, or something fancy?"

"Burgers," Tony said immediately

"Fancy," I said, almost on top of him.

Gage's lips twitched. "Fancy with a burger option on the menu, coming up. Just a sec…"

He went back to his phone again, tapping and scrolling.

"It's gonna be like, rhinoceros burger with gold leaf instead of lettuce, or something," I teased Tony, relishing the feeling of ease that seemed to have settled between the two of us.

"It is *not* going to be a rhinoceros burger," Tony said under his breath. "They're endangered. And you can't *eat* gold." He hesitated. "Can you?"

"Hello?" Gage said into his phone. "I'd like to make a reservation for three, at seven p.m. tonight." He paused as the person on the other end spoke. "Yes, sorry, I know it's last minute—"

I blinked. Huh? Since when was letting a restaurant know that you were coming eight hours ahead of time considered *short notice*?

" —but I'm with the Knockley pack," Gage continued. "We would take it as a personal favor if you could find a table for us tonight."

More unintelligible speech from the other end.

"Thank you," Gage said. "I appreciate the accommodation, and we'll make sure to give you some positive press in return."

He hung up. I raised a suspicious eyebrow.

"Positive press?" I echoed. "What's that supposed to mean?"

Gage slipped his phone into the pocket of his tailored trousers and met my gaze evenly. "I do want to be clear about this, kitten. Part of agreeing to let Knox fix your I.D. problem is going to be letting yourself be seen with us in public."

I frowned. "Well… yes. Isn't that what we're doing today?"

"It is," he agreed. "But I don't think you understand what that's actually going to mean. I'm not the main attraction of Knox's pack. He is. But people still know who I am… and they're going to be interested in any omega I'm wining and dining and buying jewelry for." His earnest hazel eyes moved to Tony. "That'll be the case for you, too—to an extent. But you'll have the freedom to shape that narrative more than Jez will. You can be the beta moving up in Knox's organization. Or you can be more."

Tony took a physical step backward, even as I tried to digest everything he'd just said.

"I'm just an employee," Tony said quickly.

Gage nodded as though it wasn't a big deal. "That works. If that's what you want, that's what we'll go with."

I bit my tongue to keep from pointing out that after everything Tony and I had talked about, it clearly *wasn't* what he wanted. How had *I* become the love interest in this romance movie, when Tony was the one who'd actually caught feelings for Heath?

"Fine," Tony said. "Good."

"Yes, fine," I agreed. "Can we go now?"

"Sure," Gage said. "I'll drive."

———————◆———————

Gage's SUV was exactly the kind of vehicle I'd have expected him to drive. It was big and silver and angular—taking up space on the road without being overly flashy. He was a relaxed and confident driver, so I quickly found myself sightseeing as we headed toward the part of the city where rich people hung out.

I'd been to Navy Pier a couple of times, and I'd sniffed around the edges of the Magnificent Mile to see if it was a good target for panhandling. After a couple of attempts, I'd set my sights lower, in places where Chicago's finest weren't quite as concerned with keeping things postcard-perfect for the tourists.

I'd thought Gage might head for one of the big department store buildings like North Bridge or Water Tower Place, but instead we ended up walking on the side streets just off Michigan Avenue. Tony whistled, looking at the store names like Hermes and Prada, and several others I'd never heard of.

"Shoes first," Gage said, leading us into a Christian Louboutin store.

Tony blanched. "Are you sure it's okay to spend this kind of money on, y'know, *footwear?*"

Gage turned and came to a halt, placing a big hand on Tony's shoulder. Tony's cheeks, which had gone pale at the prospect of spending a thousand dollars on a pair of loafers, went bright pink beneath the alpha's touch.

"Yes, I'm sure it's okay to spend this kind of money on shoes," Gage told him solemnly.

Tony gulped as the big alpha gestured a pair of associates toward us and exchanged a few low words with them. Moments later, we were whisked off in different directions. I disappeared into a wonderland of slings, sandals, pumps, and platform boots.

"What sort of occasions will you be needing shoes for?" asked the stylish male omega who'd taken charge of me.

"Um..." I hesitated, remembering what Gage had said about being seen with members of the pack. "Just... nice dinners, and maybe... parties? Or clubs?"

"Perfect!" the omega enthused. "Yes, I have several options that would suit you wonderfully. Let me bring some out in your size."

What followed was a whirlwind of trying on fairytale footwear with flashy red soles. I ended up with a pair of low-heeled slingback pumps in a pretty ivory color with little crystals embedded in the shape of flowers, and a pair of dramatic red stilettos with a strap at the ankles.

Tony emerged from a different section of the store, looking like a tornado had just spit him out and carrying a pair of leather loafers in black patent leather, with the toes tapering to an elegant point.

Gage ran an assessing eye over our prizes and gave an approving nod. "*Nice*. We'll take them."

The process continued at different stores catering to different things—handbags, jewelry, menswear, dresses, coats. Gage whistled when I emerged from a changing room wearing a tailored cream cocktail dress with an adorable matching pillbox hat, and a tiny mesh veil that covered one eye and cheekbone.

Both Gage and I blinked rapidly in surprise when Tony emerged in a different store—a perfectly fitted charcoal suit accentuating the lean lines of his body that he usually hid under baggy jeans and shapeless shirts.

"Tony," Gage said. "My *dude*. Don't take this the wrong way, but whoever taught you to hide all that under hoodies needs to be taken out to the woodshed and *whipped*."

I froze for a moment, because I could tell Gage *exactly* who'd taught Tony to hide himself away. I should know. I'd been the one to bash the asshole's skull in with a table lamp.

Tony, too, went unnaturally still for a beat. But then he took a deep breath, let it hiss out, and said, "Yeah, it doesn't matter now. Maybe it's time to stop hiding from what happened in the past."

"You look amazing," I whispered, standing on tiptoe to speak in Tony's ear. "Heath's an idiot, and if you weren't batting for the other team, I'd do you in an instant."

Tony blushed and gave an uncomfortable little laugh. "It feels like I'm wearing a Halloween costume. But you're right about one thing. Heath *is* an idiot."

The shopping expedition continued. As the afternoon wore into evening, the number of designer shopping bags in the back of Gage's Yukon grew to truly obscene levels. I'd ended up wearing the cream dress and slingback pumps, while Tony was in his new suit, with the addition of a striking maroon silk buttondown and matching pocket square.

As we entered the high-end restaurant Gage had blackmailed into taking our reservation, the three of us drew a number of interested looks. I tried not to shrink back, knowing that—just like Tony—I would have to get past my instinctive desire to hide in the shadows if I was going to play this role successfully.

Did these random people recognize Gage? Or was it the expensive clothes?

Maybe it didn't matter. The restaurant staff was polite and welcoming. Our table was tucked away enough to feel at least somewhat private, while not being truly hidden from the other diners.

"You know, if you get rhinoceros-burger juice on that suit, you're never going to forgive yourself," I murmured to Tony, as I scanned a menu full of food I'd never even heard of.

Tony glanced down at the clothing that cost more than I could panhandle in a year. He cleared his throat. "Yeah… maybe I'll pass on the hamburger after all. Gage, do you know what's good? Could you order for me, please?"

"Order for both of us," I said. "I don't even know how to pronounce most of this stuff."

Gage gave a little chuckle. "You assume *I* know how to pronounce it either? But, yeah, I can do that."

I ended up with a fancy-looking pasta dish containing little red and white bits of seafood that looked like shrimp, but were apparently… baby lobsters? Tony had a steak and some kind of puffy, cheesy potato thing.

"Mmm. Best rhinoceros I've had all week," he deadpanned, cutting through the succulent red meat.

Gage had some kind of tiny roast birds in a mushroom sauce, with asparagus and almonds on the side. For dessert, we shared a chocolate cake thingie that had a different flavor of fruit jam between each layer, and a rich vanilla buttercream frosting slathered on the outside.

I noticed that Gage was only pretending to eat it, instead watching Tony and me devour the thing like it was the last food on the planet.

"Oh, my *god*," I groaned, once we'd fought a fork-duel to scrape up the last bits of jam and icing. "That was the most amazing meal I've ever eaten."

"And now the food coma is coming for me," Tony agreed, looking as wrecked as I felt. "Crap—are we supposed to get up from the table now?"

Gage was smiling his secret little smile again—the one that said he was an alpha who'd successfully fed his charges until they were about to pass out from bliss. "Pretty sure they frown on sleeping at the tables. Sorry." He stretched, taking a look around the dining room as though to catalog the other customers. "Well, the good news is, we're only a block or so from the parking garage."

Tony snorted. "It's almost like *someone* was thinking ahead."

"Always," Gage said, running a satisfied, proprietary eye over both of us.

The trip back to the pack house was uneventful. As Gage and Tony hauled our shopping bags up to the front porch, I was busy wondering if Gage would let me crash in his room again tonight, rather than slinking back up to the attic.

That was my excuse for yelping in surprise and nearly jumping straight back into Tony as the door opened to reveal Heath, car keys in hand—eyes bloodshot and slightly wild as he took in our presence in front of him.

THIRTY-FOUR

Jez

THE FOUR OF US stared at each other without moving for a long beat. Then Gage raked his eyes up and down Heath's hunched form, took in the car keys in his hand, and scowled.

"I don't need a pack bond to tell that you're about to do somethin' stupid," he said, sounding more tired than anything else. "Turn around. March your ass back inside, and we can all pretend you weren't busy making poor life choices."

Heath's lips peeled back in a snarl. "I don't need a *babysitter*." The cracked wall inside my head shifted once more on its foundations.

I was beginning to hate that feeling.

"Don't you, though? Because it sure looks like you were about to go out and get wasted after staying sober for almost two years," Gage said, unimpressed. "Where's Knox?"

"How should I know?" Heath snapped. His green eyes snuck first to me, and then to Tony. His pupils blew wide as he took in the picture we made, dressed from head to toe in the latest designer fashion. He jerked his gaze away an instant later, staring past Gage's shoulder instead. "Buried in work, probably."

"Fine," Gage said. "In that case, you three are having that talk now."

"What?" Tony yelped.

I would have echoed him, but there was a terrible sense of inevitability about the cluster-fuck to come. I was relaxed and well-fed, clean and wearing amazing clothes. Maybe having this conversation in the rearview mirror would be better than dreading it in the future.

"*Inside. Now.*" Gage had the decency not to bark, but it was clear we'd all be doing what he said, or else we were going to find ourselves dragged in by the scruffs of our necks.

"Come on," I told Heath with a sigh. "Whatever shit you want to pile on me, you might as well do it and get it over with. Plus, you and Tony really *do* need to talk."

I trudged forward and shouldered past him, trying to ignore the spark of lightning that thrummed along my nerves in response to the brief contact. After a long hesitation, other foot-steps followed mine.

"Where are we doing this?" I asked, not looking back.

"Kitchen," Gage said.

The kitchen was bright and airy as always. I hadn't been wrong about the scruff of the neck thing, either. Tony and I slunk inside under our own power, but Gage had Heath by the back of the shirt and deposited him physically in a chair.

I found a spot leaning against the counter and took a deep breath. Might as well get this over with.

"Did Knox tell you about his plan to get me a new identity?" I asked.

For an alpha, Heath seemed to be having an awfully difficult time looking at me.

"Yes," he said. "He said you intend to get your mating gland removed as soon as it can be arranged."

"That's right," I agreed, ignoring the part of me that wanted to wail and throw things in protest. I was coming to hate that selfish and stupid piece of myself. "I won't make you put up with my presence in your head any longer than absolutely necessary."

For some reason, *that* made him wrench his gaze up to meet my eyes.

"I'm doing my best to keep it blocked," he said, sounding defensive.

"I didn't say you weren't!" I shot back, not sure what I'd said to make him even more upset. Maybe he was pissed that I'd let Knox talk me into using a real doctor? Finding someone in the city would be quicker—

"Because we all know your stance on long-term relationships," Tony muttered, as though the words had been pulled from him.

Heath's eyes moved to him.

"What?" he asked, sounding genuinely bewildered.

Tony's cheeks flamed, and he turned his face away. "Nothing."

Abruptly, my patience for their cluelessness disappeared like smoke.

"Tony has a thing for you," I said. "But he's scared to tell you, because you had a one-night stand with him and then shoved him back to arm's length as though it never happened."

"Wh-*what*?" Heath repeated, at a higher pitch this time.

"*Jez!*" Tony squeaked, sounding completely appalled.

I stared him down. "Well, it's not like *you* were going to say it if I didn't."

Heath's mouth worked, but no sound came out. He snapped his jaw shut and swallowed before trying again. The wall shielding the bond started to shake. The cracks running through it widened, until huge chunks began to tumble free.

"Is this true?" he asked hoarsely.

Tony balled up his fists. "Of course it's fucking true! I've wanted you since the day you showed up at my apartment and cleared away a body for me as though it was nothing!"

Heath made a choking noise and shoved away from the table, staggering to his feet. His mental wall crumbled to dust as he crossed to a bare section of wall and slid down it, sitting hard on the floor. His presence flooded into me, unfiltered. I gasped, clutching at the edge of the counter behind me to keep from following him down.

Gage looked between us, clearly worried and unsure what to do.

A terrible wave of guilt, every bit as strong as what I felt over Knox, slammed against me — threatening to wash me away beneath its force.

But... why would *Heath* feel guilty? *I* was the one who'd fucked everything up —

"You should both stay as far away from me as possible," Heath rasped. "You two, of all people..."

Gage was still hovering, unsure who to fuss over.

"Heath, you need to talk to us properly," he said. "We don't understand what you're saying... and we need to understand."

Heath slammed a fist into the unyielding tile floor. It echoed with a meaty *smack*.

"I would have raped a kid!" he shouted. "Is that fucking *clear enough* for you? They injected me with drugs, and I would have become the same kind of monster we fight, if my scent match hadn't been locked up down the hall! If she hadn't broken out and rescued that... that *child* from me! *He was just a child*!"

My fingernails dug into the counter as I gasped for air, caught in the undertow of my mate's horror and self-loathing. The echo of long-ago hands pawing at me blotted out the pleasant kitchen, and my own moan of denial emerged from Heath's mouth instead of mine as he felt what I felt.

"*Shit*." Gage's curse barely reached me through the maelstrom. "Stop it — *both* of you!"

I felt a jolt and peered through blurry eyes, finding Gage crouched in front of Heath and giving him a sharp shake of the shoulders. Amazingly, it helped a bit.

"You wouldn't have hurt the kid." Tony's voice was shaky, but his words had the ring of certainty behind them.

"You don't know that," Heath said, still sounding like he'd swallowed sandpaper.

"The *hell* I don't." Tony was gaining strength now, stepping toward Heath and pointing a finger down at him accusingly. "I saw you afterward! You'd clawed furrows in your own goddamned face! You'd have torn your own throat out with your bare hands if that's what it took to keep that poor kid safe! I *know* you! You think I'd let just anyone stick their dick up my fucking ass, after what was *done to me*? Of *course* you wouldn't have hurt him!"

I drew in great lungfuls of air, as the force of Tony's words broke us both free of our spiraling emotions. Tears were streaming down my friend's cheeks.

"*Tony…*" Heath said weakly.

"Yeah, I'm with him, actually," Gage put in, his tense stance easing a bit. "Now, why don't you talk to him about why you pushed him away after you slept with him?"

Heath looked up at Tony imploringly. "You literally told me that was all you wanted! I figured if a one-night stand was all I was going to get, it was better than nothing!"

Tony gaped at him. "You… would have said yes if I'd asked for more?"

Heath made an awful croaking noise that was probably a laugh. "I would have warned you off, because I'm an emotionally stunted alcoholic asshole, and you deserve better. But... yeah. And then you would have regretted it within a month."

Tony flopped down on the floor in front of him as though his knees had decided to stop working.

"Oh," he whispered.

Gage crossed his arms and huffed. "So, can we all agree that the people to blame for putting that omega kid in danger—and for setting Jez up to get bitten without proper consent—are the ones that kidnapped you and injected you with stim shots?"

"Yes," I said, because despite what Heath seemed to think, there was really no arguing with that.

Gage nodded. "And can we agree that the person to blame for Jez going after Knox is this Adrian character? And whoever else put him up to it?"

"No," I said.

"No," Heath agreed. His eyes met mine properly for the first time. "You could've looked into Knox's background more. Not just taken some omega asshole's word for what was going on."

"Yes," I told him, not looking away. "I should have done that, and I didn't."

"But we lucked out," Gage said. "Because nothing that's happened is permanent. Knox survived, and he's going to be okay. And Jez, we can get you the surgery, so the mating doesn't have to be forever."

"Right," I said gamely. "Things could have been way worse."

Now that our mutual PTSD episode had subsided, it no longer felt like I was drowning in the bond. Instead, an echo of the same magnetic pull I'd felt when I was in heat tugged at my insides. I licked my lips.

"You… uh, you don't have to try and keep the wall up all the time," I told Heath. "If you can stand having me in your head, I mean. I think having the wall there feels worse than just having the bond."

His gaze skittered to the side. "Oh. Well, that's… just as well. I'm not sure I could have kept it up for much longer."

"Okay, then," I said.

"Okay," he echoed.

I wrapped my arms around myself and squeezed, aware of what a pathetic bunch we were, expensive clothes and all. I wondered at what point Tony would realize he was sitting on the kitchen floor in a brand new two-thousand-dollar suit.

At least it was a clean floor.

Gage caught my eye. He looked tired, too… although not as utterly wiped out as the rest of us.

"You and Tony stay here for a few minutes while Heath and I go set something up. Promise?" he said.

I nodded. I was too tired to run anywhere, and Tony was still in shock, from the looks of it. "Sure."

Gage reached down and grabbed Heath by the upper arm, hauling him to his feet.

"Get off," Heath said—but there was no force behind it.

He let Gage shuffle him out of the room, giving Tony a wide berth. I kicked off my new red-soled pumps and leaned against the counter again, probably putting creases in the nice cocktail dress I was wearing. Tony didn't move... didn't even look up at me.

Eventually, he spoke.

"Was that as bad as I think it was?"

I considered. "I'm pretty sure it wasn't. Now Heath knows how you feel, and it sounds like he feels the same. That's a good thing, isn't it?"

Tony hesitated for a long moment. He stirred enough to take off the expensive suit jacket, looking down at it in his hands like he wasn't sure where it had come from.

"I don't know," he said. "Because now I have to do something about it. Before, I didn't."

It wasn't like I was in any position to give relationship advice, so I just shrugged.

Gage returned a couple of minutes later. "Let's go," he said. "We're sleeping."

"That sounds good." Tony accepted a hand up. "I probably shouldn't try to drive. Where do you want me? A couch is fine."

Gage took the jacket from him and draped it over a chair back. Then he reached a hand out toward me. I took it without thinking.

"You're not listening," he told Tony. "*We…* are *sleeping*. Come on."

He led us deeper into the house, to a room I hadn't explored before. It was some kind of big family room. There was a huge TV on one wall, and a sectional sofa pushed to one side. Someone—Gage and Heath, presumably—had dragged in a couple of huge mattresses and shoved them together. Piles of bedding and pillows lay all around. Heath sat crouched in the middle of the makeshift nest, his elbows resting on his knees and his face buried in his hands.

"Down you go," Gage said, and basically shoved Tony on top of him.

Tony made a strangled noise, and Heath's arms came around him mostly in self-defense. The pair sat frozen for a painful moment. Then Tony let out a strangled whimper and clung to the alpha he'd tried so hard to push away. They both fell back to lie on the mattress; their bodies tangled together from chin to ankle.

The feelings flooding through the bond made my breath catch. Guilt and regret and fragile hope, all wrapped up with silvery threads of painful yearning. Gage took my hand again, drawing me down with him.

"The dress," I said stupidly, thinking of stains and sweat and wrinkles.

"Forget about the dress," Gage rumbled, as I settled into the space between his big body and

Heath's back. A moment later, he shuffled me forward until I was spooned against Heath, with Gage curled close behind me. The electric surge of contact from earlier mellowed into a deep, penetrating warmth.

It should have been hopelessly awkward. A tangle of people who had a list of reasons not to like each other, mired in misunderstanding and bitterness. Instead, something inside me that I didn't dare look at too closely untwisted itself, relaxing into a kind of security that I'd never felt before.

There was no chance to poke at the feeling, though. Because seconds later, I was fast asleep.

THIRTY-FIVE

Heath

WHEN I WOKE up, I had an armful of Tony, and there Jez was still nestled inside my head. The room was dark, but the darkness held a faintly gray edge that signaled the arrival of morning in the not-too-distant future.

"Not a dream, then," I muttered, even though the whole scene had a faint sense of unreality to it.

"Not a dream," a feminine voice whispered at my back.

Tony slept on in my protective embrace. Gage's rhythmic snoring sounded from somewhere behind me. Jez and I lay there for several minutes, loudly *being awake* at each other through the mating bond.

We had to talk. I *knew* we had to talk. She knew it, too.

Eventually, she stirred. "C'mon," she murmured. "While they're still asleep."

I felt the slip-slide of her expensive dress as she eased upright, squirming out of the tight space where she'd been lodged between me and Gage. Giving in to the inevitable, I gently settled Tony's slender body into the nest of cushions and blankets.

He made a small, unhappy noise in his sleep. I barely managed to get out of the way before the hulking form of my alpha packmate shuffled forward and took my place, wrapping his arms and legs around Tony without either of them waking up.

The idea of Tony safe in the arms of the world's most protective teddy bear made a spear of some unidentifiable feeling pierce through me. And, of course, every emotion I felt was now shared with an audience of one bonded omega.

"Yeah," Jez breathed, apparently in agreement with my reaction to the pair now cuddling in the nest. "I know exactly what you mean."

That mirrored reaction ricocheted between us, until I couldn't have said who was feeling what. I carefully got to my feet, aware that Jez was doing the same. We snuck out of the room like guilty schoolchildren, trying not to make noise.

Was Knox awake yet? Normally, he would be—but I could tell he wasn't quite as recovered as he wanted us all to think. I didn't hear anyone else stirring in the house. For lack of any better ideas, I led the way to my room, rather than to the shared space of the kitchen.

It was only when we entered that I realized this might not have been the best choice of venue. I was immediately hit with the visceral memory of everything that had happened in this room over the past several days.

I flicked on the light.

"You cleaned up," Jez said. She went immediately to the bed and sat on it, which really wasn't helping with my situation.

"Of course I cleaned up," I snapped back. "You'll excuse me if I don't actually want to sleep in dried blood and stale spunk."

She just stared at me, her gray eyes too large in her gaunt face.

How had I failed to notice how thin she was? The expensive party dress she was wearing clung to curves and angles that wouldn't have been out of place on an exclusive catwalk in Paris or Milan. But I somehow doubted her lanky, size-four frame had been cultivated for the whims of the fashion industry.

I shook my head sharply. It did nothing to dislodge her presence inside my skull.

"Sorry," I said, more gently.

She sat staring at me for longer than was comfortable. When she finally spoke, the words weren't what I'd expected.

"I know you have serious feelings for Tony," she began. "I can feel what you feel. You do understand that he only kept you at arm's length to protect himself, right? He was lying through his teeth when he told you he didn't want any strings attached."

"I… what?" I stammered, derailed.

I was still trying to wrap my head around the situation with Tony, because if I had one rule for dealing with people, it was to believe them when they told you what their boundaries were.

She sighed, and it seemed to come from down around her toenails somewhere.

"Never mind. It's not my business; I understand that." She drew her knees up, resting her bare feet on the edge of the mattress and wrapping her arms around her legs. "Look, you just need to know that I don't blame you for anything that happened. None of it was your fault. You treated me better than other people would have, after I tried to kill your pack leader. And as for the rest of it—"

Another sigh.

"Well... we'll get it sorted out soon enough, I guess. I can take a pregnancy test in about ten more days, and Knox wants us both to get tested for diseases. Then I'll get the gland removal surgery as soon as I can. It'll be like none of this ever happened."

Her emotions flowed through me in time with her words, stealing my tongue for several seconds. Sincerity... worry... guilt... grief.

"I'm so sorry for what I did to Knox," she finished, the guilt swelling to the forefront. "I just... need you to believe that, even if it doesn't change anything, really."

"It changes things." The whispered words were out of my mouth before my brain could vet them.

She looked up at me with wet eyes. As I watched, a tear overflowed to trail down her cheek. She dashed it away impatiently.

"There's something else you should know," she said. "Tony is a good person. In fact, I think he might be the best person I've ever known in my life." Two more tears tracked down her cheeks. "Please give him a chance and treat him right, because something as wholesome as his love for you doesn't come along every day."

"He deserves better than someone like me." Again, the words were out before I could stop them.

She gave a little shrug. "Maybe. But you're the one he wants. And people like Tony and me... we're very careful about what we want."

It felt like all the fight had drained out of both of us.

"I wasn't exaggerating when I said you saved me in that cell," I said, because it suddenly seemed important for her to understand that. "The others don't think I would've hurt the kid... but they have no clue what it was like to be stuck in that chemically induced rut."

I examined Jez's face. She'd gone to sleep with makeup on, but her tears had melted the foundation along her cheek. Beneath it, I could see the half-healed scar where a kidnapper's blade had sliced along the delicate skin.

I swallowed hard. "It was complete insanity. The others can't understand that feeling of being out of control... of believing with every fiber of your being that if you don't fuck, you'll *die*. Jez... your scent—knowing you were nearby—it gave me the strength to hold on until you could get to me."

Her face crumpled, and a silent sob shook her small frame.

"I wish I could have met your pack the right way," she whispered, more tears washing away the façade of makeup she'd put on to cover up her pain.

Yearning flooded the bond. Mine or hers… maybe ours together.

I pushed away from the wall, crossing to her. My hands might as well have belonged to someone else as they cradled her jaw. I pressed a kiss into her rumpled, pale blond hair.

"Me, too," I said, as I straightened away. The truth of the words echoed through me, taking me by surprise.

Rather than giving in to her tears completely, she closed her eyes and steadied her expression before opening them again and meeting my gaze.

"Promise me something," she said. "Don't let Tony leave the house without talking to him. *Properly*. If he wants you, and you want him, then for god's sake, *have each other*. This world sucks too bad to throw the good things away when you find them."

I couldn't refuse her. Not when she was so very, very *right* about that.

"I promise," I told her, and there was nothing artificial about her relief through the bond.

"Good," she said, sniffling.

After taking another moment to compose herself, Jez led the way back to the TV room. The others were, miraculously, still asleep. She didn't waste any time, shaking them both awake with practical effectiveness.

"Wha…?" Tony muttered, coming back to consciousness to find himself in a different pair of arms than he'd fallen asleep in. He twisted around to look at Gage in the early morning light. "Um… hi?"

Gage, who always woke up just about as gracefully as a hibernating grizzly, blinked at him. "Hi. You're good to cuddle."

Pink flooded Tony's cheeks. Gage let him go and he struggled into a sitting position.

"… thanks?" Tony said uncertainly.

Affection flooded through me despite my best efforts, followed closely by a wash of smugness not my own.

"Get up," Jez commanded, grabbing Gage by one meaty bicep and tugging. "You're taking me back to your room. Tony and Heath need privacy for a talk."

"Oh," Gage said, still noticeably out of it. "Okay."

Jez got the big guy upright and marched him out of the room efficiently. Just like that, I was alone with Tony.

He scooted back until his shoulders rested against the front of the sectional couch, rolling his lower lip between his teeth nervously.

"Erm…" He hesitated, then spoke in a rush. "I'm really sorry I lost my shit with you over the phone. I meant what I said at the time… but it wasn't fair, and I was upset."

"You had plenty of good reasons to be upset," I said, trying not to wince as I thought back to all the things Tony must have seen while Jez and I were out of our minds with lust.

"I know," he said. "But I still shouldn't have unloaded at you like that. What happened, happened. And anything you and I might have had together —"

"Stop," I said.

His jaw clicked shut.

My stiff joints creaked as I lowered myself to sit next to him, within arm's reach but not touching.

"Someone just told me that the world sucks too much to throw away the good things when you find them." I met his eyes — deep brown and slightly bloodshot. "Now, I wouldn't normally take advice from this person, but in this case, she was absolutely right. I want to be with you, if that's what you want, too."

His breath caught in his throat, and he swallowed noisily.

"But... the mating bond," he said hoarsely.

"Is temporary," I retorted, not acknowledging the wave of unpleasant emotion that came on the heels of the words. "Maybe we need to talk about how packs work. Sometimes I forget you're a beta."

"You guys don't really act like a pack, though." Tony's eyes darted nervously away, and then back. "I mean, no offense. But I didn't think any of you *did* relationships. Like, *at all.*"

The sad part was, he was right.

"Well... maybe that needs to change." Saying it felt like jumping off a cliff; the water churning far below. I took a deep breath and forged onward. "Packs sometimes include betas. I would like you to be my—*our*—beta."

Tony's breathing grew faster; a little ragged. He licked his lips.

"I, uh… I knew a pack in St. Louis. They… helped me. They had a beta, but I thought it was a special case. He was already married to their omega before the pack met them."

"*Every* pack is a special case," I told him. A small snort of amusement took me by surprise as I added, "Although, this one might be a bit more '*special*' than most."

He huffed out a breath of laughter. "Yeah, maybe." Then he sobered, holding my gaze with unblinking intensity. "You mean it, though? You'd really… want that?"

My throat ached. "I don't think either of us are very good at wanting things. Maybe it's time to work on that."

Apparently, it was my job today to make other people cry. Tony's face contorted, but before I could stammer out an apology, he'd turned and scrambled into my lap, his lips crashing over mine. I tasted his single sob more than I heard it—but an instant later, it was lost beneath the sea of relief and rightness at having him in my arms.

THIRTY-SIX

Jez

GAGE'S ROOM WAS right down the hall from Heath's. Which was good, because the big alpha was still stumbling around, half-asleep. Meanwhile, all sorts of uncomfortable feelings had started flooding through the open bond.

I wanted Tony to be happy, because I couldn't be. It made a sort of sense that since he was the good guy, and I was the villain, maybe he could get enough happiness for both of us. I'd liked seeing him curled up safe in Gage's arms—as though he could somehow stand in for me with this pack that should have been mine, but wasn't.

He wasn't an omega, it was true. But I was pretty sure he would have made a good one, if only he'd been born that way. A better one than me, certainly.

I closed the door to Gage's room and turned to find him looking at me. Most of the fog of sleep had cleared from his expression as he examined my face.

"You've been crying," he said, with a deepening frown. "Did Heath do something? Or say something?"

I let out a ragged laugh. "Heath said plenty. So did I. It was all stuff that needed to be said, and none of it was bad."

The furrows in his heavy brow deepened. "Then why—"

"Because this could have been so amazing, if I'd only met you three in the right way," I interrupted. "Because if I'd just *done better research* instead of assuming that Adrian wouldn't lie about something like his little sister being taken, none of this would have happened."

Gage let out a deep sigh and closed the distance between us. He put an arm around my shoulders, leading me to the bed and pulling me down to lie on top of the covers with him. I burrowed against his side shamelessly, feeling like I needed to hoard as much of this feeling as I could get, in preparation for the long years of loneliness ahead.

"First off," he began, "If you'd run for the hills when Adrian tried to hire you, then you're right. *None* of this would have happened."

I pressed my ear against his chest, feeling the vibration of his words.

"We wouldn't have met you. Tony and Heath would still be dancing around each other. We wouldn't have found the baby omegas being held at the silos." His hand stroked through my hair. "And I would never have gotten to see what you look like when you're making O-faces over fancy chocolate cake in a nice restaurant. And second—why the hell do you think Knox would've been safe if you'd turned Adrian down? You think Vozzina would have shrugged and decided to leave him alone?"

I lifted my head, looking down at him in surprise.

He met my gaze and scoffed. "He would've found someone else to do it. Another dupe, or just someone with a good rifle scope and a background as a military sniper. And maybe they wouldn't have missed. Don't take this the wrong way, kitten—but knowing how you were living before you came to us, it seems real likely that you were just his cheapest option for the job."

Offense rose up in my chest, building there for a beat before reality set in, and it deflated like a pricked balloon. I flopped back on the bed.

"I wasn't doing it for the money," I muttered, heat rushing to my cheeks and ears.

Gage snorted. "Yeah. That much was pretty clear. Sweetheart... you have no idea how much assassins get paid, do you?"

I glared at him sideways. "And you *do*?"

He made a considering noise. "Never had cause to hire one myself, it's true. Although I might start rethinking that after getting a closer glimpse into Lorenzo Vozzina's operation. Let's just say, assassins who kill people successfully and don't get caught afterwards can usually afford to pay for rent and groceries."

"I *did* get caught," I pointed out, ignoring the sour taste at the back of my throat.

Gage rolled onto his side, propping himself on an elbow. "Yeah, you did. And Knox surviving messed up your perfect record of successes, too. Can't say I'm unhappy about either of those things."

I closed my eyes, trying not to get distracted by the rollercoaster of emotions coming at me through the bond as Heath and Tony talked. *Not my business.*

"You can't just pretend I didn't try to kill Knox," I said. "Gage, be serious. There are mistakes you can't come back from."

He raised an eyebrow. "Funny. You were *all about* pretending, that night you and I slept together. Seemed to work out pretty well, as I recall."

My face burned hotter as I remembered that night, when I'd begged Gage to let me feel what a different life might have been like. "That was differ—"

I cut off with a gasp as sudden lust slammed through the link with Heath.

Gage sat up abruptly. "Kitten? What's wrong? What is it?"

I couldn't stop a moan. Heat that had nothing to do with embarrassment roared through my veins, heading southward like it was on a mission from god.

"Jez!" Gage sounded almost panicked.

I shook my head frantically, trying to play it off. "No, sorry, it's nothing. Heath and Tony, they're… um…"

Gage leaned down and took a cautious sniff. His eyes widened, presumably at whatever he was smelling in my pheromones.

"Oh," he said. "*Oh.*"

"Yeah," I agreed, the word emerging strangled. "S-sorry."

"*Sweetheart,*" he rumbled. "Do *not* be sorry."

I tried to rally. "I guess they got things figured out. That's good, right?"

"Course it is," Gage said. "Little awkward for you, though." He seemed to hesitate. "You want to let off steam? With me, I mean? You an' me have danced before, and it'd kind of serve Heath right after he blindsided you like that. Only if you want to, obviously."

Gage's trousers were wrinkled and creased from sleeping in them all night, but that did nothing to hide the bulge growing beneath them. I drew in a breath, mentally weighing the prospect of riding out Heath and Tony's hookup with no relief, versus the prospect of riding Gage into the sunset while also reminding Heath that the bond went both ways.

"Fuck it," I said, and dove for Gage's fly. "Just… be a little gentle? I'm still kind of sore… down there."

Honestly, if you'd asked me fifteen minutes ago, I'd have said that the idea of a knot inside me was about as appealing as a fork in the eye. Apparently, all my pussy had needed was a swift kick of horniness from my temporary mate. Because now it was whispering about how good it would feel to get filled up while it was tender and aching from the aftermath of my disastrous heat.

"I can do gentle, kitten," Gage promised. "Tell you what; you lead. I'm all yours... as much or as little as you want."

He gently moved my fumbling fingers away from his trousers and began efficiently pulling off clothing. I turned my efforts to the cocktail dress, not giving the garment nearly the amount of respect it deserved for its price tag. Mind you—I'd already slept in it, so at this point it probably didn't matter.

Underwear followed, and Gage—now naked as well—rolled onto his back with an appreciative purr as I debated where to start. Remembering the sweet torture of his mouth, I climbed up the length of his body to straddle his head. Strong hands grasped my hips, guiding me down until my pussy brushed his lips.

A shudder of relief rolled through me as Gage began delicately caressing and teasing along my folds, feeling out my response. It was a soft counterpoint to the wild, almost violent feelings crashing through the link, and before long, I was grinding against Gage instead of brushing against him.

He let out a possessive growl, the vibration going straight to my core as his tongue delved deeper, matching me stroke for stroke.

Soreness? *What* soreness?

Within minutes, a shuddering climax wracked its way through my muscles. The feedback through the bond built impossibly higher, making my mouth water. I needed something to fill it, because my body wasn't done yet—not even close.

Clambering off Gage only long enough to get turned around, I clamped my knees on either side of his broad shoulders and went back to smothering his face with my slick, squirming around until I could stretch down and get the tip of his cock in my mouth at the same time.

He gasped against my sensitive nerves, his body trembling as he tried to keep from thrusting up. I wrapped a hand around the part of him that I couldn't get in my mouth and went to town. The hands on my hips tightened; the faint hint of neatly manicured fingernails digging in.

I lost myself to the physical sensations flying at me from all directions, wondering vaguely if Gage would stop me before I made him come like this. I didn't think he would, and my desire not to waste his knot warred with the appeal of watching him come undone while he was helpless to stop it.

The thick length twitched hard in my mouth as I gushed another release over his face. He bucked, unable to control the movement, his tip shoving toward the back of my throat. Through the bond, Heath lost control as well, his orgasm pouring over me.

My aching need to be filled overrode everything else. I pulled off Gage's cock and scrambled inelegantly down his body, straddling his hips instead of his head so I could get him inside me. He let out a choked cry as I slammed down, taking his cock in a single, brutal stroke.

He'd already been too close, because that was all it took to push him over the edge. He spurted into me, jerking once, twice, three times. I groaned as his knot swelled, stretching tissues that had been abused for days, but were already begging for more.

A third release, deep and slow, washed along my nerves. The knot inside me jostled as Gage pushed himself into a sitting position behind me. He cinched my back against his front with an arm around my stomach and carefully shuffled both of us back until he could lean against the headboard.

I shivered, then lolled back against him as all the tension flowed from my body. Through the bond, Heath, too, had gone soft and quiescent. There was a kind of blank awe buzzing across the connection, low and confused.

I shouldn't have liked it as much as I did.

"What was that you said about being gentle?" Gage murmured against the exposed skin of my throat. Amusement laced through his tone.

"Umm..." I said brilliantly.

He chuckled, the puff of air whispering across sensitive flesh.

We rested together, his knot seated warm and deep inside my body. His fingers trailed up my arm and across my shoulder, pausing to trace the mark of Heath's teeth in my mating gland. After a moment, they stilled.

"I'm gonna say something kind of crazy," Gage murmured, his light touch still resting over Heath's mark. "Because this whole thing has been crazy, right?"

I made a humming noise of curiosity.

"It's just that... you've already decided to have this removed," he went on, tracing my gland. "So, I'm thinking—what's stopping us from mating, too?"

My breath stuttered. I rolled my head, meeting his hazel eyes as best I could in this position.

"You told me once that you wanted to feel what it would be like if you'd chosen all this," he said, holding my gaze with his steady, comforting presence. "And... we could choose it now. You could have a mate that you'd chosen, and I could know what it feels like to be bonded to my amazing, beautiful scent match."

My throat bobbed convulsively as I pictured what he was proposing. A mate who actually seemed to care for me... a connection that I could choose because it was something I wanted.

It will only make things harder when you have to let go, I tried to tell myself.

But would it really? Could anything be harder than going back to my stupid, meaningless life after all of this?

"What do you think?" Gage asked, worry creeping into his voice as my silence stretched too long.

I swallowed hard. Once. Twice.

"Yes," I whispered, the word a hoarse rasp. "Yes. I want that."

THIRTY-SEVEN

Tony

HEATH WANTED ME. My heart had been pounding with adrenaline, throughout our entire agonizing conversation after Jez and Gage had left—but now those three words were all I could think about.

He hadn't just said that he wanted to keep sleeping with me. He'd said he wanted me to be their beta. There was so much to unpack with that. Things like the way it had felt to wake up in Gage's arms, when I'd fallen asleep in Heath's... or the fact that no one had talked to Knox, the pack leader, about this.

And then there was Jez.

But Jez wasn't here right now. Whether she broke her mating bond with Heath, or whether she didn't—all of those things were worries for the future, not the present.

"You mean it, though?" I asked, needing to hear Heath say it again. "You'd really want something like that?"

And the part that went unsaid. *You'd really want... me?*

His green eyes were tired and sad. "I don't think either of us are very good at wanting things. Maybe it's time to work on that."

I should have come up with some kind of witty, devastating banter to toss back to him. Instead, the achy thickness in my throat bubbled up and spilled over in the form of tears. It wasn't how I wanted him to see me. Those tears didn't belong to the strong, independent person I needed to be.

Throwing myself at him and trying to stick my tongue down his throat seemed at the time like a completely rational way to keep him from noticing that I was sobbing. Then strong arms closed around me, holding me in place, and tears became the very last thing on my mind.

It made no sense whatsoever that my brain had randomly decided a year ago that Heath was the *safe one*. I should have been terrified of male alphas. According to society, they embodied everything that had hurt me so badly as a child. Overwhelming physical strength. Out-of-control libido. Rabid possessiveness. Toxic masculinity.

Stereotypes were just stereotypes, though.

Heath slid a calloused hand up to cradle the back of my neck, using the light grip to gentle the kiss until we were no longer clashing teeth and bumping noses. I whimpered as he tilted my head back further and nipped his way from my lips, along my jaw, and down the length of my exposed neck. His soft beard tickled my skin.

"Shh," he murmured against my throat. "Let me take care of you." Another nip. "I'm sorry I didn't understand the things you weren't telling me." Teeth scraped along my collarbone. "I'm sorry for all of it. So, so sorry."

"Don't be sorry," I begged. "I don't want sorry. I just don't want to be alone anymore!"

That was no better than the tears had been. But the words had been building in my chest for so long, even if I hadn't realized they were there. Now that they had a chance to escape into the real world—now that they had a chance to be heard—there was no stopping them.

Heath rested his forehead against my shoulder for a beat. "Then don't be alone. Be with us."

A shivery feeling took up residence in my bones at the idea I could say yes to this. The idea that I could actually get all the things I'd secretly desired, since Heath had swooped in and rescued me from the dead body in my apartment.

Before I could blurt out anything else embarrassing, Heath slid a finger along the open collar of the designer button-down shirt I was wearing.

"How much did this thing cost?" he asked, without lifting his head from my shoulder.

I swallowed noisily, my pulse picking up again. "Um… a lot?"

Hands eased me away by the shoulders until I was sitting upright, straddling Heath's thighs.

"Pity," he said, grasping the sleek maroon fabric and jerking the shirt open.

Thread ripped, buttons popping in every direction. A couple pinged against the walls;

most of them disappeared silently into the rumpled bedding and couch cushions.

"*Christ*," I gasped, blood rushing painfully to my dick

Heath spilled me backwards off his lap. I landed in a heap on the mattress where the four of us had been sleeping. He leaned over me, bracing a hand next to my ribs—his arm caging me in loosely.

"I'm sucking you off until you come in my mouth," he said matter-of-factly. "Afterward, I'll do anything you want, as long as it doesn't hurt you. But first, I want to watch you come undone without any distractions."

What did a person even say in response to something like that?

"Okay?" I managed.

He sat up, freeing both hands to open the fly on my expensive new suit trousers—thankfully without ripping them. I swallowed an undignified noise as he reached in and freed my desperate cock from my underwear.

I lay shaking with anticipation as he looked down at me. He was still fully dressed, and I was on my back in a ruined shirt and thousand-dollar trousers, my dick hanging out as he gave it an assessing squeeze.

Lightning raced from my shaft to the base of my spine. I squirmed beneath his touch. A bead of precome dripped in slow motion from my tip to the trail of dark hair on my belly.

"Please," I whispered, struck once again by how safe this felt, as long as Heath was the one doing it.

The gruff, sharp-tempered alpha bent down. His lips engulfed the head of my cock, his tongue rasping over the slit to gather up the wetness there. My eyes crashed shut as my entire world narrowed to slick heat and suction.

I could count on one hand the number of times someone had sucked me. Always before, it had been another random, harmless twink. Someone like me, who preferred to bottom, and who didn't have an aggressive bone in his body.

This… was nothing like that.

Heath possessed me with his mouth, taking ownership until there was no question of staying in control… of keeping my cool as my body's responses rose in an ever-tightening spiral.

"Oh, god," I choked. "Heath… *Heath!*"

I was worried that I'd shoot off like a rocket before a full minute had passed. Yet somehow, my pleasure kept building and building, long past the point when I expected it to blow. A faint buzzing noise echoed in my ears, punctuated only by the wet sounds of Heath's mouth working, and my own thundering heartbeat.

Shush-shush. Shush-shush. Shush-shush.

I listened to the soothing rhythm, following its gradual rise in speed and volume. It was almost a surprise when my muscles clenched, my balls drawing up to shoot hot and heavy into Heath's welcoming mouth. My whole body trembled with reaction, as though I was dumping an entire year's-worth of tension instead of a single mouthful of spunk.

Heath groaned, swallowing around my softening length.

I felt oversensitive; lightheaded.

"I want your knot," I whispered, as Heath pulled off with a pop. My half-hard dick flopped into the crease of my thighs, still twitching weakly.

He straightened, looking down at me. "You're still not taking an alpha knot without a lot of prep first," he said, echoing what he'd told me the first time we'd had sex. "But I'll give you as much as I can without hurting you, pet." He chuckled. "Looks like you're plenty relaxed, at least."

"Can I see you naked now?" I asked, my brain-mouth filter conveniently offline.

"Course you can, not that there's much to see." He started taking off his shirt, only to freeze, inhaling sharply.

I rolled up on an elbow. "What's wrong?"

His eyes darkened, but after a moment, he shook his head and let out the breath he'd been holding.

"Nothing," he said. "It's nothing. Get out of those trousers, why don't you. Because as much I like the idea of you shooting your load all over that brand new Armani, Gage would probably kill me."

I wriggled out of the suit pants and my underwear with uncoordinated movements, then shed the ruined shirt for good measure.

"Stay here for a minute," Heath said. "I need a couple of things, if we're going to do this proper. See if you can get that pretty cock hard for me again while I'm gone."

I blinked at him, unable to miss the way his own dick was thickening and twitching beneath the trousers he was still wearing.

"'Kay." I obediently reached for myself and started stroking, even though I doubted I'd be getting hard again so soon.

Heath disappeared, his unbuttoned shirt hanging open, and reappeared shortly afterward with a condom and a packet of lube. His expression, which had been surprised and uncertain before, had grown sharp, almost desperate.

I rolled onto my stomach, hitching one leg to the side in anticipation of the thing I always wanted, and almost never let myself have.

"Gimme," I said brilliantly.

Heath snorted. "Yeah, I'll give it to you, all right. *Brat.*"

The last was said with affection, and I hid my smile against my crossed arms.

As he had during our first hookup, Heath hefted my hips up and shoved a couple of pillows beneath them, lifting my ass in the air. I floated in a pleasant haze, all of my usual worries and fears growing faraway and unimportant. Slick, blunt fingers probed my hole, circling and scissoring. Heath was patient and thorough, but there was an edge of something behind his movements that I hadn't felt before.

"Ah… you're ready," he purred, once I felt loose and easy around his touch.

"So ready," I agreed, my voice distant in my own ears. "I want it hard this time, alpha. Please give it to me hard."

Heath let out a low rumble that shivered along my nerves. The thick, blunt head of his shaft nudged at my entrance and pushed inside, slow but inexorable. My muscles turned to jelly as my body surrendered to the assault, sparks zipping up my spine.

Feeling my readiness, Heath began to move in slow, deep strokes. Not rough, but powerful. Hands adjusted my hips, moving me this way and that until the head of his cock hit my prostate. I whined, fresh blood flowing to my own spent dick. With his target successfully acquired, Heath took up an unforgiving rhythm, holding my hips in place as I twisted and squirmed. My newly awakened erection rubbed against the pillows beneath me with every thrust.

"You're going to come again for me," Heath panted, his voice nearly a growl. "Come apart with me inside you."

There was a wildness in his tone and movements that sent new shocks through my body. In an embarrassingly short time, I was on the edge for the second time.

"Yes!" I said breathlessly, thrusting my hips back to meet him, then forward to rub my aching hard-on against the pillows. "Yes, *yes!*"

This climax was deep and devastating, rather than sharp and violent. It rolled through me, prickling the hair on my scalp and curling my toes. My ass milked the thick cock filling it, as though begging Heath to shoot inside me.

With a groan and a curse, his thrusts turned sloppy as he spurted into the condom.

"Fuck..." he moaned. "*God.*"

I whimpered as he pulled out, a bit too abruptly.

Hands rolled me onto my side, away from the mess I'd left on the pillows. Heath urged me to lie with my thighs pressed together. His heavy cock nudged into place where my thighs met my ass cheeks, his knot already swelling inside the warm, protected space.

"This good?" he slurred, tugging me snugly against his front.

"So good," I agreed sleepily. "Still gonna take that knot someday, though."

He hummed something that I chose to interpret as agreement.

I wasn't sure how long we lay there, dozing. But I jerked awake when he gasped and flailed upright behind me, his now-soft dick sliding free of my thighs.

"Whu...?" I asked, craning to look over my shoulder at his slack-jawed face.

His mouth moved for a moment before words formed.

"Sh-she just..." he shook his head as though to clear it. "*He* just..."

I blinked up at him in utter confusion. His green eyes met mine, full of shock.

"*Fuck*," he said, with feeling.

THIRTY-EIGHT

Gage

THIS WAS *NOTHING* like the handful of times I'd playfully bitten someone during sex. The blood in my mouth tasted like a drug; like addiction painted red and caged in iron.

Jez had trusted me to be inside her body — my knot still nestled within the space that had been perfectly made for it. Now, she was inside me, as well. Her mind held the same sharp, metallic edge as her blood. She was a steel blade, but that blade was double-edged. One side sliced outward, seeking vengeance against those who'd hurt her, and countless others like her. The other side of the blade faced inward, and that was the razor-sharp edge that stopped my breath for a long moment.

My mate lay bound under a guillotine of her own making. I sensed the peril that hung over her, every hour of every day. The need to *fix it* made my muscles twitch.

I could feed her chocolate cake and dress her in fine clothing, but none of it touched the bright line of pain at the center of her being.

I jerked my teeth away from the fresh mark I'd made, breathing hard. Instinct urged me to lick the wound closed, but it also urged me to protect the other part of my soul at all costs, even if the thing she needed protecting from was herself.

"*Jez*," I said hoarsely. "Why didn't you tell us that you don't want the surgery to remove your gland?"

I could *feel* the ache of it… the grief for another part of herself that was about to be taken against her will. Alpha instinct to step between my mate and the thing threatening her swelled, until I felt like I'd grown to three times my normal size. Inside me, a growling, slavering monster raged. A monster that needed to destroy every single thing that might hurt Jez.

Beyond the all-consuming newness of the mating bond, a second presence lurked.

Heath.

Alarm trickled through the two-way connection, muted by distance and the immediacy of Jez's distress. I ignored it.

Instead, I gathered Jez up in a tight embrace. "Kitten, *talk* to me," I begged.

She shook her head almost violently. Fresh blood welled from the mating bite.

"There's nothing to say." The words sounded broken.

My knot had begun to deflate under the force of her sadness. It slipped free from her body, separating us even though I wasn't ready.

"There's *plenty* to say," I shot back. "If you don't want the surgery, you shouldn't get the surgery!"

Instead of making things better, this only seemed to upset her more.

"But I *have* to!" she said, her voice wavering. "Heath doesn't want the mating bond! I can't *make him* stay mated to me!"

I could still sense Heath through the bond, even if it was harder to untangle the feelings he was putting out. I got the sense of movement, though. Of action.

"Yeah?" I shot back. "Well, what if *I* want the bond? What then?"

"I don't know," she whispered.

I sealed my mouth over her precious gland, laving my tongue across the raw toothmarks to heal them. She melted beneath the soothing touch, making my heart swell even bigger. When the bleeding stopped, I reluctantly pulled away.

"From where I'm sitting, that makes the vote two to one, against the surgery," I told her. Then I sat up and rummaged around for my discarded shirt. "Here, sweetheart. Put this on for me. I think we might be about to have a visitor."

She seemed very small as she let me help her into the oversized garment. I untangled the trousers I'd tossed aside and pulled them on, just so I'd have something as a nod toward modesty in case Tony showed up, too.

No sooner had I returned to the bed and pulled Jez into a protective embrace against my side than a harsh knock sounded at the bedroom door. Heath yanked it open without waiting for a response.

He looked wild-eyed and disheveled. And, sure enough, I could just make out Tony's uncertain form, half-hiding behind him. Jez cringed and huddled closer against me, hiding her face in my neck.

"What. The *fuck*," Heath said, in utter bewilderment. "Gage, *what the fuck?*"

Tony pushed forward just enough to be seen behind Heath's shoulder, although he very pointedly kept his eyes averted from the bed.

"You really mated her?" he asked, less loudly than Heath, but with just as much shock in his voice. "Jez, did you consent to this? Are you okay?"

I tried not to be offended by that. I really did. But all the emotions were too big right now, and most of them weren't even mine. A growl rose in my chest.

"You think I'd mate someone *against their will*?" I demanded—only realizing after the words were out how that might sound to Heath.

He flinched, both physically and through the bond. Jez flinched in sympathetic response.

Tony was trying his best to act like someone who wasn't scared of alphas and big feelings—standing his ground in the face of my anger, even though it looked like all he wanted to do was run away.

"I want to hear it from her," he said. "Jez… *please*."

There was a terrible pause.

"I wanted it," Jez said in a tiny voice. She looked up, lifting her head away from my shoulder. "It was supposed to be temporary. Just like *all* of this is temporary. But—"

She trailed off.

"But she doesn't want the surgery," I finished for her. "She never did. How the *fuck* did you not know that, Heath?"

Tony's eyes went very wide, and Heath looked like he'd been pole-axed.

"I… I was trying to block the bond," he stammered. "It was nonconsensual, and I thought it would be easier for both of us if I walled it off. As much as I could, at least."

"Yeah, and you stopped doing that last night," I told him. "I was *there*, remember? So, again, *how the fuck did you not know?*"

Tony's brown eyes darted between us. "There were a few other things going on at the time," he said. "As you might remember."

Some of my righteous indignation drained away.

"No, he's right," Jez agreed. I could feel the fine tremor of stress in her muscles, her earlier relaxation gone without a trace. "And I wasn't really thinking about the surgery until you… until we…"

Her voice broke.

Awkward silence fell over the room.

"It's true, though?" Heath asked, when it threatened to grow too thick. "You want to keep your mating gland? Keep the bond?" He hesitated. "Or… bonds, rather?"

Jez lifted tear-filled eyes. "I don't want to be an omega without a mating gland. I know you hate me for what I did—"

Heath's head snapped back as though he'd been struck. "I don't *hate* you."

Tension stiffened Tony's shoulders.

"Maybe I should, um… leave now?" he said. "I'm just making this more complicated—"

"*No*," Jez and Heath said in unison.

I shut my eyes for a moment, trying to pack away all the strong feelings ricocheting back and forth through the three-way mental connection. Jez and I had made an impulsive decision—and I, at least, had done it without having all the information. The longer we talked, the more I thought that maybe Jez hadn't had all the information, either.

She hadn't been lying about intending to get the surgery. I was beginning to think she just hadn't considered that there was any other option.

We all needed to lower the emotional temperature before things got out of hand, and people started saying stuff they'd regret later. Then, we needed to face the music head-on… because keeping shit in the dark hadn't worked out too well for us, so far.

"Okay," I said, opening my eyes. "Here's what's happening. Everyone's getting cleaned up. Take a shower, get some fresh clothes. After which, the four of us are gonna go tell Knox what's happening."

Three faces went sheet-pale.

I looked at the ceiling for strength. "That's not negotiable, okay? He's our pack leader.

Plus, he's been operating under the same misconception as the rest of us, right? He thinks Jez *wants* the surgery. So, we'll go let him know about the mating, and what Jez actually thinks… and whatever you and Tony need to tell him, Heath."

Jez winced. Tony went even paler.

"All right. But… are we really, *really* sure that his heart's okay now?" Jez asked, in a tiny voice.

"Guess we're about to find out," I said.

THIRTY-NINE

Knox

I WAS DRAGGING this morning, just like I'd been dragging *every* morning since I was released from the hospital. It didn't help that I could hear other people moving around, interspersed with voices talking and arguing.

I couldn't make out the words, but the rise and fall of it kindled a fresh sense of unease in my gut. Maybe I'd been deluding myself—Heath and Jez needed to work out their shit, and I'd believed it would be better if they did that without me breathing down their necks. Now, though, I was struck with the inexplicable certainty that something else had happened while I'd been asleep.

Grimly, I slogged through my morning routine. Shower, shave, dress for a day of dealing with nervous investors and business partners who still seemed to think I had one foot in the grave. I'd just draped a sober dove-gray tie around my neck when a purposeful knock sounded at the bedroom door.

Well.

At least they were coming to me, instead of making me chase them down later.

"Come in," I called, turning from the oval mirror just in time to see Gage open the door.

"Hey, boss," he greeted. "How ya feeling this morning?"

"Fine," I said cautiously, sensing a slightly more veiled version of the 'how's your heart?' conversation that seemed to be plaguing me since Jez's attack. "What can I do for you all?"

Three other figures hovered behind Gage's broad shoulders. I'd thought I'd heard Tony's voice in the mix earlier, and I'd wondered if he and Heath had successfully hashed things out. On the one hand, they had a pretty big age gap, and any relationship between the pair was likely to make things complicated as hell while Heath remained mated to Jez. On the other hand, Tony was a good kid, and both he and Heath deserved some joy in their lives.

Gage cleared his throat and came inside. Heath followed, looking like death warmed over. Jez and Tony stayed close to the doorway, either for ease of escape or because they weren't comfortable taking up space in my room. Although, to be fair, the presence of three alphas arrayed in a tense triangle made the generous bedroom feel smaller than it actually was.

The scent of caramel coffee wafted around us, making my spine tingle.

"So…" Gage began, rubbing at the back of his neck in a habitual nervous gesture. "Jez and me mated each other last night."

The tight ball of misgivings that had been gathering in my stomach abruptly turned to lead.

"Because, y'know, if she was going to get a glandectomy, it wouldn't be permanent anyway, right?" he hurried on.

Which… was admittedly true. My shoulders relaxed a bit.

"Except, it turns out she doesn't really want the surgery," Gage said. "She just thought she didn't have a choice."

My eyes flew to the wide-eyed omega waif poised by the doorway as though ready to flee at the first sign of trouble. "Is that true, Jez?"

She rolled her lower lip between her teeth, but I could read the truth behind her huge gray eyes. The weight in my stomach turned to queasiness. Had my pack and I unwittingly steamrolled this woman into agreeing to a life-altering surgery against her will? I tried to think back, seeking any hint that she'd been under duress.

I'd assumed from the beginning that it was what she would want… because it's what *I* would want, if I was an omega who'd been mated without proper consent. Every time we'd talked about it, she'd agreed with me immediately.

My queasiness grew worse.

She'd agreed with the rich alpha who had the power to put her in prison with a snap of his fingers. Whose house she was staying in… whose food she was eating… whose life she'd tried to end because she'd bought into a calculated lie.

"You didn't think you had a choice," I echoed, appalled.

But she shook her head almost violently.

"No, I mean… I thought it *was* what I wanted." She picked at the cuff of her shirt, not making eye contact. "It's the only thing that makes sense, you know? It's not fair to Heath to make him stay mated, and it isn't as though I wanted to be bonded to someone who has so many reasons to hate me."

Heath had been standing frozen, almost statue-like during the exchange. But at that, he came to life. "I told you; I don't *hate* you, Jez. I was angry. I'm *still* angry, but I also know now that you were a victim, too. You hurt Knox. You also saved me, back at the silos. And I don't know where that leaves us—but whether you let surgeons cut out a part of your body is *your* choice, not mine."

Jez's jaw, which had been hanging slightly open, clicked shut.

Heath sighed deeply. "I know it's still complicated as hell." He turned to me. "And I'm about to make it even more complicated. Tony and I want to pursue a relationship. I'd like to make him part of the pack."

Gage looked smug. "Bout time," he muttered.

As for Tony himself, he looked like if he tried hard enough, he might be able to sink through the floor and disappear.

"I have no problem with that," I told him, gentling my tone as much as I could. "You're welcome here, Tony. Sorry about the non-stop batshit insanity lately. Believe it or not, it isn't always like this."

That startled a snort from him. "Um… thanks. And good to know, I guess? Now, if that's out of the way, would anyone object if I disappeared back to my apartment so I can rock quietly in the corner for an hour or two with no interruptions?"

Heath looked like he wanted to object, but he caught himself. "Whatever you need. You'll let me know if there's a problem, though?"

Tony's dark eyes softened. "Yeah. Sorry — I'm used to dealing with stuff on my own. Well… aside from inconvenient dead bodies, anyway. It's going to take some adjusting, is all."

"For him, too." Gage hooked a thumb at Heath. "Don't worry, though. We're going to get this figured out and make it all work. You'll see."

Tony mustered a smile. "I know better than to disagree when you make a prediction about something, big guy. Jez, are you okay here?"

Jez still looked more like someone staring down the gallows than someone staring at a tastefully decorated bedroom, but she nodded.

"I'm fine," she said.

I made a mental note regarding how quick she was to lie about her own emotions. That was something I should've pegged sooner, even though I hadn't exactly been at my best for the past few days.

"Okay," Tony told her, accepting it. "You know where to find me if you need me."

I waited until he'd left, before catching Heath and Gage's eyes. "I think it would be best if I had a word alone with Jez."

Gage looked at her. "That all right with you, kitten?"

She nodded, and I took comfort in the knowledge that Gage would be able to tell if she was lying.

He turned back to me. "I know we made things even more complicated by mating last night, but I ain't gonna apologize for it. You don't throw away your scent match just because things are difficult."

He grabbed Heath's arm and propelled him toward the door. Pausing, he leaned down and pressed a kiss to the top of Jez's head.

"Remember… we are *going* to make this work," he told her. "Promise."

She didn't look like she believed it, but she did paste on a wan smile for him.

He and Heath left, leaving the door open behind them. I saw Heath shoot an unreadable glance over his shoulder before the pair disappeared down the hallway.

Alone with my would-be murderer, I let out a sigh, crossed my arms, and rested a hip against the heavy dresser.

"I think I steamrolled you before, and I didn't even realize I was doing it," I told her. "I have no idea how you and I are supposed to navigate this situation, but that's not an excuse for forgetting what a power imbalance looks like."

She hesitated for a moment. "It didn't make sense for me to keep my gland. I was ready to get it cut out in a back alley. It's what anyone would expect me to do."

"Maybe," I agreed. "But you're still the one who needs to make that choice. Sure, Heath is part of it. Gage too, now. But it's your body that's on the line, not any of ours."

The silence stretched longer this time.

"Whenever I think about having my mating gland removed, all I feel is sad," she said eventually. "But I've been sad about a lot of things that still needed to be done. Wanting something hasn't exactly been a big reason for doing things in my life… or for *not* doing them. Survival has."

I could only imagine.

"You wanted the bond with Gage, though?" I probed. "He certainly seems to want it with you."

"I did," she whispered. Then she squared her shoulders. "I do."

"And what about Heath?"

Her shoulders slumped again. "I don't know. It seemed so right when I was in heat. So simple."

"But you're okay with him and Tony being together?" I asked.

She frowned. "Of course I am! I told Heath he was being an idiot if he turned down someone as sweet as Tony."

I filed that little tidbit away as being extremely interesting.

"And he listened to you," I mused. "So, it sounds like you and he might have found some common ground, at the very least."

"Maybe," she allowed, but her expression was unsure.

I took a centering breath. "Lorenzo Vozzina tried to have me killed, using you as his weapon," I said, not sugar-coating it.

She looked down at her bare feet. "Yes."

"As far as I'm concerned, your mating bonds with Heath and Gage are completely separate from that," I went on. She looked up again, surprised.

"But—"

I cut her off, shaking my head. "It's true that our shared past still hangs over us. I can't forget that you're my scent match, any more than you can forget I'm yours. But I don't think trying to act on that would be fair to either of us. Not after everything that's happened."

I ignored the surge of alpha stubbornness that snarled in disagreement with the words. This situation was going to be difficult enough to navigate without letting animal instincts steer the boat.

"No," she breathed. "I guess it wouldn't be."

It was time to change the subject, before the soft scent of sadness beneath her omega perfume further roused the beast inside me.

"Regardless of everything else, we still need to get your identity papers, and publicly establish you as part of the pack," I said briskly, straightening away from my perch. "There's a charity gala coming up… one that I need to be seen at, so everyone knows I'm back at work and fully recovered."

Of course, *fully recovered* was a stretch. But the business world was full of sharks, and I had no intention of becoming chum in the water.

"You want me to come with you to this gala?" Jez asked.

"I'd like to make it a pack affair, yes. In fact, I'd like Tony to come as well, if he's willing."

She seemed to consider that.

"I've never been someone's arm candy before," she said, and I thought I could hear a touch of genuine amusement in her tone.

"I sincerely doubt Tony has, either," I quipped back. "Although, to be clear, I object to the term in both cases. You're both part of this pack, no matter how unusual the circumstances that brought us to this point."

"All right," she said. "I'll come."

"Good," I replied. "Oh… there's one more thing. I need to finalize the name we'll be using for your paperwork. Jez is short for…"

"Jezebel," she said, without much enthusiasm.

"Are you okay with something a little less unique?" I asked. "I was thinking Jessica Smith? Although it will be Jessica Knockley, now."

Her expression cleared. "Jessica is good. Funny… back in school I used to tell people that's what Jez was short for. I always hated Jezebel. My dad chose it."

I ached for a little girl who'd been branded deceitful and immoral before she could even talk. Idly, I wondered if Jez's father was still alive, and if he'd ever faced any consequences for what he'd done to her.

"Jessica it is, in that case," I said. "And while I may not be able to promise you another mate bond, you're more than welcome to my last name."

Jez's eyes went far away. "It's been a long time since I had one of those," she said.

FORTY

Tony

IF YOU'D ASKED ME for reasons why I might be required to wear a tuxedo someday, I might've joked that I'd already missed my high school prom, and I was highly unlikely to ever be recruited as anyone's groomsman... much less a groom.

I would *not* have said that I might have to go to a black-tie gala recognizing the economic impact of regional leaders in international trade. Because, up until recently, the closest ties I had to international trade involved ordering cheap electronics off of eBay and waiting weeks for them to arrive from China.

When Jez had told me that Knox wanted me to attend as part of the pack, I'd thought she was joking.

Spoiler alert—she hadn't been joking.

"We're going to be *arm candy*," she'd told me solemnly, blinking huge gray eyes up at me in a way that completely failed to hide the devilish glint behind them. "That means we both have to dress up real pretty for the alphas."

I'd blinked back at her, probably with much more of a 'deer in the headlights' expression than she was wearing. "Um... how pretty are we talking about? Will I have to find a tie to go with that expensive suit?"

The look she gave me as she patted my cheek had been pitying.

"Sure, something like that," was all she'd said.

And so, once again, I'd found myself being measured and examined by a well-dressed store clerk with a tape measure literally hanging around his neck. But this time, I'd emerged from the store with a slim-cut black tux in a garment bag, complete with starched shirt and bow tie.

It was not what one would call a comfortable outfit. And yet, somehow, I found that I was enjoying wearing it. That might have been due to a poorly hidden teenage James Bond fantasy… or it might have had more to do with the way Heath had been eyeing me like he wanted to tear the tux off my body with his teeth. Gage had also been shooting me occasional admiring looks, and even Knox had whistled low when he saw me.

Still, when it came to arm candy, I was nothing compared to Jez. I'd wavered for hours before finally gathering up my courage and applying a bit of subtle guyliner around my eyes. Meanwhile, she'd spent an afternoon with some high-end stylist, having her hair and makeup professionally done. With the addition of a stunning emerald mermaid gown that hugged her slender from bust to knees before flaring out in layers of tulle and lace that brushed the floor, she looked like visiting Nordic royalty.

When he wasn't subtly checking me out, Gage had been staring at Jez like a love-struck puppy. Knox had also done a startled double-take, while Heath looked like he was in danger of having a stroke.

None of this felt real. Not the limo ride from the pack house to the historic Greystone Hotel, where the ultra-rich hosted weddings and galas in an updated hundred-and-forty-year-old, four-story building with a view of the lake. Not the bevy of waiters and attendants scurrying around us as we were seated at a table near the raised stage at the front of the banquet hall, or the glittering guests milling and chatting over the sounds of an honest-to-god string quartet.

Amazing food started arriving as soon as we were seated—plates of tiny appetizers and bottles of champagne, little bowls of chilled soup and fruit cut into intricate shapes. Jez and I exchanged a glance, our lips pressed tightly together to keep from descending into stupid giggles as we eyed the dizzying array of different-sized forks set before us.

Still battling for control of my expression, I picked one up at random and speared a piece of shrimp rolled in a translucent wrap with greenery poking out of the ends.

Knox looked us over with faint amusement. "Enjoying yourselves?" he asked mildly.

I chewed and swallowed, gesturing at him with the fork tines. "I'm going to try every single food they have, and gain twenty pounds in a single sitting."

Gage smirked.

"I like the music," Jez said. "There was an old man who used to play violin near the Flat Iron building sometimes. Do you remember him, Tony? He used to play things like this."

"Yeah." An odd kind of nostalgia tugged at me. "I do remember him. I wonder if he's still around?"

"We could go look for him sometime," Gage said. "If you wanted."

Across the table, Heath tensed. His eyes widened for a moment at something behind me, before his face went cold and stony.

"Oh, *hell* no," he said, and I had a moment's panic that he was angry for some reason about what Gage had said. Then he added stiffly, "You might have mentioned that the *fucking Vozzinas* were invited to this party, Knox."

Knox followed his gaze, and despite myself, I craned around to look as well. Next to me, Jez went very still. I couldn't tell who they were looking at, since there were a bunch of people in a group.

"I wasn't provided with a full guest list," Knox said, bringing his attention back to Heath. "It isn't a huge surprise, though. Is that the omega? Lorenzo's new mate?"

"That's Adrian," Jez said tightly.

"Paolo," Heath growled. "His real name is Paolo Vozzina."

A cold feeling spread through my stomach. "The guy who kidnapped you and tried to kill Knox is *here*? Should we leave? Or, I dunno… call the police or something?"

Knox raised an eyebrow. "He's hardly going to attack us in the middle of a major society event. Let's just say, I've already put legal wheels in motion when it comes to the Vozzinas."

"You have?" Jez asked, her gaze flickering between Knox and the mystery omega behind me.

"I have," he confirmed. "But the process has to happen in a somewhat roundabout way."

Gage frowned. "Or else Jez'll get dragged into the mess. Right."

Heath had been gripping the edge of the table in such a way that suggested it might crack beneath the strain at any moment. At that, he pushed his chair away and stood up.

"I need some air," he said.

On the stage, the emcee tapped her mic and began talking about the awards that would be handed out tonight to various businessmen, including Knox.

"Heath—" Knox began.

"Don't worry. I'm not going to wring his scrawny neck," Heath said in a low monotone. "But I'm also not sitting here while that little snake and his alpha sugar daddy simper to the crowd."

With that, he spun and stalked off.

I started to stand up as well. "I can go after him—"

But Jez raised a hand. "It's okay, Tony. I'll go. You're enjoying this. So, keep enjoying it. I'll talk to him."

"You sure, kitten?" Gage asked.

Jez nodded. "Yes. Believe it or not, we don't do too badly together, when it's just him and me."

"I don't see any sign of Lorenzo," Knox told her. "I don't think he's here… and even if he was, I sincerely doubt either he or Paolo would recognize you in that dress unless they got within scenting range. Even so, stay aware of your surroundings."

"Right," Jez said, tapping the side of her nose. "Remind the street kid to watch out for danger in unfamiliar surroundings. Got it."

She headed after Heath, and I sank back into my chair.

"You really think she and Heath will be all right on their own?" I asked, unable to completely contain my worry.

"I think they'll need to *learn* to be all right," Knox said. "Under the circumstances."

The emcee had been droning on throughout this exchange, but now, she gestured grandly toward the table the others had been watching.

"Our first award for outstanding community development goes to… Lorenzo Vozzina, of Vozzina Associates! Please come up to the stage and say a few words."

There was a murmur among the guests as a slender omega stood, smoothing down his maroon tuxedo jacket and strutting toward the stage like a model on a runway. His dark gaze fell on Knox as he approached, holding there for a moment too long. The skin at the back of my neck prickled as he passed behind me.

"Smarmy little prick," Gage muttered, hopefully too low to be heard by the smarmy little prick in question.

Paolo mounted the steps in three light strides and accepted a microphone, smiling widely at the audience. *"Good evening, ladies and gentlefolk! I know I'm not quite who you were expecting, but my dear mate had to beg off tonight thanks to a nasty flu bug. We couldn't have Chicago's glitterati catching a virus, now could we? However, I'm honored to accept this award on his behalf…"*

Gage made quiet gagging noises as Paolo continued to enthuse to the crowd.

I stared at the slimeball who'd manipulated Jez into hurting Knox, and hurt both her and Heath so badly at the silos. An unfamiliar feeling that might have been hatred swelled in my chest.

"I could stick a foot out and trip him when he walks back to his table," I suggested, only half-joking.

"No, you will not trip a rival pack's omega in the middle of a charity gala," Knox said sternly.

"*As you know,*" Paolo's smug voice boomed through the sound system. "*I was only recently mated to Lorenzo, and may I say what an incredible honor it is to be accepted such an illustrious pack. It's gratifying to see the Vozzinas getting the recognition they deserve in this city, and...*"

I turned to Gage, about to suggest bribing one of the waitstaff to smash a pie into the little twerp's face or something, when a deafening *boom* rocked the building. The lights flickered for a moment and went out, instantly plunging the huge room into darkness as dust choked the air.

A terrible rumble vibrated my bones.

"*Christ!*" Knox's curse barely penetrated past the ringing in my ears.

A heavy weight toppled me to the ground, knocking the remaining breath from my lungs. I tried to gasp, the scent of citrus and yeasty bread surrounding me as a large body caged me in. Panic gripped me... I still couldn't see anything except blackness. The sound of terrified screams felt distant, as though they were coming from across the length of a football field.

The floor was still vibrating, and the screams became punctuated with muffled crashing sounds. A heavy impact jolted the body covering mine, pinning me beneath weight that made it impossible to breathe. Another impact followed, and another, and another. The blackness surrounding me closed in until there was nothing else, muffled sounds flattening into a low whine.

Something hard glanced against my temple, and even the whine disappeared into silence.

FORTY-ONE

Jez

THE FANCY LOUBOUTIN heels I was wearing suddenly seemed a lot less desirable, when I was trying to catch up to a tall alpha with a long stride and a chip on his shoulder.

"Heath!" I called. I didn't want to make a scene, but I also didn't want to break an ankle trying to speed-walk across a polished marble floor.

Heath either didn't hear me—possible, given the ambient noise from the guests and the sound system—or didn't acknowledge me. I gritted my teeth and sped up my steps, feeling vaguely ridiculous with the way the mermaid gown shortened my stride. Even if I took the shoes off, running was out of the question.

The red-haired form disappeared from view, blocked by other bodies. He'd been heading toward the building's main entrance, though, so that's where I went, as well. It was only when I pushed through the glass double doors and into the rapidly cooling night air that I caught sight of him again. He hadn't gone far; just to the end of the wide awning that spanned most of building's frontage.

His presence in my mind felt like a pot about to boil over. As I slowed down and approached him, he hunched over and lifted a glowing flame to his face. A moment later, a puff of smoke emerged from his lips, pale gray under the streetlights.

"I didn't know you smoked," I greeted, wrinkling my nose.

He took another drag and lowered the cigarette. The glowing tip shook faintly in his grasp as he blew out another cloud.

"I don't," he growled. "I quit at the same time I stopped drinking."

His frustration vibrated through the bond.

"I came out to make sure you were okay," I said. "Tony was going to follow you, but he's enjoying the party, so I told him I'd do it. Should I have let him come instead?"

"I don't want to talk." Heath stubbed the cigarette out against the stone block wall with an angry gesture. "I want to be somewhere that skinny little arsehole Paolo *isn't*."

I turned and leaned against the wall a short distance away from him, blowing out a breath through my pursed lips. An artfully arranged platinum curl bounced against my cheek. "I'm not thrilled about being in the same building with him, either."

A silence fell between us that wasn't *comfortable*, exactly... but neither of us felt the need to rush and fill it.

"Knox says he's going to deal with it," I said eventually. "Legally, I mean. Do you think that'll work?"

Heath let his head fall back against the stone. "When Knox says he's doing something, it usually gets done. But if we're talking about the legal system, I wouldn't bank on it getting done *fast.*"

I thought about that for a moment and nodded. "But they'll end up in prison at some point."

Heath shrugged a shoulder, noncommittal.

"Are the Vozzinas the ones behind trafficking all the omegas around here?" I asked. "I mean, not just the ones who were being held at the silos… but the ones that were in your house the night Gage took me there?"

Heath lifted his head, but only so he could thump it gently against the wall a couple of times.

"Can we prove that in a court of law? No," he said. "But… yeah, probably."

I chewed the inside of my cheek, trying to push down old memories that had begun to rise. "Maybe Knox has got something on them now," I said. "Something that you didn't have before."

"I sure as hell hope he does," Heath said.

"Me, too," I agreed. Then, I hesitated before continuing. "Look, this probably isn't the time. Or the place. But… about what Gage said. About me not wanting the surgery, I mean. I know it's not fair to ask you to have a bond that you didn't ask for—"

Heath drew breath to say something, only to be cut off as the sky above us exploded. Orange fire lit the top of the old hotel, and half a second later, a blast of hot wind ripped downward. The heavy canvas awning tore like tissue paper.

"Fucking… *fuck!*" Heath shouted, grabbing me and wrapping his body around mine.

The sidewalk rumbled beneath our feet. Or… no. Not the sidewalk. The *building*. Panicked screams pierced through the night air.

"What's happening?" I cried, clinging to Heath's tuxedo lapels.

In the next instant, crippling pain ripped through the mating bond. Not Heath. *Gage*. My knees buckled, until Heath's grip was the only thing keeping me upright. The shrill screams sounded closer now, for some reason—echoing inside my head.

Oh. Right. Those screams were coming from *me*.

The punishing blows kept coming, battering a body that might as well have been my own. Heath was reeling, too. He staggered sideways, his shoulder hitting the wall of the shaking building.

"*Jez!*" His rough voice sounded far away, the tone oddly flattened. "I think the building's coming down! We have to get away from it!"

Past the agonizing pain of someone else's injuries, I could feel his stabbing guilt over the idea of moving farther away from our pack. But the strong arms holding me tugged me sideways, and then we were stumbling like drunkards toward the street.

"*No!*" I set my feet, digging stiletto heels into the concrete, and nearly sent both of us tumbling to the ground. The shriek of my alpha's damaged bones and muscles made another scream lodge in my throat, but I rooted myself in place and refused to budge.

"Jez—" Heath said again, tugging at me.

"Our pack is in there!" I yelled, directly in his face.

In the distance, sirens wailed.

His hands clenched convulsively around my shoulders. "We can't get to them! That bomb brought the roof down—it'll take search dogs and specialized equipment to find anyone buried under the rubble!"

My lips curled back in an ugly snarl. Inside my mind, an invisible, silken rope tugged me inescapably toward the destruction. "*I can find them! I can find Gage!*"

"What?" Heath's mouth worked silently for a moment. "Jez… no! That's not how mating bonds work!"

I grabbed his forearms, my newly manicured nails digging into the fabric of his jacket. "*I can find him!*"

Still, he hesitated.

"Tony's in there, too!" I shouted. "God-damn it! If you won't help, then *let go of me!*"

Heath's hands released their grip as though I'd suddenly become red hot. I swayed, and would have gone down if not for my clasp on his forearms. He steadied me.

"Let's go, then," he said, his face deathly pale. "You'll have to lead the way. I can only feel that Gage is hurt. Not where he is."

We were still under one end of the damaged awning. It hadn't come down on top of us, but getting back to the front doors required shoving through a section that had torn and fallen, draping across the sidewalk like a tent. Part of it was on fire. Heath once again covered me with his body, hissing in discomfort as we pushed past the smoky heat.

The power was out. Heath pulled out his phone one-handed and turned on the flashlight. One of the glass doors had shattered, while the other had blown half off its hinges. There was a gap large enough for me to slip through, broken glass crunching under my heels.

Heath cursed and struggled, forcing his larger body through the narrow space. The mental rope pulling me deeper into the building wavered in and out of focus, its ends fraying. Only Heath's hand around my wrist kept me from stumbling blindly forward into the darkness before he'd managed to get inside with me.

With a final grunt of effort, he squeezed through. The flashlight panned across the floor, playing over people in expensive evening wear groaning and pushing to their feet. Clouds of gray dust billowed in the beam of light, coating the figures and making them look like ghosts. I coughed convulsively, covering my nose and mouth with my hand.

"Everyone get outside!" Heath bellowed. "Help the injured and get away from the building! Police and fire rescue are coming!"

More phone flashlights flickered on, criss-crossing the grand entryway with yellow beams. People started staggering toward the broken doors, some of them pausing to help lift others who hadn't yet risen.

Heath and I pushed against the slow tide of bodies, heading toward the very place that everyone else was fleeing. The wall separating the reception area from the huge, high-ceilinged banquet area had a massive crack in it. The arched double-doorway looked like a photograph someone had torn in half and tried to glue back together, the edges no longer meeting up.

Beyond, the sound of screams and groans of pain echoed eerily.

Heath lifted his phone's flashlight, shining it past the fractured doorway… and illuminating a scene straight from the depths of hell itself.

FORTY-TWO

Heath

THE BANQUET HALL looked like a vision from another planet. The huge event space had taken up the entire center of the old hotel, open all the way to the ceiling of the four-story building, thirty-odd feet above our heads.

Based on the explosion we'd seen and felt earlier, someone had planted a bomb on the roof. That roof was now lying in pieces on the floor, while the rest of the building rumbled ominously around us. Great clouds of choking gray dust billowed in the light of my phone's flashlight.

Next to me, Jez bent over. Her hand gripped my arm for balance as she pulled off her fancy shoes and tossed them away. She hiked the tight skirt of her gown up to her hips, and before I could get words out, she was away, scrabbling around and over fallen chunks of concrete.

She moved with utter fearlessness… with a complete lack of care for the injuries she was sure to get as she grabbed sharp-edged handholds and stepped over broken glass and wood.

I gaped after her for a precious second, unable to comprehend how she was even *functioning* with Gage's pain pouring through the bond. I was only getting it secondhand, and it was very nearly crippling.

Keeping the flashlight beam as steady as I could in one shaking hand, I lunged after her. Groans and sobs from partygoers trapped in the rubble formed a nauseating symphony around me. The occasional human limb coated with sickly gray dust stuck out from random gaps.

Through it all, Jez scrambled ahead of me in an absolutely straight line, climbing over any obstacles that stood in her way as though an invisible elastic band was dragging her forward.

I coughed and choked on dust as I did my best to keep her in sight. My stomach plunged as her small form dropped behind a pile of debris, disappearing from view. But when I reached the spot, it was to find her running across a relatively clear area of the floor.

Stupidly, I paused and looked straight up. Beyond the haze of dust, patches of stars twinkled in the night sky where the roof had once been. The sirens that had been blaring in the distance sounded nearly on top of us.

"*Knox!*" Jez shouted, jolting me out of the surreal haze of the destroyed building and Gage's pain.

I ran after her, stumbling over toppled chairs and smaller chunks of debris. My phone's light wavered wildly before playing over a gray-coated figure crouched beneath the slant of an upended table.

"*Get out!*" Knox choked, his voice wavering with effort. "It's not… safe—"

Horror suffused me as my brain made sense of what my eyes were seeing. The half-destroyed table was jammed like a lever beneath one end of a much larger section of fallen concrete; Knox using his own body to keep it from collapsing and crushing the unmoving body trapped beneath it.

No. Not body. *Bodies.*

I dove in next to Knox, shoving my shoulders against the creaking wood of the broken table to take some of the strain.

"Gage!" Jez shouted, "Tony! *Wake up!*"

"Can't," Knox grunted. "I can't hold it…"

I jammed my shoulders harder against the underside of the table, my back and thigh muscles screaming as I took more of the weight.

"Jez," I grated. "Can you pull them out?"

It seemed impossible on the face of it. She was a tiny wisp of a thing, and Gage was a mountain of an alpha—but we were short on options.

She grunted and cried out. More pain flared through the mating bond.

"His leg is trapped!" she said, sounding near tears. "And most of his weight is on Tony! I can't move them!"

I clenched my jaw and threw my full strength against the table. "Knox, go help her!" I managed past gritted teeth. "I'll hold this!"

Knox coughed out an acknowledgement and slipped past me. My spine popped and creaked in protest as I took the remaining strain. Christ—how long had Knox been bracing this thing before we got here?

Something behind me shifted, and there were more groans of effort.

"We have to get them out!" Jez's voice held more than a hint of hysteria. "Come on... *come on!*"

The pile shifted again, and the pain through the bond grew white-hot. My vision wavered; a haze of red closing in from the edges. Jez's cries grew into screams.

I couldn't lose consciousness. I *couldn't* lose consciousness.

I could feel the table I was bracing pressing my body down. My muscles shook. The heels of my shoes squeaked against the dusty tile of the floor. A rasping cry of denial clawed its way up from my throat—

Two bulky bodies shoved themselves in on either side of me.

"Hold on, sir." The voice sounded alien... flattened by a respirator mask. "Chicago Fire Department. We'll get your friends out."

The crushing weight on my shoulders eased. I still couldn't breathe properly past the dust and smoke, but the tunnel around my vision receded enough to make out the figures on either side of me, both wearing full gear.

A third firefighter pulled me out from under the table and took my place.

"One... two... *three!*" The respirator-flattened voice counted down, and the table tilted as the three people beneath it heaved.

I stumbled around to the side and eased Jez away, taking her place and grabbing Gage beneath the armpits as another firefighter levered up the beam that had been trapping his leg. I heaved, pulling my packmate free. Knox and Jez pulled Tony out of danger immediately afterward, now that he no longer had a two-hundred-twenty-five-pound alpha on top of him.

"Stretchers!" called one of the firefighters. "We need two stretchers over here!"

Gage was alive—the pain through the bond proved that much, even if he was barely conscious. The need to crash to my knees next to Tony's body and check his pulse was nearly overwhelming—but Jez, Knox, and I were immediately elbowed out of the way by the knot of first responders surrounding the pair.

The wreck of the banquet hall was now a confusing blur of moving, high-powered flashlight beams. Rescuers swarmed the area, shouting orders and calling for more stretchers.

Gage and Tony were efficiently strapped onto backboards and transferred to the first two stretchers.

"Go with them," one of the firefighters said. "We need to help the people who aren't ambulatory. This building isn't stable."

Knox grabbed my arm, keeping me from following the stretchers. "Thank you," he told the man. "You and your team saved our lives."

The firefighter gave a brisk nod, but then he immediately disappeared to rejoin the search.

"Jez." Knox's voice was a bare rasp, but Jez dragged her eyes away from Gage and Tony's stretchers in response, meeting his gaze. "Go with them," he told her. "We'll be a few minutes behind you."

Her dusty face wrinkled in a confused frown, but then the stretcher bearers were already carrying their injured burdens in a slow trek through the rubble. She looked torn for a moment, but then she nodded and limped after them.

Worry, fear, exhaustion, throbbed through the mating bond, a counterpoint to the pain of Gage's injuries. I swallowed hard and choked on grit. Knox still had me by the arm.

"We need to get out," I told him hoarsely.

His dark eyes glittered in the light of the firefighters' emergency lamps, hard despite the bloodshot whites. "In a minute."

He tugged me toward what I was pretty sure had been the stage area, where pitiful whimpers and groans came from the shadow of a pile of rubble. I'd dropped my cell phone in the confusion of saving the others. It was probably crushed under the table at this point — the second phone I'd lost this month. Knox still had his, though. He played the flashlight beam along the base of the pile until it illuminated a familiar face.

Adrian… *Paolo*… sobbed and flinched as the light hit his eyes. He lifted an arm weakly, as though to fend us off.

I took an abrupt step back. "Knox, *what the fuck*. Let him rot."

Hatred roiled in my gut as I stared down at the slimy little weasel who'd orchestrated not only Knox's attempted murder, but also the shit-show at the silos.

"No," Knox said in a monotone. "I don't think so. Help me get him free."

He propped the phone nearby and grabbed the first chunk of concrete, rolling it aside. I hesitated, but the instinct to obey my pack leader won out over the instinct to get my hands around Paolo's scrawny neck and squeeze.

Barely.

The collapse that had trapped the omega didn't include any debris too big for us to move. The first responders were still dealing with the area where most of the guests had been seated. They didn't appear to have noticed us over here in the shadows.

My hands slipped when I pulled a chunk away from the asshole's leg. The concrete was wet with blood, and so were my hands when I dropped it on the growing pile next to me. The rest of the debris covering his lower body fell away easily, revealing more blood.

Even though he was no longer trapped, Paolo just lay there—staring up at us with terrified eyes. The leg I'd freed was twisted at an unnatural angle, and his stupid maroon tuxedo trousers were shredded. Worse, though, was the source of the blood soaking the floor around him. It wasn't just pooling sluggishly. It was pulsing from a gash in his thigh.

He was bleeding out as we watched.

"Don't... don't hurt me," Paolo whimpered. "I'm sorry, I didn't mean to... to..."

"See, here's the thing," Knox said to me, ignoring the omega's cringing and begging as he shed his jacket and unfastened his suspenders. "Maybe Lorenzo Vozzina was the one who planted a bomb in this building, and maybe he wasn't."

He wrapped the suspenders around Paolo's leg above the wound and yanked them tight, drawing a weak cry of pain from the injured omega. The bleeding slowed to a trickle.

"Maybe he was trying to kill us, and maybe he wasn't," Knox continued. "One thing's sure, though— if Lorenzo was behind the attack, it means he sent his brand-new trophy mate here to stand directly under a bomb when it went off, while he stayed safely at home, out of the line of fire."

"Wh-*what*?" Paolo squeaked.

Knox smiled at him. There was no humor whatsoever behind the expression. "You might want to ponder that before you crawl back to him, Paolo. And if you decide to make a different choice, my door is always open." He calmly pulled a business card out of his pocket and slid it into Paolo's jacket, hiding it behind his rumpled pocket square. "Heath, get us some help over here, please. My voice is shot to hell."

I stared for a long moment at the cold, calculating sonuvabitch who led my pack, trying to peer into his skull and see whatever schemes were hatching there. Then I turned and bellowed, "Medic! *Medic*! We've got a serious injury over here!"

We waited until a pair of firefighters started heading our way. Then Knox picked up his phone, slung an arm across my shoulders, and let me support his weight as we turned and limped toward the path that the first responders had cleared, leading to the exit.

FORTY-THREE

Jez

NORTHWESTERN MEMORIAL Hospital was a madhouse. Back at the destroyed hotel, the EMTs who'd loaded Gage and Tony into one of the first ambulances to arrive at the hotel had tried to tell me I couldn't come with them. I'd showed them the bloody scrapes on my hands and feet, and they'd relented, squeezing me onto a jump-seat in the gap between the patient area in the back and the place where the driver sat.

The sirens hurt my ears as we hurtled down the road, Gage's pain battering at my nerves like fire. It didn't look like the ambulance was designed to hold two injured people; much less three. But there had been dozens of casualties in the demolished banquet room, so I guessed they were bending some rules to get everyone to the hospital as fast as possible.

Gage was on the gurney in the back. They'd braced Tony—still on his stretcher—crosswise across the cabinets set on either side of the work area.

"Broken femur," the EMT reported, prodding at Gage's unmoving body. "Possible cracked ribs, possible cervical spine injury. Good thing he's an alpha."

"What about Tony?" I asked, my voice wavering.

The nicer of the two men—the one who'd let me on the ambulance—glanced at me. "His vitals are stable. Looks like a head injury, but they'll check him out properly once we get to the ER. Try to stay calm, miss."

I wrapped my arms around myself, the sting of my raw palms disappearing into the overall throbbing agony of the bond. I bit my lips to keep from bothering them while they were trying to work. The ambulance jounced around a curve at high speed, and I nearly cried out as Gage's injuries flared white-hot.

When we arrived, two other ambulances were already unloading patients. The EMTs flung open the doors and started readying Gage's gurney for transport. I stood up, only to fall to my knees with a poorly stifled scream when they lowered the gurney to the ground, jolting Gage's battered body with the impact.

The nicer EMT cursed under his breath. "Miss? What's wrong? Is it your feet?"

I tried to speak and couldn't.

The man's partner hopped back up, ducking under Tony's stretcher to get to me. "She's got a recent mating bite. Ma'am… is alpha this your mate?"

I managed a wordless nod, tears of pain squeezing from the corners of my eyes.

"Christ, how are you still conscious?" he muttered, low enough that maybe I wasn't supposed to hear it. Then he spoke in a more normal tone. "You should have said something.

Bill, let intake know about this. They'll want her nearby to keep him calm."

"Will do," the other EMT said briskly.

Things got confusing after that. Strong arms helped me out of the ambulance. Orderlies showed up to move Tony's stretcher, but I lost track of him in the press of bodies inside.

I didn't want all these people touching me, but they were helping me stay near Gage. Someone deposited me on an uncomfortable chair in a treatment room. Someone else—probably a nurse—glanced at my hands and the soles of my feet.

"She'll have to wait," she said. "This is a mass casualty event, folks. We're about to get slammed like you've never seen before."

They hooked Gage up to a bunch of beeping and pinging machines. I couldn't see exactly what they were doing with so many people coming and going, but I sure as hell felt it when the unrelenting pain pouring across the mating bond was abruptly snuffed out, leaving echoing nothingness in its wake.

I shot to my feet, aware of the pain of my own injuries in a way I hadn't been before. *"Gage!"*

Hands grasped my shoulders and urged me to sit again. I resisted, trying to look past the body looming in my field of vision and see what was happening.

"Please calm down, ma'am," said the nurse. "Your mate is unconscious, but we're taking good care of him. He had ID in his wallet;

can you please confirm that his name is Gage Huxley?"

I stared at her. I was mated to Gage, and I hadn't even known his last name. Slowly, I nodded.

"Thank you. And does he have medical insurance?" she went on, oblivious to the stillness in my mind where there was supposed to be pain.

"I... don't know?" I rasped. "Probably?" His pack leader was rich... but maybe rich people didn't need to bother with insurance?

She let my shoulders go and picked up a clipboard. "Okay, we'll deal with that later. What's your name, please?"

"Jez," I whispered. But that wasn't right anymore. "I mean... Jess. Jessica."

"Jessica what?"

I couldn't remember the last name Knox had told me. It hadn't seemed real then; it didn't seem real now. Or was I Jessica Knockley already? But that wasn't Gage's last name... or Heath's.

"I... I don't..." I stammered, beginning to panic.

The doctors leaning over Gage backed away, and orderlies started pushing his gurney toward the door.

"Wait!" I cried, trying to push past the nurse and follow them. She grasped me by the shoulders again.

"Jessica!" she said sharply. "Please try to stay calm."

"Let me go!" I yelled, shoving at one of her forearms, then yelped as the pain in my palm flared.

"Ma'am!" Her grip tightened. "You need to calm down! If you try to get physical with me, I *will* have you sedated! We've got enough to deal with already!"

I reared back, my panic overflowing at the idea of being drugged and helpless in this unfamiliar place, with Gage and Tony being taken who-knew-where, to have who-knew-what done to them.

"Dan! Jorge! I need some help over here!" The nurse's voice grew alarmed as I tried to jerk myself free of her hold.

Two large men turned toward us. One of them was an alpha. A whine of fear lodged in my throat.

A protective presence stirred in the back of my brain, someone else's alarm joining my growing terror. Not Gage. *Heath.* I drew in a sharp breath, straightening and leaning toward the door like a dog testing its chain.

A pair of tall figures appeared in the doorway—one limping heavily, both coated head to toe in dust. The smell of cedar and campfire smoke, whiskey and oak tickled my senses.

"*That's our pack's omega,*" Knox called, his voice still hoarse, but pitched to carry across the confusion in the room. "Please step away from her."

The two orderlies hesitated. The nurse's grip on my arms loosened. I took the opportunity to twist free and duck past her. There wasn't a rational thought in my head as I shoved through the crowd of medical personnel and threw myself at the source of fierce protectiveness coiled on the other end of my mate-bond.

Heath caught me with a small *oof* of surprise. He tensed for a moment, then his arms tightened, pressing my face against his battered tuxedo jacket to shield me.

"We've got her," Knox said, still with infuriating calmness. "I'm Matthew Knockley. You may recognize the name from the new wing in the biomedical research center, which I paid for three years ago. We'll need a private room suitable for a pack of five people, and regular updates on the status of Gage Huxley and Anthony Scalise. Aside from that, we'll stay out of your hair."

Everyone in the room went quiet and still.

"Um…" said the nurse who'd tried to restrain me. "Yes, sir. I'll, uh, see what I can do. If you'll follow me to the nurse's station, please?" She eyed Knox warily. "Do you need medical assistance?"

"Not badly enough to take personnel away from the seriously injured," Knox said. "Thank you. Please lead the way."

Heath started to lead me after Knox and the nurse, but at the first step, my injured feet screamed a protest at me. Heath flinched in sympathetic reaction, then promptly scooped me up in his arms and carried me.

I wanted to hate it… to resent this bad-tempered alpha who'd never asked to be mated to me. Instead, I curled into him and pressed my nose to his neck, breathing in the scent of aged oak barrels even though the dust on his clothes made me sneeze.

In a shockingly short time, we were taken to a large room with two futuristic-looking medical beds, a scattering of chairs, and one large, normal bed that looked like something you might find in a hotel room. The harried nurse dropped off a load of first aid supplies and then made a quick exit.

"Get cleaned up, you two," Knox said. "I'm going to get a proper update on Gage and Tony, even if I have to extract it with a pair of pliers."

He limped out again, the door swinging silently shut behind him.

Alone with me, Heath cleared his throat awkwardly. It sounded like he had gravel stuck in there. I could relate.

"There's a bathroom with a shower," he said. "Do you want me to look at your feet first, or…"

I shook my head. He carefully set me down.

"What you did back there in the hotel," he went on. "It was…"

"Reckless?" I offered in a small voice.

"Awe-inspiring," he said. "You saved them, Jez. If not for you, Gage and Tony would be dead."

"I can't feel Gage," I blurted out, my voice breaking on his name. "Like, *at all.*"

Big hands framed my face, the familiar buzz of warmth spreading outward from the contact.

"Sweetheart," he said. "He's your *scent match*. If he were dead, you wouldn't be able to feel anything else except the pain of the broken bond. He's just unconscious. Probably because they anesthetized him for surgery."

I gave a reluctant nod. "Okay." Now that the panic had abated a bit, something else was bothering me, though. "How did you and Knox find me? It's a big hospital."

Heath's green eyes slid away from mine for a moment.

"I couldn't feel where Gage was, like you could," he said. "But it turns out, when I'm not blocking out the bond, I can track *you*."

I thought about that for a few moments. "Is it… because of the scent match? You said earlier that bonds aren't supposed to work like that."

"I think it must be," Heath said, with a helpless shrug. "Right now, let's just be grateful for it, whatever the cause."

I hesitated, then nodded. "Yeah."

He let out a slow breath. "Go wash off the dust. You'll feel better. There are hospital gowns with the first aid stuff. When you're done, I'll bandage your hands and feet."

I poked at the empty blankness where Gage was supposed to be.

"We can both shower. It'll be quicker." The words were out before I could stop them.

I felt Heath's thoughts stumble to an abrupt halt.

"Please," I forged on. "I don't want to be alone."

There was no room for misunderstanding through the mental link. He knew I wasn't talking about sex, or anything like that. I meant exactly what I said—I wasn't sure I could hold onto my sanity if I was left alone with Gage's emptiness. As strange as it felt to even think it, Heath was all I had left right now.

After a beat of complete stillness, a faint shudder went through him.

"All right." He gently took my shoulder and turned me toward the bathroom door. "Come on. Let's be quick. Knox'll be back with news on the others before long."

FOURTY-FOUR

Jez

WHAT HAD CHANGED inside me, these past weeks? What switch had been flipped? Although maybe it was obvious. I was mated now.

I still flinched away and panicked at the prospect of an unfamiliar alpha touching me when I wasn't braced for it, like the orderly in Gage's treatment room. But I'd lasted all of fifteen seconds naked in the shower with Heath before I'd ended up wrapped in his arms again, trembling with reaction.

And the thing was, he was shaking, too. His presence inside me, a sharp light that I'd come to recognize as Heath's unfiltered self, felt as though it might break apart at any moment.

"Are you worried about Tony and Gage?" I asked, because they were all I could think about.

His arms tightened convulsively for a moment. I felt him wrestle his emotions back under control. Instead of answering immediately, he very deliberately loosened his hold, turning me so the shower spray hit more of my body. Nasty, clay-colored muck flowed across the shower floor and down the drain.

"Of course I am," he said. His voice still held that gravelly hoarseness from earlier, but I was less convinced now that it was because of the dust. "I think I'm more worried about myself, though," he added in a mutter.

I turned my head to look at him. "What do you mean?"

An ugly, heavy sense of self-loathing inside my head spiked. I was pretty sure it wasn't coming from me.

Heath hesitated for long enough that I wasn't sure he would answer at all. Then he stepped forward, easing me to one side so he could get his head under the spray. Gray mud sluiced out of his hair and beard, revealing its dark copper color when wet.

He put a hand out and braced it against the plastic shower wall, staying hunched over as he finally spoke.

"If I'd been alone, back at the hotel... if you hadn't been there with me when the bomb went off, Tony and Gage would both be dead. Maybe Knox, too, since he'd have snapped his own spine in half trying to save them."

I frowned, not sure what he was trying to say.

"What kind of packmate does that make me?" he asked.

I still didn't understand where he was going with this.

"One who's not psychic?" I suggested. "You'd never have been able to find them in the debris if I hadn't been mated to Gage. None of them would have wanted you putting yourself at risk like that. Not when there was no chance."

He made a sound that was probably a laugh, although it had a suspiciously choked quality. Straightening, he swept his soaked hair back and scrubbed a hand down his face to clear the water from his eyes.

"That's my point." Once again, he urged me under the spray. This time, he grabbed the shampoo and squirted some into his hands, rubbing them together before digging his lathered fingers into my hair. "At the silos, I'd have done something terrible if you hadn't broken out of your cell and saved me. At the hotel, I'd have stood around like a useless piece of shit while my packmates were crushed to death, if you hadn't been there and physically dragged me back inside to save them."

The gentle scratch of his fingertips along my scalp sent tingles rushing down my body, making it hard to think. This was important, though. I grabbed his wrists, bringing his hands down to curl between us.

"In the silos, I *had* to get to you," I told him. "It wasn't a conscious choice. I just knew that it didn't matter what was standing in my way. I had to climb over it or dig under it or smash through it, because it was stopping me from being where I needed to be. It was the same with Gage in the hotel. I didn't *choose* to drag us back into danger. I needed to be with him, and it didn't matter what was separating us."

Heath's head bowed again, over our joined hands.

"We can choose now, though," he said, not looking at me. "I ought to hate you for what you did to Knox. You ought to hate *me* for holding you prisoner in the attic... for biting you without your consent. But... *Jez*. You being here makes me a better person than I would be otherwise. We could choose... to be better together."

My heart stuttered, because this was something more than tolerating an unwanted mate-bond so that I wouldn't have to get my mating gland removed. Just like Heath had said, *this*... was a *choice*.

I swallowed, even though it felt like gargling broken glass.

"I think... I'd like that," I managed. "If you would."

He drew breath, but we were interrupted by sounds coming from the hospital room outside.

"*Heath? Jez?*" Knox's muffled voice filtered past the closed door and the sound of running water.

"We're cleaning up! Out in a minute!" Heath called back, color rising to his cheeks above his beard. The flush of pink highlighted the scars on his face and neck where he'd clawed his own skin to shreds while he was in rut, in an attempt to maintain control.

He briskly soaped himself, avoiding my eyes.

"Rinse your hair," he muttered.

We emerged wearing our underwear, covered up with stupid-looking hospital gowns. Mine was too big for me; Heath's was too small for him.

Despite feeling ridiculous, I couldn't help a twinge of sympathy for Knox—still limping and covered in dust. If he had opinions about coming back to the room to find us in the shower together, he kept them to himself. I suspected Heath and I were equally thankful for that fact.

"Did you get any news on the others?" Heath asked, once more vibrating with tension.

Knox looked longingly at one of the chairs. Seeming to realize that if he sat down in it, he'd make the chair as filthy as he was, he sighed heavily and remained standing. "Gage is in surgery for several broken bones. Tony has a mild concussion, but he's surprisingly not in bad shape, all things considered. They should be bringing him up here to join us before long."

Heath sagged with relief in response to the news about Tony. The way it transmitted through the bond made me feel lightheaded.

"Will Gage be okay?" I asked.

"His prognosis is guarded, but positive," Knox said. At my blank look, he added, "In other words, he's badly hurt, but they think he'll recover."

I closed my eyes.

Alive. They're both alive. Focus on that.

"Is there anything else we have to know right now?" Heath asked. "Because if not, you need to take a shower and sit down for a bit."

Knox shook his head tiredly. "That's all for now. We'll all have plenty to talk about later, though."

His tone went hard on the last sentence, and I shivered. Even now, it was hard to remember that the granite in his voice probably wasn't because of me.

"Paolo?" Heath said.

I looked at him sharply.

"Sorry," he went on, addressing me directly. "There's too much going on; I didn't think to tell you. After you left, Knox and I pulled Paolo free of the rubble. We kept him from bleeding to death until the medics got to him."

"It's just possible he's learned a valuable life lesson about how much value he holds in Lorenzo Vozzina's eyes," Knox added. "Which is to say, *none*."

I put two and two together. "You believe Vozzina planted the bomb, and he made sure Adrian — *Paolo* — was going to be right there at ground zero when it went off. You think Paolo will be pissed off enough to rat him out?"

If so, this was *huge*. Game-changing, even. As much as I hated the idea of having any further contact with the omega who'd lied to me and betrayed me, he was one of the few people who might be in a position to bring the Vozzina pack down for good.

"We'll see," was all Knox would say.

After that, he disappeared into the bathroom, giving in to the lure of the shower. The sound of running water followed a minute later. Heath and I waited in awkward silence, both of us too tightly strung to rest as we waited for whatever happened next.

The first person to show up at our hospital room wasn't Tony, but rather Knox's driver.

"Bud," Heath greeted, meeting him at the door.

I hung back, feeling uncomfortable in my shapeless hospital smock in front of a man I barely knew.

"Heath," Bud said, sounding harried. "I got a call from the boss saying to bring clothes and toiletries. Was anyone badly hurt?"

Heath quickly filled him in on what we knew about the others, before taking the bags he was holding and thanking him. "We appreciate the quick turnaround. I don't know about the others, but I really don't think hospital chic suits me. What's the news coverage look like so far?"

"Yeah, you're right. It really doesn't suit you," Bud agreed, sneaking a look downward at the comically short hospital gown. "Law enforcement is playing things close to their chest so far, but the FBI is involved. They're reporting it as an explosion of unknown origin, last I heard."

"Right," Heath replied dryly. "Because the roof blowing off like that could've been *anything*. Happens all the time."

Bud shrugged. "It's early days yet. Give 'em time. I'll check in a bit later in case you need food that doesn't come from a hospital cafeteria." He turned, only to pause. "Oh, look! It's the kid. Hello, Tony."

I rushed forward to peer out the door past Heath, my discomfort forgotten. Sure enough, a nurse was wheeling Tony toward us in a wheelchair.

Bud stood aside and patted Tony on the shoulder as he rolled past. "Guess I'll leave you folks to it. Tell the boss there's been no word yet about which hospital that little asshole Paolo ended up at."

"Right..." Heath said absently. "I'll tell him."

All his attention was on Tony, who looked pale and exhausted. Then again, didn't we all?

"You're both okay," Tony said with relief. "Thank god. They wouldn't tell me anything."

"Gage is in surgery for broken bones," I told him. "Knox is in the shower. We were so scared for you, Tony."

My voice wobbled, and I swallowed hard against tears.

"Here, Mr. Scalise. Let's get you settled in," the nurse said briskly, wheeling Tony over to the large bed at the center of the room. He cast a glance at Heath. "He should be fine with plenty of rest and some time to heal. We're short-staffed tonight, as you might imagine, but someone will be by to talk to all of you in a few hours. In the meantime, just keep an eye on him and make sure he doesn't become unresponsive. Otherwise, let him sleep. He needs it."

I hugged myself as Heath and the nurse got Tony settled on the bed. My hands and feet still throbbed unhappily, even after Heath had covered the worst of the scrapes with bandages while we were in the bathroom.

The moment the nurse left, so did the last shreds of my self-control. Not sure where the impulse had come from, I climbed onto the bed and wrapped my body around Tony, holding him close. He caught his breath, going still with surprise.

I knew I was supposed to ask him first if this was okay, but all I could do was cling. After a moment, Heath's weight dipped the mattress on Tony's other side. His long arm snaked around both of us, and Tony's tension broke. He relaxed between us with a small noise, like a whimper of surrender.

"She's right, you know," Heath murmured. "We were so worried."

"Gage saved my life," Tony said in a tiny voice.

"And Jez saved his," Heath said. "I've got you, Tony. Both of you. It's going to be all right."

I curled into them, Tony's steady heartbeat thudding against one ear, and the muted sound of the shower running in the other.

FORTY-FIVE

Knox

THE HOT STING of the hospital shower made me feel slightly less like a fugitive statue from Medusa's cave of petrified Greek warriors, and more like a functioning human being. Gray dust turned a muddy brown as it circled down the drain, but it still felt like I had a pound of that shit grinding against my eyeballs. I tilted my face into the spray, trying to rinse as much as possible from my lashes and eyelids without accidentally doing more damage by scrubbing at them.

Something inside my right knee was fucked up, and I was running on fumes. For the first time in years, I found myself second-guessing the life I'd chosen to lead. It was one thing to crash my own ship against the jagged rocks. But these days, I'd started dragging people I cared about along with me.

In a couple of months, it would be the twentieth anniversary of the day my twelve-year-old sister Maria had been kidnapped from her after-school soccer practice. It wasn't the kind of anniversary anyone wanted to celebrate.

My twin and I hadn't fit the stereotype of being close; not at that age, anyway. If anything, we'd kind of hated each other. Sibling rivalry at its finest.

"Stop calling them twins," my alpha father would always tell my beta mother. *"They're just littermates."*

And every single time, she'd reply, *"They came out of my uterus thirty minutes apart, George, and I'm not built to squeeze out five babies at a time like an omega. They'll always be the twins to me."*

In the end, 'always' had ended up being twelve years, nine months, and two days. First, my sister was taken, disappearing into the black hole that was the shadowy world of omega child trafficking. My mother only made it six months after that before she took her own life.

I'd been too young to fully understand that Mom's tendency toward sadness and apathy for most of my childhood had been undiagnosed clinical depression. I also hadn't understood until much later that my sister didn't simply vanish from existence one day. She'd been dragged into the depths of hell, and she'd suffered there for who-knew-how-long.

By contrast, my mother possessed an adult's understanding of what had happened, paired with a parent's irreconcilable guilt over what she saw as her own failure to protect her daughter from the world's monsters. She had eventually decided that overdosing on pills was preferable to suffering that unrelenting pain day after day.

My father limped along for another thirteen years before dying of cancer, but he'd been a shell of a human being for most of that. I took over much of the running of his business at a ridiculously young age—behind the scenes, at least.

Very little of the wealth I enjoyed today was because of anything I'd built myself. I was just competent enough at doing the work my father had started that I didn't lose his fortune, once it fell into my lap at the ripe old age of twenty-six.

Trying to help trafficked omegas behind the scenes was my attempt to fill the hole in my past where my family should have been. And now, here I was, watching the new family I'd built nearly lose their lives because of it.

I leaned back against the shower wall, feeling a bruise on my shoulder twinge as I gently thumped my head against the cheap plastic enclosure.

"What the fuck are you even *doing*, Knockley?" I growled at myself.

There was no time for this kind of self-indulgence, though. God alone knew why, but there were people outside who'd placed their futures in my hands, and it was up to me to make sure they didn't end up in the same kind of mess as my birth family.

Somehow, leading a small bachelor group of alphas had felt completely different than being the head of a mated pack with a scent-matched omega and a vulnerable beta tossed into the mix. It also said a lot about the current situation that Jez's attempt on my life had become a mere blip on my radar at this point.

I'd been surprised to find her in the shower with Heath, but not massively shocked by it. Heath had always been intensely loyal to me… probably more loyal than he should be. However, from what I was able to gather, Jez had basically saved our lives back at the hotel. If Heath decided that the scales were balanced now, maybe he had a point.

I reserved the right to hold a grudge against the caramel-coffee scented omega who'd nearly put me in a matching grave next to my mother and father's. But the equation started to look quite a bit different after she'd saved Gage and Tony, especially at the risk of her own life.

Giving my face a final scrub, I turned off the shower, dried myself with aching arms, and gingerly limped over to the vanity. The mirror was fogged over, and that was probably just as well. Bud was on his way to bring replacement clothing to the hospital, but for now I followed Heath's lead and wrapped a cotton hospital gown over my underwear.

At least I hadn't pissed or shit myself while I'd been trying to keep a massive concrete slab from crushing the others. That was something, anyway.

When I opened the door, it was to find Heath wrapped around Tony and Jez on the room's large bed. Bags of clothes sat abandoned on the floor nearby. I'd been so out of it that managed to completely miss the sound of people coming and going.

Heath turned to look over his shoulder as I closed the bathroom door behind me. He looked as tired and drawn as I felt.

"How is he?" I asked quietly, tilting my chin toward Tony. Both he and Jez appeared to be fast asleep, and I couldn't help an irrational twinge of jealousy at Heath's intimate position with them.

"Concussion, just like you said," Heath reported, his voice equally low. "They told me it's okay to let him sleep. Bud brought us some stuff. He says to tell you he hasn't been able to find out where they took Paolo. No new word on Gage yet."

I nodded to show I'd heard him, and debated if my battered back could cope with resting in the chair again.

"You've gotta sleep too, Knox," Heath went on. "You're dead on your feet."

There were a hundred things that needed doing. Unfortunately, I was self-aware enough to know that if I tried to do any of them right now, I'd either pass out or screw something up without realizing it. I eyed the two medical beds, struck by a kind of gut-level revulsion at the idea of crawling into one after having spent the better part of a week in an identical bed, elsewhere in this very same hospital.

Heath followed my gaze. "Just lie down here. It's not like we're short on room, and I'm ninety-nine-point-nine-nine percent sure she's not interested in killing us anymore."

I sighed. I was ninety-nine-point-nine-nine percent sure he was right, but I still hesitated. This was one of the handful of pack-friendly rooms in the hospital's patient wing, designed specifically for things like supervised, medically risky heats and pack births. The bed had an Alaskan King-sized mattress, and two small people with an average-sized alpha wrapped around them didn't even take up half of it.

It was the scent that finally got me. They'd showered, but already, a hint of sweet coffee laced with aged whiskey had begun to permeate the room. That, along with the sight of an omega with her back exposed when the pack was in danger, tipped the scales. Heath had his arm stretched around both Tony and Jez, but that unguarded back ate at me.

Goddamn it, I thought, and stiffly eased myself into the space between Jez and the edge of the bed.

My bruises and strains throbbed with a deep ache in time with my heartbeat, but I didn't want to shift around for a more comfortable position and wake the pair of sleepers. I'd give myself half an hour to get a second wind. After that, I needed to badger the nurses for an update on Gage, and check in with Bud to see if he'd been able to track down Paolo's location yet.

In the meantime, I really needed to come up with a better plan when it came to the Paolo situation. By the time I found out what hospital he'd been taken to, Lorenzo Vozzina would already know. The question was, how far would the man go to get rid of his unwanted trophy omega?

If I was going to get Paolo to testify against his pack, I needed to keep him safe. But I couldn't keep him safe when I didn't know where the hell he *was*. My mind spun in useless circles, rehashing the same facts over and over while getting nowhere.

It occurred to me that I should open my eyes and check the time, because it had probably been half an hour by now. Unhelpfully, my eyes chose not to cooperate.

Just five more minutes, I promised myself. *Five more minutes won't hurt.*

Daylight was streaming in through the window when a small form next to me jolted upright with a loud gasp, dragging me abruptly from deep sleep.

"Gage!" Jez squeaked, her hand hitting my shoulder as she flailed.

A sickening feeling of dread dragged at me, even as Tony stirred, and Heath bolted upright on the other side of the bed. Jez and Gage were mated. If the bond had roused her from sleep, that might mean that he was—

"He's awake," Heath said, reaching out a hand to clasp Jez's shoulder, steadying her. "I'm only getting this secondhand, but it feels like he's coming out from under the anesthetic."

FORTY-SIX

Jez

IT WAS ALL I could do to follow Knox's raspy command to get dressed. Gage's emotions flailed in my mind like a newly blinded person trapped in an unfamiliar room, and I *needed to get to him*.

Confusion. Anxiety. Pain. Maybe if I had more experience controlling the bond, I would've been able to send him calming thoughts. As it was, he was probably getting my own frantic worry mirrored back at him.

"He's right." Heath's hand was a grounding weight on the back of my neck. "Stop for a second. Breathe. Someone will probably be here in a few minutes to take you to him, and there's no point in walking the hallways with your ass hanging out of a hospital gown if you don't have to."

Knox still looked like he'd been run over by a truck, but he blearily pawed through the bags the driver had brought. A moment later, he handed over a T-shirt, track pants, and a pair of sneakers in my size.

I rushed into the bathroom to change, pulling the hospital gown over my head to save time. The scrapes on my hands felt more tender this morning than they had last night, and I felt a fresh burst of protective worry through the bond as the nagging pain flared.

Worry about yourself, I tried to send to Gage, even though the bond didn't work like that. *I'm fine. I'm coming just as soon as I can.*

Maybe something about that second part got through, because the tension in the back of my head waned slightly. I pulled clothing over yesterday's underwear, jammed my feet into the sneakers, and tied the laces hastily.

When I burst out of the bathroom, it was to find Heath shrugging into a white polo. I blinked as the soft material slid down over pale skin stretched across sleek muscle and peppered with bruises.

In the corner, Knox had been slower to get changed. He was still bare-chested, holding a shirt in his hands. I might've seen the man convulsing on a bed as his heart gave out, but I'd never seen him bare above the waist before.

He gave an awkward cough and turned his bruised back to the room when he noticed me looking. Helplessly, I met Tony's wide eyes, and we shared a moment of overwhelmed solidarity in the face of exposed alpha muscles.

It was broken by a rapid knock at the door. I tore myself away from the vision of hot alpha pecs and jogged over to open it.

The nurse standing on the other side looked like she'd seen some shit. She also looked like she'd been on her feet for at least twenty-four hours straight. Still, she was brisk and professional as she took in my appearance and cleared her throat.

"Good morning. You are Gage Huxley's mate, yes? He's showing signs of emerging from sedation, and it would be best if you were there when he wakes up properly."

"He's already waking up," I said blankly.

"I'll take you to him right now. Come with me," the nurse replied.

"We'll both go." Heath appeared behind me, his scent enveloping me like a reassuring cloud. "I'm Gage's co-mate."

Something shivered down my spine at the no-nonsense way he said it, like it was an immutable fact of life.

"Of course," said the nurse. "This way, please."

———◆———

The woozy presence through the bond went intermittently still and quiet between bouts of almost violent worry. I kept trying to send reassurance past my own fears—*I'm coming, I'm coming… hold on, I'm coming.*

Heath took my hand as we power-walked along endless hallways. The sudden physical contact startled me, but almost instantly, some of the tension began to drain from my shoulders.

"Can you update us on his condition?" Heath asked, not slowing down.

"It would be best for one of the doctors to give you the details," the nurse told him. "But he underwent surgery promptly, and he's obviously a strong and healthy alpha."

I didn't like the sound of that. Before last night, my only experience of hospitals had been that people on the streets who got shot, or beaten, or starved, or sick, tended to disappear in ambulances and either not come back at all, or else they came back in pretty much the same condition as before, only with more bandages.

Heath squeezed my hand. "We'd like to speak to his doctor as soon as possible, in that case," he said.

The nurse nodded tightly. "As you're aware, things have been crazy overnight. I'll pass that on for you, though."

We crowded into an elevator containing two orderlies and an unconscious woman on a gurney, squeezing to one side in an attempt to stay out of the way. When the doors dinged open, we entered an area with a lot more activity than the quiet wing with the pack room. People in masks and scrubs jogged down the corridor, while others rushed around with clipboards.

The harsh lights and overlapping, hard-edged voices scraped against my overstretched omega nerves like sandpaper. My fingers tightened convulsively around Heath's. I felt him puff up next to me, easing a half-step sideways to tuck me behind his shoulder.

"He's in post-op right now," the nurse said. "It's just around the corner, and things are a bit quieter there—I promise."

I let Heath lead me after her, poking hesitantly at this strange feeling of someone else looking out for me. It wasn't a grand gesture. Heath wasn't stepping in front of a bullet for me, or rescuing me from the edge of a cliff.

My anxiety had spiked because of bright lights and loud talking and stressed people hurrying around me. It was stupid. Irrational. Heath would have been completely justified in snapping at me to hurry up and stop acting like a baby. But instead, he'd taken my hand and moved me behind him, sending reassurance through the bond like a warm fire on a freezing night. Just because I was an omega, and he was an alpha.

Because he was… *my* alpha.

I nearly stumbled over my own feet as the idea settled into place. We'd talked about choosing to be better, *together*. And this moment… *this very moment* was what that looked like, in reality.

Heath glanced over his shoulder at me, looking equally startled. As though it hadn't even occurred to him that his actions might be a big deal.

It was a big deal *to me*.

I stared at him, only to gasp when Gage's consciousness resurfaced, near panic.

"Here we are." The nurse pressed a pad, and a pair of double doors swung open. The area beyond was separated into a dozen alcoves with hanging gray curtains, but as promised, it was much quieter here. The lights were dimmer, too.

Letting go of Heath's hand, I darted forward, following the tug toward Gage. He hurried after me, both of us ignoring the nurse's startled, "Wait!"

I skidded to a stop at the second alcove from the end and shoved past the curtain blocking my way. Heath was right behind me.

"Gage!" I rushed to the side of the hospital bed, where Gage lay twitching, a heavy frown wrinkling his brows.

"Jesus," Heath breathed, coming to stand at my shoulder.

Gage's left leg was encased in a cast from his hip to the ball of his foot, only his toes visible at the bottom. He wore a neck brace, like a car accident victim. A weird set of straps criss-crossed his shoulders, like the straps of a backpack, but there was no pack. A square patch had been taped over the right side of his ribcage.

He moaned, and I lunged forward to take his hand in mine.

The nurse came puffing in, out of breath. "Please keep him as calm as you can, and don't let him dislodge the cool pack on his ribs. He should wake more easily now that you're here, but don't be alarmed if he seems confused at first. I'll see if I can get the doctor in here for you."

"Thank you," Heath told her—which was just as well, since I couldn't look away from the dark circles under Gage's flickering eyes.

"Gage," I said again, mournfully. I'd known he was badly hurt, but seeing him like this was somehow worse.

Another pained groan forced its way past his lips. His fingers twitched hard against mine.

"That's it," I told him. "C'mon. Wake up for us, please? We're here. Everything's okay."

Everything was *so* not okay. And that fact was probably coming through the bond, loud and clear.

"Where—?" Gage rasped, his hazel eyes blinking open. He stared at the ceiling, his gaze unfocused.

"You're in the hospital," Heath said. "You're pretty beat up, but the doctor should be here soon to give us more details."

Gage's eyes widened in alarm. He sucked in a sharp breath, and secondhand pain flared through the bond. "Hotel," he gasped. "*Tony.* Is… is he—?"

I squeezed his hand hard. "He's all right. He will be, anyway."

"You saved him," Heath added, in a quiet voice. "You saved Tony's life, Gage."

FORTY-SEVEN

Gage

MY HEAD FELT all kinds of fucked up, like I'd taken bad drugs and wrapped my car around a utility pole. But it sounded like Jez had just said Tony was okay… and also like Heath was near tears.

I tried not to think about the way parts of my body weren't working right, and other parts felt numb. One thing at a time.

"Say that again?" I asked—not sure why my voice sounded so weak and out of breath.

The small hand clasping mine gave another squeeze. "You saved Tony. Part of a building fell on you both, but you're going to be okay." Jez said. "Knox, too."

The jittery fear that had been coming through the bond was beginning to ease a bit, and that, more than anything else, made me believe that maybe everything really was going to be all right. Then, the sense of what she'd just said penetrated through the layers of fuzz surrounding my brain.

"Th' what did *what*?" I slurred.

The details of whatever had happened at the hotel were still swimming in and out of focus, bits of memory darting to the surface like shiny silver fish, only to sink back into the depths a moment later.

Heath still sounded shaky when he took up the tale. "We think someone set off a bomb on the roof while Jez and I were outside. The ceiling over the banquet area came down on top of the guests. We found you protecting Tony with your body, while Knox was holding up one end of a concrete slab that would have crushed you both."

That was a lot of words all at once, but it made sense with the bits and pieces I remembered before everything went black. I'd have to remember to buy Knox a nice bottle of whiskey at some point.

"And by '*someone*,' you mean…" I began.

"Probably Lorenzo Vozzina," Jez said grimly. "No proof, though."

"Last we heard, the authorities weren't even calling it a bomb yet," Heath added.

"Oh." I frowned as a new silvery fish swam to the surface. "Hang on a minute. Wasn't what's-his-ass there? You know, the omega shit-stain?"

"Paolo," Heath said. "And yes."

"Heath and Knox pulled him out of the rubble," Jez went on. "Knox thinks he might turn on the Vozzinas if he believes his mate tried to blow him up for funsies."

Holy shit. That was cold, even for Lorenzo.

"Oh," I said again—because stringing words together was getting harder, and the weird feedback from my body seemed to be getting worse.

Worry started to creep through the bond again.

"How are you feeling?" Jez asked. "I mean, sorry… that's kind of a stupid question. And I probably should have asked right away—"

"It's not a stupid question," Heath said. "Gage, we can feel that you're still fuzzy from the anesthetic. Do you need painkillers?"

"Think they musta gave me some already," I managed. "Wha's wrong with me, 'zactly?"

"We're still waiting on a doctor to give us details," Heath said. "But from the look of things, a broken leg, something with your ribs, and something with your neck."

"Collarbone, too," Jez added unhappily. "It's all swollen, and I think that's what the shoulder straps are for."

"Fuck," I said. "Tha's a lot of different stuff."

At which point, staying awake suddenly felt like extra work that I wasn't prepared to put in right now. As long as the others were mostly okay, a nap sounded like just the thing. My heavy eyelids fell closed, and I settled into the steady, reassuring hum of the bond.

"Might sleep for a bit, 'kay?" I muttered, and gave up the fight to pay attention to my surroundings.

———◆———

When the annoying sound of beeping machines woke me sometime later, the first thing I noticed was that Jez felt further away. The second thing I noticed was that whatever drugs had been making my body feel numb and distant before were wearing off… and that broken bones *fucking hurt.*

"Ow, *fuuuck*," I groaned, discovering pretty quickly that groaning aloud made several things in my chest grind together unpleasantly.

"Easy there." The hand that landed on my forearm was larger and callused, rather than small and delicate. I blinked open bleary eyes to see Heath leaning over me. "Try not to move more than you have to."

"Kay," I said.

Heath let go of me long enough to drag a nearby chair up to my bedside and sink down in it.

"The doctor finally showed up. Turns out, you're rocking a simple fracture of the femur, three broken ribs, and a broken collarbone. They were worried about a spinal fracture in your neck, but it turned out to just be whip-lash."

I thought about that for several moments.

"That sucks," I decided.

"It's not great," Heath agreed grimly. "Be glad you're an alpha. A beta would be laid up for six months. Even for you, you're looking at six to eight weeks until that leg is back to one hundred percent."

Jesus. Six to eight weeks? I got fidgety when I had to sit still for twenty goddamned *minutes.*

"Where's Jez?" I asked, rather than think too closely about it. I could feel the direction she was in, like there was a thread tied to both of us, tugging me toward her. But since I clearly wasn't getting out of this blasted hospital bed to follow it, I figured it was easier to ask.

"She went back to let the others know what the doctor said." He hesitated. "Knox scored us a pack-friendly room by waving his big dick around. Tony has a mild concussion, and Knox is pretty battered, although I don't think any of it is too serious. Hopefully they'll move you up there with us soon."

I started to nod… and rethought the movement just in time. "Yeah. Could use some of those painkillers right about now, if they're still on offer."

Heath reached over and pressed a button I hadn't noticed before, mostly because my head was stuck in some kind of weird BDSM dungeon contraption that kept it from turning to the side.

"The nurse should be here in a few minutes," he said. "Things are still pretty insane, but not as bad as last night."

"Any news about the explosion?" I asked, reassured that I at least remembered what he and Jez had told me about it before.

"Yeah, the news outlets are admitting it was a bomb now." He huffed out a breath. "Not that there was much question. The place is swarming with police and FBI, but I don't expect Vozzina will have left anything behind that ties it to him."

"Assuming it really *was* him," I said, and winced when my ribs reminded me how little they liked breathing right now.

Heath shrugged a shoulder. "Helluva coincidence that he was too '*sick*' to be there, while all the people he'd love to get rid of were conveniently gathered in one place, right around the stage."

I tried to wrap my brain around the idea of an alpha trying to murder the omega he'd mated. It made me feel nauseated in addition to feeling broken.

"Can't believe he'd do that to Paolo," I wheezed. "'S fucked up."

"Yeah." Heath sounded sour. "Much less fucked up for your scent match to try and kill you *first*, and for the mating to come afterward."

I peered at him, because the tone didn't match what was coming through the bond. "You and Jez still at each other's throats?"

He shook his head and rested his elbows on the edge of the mattress. "No. No… we're actually not. We had a talk. A couple of talks. Which doesn't totally cancel out the fucked-uppedness of the situation. But… I think we're good. Still not sure about Knox, though."

That was fair. Jez had tried pretty hard to kill both Heath and me when we'd been holding her prisoner in the attic, but not in the same cold-blooded way she'd almost killed Knox. It was a lot to get past, on both sides.

"Glad you're working it out," I told him. "Is Tony okay with it, d'you think?"

Betas could be tricky. Relationships looked different for them. I sometimes wondered what it would've been like, back in ancient history when alphas, betas, and omegas were all kind of jumbled up together… before everything got so segregated.

Heath scrubbed both hands down his face. "I don't know. But I think… maybe? It's complicated, but they were friends before." His gaze met mine and held. "I didn't say this like I should have, earlier. What you did for him… he'd be dead if you hadn't protected him. I can't ever pay you back for that, Gage."

A thin thread of surprise pierced through the pain. Heath didn't say things like that. Not with those big, wet, red-rimmed green eyes pinning mine, and without so much as a flicker of sarcasm anywhere to be seen.

I made myself smile up at him, hoping it didn't look too much like a grimace of discomfort. "Don't need to pay me back, idiot. We're pack. Besides, he's adorable. Think I might be in with a chance, if I play my cards right?"

It probably would have been more effective if I didn't sound like a wheezing old man, but Heath let out a little amused huff anyway.

"You'd have to ask him yourself," he said. "Just as long as he doesn't get a taste of you and suddenly realize what a bitter old asshole I am.

I swear to god, you're too fucking good for this world sometimes."

"I'll make it clear we're a package deal," I promised. "And only if Jez is okay with it, obviously."

"Fair." Heath paused, sobering. "I'm starting to worry about how Knox fits in with all this. You know what I mean?"

I snorted, and immediately regretted it.

"I'm more worried about people trying to blow us up, to be honest." He had a point, though. "But… yeah. Guess we're going to need a few more pack meetings, huh."

FORTY-EIGHT

Tony

AFTER JEZ AND HEATH went to be with Gage, I was left alone with Knox in the huge hospital room. I'd never really felt awkward or tongue-tied in his presence before, but I'd also never watched him change clothes right in front of me.

Down, boy.

Maybe a concussion lowered your inhibitions or something? At least, that was going to be my excuse until someone with a white coat and a stethoscope told me differently.

Knox seemed oblivious to my discomfort as he sat down in one of the chairs across from the bed. He flinched as he settled back, and I couldn't help wondering if he was hiding more injuries than whatever was making him limp around on his right leg.

"How much did the others tell you about what happened, when I was in the shower last night?" he asked.

Do not picture Knox in the shower.

Do not picture Knox in the shower.

Do not picture Knox in the shower.

"I know Gage saved me when the roof came down," I said. "There was an explosion, right? I didn't imagine that part?"

Knox nodded. "A bomb, yes. Probably Lorenzo Vozzina's work, although that's just a theory so far."

I wavered between being shocked, and being decidedly *not* shocked. Then something else occurred to me. "Hang on. When they were wheeling me in here last night, Bud was here. He said something about Paolo being hurt? But… if Vozzina was behind the bomb… wouldn't that mean—"

"That he saw a way to kill multiple unrelated birds with one stone? Yeah, it would." Knox's normally affable expression settled into hard lines, and I couldn't help a little shiver of reaction.

"Wow," I said inadequately. "That's *cold*."

I wasn't sure there were any circumstances that could make me feel sorry for Paolo, after everything he'd done. It was still chilling to think about it, though.

"The Paolo situation is sitting right at the top of my to-do list." Knox's tone was as stony as his features. Then his face softened slightly as he met my eyes. "Well, *almost* at the top, anyway. Tony, I'd like you to stay with the pack, once they release you from observation. I'm not comfortable with you being alone in a low-security apartment."

My thoughts stuttered like a needle jumping tracks on an old vinyl record. "You want me to stay in the pack house?"

"We're not going back to that house," Knox said, confusing me even further. "I have other properties. Aside from not wanting to be in the place where Lorenzo Vozzina will expect us to be, I also have no intention of asking Jez to live in the same house where she was held prisoner. She's mated to my packmates, and it looks more and more as though that won't be changing anytime soon. She doesn't deserve a constant reminder of how things started out."

Yeah… this conversation probably would have been easier without the concussion.

"Okay," I said. "Sorry. This is kind of a lot to take in."

Knox's half-smile was grim. "I know. No need to apologize. And no one's going to force you to pack a bag and come with us—but I hope you will. If for no other reason than the fact that Heath is going to be a basket case if he has to worry about both you and Jez at the same time."

Something about that idea made warmth bloom in my stomach. "You think so?"

I tried to make the words sound skeptical, but I was pretty sure they just sounded hopeful.

"I don't think. I *know*," he shot back. "Look, you don't need to answer right away…"

"I'll come with you," I said, too quickly. Because, *sure*? Why not upend my entire life for a relationship that was barely a few weeks old?

"Good," Knox replied. "I'll arrange movers to transfer anything you'd like to bring from your apartment."

Wasn't it supposed to be lesbians who kept U-Haul on speed dial?

"If you're sure," I said. Then, partly to change the subject, and partly because I was genuinely curious, I blurted, "Isn't it weird for you, having Jez mated to the others? After, you know…" I gestured in a rapid circular motion with one hand. "… *everything*."

Knox gave that a moment's thought.

"I suppose it should be." He rubbed his knuckles over his jaw, where black stubble was beginning to darken his skin. "But… the others may not have mentioned the fact that while it was Gage who saved you when the bomb went off, Jez was the one to save all of us in the end. She can sense Gage's location through the bond—maybe because she's his scent match. She can probably sense Heath's location as well… but the point is, she and Heath ran back into the collapsing building to get to him, and rescued you before the slab of concrete hanging over both of you fell."

I shivered, trying not to picture it.

Another of those grim not-smiles flickered over Knox's face. "And, all that aside, I kind of like her. As a person, I mean—now that I've seen the parts of herself that she tries to keep hidden." A sigh gusted out of him. "Which is probably fodder for six months of therapy, at a minimum."

"It's better than hating her, surely?" I suggested.

"I suppose it is, yes." He lifted an eyebrow, the barest hint of a twinkle entering his dark eyes. "And don't call me Shirley."

That startled a laugh out of me, which I immediately regretted when my skull throbbed. "Holy crap. You've seen that movie?"

"Tony, *everyone* has seen that movie." He ran a critical gaze over me. "Now get some rest."

Still hiding a smile, I settled down on the soft mattress and rearranged the blankets around me. I was starting to think that a person could get used to having an overprotective alpha guarding them while they slept.

The sound of the door opening woke me from a dream about going for ice cream with the pack, and not being able to read any of the labels showing the different flavors. I craned around, my bleary gaze settling on Jez. She closed the door gently behind her.

"Everything all right?" Knox asked.

"How's Gage?" I added.

"The doctor finally showed up with a report," she said, crossing to one of the room's other chairs and dropping into it. "He's asleep right now. They say he has a fractured femur, three broken ribs, a broken collarbone, and whiplash."

Knox's face got that hard-edged look again. I decided I wouldn't want to be in Lorenzo Vozzina's shoes anytime soon.

"Thank you for letting us know, Jez," he said. "I assume Heath is staying with him?"

"Yes," Jez said. "The doctor said he'd probably be out for a while, with all the painkillers and the anesthesia. Heath sent me back here to rest." Her tone turned dry on the last sentence.

"And so you should," Knox told her firmly. "You'll be able to tell if Gage wakes up and needs anything, whether you're in the room with him or not. How are your hands and feet doing?"

Jez instinctively stuck her bandaged hands beneath her arms, as though hiding them. "Fine. What about you? Are you going to let a doctor look at you?"

I frowned and sat up abruptly, ignoring the way it made my head pound. "*What*? You haven't been seen by a doctor yet? What the *hell*, Knox?"

"There's nothing serious enough to warrant taking doctors away from the other victims," Knox said. "I'll get my knee looked at eventually, but I'm already the rich alpha who demanded high-end pack accommodations during the middle of a mass casualty event. I don't intend to also be the rich alpha who dragged a doctor away from emergency surgery to look at a twisted knee and some bruises."

Jez glared at him. "You singlehandedly held up a huge concrete slab for how long? I'm surprised you didn't break your goddamned *back*."

Knox shot her a wan smile. "Nice to know you care."

"Of course I care!" Jez flared—but I was too busy making mental connections.

"Wait," I said. "You told me there was a concrete slab about to fall on me and Gage!"

Jez scoffed. "*About* to fall? It *did* fall. That was probably what snapped Gage's leg. We found Knox using a broken table as a lever to keep the other end from dropping and crushing you both! Or did he forget to mention that part?"

My eyes flew back to Knox.

"Of course I did what I could," he said evenly. "It's my duty to keep all of you safe, Tony. I didn't do a very good job of it yesterday, but thanks to Jez and Heath showing up when they did, everyone's still alive. I intend to do better in the future."

I stared at him so hard that my eyes began to burn. Except... fuck. *Fuck.* Those were tears. I was going to break down crying in front of the guy who'd been my boss for the last year-and-change. And who was now my, what? My pack leader?

I pressed my lips together in a hard line.

Jez sighed and flopped down next to me on the bed. "It's okay, Tony. From what I can tell, that's just how these guys are. I swear, it's like something out of those romantic movies you used to drag me to."

"I don't think anyone's ever cast me in the role of leading man before," Knox said dryly. "Thanks, I think."

Fortunately for my self-esteem, Knox's phone rang before I could genuinely start bawling.

He dragged it out of his pocket and answered. "Yes?"

I couldn't make out the voice on the other end, but his expression sharpened like a junkyard dog that had just been offered a bone.

"Is that so?" he said. "I'm glad to hear it. Did you send the flowers?"

More indistinct speech.

"Perfect," Knox replied. "Thank you for the update, Bud."

He disconnected the call.

"Was that about Paolo?" Jez asked.

"It was," Knox said with satisfaction.

"You're sending Paolo… *flowers*?" I asked, my burning eyes forgotten in the face of my bewilderment.

"A bouquet with a note attached," Knox explained. "A note with a reminder about the phone number that Paolo might consider calling, if he doesn't want his trophy mate to have a second chance at making him disappear."

Jez's gray eyes narrowed. "And that phone number belongs to…"

The phone in Knox's hand rang again, and a slow smile crossed the alpha's face as he tapped the answer icon.

FORTY-NINE

Jez

IT WAS BAD ENOUGH that Knox smelled like heaven and had more money than god. Apparently, he also had to be smarter than everyone else in the room, even when the room in question was surrounded by actual brain surgeons.

What was it Tony had called it once, when he was talking about the pack in St. Louis that had helped him get away from his fucked-up family? *Competence kink.* I had a competence kink for the guy I'd tried to kill.

Help.

Knox lifted the phone to his ear. "Hello?"

I couldn't hear the voice on the other end, but I exchanged a look with Tony. Once again, he looked about the same way I felt.

I knew on some level that as an omega, I was supposed to be a territorial crackhead when it came to alphas—especially ones I was scent-matched to. So, why was it that when I thought about sharing them with the beta guy I'd called my best friend, all I felt was relief?

It felt like maybe if I had someone to confide in—especially someone less messed up in the head than I was—I could somehow avoid blowing everything to hell the first time my demons got the better of me.

But there was no time to dig into those feelings now.

"I'm glad you called, Paolo," Knox said in a painfully neutral tone. He lowered the phone and put the call on speaker.

"Why should I trust you?" The familiar voice was weak and raspy, but I could hear the terror hidden just under the surface.

"Well," Knox replied, "the obvious answer is that I've never tried to murder you."

The silence that followed felt like a stone dropping into a pond.

When Paolo finally found words, he wrapped them in a blanket of disdain that didn't sound completely convincing.

"Right. You're just doing this out of the goodness of your heart. Sure."

Knox, still completely unperturbed, said, "Not at all. I'm banking on the fact that you want to stay alive badly enough to help me put Lorenzo Vozzina and the rest of his trafficking operation away for good. Tell me, does he know what hospital you're in? Has he bothered to visit you?"

Another pause.

"Who else is there? I can tell you put me on speaker."

Knox's neutral tone hardened. "No one you need to concern yourself with."

"Is Jez there? I saw her hanging all over your pack at the gala, before —"

"Before your mate tried to drop a hotel on you?" Knox suggested.

"I'm here," I said.

The words were out before I could decide if they were a good idea. With a nervous glance at Knox, I walked over to the chair he was sitting in and hovered next to it. He gave me a speculative look, but didn't protest.

"*I want to talk to her,*" Paolo said, the tremor in his voice growing more pronounced. "*Privately.*"

Knox's eyebrows went up.

"Jez," Tony said, his tone half-concern, half-warning.

Knox muted the call. I could see the calculations running in his head as he weighed how to respond. Was I trustworthy? Did saving him and the others in the hotel cancel out my attempt to kill him? That was what he should have been asking himself, certainly.

But what he said was, "You don't have to, Jez. After what he did to you, as far as I'm concerned, you don't ever have to acknowledge the little snake even exists."

I took in a deep breath. "No, I'll do it."

He unmuted the phone and handed it over. Chewing my lip, I lifted it and headed for the bathroom, closing the door behind me.

"Okay," I said, sitting on the closed toilet seat. "I'm in the bathroom. It's just me."

"*He's going to make me disappear.*" The fear Paolo had been attempting to hide poured into the open, and for a moment I thought he was talking about Knox.

"He's not—" I began, unsure exactly how I was supposed to be playing this.

Paolo cut me off. *"He is! He's been blocking the bond for days, and when he finally showed up at the hospital, his eyes were just… dead! He looked at me like I was a bug that needed squashing!"*

"Oh," I said. "You mean Lorenzo. Yeah, I expect he's plotting some kind of unforeseen medical crisis for you as we speak."

A pathetic whimpering noise crackled across the connection, and I absolutely did not take pleasure in it.

"Matthew says he'll hide me at a private clinic so Lorenzo can't find me, but we'll still be mated! I can never get away from him!"

It took a beat longer than it should have to connect the name Matthew to Knox. The instant it did, every bit of omega territorial rage that should have been directed at Tony rushed into my chest like hot lava.

The urge to squeeze myself down to microscopic size, fly into the phone speaker, and follow the cell signal back to its source so I could rip this interloper's tongue out for daring to *use my alpha's name* was nearly overwhelming.

An animal snarl caught in my throat, choking me.

And… *what*? What the actual *fuck*?

Knox was not my alpha.

For a second, I couldn't breathe. But I was supposed to be talking to Paolo for a reason. I squeezed my eyes shut, willing the red haze to recede. Knox needed Paolo to testify against the Vozzinas. Paolo wasn't going to steal my mates, even if Knox had been one of them. Which he very much *wasn't*.

The alphas all hated him as much as I did.

I drew in a shuddering breath and let it out slowly.

"So, get your gland removed," I told him in a completely flat voice. "Knox is loaded. He'd probably pay for it. He offered to pay for mine."

"*I can't get my gland removed!*" Paolo's pitch went up half an octave. "*I'd be—*"

The word 'worthless' hug in the air, unspoken.

"Yeah?" I prodded, the tough-girl persona that had kept me alive on the streets pushing to the fore. "Aw… *boo-hoo*. Life sucks, and then you die." Then, inspiration struck. "Though, I guess there's also a third option—if you've got the spine for it."

"*What do you mean, a third option? You're either mated or you're not!*"

And didn't I know all about that, after the past few weeks.

"You're either mated, you get a glandectomy … or he dies," I said. "It's only Lorenzo that bit you, right? No one else in his pack?"

"*Y-yes?*" Paolo replied in a tiny voice. "*But what do you—*"

I interrupted again, needing to keep him off balance. "I'm not offering to kill him for you, idiot. Tell me, how many capital crimes has he committed? And—more importantly—how many could you prove to a jury?"

The resulting silence went on for so long that I pulled the phone away from my ear to make sure the call was still connected.

It was.

"Matthew said he wants me to talk to the cops."

The red haze descended again. My pulse throbbed in my temple. I gritted my teeth.

"*Mr. Knockley* is probably your best bet to stay alive at this point," I managed.

That hadn't come across as too murderous, had it?

"How do I know I can trust him?" Paolo asked. He sounded near tears.

That part, at least, I could answer.

"I nearly killed him, and he still forgave me," I said. "Admittedly, you *also* tried to kill him… but like he told you just now, he needs you. From the sound of it, you need him more."

The silences were doing a lot of heavy lifting in this conversation. I let this one stretch.

"Let me talk to him again."

The entitled tone made me want to gouge his eyes out. Enough of my feelings had started leaking through the bond that Heath was sending me questioning nudges. Good thing Gage was still sleeping, or he probably would have been hobbling full speed through the corridors on crutches to find out what was happening.

"Sure," I said sweetly; the politeness a thin veneer over a cauldron of bubbling poison.

I left the bathroom and held the phone out to Knox. "He wants to talk to you again."

I only realized that my fingers were curled around the cell like claws when his first gentle tug didn't pull it from my grip. I made myself relax my hand.

"This is Knockley," Knox said. "Have you thought about my offer?"

He hadn't put the call back on speaker, so I couldn't make out Paolo's answer.

"I see," he said, after a few seconds. "We'll have to discuss that condition. Hang on a moment."

He muted the call again.

"What is it?" I asked, a nervous churn taking up residence in my stomach. The scent of cedar and woodsmoke wrapped around me, more reassuring than it should have been.

Knox frowned. "He's agreed to let me relocate him to a more secure facility—but only if you're there as a show of good faith." A wry twist tugged at one corner of his mouth. "Apparently, he's decided you're on his side."

Tony let out something between a laugh and a scoff. "Right. Little dude-bro also thought *Lorenzo Vozzina* was on his side."

"There are bad judges of character, and then there's whatever the hell *he* is," I said, unable to hide the venom.

"I won't send you in alone," Knox said. "I won't send you at all if you say no. Heath will be leading a security team of a dozen alphas for the transfer. If you want to go with them, I'm going to need your word that you won't kill this little asshole while the others' backs are turned."

My teeth ground together as I pictured being in the same room with the slimeball who'd nearly destroyed my life... and who dared to call Knox 'Matthew' in that disgusting simper. Then I pictured Lorenzo Vozzina being hauled away in handcuffs and an orange jumpsuit for the crime of trafficking omegas.

"I'm not going to kill him," I said. "We need him."

FIFTY

Heath

GAGE WAS SLEEPING again, which was probably what he needed. Seeing how badly he was hurt had shaken me, but the doctor had been clear that he would heal, given time.

The idiot still didn't understand how much I owed him for saving Tony, and he probably never would. Hell, he probably would have done the same for a total stranger who just happened to be next to him when the hotel roof came down.

I hoped Tony wouldn't be too freaked out when he discovered that I wasn't the only alpha in this pack who wanted him. I honestly wasn't sure. On the one hand, Tony had a background with packs—or at least, a pack had helped him once before. On the other hand, he seemed to believe it was a fluke that *anyone* wanted him, which was crazy as hell.

Between him and Jez, we had a lot of making up for things to do.

And speak of the devil…

The sense of Jez getting closer to me had me straightening from my slouch in the uncomfortable plastic chair by Gage's bedside before the privacy curtain slid open. I had to do a double-take at the sight of her and Knox slipping in, shoulder to shoulder like maybe he'd been leaning on her to walk.

Who would have thought it?

"Hey," I greeted, assuming they'd come to check on Gage. "He's asleep. We were talking earlier, though, and he seemed a lot more lucid. Is Tony okay?"

"He's fine," Knox said, keeping his voice low to avoid waking the big lump on the bed. "It's actually you I need to talk to, although I'm glad to hear Gage is doing better."

"Talk about what?" I asked, not sure if it would be polite to prod at Jez's feelings through the bond. She'd been pissed as hell at someone earlier, but it clearly hadn't been at Knox.

Which was good.

"Paolo called," she replied for him. "He's agreed to let Knox move him somewhere safe, but only if I'm there as… honestly, I don't really know why he wants me. Insurance, maybe?"

"Reassurance, I'd have said," Knox added. "For some reason, he seems to believe that Jez is on his side."

"No way." The words were out of my mouth before I even thought about it.

Jez's eyes narrowed. "'*No way*'?" she echoed. "'No way,' what?"

"I don't want you within a mile of that slimy little fucker," I said, my hackles rising at the very idea.

She stepped up to me and very deliberately poked a finger into the center of my chest. Since I was still sitting down, she didn't have to reach up to do it.

"Let's get one thing straight," she said, poking me again for emphasis. "Just because we're not trying to kill each other anymore, it doesn't mean you get a say in where I go or what I do. I'm not locked in your attic now."

And, yeah… I flinched at the reminder.

Good god, was this how it was going to be now, being mated? Suddenly, all the stupid TV romcoms about omegas ruling the nest made a lot more sense.

"Whuz goin' on?" Gage slurred from the bed.

"Knox is about to do something clever, and we're fighting about the details," Jez told him. "Go back to sleep. We've got this."

"Kay," Gage muttered, his eyes sliding shut again.

I stared at Jez in disbelief.

Knox stepped in before the free-for-all pussy-whipping could continue.

"Heath—I have a twelve-person team on standby to transfer Paolo to the private clinic. I need you to lead it, since having me limping around like an invalid wouldn't help with the impression I'm trying to make. Jez has already agreed to go with you—"

"And I also promised not to slit Paolo's throat while no one was looking," she interrupted. "I might try to make him cry, though."

"I have no problem with that," Knox told her. "But maybe wait until he's in the ambulance. We don't want to scare him off completely."

Knox and Jez were… *bantering*? What the hell?

If I tried to unpack all this, my brain would explode. I made a conscious decision to move past it.

"Paolo's agreed to testify against Vozzina?" I asked, because if he had, that was *huge*.

Jez examined her fingernails, which were still cracked and torn after clawing at rubble. "I told him the only way to get out of this mating with his gland intact was to make sure his mate died. Then I asked him how many capital crimes he could prove Lorenzo was behind."

I continued to stare at her. "Who even *are* you?" I demanded, only half joking.

"Right now, she's our key to getting Paolo away from the Vozzina pack," Knox said. "The nurse down the hall said they were about to transfer Gage to the pack room. Let's get him situated, and then I'll let Bud brief you both on the details of the extraction operation. I want that little shithead moved as fast as possible."

<hr>

Two hours later, Jez and I were in the back of a car — part of a convoy heading southwest toward Saint Anthony Hospital in North Lawndale.

Every time I so much as drew breath to suggest she stay in the car during the transfer, I received a glare so murderous that I snapped my jaw shut. Eventually, I bowed to the inevitable and changed my approach.

"Why are you so set on this?" I asked. "I get that Knox asked you to do it—"

"He didn't," she said shortly. "I offered."

I frowned at her. "Then why would you voluntarily get anywhere near this little pusbag, after everything he's done?"

She didn't even blink. "Because I want Lorenzo Vozzina dead. And I want Paolo to suffer and be humiliated in the court of public opinion. I can't get either of those things if Vozzina manages to kill him before he can testify. Also, Paolo wants me there, or else he'll pitch a fit and maybe back out of the whole thing. So, I'm going."

It was a completely rational assessment, with only one hole in it.

"You should know that Illinois doesn't have a death penalty," I said.

She scoffed. "There's a federal death penalty, right? They killed that guy who blew up a government building a few years back. And omega trafficking is international. I should know; I was brought here from Canada."

I'd had no idea she was Canadian.

Why hadn't I known that?

I cleared my throat. "Fair point. Just so you're aware, it can be really hard to get that kind of a sentence."

I'd never seen her expression grow so hard.

"Paolo's pretty motivated to succeed."

After the idea she'd planted in his head, I didn't doubt it.

"Did you ever think about killing me to get rid of our mating bond?" I joked. At least, I sure hoped it was a joke.

Her face softened. If anything, she looked sad now.

"No. Just the glandectomy." To my surprise, she reached across and covered my hand with her bandaged one. "And anyway, this is much better."

I turned my palm up to interlace our fingers. The sting from my own scrapes and cuts felt appropriate, somehow. "Yeah. Sorry I tried to go all alpha on you, back at the hospital."

That part was going to take some work, because the things my instincts tried to tell me about protecting my omega weren't going to fly in this relationship—whatever it turned out to be.

She squeezed my hand. "Thanks for that. Maybe channel some of that protectiveness toward Tony instead. I think he'd appreciate it more."

"You really are all right with that? With Tony and me?" I said, unable to keep the wonder out of my voice.

"Yes," she agreed. "I really am. It's funny—I'm *relieved* that Tony is becoming part of the pack, because it means if I make mistakes, there's… I don't know… a buffer, I guess?" She looked away, her cheeks pinking. "But the moment Paolo called Knox by his first name over the phone, I was ready to start clawing out eye-balls."

My eyebrows flew up in surprise. "Were you, now?"

She shrugged, still not meeting my eyes… but not letting go of my hand, either.

I sighed. "You should know that Gage is going to talk to you about something when he isn't so loopy. He wants to know how you'd feel about him pursuing Tony as well. Assuming Tony is interested, of course."

Her eyes shot to mine, and her sudden, wide smile was completely unexpected. "*Really?* Oh, my god. They'd be *so* cute together."

I couldn't help a startled laugh.

Then a different kind of light came into her eyes. "I think… I'd like to see that. To watch, I mean." She chewed her lower lip, and I cursed the sudden southward migration of my blood in response. "I'd like to see Tony with you, too," she said, and now there was no mistaking the spark of arousal ricocheting through the bond. "If everyone else wanted that, I mean."

I couldn't help it. I reached out with my free hand and cupped her jaw, guiding her to me for a kiss.

It was completely inappropriate while we were on a job, even if there was dark glass sep-arating us from the car's driver. But her delicious scent wrapped around me, and the bond flared with hot tingles… and it was all I could do to keep the brush of lips from turning completely filthy within seconds.

Pulling away felt like ripping Velcro apart, and it didn't help when she let out a little whimpering noise, chasing after my lips. I closed my eyes and pressed our foreheads together.

"Later?" I said, not even sure what I was asking for.

There was a long hesitation, and then she nodded. "Later," she agreed.

The car turned, and I looked up to find that we were entering the hospital grounds.

———◆———

Knox's operations were always planned and organized flawlessly. This one was no exception. Bud reported that Vozzina had two men on Paolo's door, which was why Knox had sent twelve alphas of his own, plus Jez and me.

The transfer paperwork was already handled. It only required Paolo's signature. While three of our alphas surrounded each one of Vozzina's goons, silently daring them to make a scene, Jez shoved the papers under Paolo's nose and said, "Sign these, and don't whine about it."

Once he'd done so, she swapped his phone for a burner from Knox's stash, stomped on the old one, and handed it to me—ignoring Paolo's wail of protest. I pulled out the sim card and snapped it in two, then dropped it and the cracked phone case in the nearest trash can.

"He may have put a tracker somewhere in your belongings," Jez explained. "Change into a hospital gown. Leave everything else here. Knox will buy you whatever you need once we get where we're going."

She bodily hauled him out of bed, shoved the gown into his hands, and dragged him, limping heavily, to the bathroom. He emerged a few minutes later holding his silk pajamas clutched in one hand and wearing Hospital Couture. Tears were already tracking down Paolo's pale cheeks, and she'd barely even had to try. I covered my mouth and fake-coughed to hide my shark's smile.

Also, this wasn't doing a damn thing to quell the lust humming through the bond.

A nervous-looking nurse arrived with a wheelchair. Jez pointed to it imperiously. Paolo balked, looking at her with wet eyes.

"You're sure I'll be safe?" he asked.

"Once you get out of here?" she said. "Yes. Until then? Not so much. Now, *move*."

Paolo plopped down in the wheelchair as though he'd been pushed. I handed the paperwork to the nurse, who flipped through it to check the signatures. While she did that, I stepped outside and addressed the team, pointing at Vozzina's men.

"Four alphas each, remain here and make sure these goons don't leave for the next hour. No phone calls in or out; no discussion of any kind."

Everyone nodded. Once we were long gone with no possibility of being followed, the ones who'd remained behind would return to the security agency Knox had hired them from, yielding no useful information for Vozzina about where we'd transferred Paolo.

The rest would act as a motorcade for the ambulance, in case Bud had missed something and we were being followed after all. Once Paolo was established at the private clinic, hired guards would stay on rotation twenty-four-seven to screen anyone trying to visit him.

And after that, the lawyers would hopefully take care of the rest.

Jez and I followed the four guards flanking the wheelchair. Paolo was loaded into the ambulance with no issues.

"Wait!" he called, as the EMT moved to shut the double doors. "Jez! Aren't you going to ride with me?"

Jez tilted her head, assessing him.

"Nah," she said. "Have a good trip, though."

The doors closed and latched, cutting off Paolo's protest.

We got back in our car, where I spent the drive across the city looking out of the back window, obsessively scanning for anyone following us. We arrived safely at the clinic forty-five minutes later, took care of the intake details, and left Paolo looking like a pale, kicked puppy in the middle of the comfortable opulence of his private room.

"Wait, please—" he said again, as we turned to leave. "I thought you were going to stay with me!"

We ignored him, letting one of the two guards remaining behind on duty close the door after us. Once we were back in the car, I turned to Jez, looking down at her slight form.

"Back to the hospital?" I asked.

"Back to the hospital," she agreed.

FIFTY-ONE

Jez

AFTER GETTING PAOLO safely to the clinic, I expected more... I dunno... *drama*? I was still reeling from the kiss with Heath in the back of the car. Was this how he and I were going to be from now on? Could the fantastical vision of the pack in my head ever become real, when their leader was still firmly standing on the outside?

When we got back to the hospital, Knox wasn't in our room. Instead, Tony had ventured from bed and pulled on some worn sweatpants with a hoodie. He'd dragged a chair over to the medical bed where Gage lay, looking halfway between being asleep and fully awake.

"You're back." Tony sounded tense. "How did it go?"

"As well as could be expected," Heath said, coming over and placing a hand on Tony's shoulder. "The little shit's safely in hiding, and he looks a lot healthier than he did when Knox and I pulled him out of the rubble."

"I made him cry, as promised," I added helpfully. "It wasn't as fun as I thought it would be, though. Too easy."

"He's probably terrified," Tony said grimly.

"Couldn't happen to a nicer omega," Heath said, without an ounce of sympathy. "Where did Knox get to, anyway?"

470

"He's finally seeing a doctor for that knee," Tony replied.

"About time," I muttered.

Tony fiddled with a loose thread on the sleeve of his hoodie. "He wants to move the pack to a different house, after we get out of here. Did he tell you guys about that?"

Surprise trickled through me. It was solely mine — Heath's emotions through the bond felt resigned, if anything.

"Not really surprising," he said. "There's no point in making it easy for Vozzina to find us."

Worry mixed in with my surprise. I turned to Tony. "You should come, too. What if he finds out where you live?"

I couldn't stand the thought of shadowy figures lurking in an apartment hallway… lying in wait.

To my surprise, Tony looked down and let out a little laugh. "Too late. Knox already asked me. I agreed." He looked up at Heath, uncertainty flickering across his expression. "I mean, if that's all right?"

Heath made a small, pained noise. Guilt washed across the bond — and I knew it was because he'd somehow made Tony think that it might *not* be okay.

"*Tony*," he said, his voice pained. "What part of 'join our pack' was unclear? Yes, obviously, I want you safe. I want you close. We *all* want you close."

"He's telling the truth," I added. "Please don't make me try to figure out how to be a civilized omega mated to a rich pack on my own. I'm going to fuck it up *so bad*, Tony. I'm not even joking right now."

That startled another breath of laughter from him. "Wait, and you think I'm going to be any help with that? Have you even *met me*, Jez?"

"Y'all talk an awful lot," Gage muttered from the bed, not opening his eyes. "Can we go home soon? Wherever home's gonna be, now."

I crossed to the other side of the bed and grabbed his hand. "Gage? How are you feeling?"

"Ohmigod," he slurred. "You guys have *got* to try these drugs. They're *so* good."

Heath snorted, his amusement sparking through the bond. "Pretty sure they frown on that here, big guy. But thanks for the tip."

Tony mock-pouted. "How come I didn't get the good drugs? My drugs *suck*."

I watched, fascinated, as Heath tugged Tony against his chest and pressed a gentle kiss to his dark hair. "I'm not sure the good drugs are recommended for someone with a concussion," Heath said.

Tony melted into the contact, only to stiffen a moment later and shoot me a worried glance. I smiled at him, trying to pour all the warmth I was feeling into my expression. I couldn't have put the mixed-up feelings squirming inside me into words if anyone had asked me, but seeing Heath's alpha gentleness was completely different from the lust I'd felt with him earlier. No one had ever modeled that kind of relationship for me... much less made me feel like it might be within my reach.

Was this how it had looked when Gage was gentle with me? I hadn't known what to do with the feelings then, either. But seeing Heath with Tony made it easier, somehow. Like I could try the emotions on for size, instead of being thrust into the middle of them.

I liked the way they fit.

Gage made a humming noise. "Mmm. Not sure what you're thinking about, kitten... but it feels real nice."

The idea of being able to trust a feeling like this was new.

"Yeah," I agreed, with a hint of wonder. "It does, doesn't it?"

The door opened, and Knox came in, leaning on a cane. He took in the relaxed scene, and the tense line of his shoulders eased.

"Mission accomplished, I take it?" he asked.

"Everything went off without a hitch," Heath assured him. "How's the knee?"

"Minor ACL tear," Knox said. "Three-to-six-week recovery time with physical therapy. Nothing to worry about."

"And your back?" I asked pointedly.

"Is bruised," Knox said. "Which I already knew. Don't worry about me. I'm fine."

"When can we leave?" Gage asked.

"Tony and I are cleared for discharge any-time," Knox said. "Heath and Jez aren't technically patients here; they're visitors. The doctors want to monitor you for another twenty-four to forty-eight hours, Gage. They need to get you started on PT, and the recommendation is for you to transfer to rehab for a week or two after that."

"Nooo..." Gage drew out the word, the drugs making him sound young and petulant. "That sounds like the *worst*. Can't you hire me some private rehab, so I can come home with the rest of you?"

"I had a feeling you might ask." Knox's tone was both dry and affectionate. "Bud's trying to set something up."

"Okay, thanks," Gage said, subsiding. "You're the *best* pack leader, Knox."

I didn't need to be mated to Knox to feel the way he stiffened in response to the goofy compliment.

"Not recently, but it's nice of you to say so," he said.

Tony, Heath, and I shared a look, but Heath gave a small negative shake of his head. We let it go... for now.

"The hospital won't complain about Jez staying here with Gage, since they're mated," Heath said. "I'm not thrilled with having them here alone, after what we just did to piss off Vozzina. But I'm also not thrilled about you and Tony being unprotected while you're getting

474

things moved to whichever property we're going to be staying at."

Knox shot him an unimpressed look. "I'm
already hiring a private security firm, Heath.
They can guard us just as easily as they can
guard Paolo. You're Gage's co-mate. You can
stay here with him and Jez. I'll get some movers
lined up, and Tony and I will take care of that
side of things. Tony, are you okay with that
plan?"

"… yes?" Tony replied. "Just don't expect
me to move furniture."

"The property is already furnished," Knox
said. "Besides, I have people for that kind of
thing, as well."

Tony and I exchanged another furtive
glance. This one clearly said, *'are we sure this is
real?'*

◆

Two days later, reality was still holding strong.
I rode in the back of an ambulance with Gage,
who had become a lot grumpier and a lot less
loopy as he was weaned off the good stuff and
onto the same over-the-counter pain meds as
the rest of us mere mortals.

"Ouch!" he grumbled as the ambulance hit
a pothole. "Goddamn it…"

I winced in sympathy. "Next time, tell
Knox to make sure the roads are fixed before his
private ambulance takes us to his private, Super
Sekrit Bat Cave."

"It's not a cave," Gage muttered. "I went with him to look at this place before he bought it. Gated community, lakefront property. Lot nicer than the main pack house, actually, but it's not—*fuck!*" The ambulance dipped and juddered again. Gage continued through gritted teeth, lowering his voice. "It's not the kind of place where someone can quietly drop off a load of omega kids and pick 'em up the next day in an unmarked white van."

The roads smoothed out. The ambulance eventually made a sharp turn and glided to a stop. Voices spoke in the front, the words inaudible. After a few moments, the ambulance pulled forward. More twists and turns, then we slowed again, and finally turned onto a different surface that vibrated beneath the tires.

When the ambulance stopped this time, one of the EMTs in the front squeezed past us with a friendly smile and opened the rear doors.

"Here we go," she said cheerfully. "Nice place! Looks like you'll have some great views while you recover."

I stepped stiffly out of the ambulance and blinked in the early autumn light. The circle drive beneath my tennis shoes was made of light brown cobblestone. Huge trees flanked the property, their leaves just starting to turn red and gold… but my eyes were drawn immediately to the house.

Mansion.

Estate?

It was *huge*. Easily twice the size of the Victorian monstrosity where the pack had been living before. This place looked modern, with big square windows and elegant arches set at regularly spaced intervals. I counted four chimneys coming out of the roof, and immediately pictured cozy fireplaces with bearskin rugs in front of them.

I was openly gaping—so taken aback by the sheer size and wealth on display that I barely noticed the ambulance crew lowering Gage out of the vehicle in his wheelchair.

"D'you like it?" he asked, and there was honest-to-god *worry* coming through the bond—like he thought there was some possibility that I'd sneer at this insane display of Knox's money.

"You're kidding, right?" I shot back. "Gage, seriously—is this real life?"

He laughed, only to wince as his broken ribs complained. "Yeah, kitten… this is how the point-zero-one percent lives, when they aren't slumming it in the woods."

A set of double doors under the main archway thingie—the portico?—opened, and a familiar red-haired figure jogged down the steps. The nice ambulance woman wheeled Gage forward, and I followed, still staring at the huge building where I was apparently going to live now.

"Welcome to the most vulgar display of money you're ever likely to see," Heath greeted wryly. He gave the ambulance woman a tight smile and thanked her politely, taking control of Gage's wheelchair. "Come on, you two. There's a patio door on the east wing that doesn't have so many stairs. Jez, once we get Gage settled in, I'll take you downstairs to see the nest."

I stopped cold, and Heath hesitated, turning to look over his shoulders at me.

My mouth felt dry. I had to swallow a couple of times before I could get words out.

"There's... a nest?" I asked stupidly. "For me?"

478

FIFTY-TWO

Jez

THE HOUSE WAS every bit as big as it looked from the outside. We'd entered through a patio door on the left side, leading into a library with dark wooden shelves built into every wall. My mouth fell open as I took in the couches and comfy chairs scattered around, along with the huge fireplace, just as I'd imagined it—right down to the fur rug.

"Oh, my god," I breathed, rushing to examine the titles on the nearest shelf. "Knox really owns *all these books?*"

"Yeah," Gage confirmed. "He's probably even read some of them, at some point. Hey, Heath—this place has an elevator somewhere around here, doesn't it?"

"It does," Heath confirmed.

"I know I can't manage the stairs, but no way do I want to miss Jez seeing her nest."

Heath grunted. "You just want me to push you around like I'm your personal nurse."

Gage snickered like a schoolboy. "Well, I mean… that, too."

"Asshole," Heath told him, not sounding mad about it. "You know I owe you five-star concierge service for the rest of my goddamned life, if you want it. Let's go, then. Do you want to grab some books first, Jez?"

I blinked a couple of times. "Can I?"

"Kitten," Gage said. "You live here now."

"You can do pretty much whatever you like," Heath added, "as long as it doesn't involve grievous bodily harm."

I flushed, but again, there was no heat behind the words. Feeling like a thief, I darted back to the bookshelf and grabbed as many books as I could carry, more or less at random.

"Didn't realize you were a closet bookworm," Gage said.

My cheeks heated further. "Libraries are good places to hang out for a few hours. They're warm in the winter, pretty safe usually, and no one throws you out as long as you're reading and not making trouble."

"Huh," Gage said, considering. "Guess I never thought about it like that."

Affection buffeted me from two directions through the bond, sending a pleasant shiver down my body.

"All right," Heath said, wheeling Gage toward the door. "Nest first. We'll do a proper tour later."

The mansion was two stories tall, but Heath had mentioned *downstairs,* so that made three, total. Compared to the old Victorian pack house with its winding hallways and steep staircases, it felt very open and airy. The central spaces were mostly painted white with the occasional brilliant blue accent, and the main part of the house was dominated by a staircase that reminded me of something you might find in a fancy modern art museum.

Public museums were another good place to spend time when you had nowhere else to go. I'd done extensive research on places like that over the years.

Anyway, the main staircase must have cost a fortune all on its own. It was curved rather than angular—a twisting banister made of intricate wrought iron spiraling gently upward and downward in the open center of the house. A massive skylight poured warm illumination over the blonde wood of the stair treads.

Heath bypassed the stairs and wheeled Gage into a little nook tucked behind the grandeur, where there was, indeed, an elevator.

"This is mostly for moving furniture and other heavy stuff," he explained. "But it'll work for a wheelchair, too—and obviously you can use it anytime you want to, Jez."

I couldn't imagine choosing to ride in a little box instead of using that beautiful staircase, but I managed a meek, "Okay," in response.

We piled in and Heath hit the bottom of the three buttons. The elevator smoothly slipped downward. My stomach barely had time to dip and bounce back up before it dinged and the doors opened.

I caught my breath as I stepped out. The main floor had been all open air and big windows and natural light. I wasn't immune to its beauty, but my omega instincts made me feel exposed, surrounded by all that space.

The downstairs—it seemed insulting to call it a basement—was completely different. The ceiling was made of arched brick, which seemed sort of weird at first, until I realized that it was made to look like an old subway tunnel or an ancient wine cellar. The lighting was plenty to see by, but there was no glare. It was more reddish orange than yellow, giving the space an intimate feel.

"Down here, the north wing is mostly taken up by the indoor pool, hot tub, gym, and sauna," Heath said, as though he wasn't speaking a foreign language.

"By the... *what*?" I squeaked.

Gage made a derisive noise and rolled his eyes. "I know, right? Rich people are really something else."

"The central area behind us has the underground garage and HVAC stuff," Heath went on, as though we hadn't spoken. "It's fully soundproofed and has a separate ventilation system, so you won't have any sounds or smells bothering you. The south wing is partly storage, though as far as I know it's not being used for anything; just empty. The rest of it is your nest. Tony went a little bit overboard trying to get things ready."

"Aww," Gage said. "Holy shit, that's so sweet."

"But you can make it up any way you'd like," Heath finished. "Knox made you an expense account at *Nestique*, so you can buy anything you need online and it will be delivered same-day."

"But—" I began, overwhelm beginning to overcome me.

Heath let go of the wheelchair and took my shoulders in his hands, waiting until I looked up at him helplessly.

"I know it's a foreign concept," he said, "but money is literally no object. Look around you. This is not the second house of a man who has to worry about the cost of nesting materials."

But I tried to kill him, I wanted to say. We'd already had that conversation, though. I swallowed the words back with difficulty, and nodded instead.

Heath let out a sharp sigh and leaned down, pressing a kiss to my hair. A callused hand circled my forearm and gave a gentle squeeze, redirecting my attention to Gage. He tugged me down and kissed the same place Heath had.

I pressed my lips together tightly and gave another nod, steadying my pile of borrowed books against my chest.

"Let's go," Heath said softly. "Don't want to keep Tony waiting."

Just like upstairs, the elevator was tucked behind the grand staircase. I could smell the faintest hint of chlorinated water in the air from the pool, but it disappeared as Heath led us toward the south wing. We passed a game room and a comfortable-looking family room before turning the corner to find Tony pacing restlessly in front of a closed door. He turned sharply as we approached.

"Hi!" he said nervously. "You're... um... you're here! That's good." He ran a hand through his messy dark hair, mussing it further. "So, I tried to get things ready for you, Jez, but I was only going off of internet sites about nesting—so if you hate it, you can totally say so and it won't hurt my feelings—"

"I'm not going to hate it," I told him, unable to keep the tremor from my voice. "Can I see?"

Tony rolled his lower lip between his teeth and nodded, pulling the door open and stepping out of the way. I crept forward, bolstered by the warmth coming through the bond, and poked my head inside to look. Tears immediately burned against the back of my eyes. The pile of books I was carrying dropped from my hands as I covered my mouth to hold in the pitiful whimper that wanted to escape.

Beyond the door lay a low-ceilinged room that was easily big enough for half a dozen people, while still seeming utterly intimate. Pretty stained-glass lamps with red shades were dotted around the edges of the room on tables, and fairy lights twinkled softly from the ceiling.

There was hardly a square foot of floor not covered by piles of pillows, beanbags, furry blankets, and low, overstuffed furniture. Only one side of the room was relatively bare, where another of the big fireplaces stood on a raised hearth, surrounded by a protective grate and with yet another heavy fur rug thrown in front of it.

I realized that some of the reassuring scent of whiskey, oak, and baking bread was coming from the room in front of me, not just the men standing behind me. As if in a trance, I walked deeper inside until I found the first item of clothing hidden among the pillows and blankets—a worn henley that had seen better days, and smelled like Christmas morning. Unable to help myself, I picked it up and held it to my nose, breathing in.

"Is it okay?" Tony asked, hovering just outside the door.

"I... it's..." My throat closed up, choking off the words in the instant before the tears I'd been holding back escaped in an ugly sob.

"I'm sorry!" Tony said, his voice going high-pitched and upset. "Seriously, you can change it if you don't like it—I didn't mean to—"

"*Tony*," Heath said. "They're good tears. You did an amazing job."

"That you did, cub," Gage added. "You ever think about getting into interior decorating? Because this room looks fantastic, and she loves it."

"Oh." Tony sounded like all the air had escaped his lungs at once. "Oh, thank goodness."

"Can we come inside with you, kitten?" Gage asked. "People are always supposed to get permission from you for that, by the way."

Permission. People had to ask permission before they could come into my nest.

The tears came harder.

"Yes," I sobbed.

In short order, Tony picked up the dropped books and set them on a table. Heath wheeled Gage in, moving enough pillows out of the way to get him to the nearest couch and help him onto it. Heath took me by the shoulders and eased me down to lie next to him, with my head pillowed on his uninjured thigh. Gage immediately started running his fingers through my hair, a rumbling purr vibrating up from his chest.

Heath lifted my feet and slid in to sit as well, resting my lower legs across his lap. Tony hesitated, then sank down on the pillows and blankets in front of us, resting his head on the edge of the seat near my stomach. Needing to thank him somehow for what he'd done, I carefully pushed my fingers into his messy hair, mirroring what Gage was doing to me. After a moment, Tony sighed, all the tension draining out of him.

The silence settled over us, warm and heavy until Heath's quiet words pierced it.

"You're home, Jez," he said. "We all are. Maybe now that we've got some breathing space, we can figure out the rest of it."

FIFTY-THREE

Knox

I TOLD MYSELF that staying out of the way while the others got Jez settled into her nest was for the best, and that doing so wasn't a hardship. I'd never been wired for sex or romance the way most alphas were. Not until that fateful night in the hotel bar with Jez, anyway.

I'd gone a good chunk of my life not giving it much thought, or having any specific word for the way I felt. Then someone had bandied around the term *asexual*, and I'd been curious enough about it to do a brief but fairly deep dive into the label—just like I did with anything I came across that seemed interesting or useful enough to bother learning about.

My quick research foray resonated to the extent that afterward, I'd privately considered myself ace-spectrum, sex-neutral, and possibly demiromantic… after which, I didn't give it much more thought. My instant attraction to Jez—not to mention my out-of-character invitation to have her come up to my hotel room— had been an aberration, I told myself.

Then, I'd walked into the pack house after Tony brought me home from the hospital, running straight into the unexpected wall of pheromones generated by Jez's heat. One breath. That was all it took for every higher brain function inside my skull to route its blood supply directly to my dick.

For a terrible few moments, the single, overriding imperative driving me had been to barge upstairs, drag Heath off of my would-be murderer, and get myself knot-deep inside her willing body.

I'd been around omegas in heat before. In our line of work, it was unavoidable. However, I'd never been around a *scent-matched* omega in heat. That fateful couple of minutes before Gage injected me with a dampener shot had rocked the foundations of a lifetime's understanding of myself.

I hadn't been in control.

I hadn't been *sane*.

Additional research was clearly in order.

That research had turned up the label '*phi-lyrasexual*,' a term specifically describing alphas who only experienced sexual attraction when they were also scent-matched to the recipient.

And now, here we were.

The only person I'd ever found myself sexually attracted to was the same woman who'd nearly succeeded in murdering me... and who'd turned out to be an otherwise amazing person, if you could overlook that one tiny fact.

Now she was mated to my two packmates, and the three of them were currently curled up in a gorgeous nest with the adorable beta who'd *also* become part of my pack. Tony had somehow wormed his way past the *demi-* in *demiromantic*... and the net result was that I really, *really* wanted to be in that nest with them, despite it being a terrible idea.

I gritted my teeth and pulled up the latest email from the law firm I'd hired to deal with the Paolo situation—making a concerted effort not to think about what might be happening inside Jez's nest right now.

Paolo, who apparently wasn't as stupid as one might infer from his horrific choice of mate, was demanding full immunity from prosecution in exchange for his testimony. I had a hunch the others would have some strong feelings about that, after everything the little douchebag had done to them.

But the thing was, Paolo wasn't going to traipse away after the trial and organize his own omega trafficking ring. Taking down Lorenzo Vozzina was more important than getting revenge against Vozzina's simpering trophy omega.

If the feds are willing to go for it, I'm fine with that, I replied, before hitting send.

Resolutely not thinking about the *other* omega I'd let off the legal hook recently, I turned to the pile of mail on my desk and opened the manila envelope sitting on top.

———◆———

The following day, that caramel-coffee scented temptation in omega form sat across the same desk from me, as I went over her newly arrived legal documents with her.

"Birth certificate, social security card, Illinois REAL ID card, passport, mating certificate," I said, fanning the items out in front of her. "These papers are enough to allow you to travel internationally, open bank or investment accounts, get a driver's license, and receive government benefits—such as they are in this country."

She looked a little shell-shocked. Uncertainty laced her scent. "So, I'm really Jessica now?"

"I'm pretty sure you're still Jez to everyone here," I told her, remembering what she'd told me once about her given name. "But Jezebel is gone forever, assuming you still want her to be."

She was quiet for a long moment before speaking again.

"That name can rot in hell with my father," she said eventually.

I nodded. "Then, may I say what a pleasure it is to make your acquaintance properly, Jessica Knockley, née Smith?" I stuck out my right hand unthinkingly as part of the joke.

She eyed it for a beat before taking it in hers and squeezing as we shook. Tingling heat rushed down my arm from the point of contact, and I barely managed to swallow my gasp. Jez didn't manage to swallow hers, and we both pulled away as though we'd been burned. My dick twitched with interest, thickening uncomfortably against the seam of my trousers.

We stared at each other wide-eyed for the space of a heartbeat. I cleared my throat awkwardly. "Erm... anyway... I was thinking we could arrange driving lessons for you. I'm assuming you never had a chance to learn?"

Her mouth moved for a moment before words came out. "Uh... no. I never did."

"Then we'll get you lessons," I said, cursing the growing ache between my legs. The faint scent of aroused slick rolling off Jez's body only made things worse. "You, er, you should also start thinking about what kind of car you'd like to own."

She blinked at me in bewilderment across the expanse of polished wood. "You're going to buy me a *car*?"

"Well... yes?" I replied, equally bewildered. "Come to think of it, Tony needs a better one as well."

Several emotions flickered across her face in quick succession. I couldn't look away, although a hint of trepidation stole over me as a calculating glint entered her gaze.

"What about a motorcycle?" she asked.

I tried not to acknowledge my flicker of panic at the idea of my pack's omega crashing a motorcycle and ending up as a gory red smear on the pavement. For one thing, it was hypocritical, since Heath had owned a motorcycle when I'd first met him, and I'd never fretted randomly about him getting hurt on it.

Was this the much-vaunted alpha protective instinct rearing its head? Jesus, what a pain in the ass.

"If that's what you want," I made myself say. "Although I'd suggest a car as well—winter in Chicago is no joke." I realized I was talking to a woman who'd lived as an unhoused person for years, and mentally cursed myself. "Which, of course, you already knew."

She gave a sharp little laugh and scrubbed a hand over her face. "Right. A motorcycle *and* a car. Why not?"

"The other thing I'd hoped to discuss with you is a bit more of a sensitive subject," I said, not wanting to get bogged down in a discussion of what she did and didn't deserve to own as a part of this pack. "Gage mentioned that you're an avid reader?"

Pink flushed her pale cheeks. "It was always a way to escape for a few hours," she said. "And libraries are safe places to spend time."

Gage had passed that tidbit on as well.

"Makes sense," I told her. "Again, I'm making an assumption here—but I'm guessing you don't have a high school diploma or GED?"

"No," she said in a wry tone. "Obviously not."

"We can remedy that if you'd like," I replied. "Along with any university-level studies you might want to pursue eventually. I only mention it so you're aware it's an option."

"Really?" She seemed genuinely shocked, as though the possibility of getting a formal education had never occurred to her.

"Really," I confirmed. "There's no pressure... it's just something to think about."

She chewed her lip for a moment before letting it pop free. I wasn't proud of the way my eyes fixated on that small movement of the tender pink flesh.

"I will," she said. "Thank you, Knox."

I managed a grim little smile for her. "Don't thank me until after you've crammed for a final exam at four in the morning," I told her.

Obviously, the smart thing would have been to pawn the details off on Heath, since Gage was out of action for the foreseeable future. And yet, that same afternoon, I found myself saying, "I need to make a quick trip to the office to sign some papers. Jez, if you'd like to come, we can set up those driving lessons on the way back."

I didn't miss Heath's double-take... or the way Jez's expression shuttered across a look of surprise.

"Um... okay?" she said. "Give me five minutes to get ready."

Bud picked us up in the limo without comment, and I watched Jez watching the city as we drove. After a few minutes, she turned with a faint half-smile.

"You know it's probably weird to show up to driving lessons in the back of a limo, right?"

I raised an eyebrow, falling into the banter despite myself. "Is it, though? I mean, it's not as though you could drive yourself there before you get a learner's permit, at the very least."

God, this would be easier in so many ways if I wasn't coming to genuinely like this omega as a person.

We stopped by my office and I signed the things that needed to be signed, but didn't linger afterward. Then Bud drove us to the best-rated driving school in the area. Inside, Jez looked around with interest as we were escorted to a registration desk occupied by a red-haired beta woman in her mid-thirties.

She smiled and batted her eyelashes, rising and gesturing toward a pair of chairs in front of the desk. I waited for Jez to sit before taking the other one.

"Good afternoon," said the woman, casting a quick gaze over Jez before refocusing on me. "My name is Francine, and it's my pleasure to assist you today. Are you wanting driving lessons for your... daughter?"

Jez, whose loose ponytail and baggy jeans did make her look young — but not *that* young — snorted.

"Not my daughter," I said in a tone that hopefully discouraged additional questions. "But, yes, Jessica here is indeed seeking lessons."

"Do you do motorcycle lessons, too?" Jez asked.

"We do," Francine replied, before once more visibly dismissing Jez in favor of addressing me. She caressed a long, red curl between two manicured fingers, stretching it out and letting it bounce back. "Here. Let me show you our various… packages."

She took a folder from a pile of identical folders, turned it around to face me, and opened it, leaning forward as she slid it toward me until I could hardly avoid the view of her cleavage within her low-necked blouse. Red lips smiled up at me.

The low growl from next to me reached my ears. An instant later, my brain tossed up the unwelcome and belated realization that the woman across the desk was attempting to flirt with me. I shifted back in my chair to put more distance between us, my eyes drawn instinctively to Jez.

By contrast, Jez had leaned forward, her hands clenched around the edge of the desk so hard her knuckles had turned white. If her fingernails hadn't still been torn and ragged from the aftermath of the bomb attack, they would have been digging crescents into the oak laminate surface.

"I'm not his *daughter*," she snarled. "I'm *mated to his pack. So, back the fuck off, bitch.*"

Francine shoved backward so abruptly that her chair squeaked across the floor. My breath lodged in my lungs, trapped there by the swell of animal lust that rolled over me like a tidal wave as my omega staked her claim with teeth and claws bared.

The three of us sat frozen in an awkward triangle for an agonizing few seconds. Then Jez sucked in a breath, the blood draining from her face as she, too, shoved her chair backward and shot out of it.

"I'm… I didn't mean—" she stuttered, backing rapidly toward the door. "S-sorry!"

The last was a high-pitched squeak, then she turned and literally ran from the office. Blood was still rushing in my ears as I stood more slowly and looked down at the beta woman, her face trapped in an '*oh*' of surprise and humiliation.

"My apologies," I said, impressed with the even tone of my own voice. "But I'm afraid we'll be seeking the services of a different provider. Thank you for your time."

After which, I hurried out, following after Jez with long strides.

FIFTY-FOUR

Jez

OH, MY GOD—what was *wrong* with me? It was bad enough when I was plotting Paolo's demise for daring to use Knox's given name in front of me. I was *supposed* to hate Paolo. But in what world did I have the right to growl and snarl over some random basic bitch flashing her cleavage at the alpha that I'd *actually* tried to murder?

I rushed out of the building, seriously considering darting into the nearest alley and disappearing into the city. The phone in my pocket—a phone that *Knox had bought me*, for fuck's sake—buzzed. I ignored it, but I couldn't ignore the concern battering me from two directions inside the bond.

That concern dragged me to a stumbling halt. In the next instant, Knox's longer stride brought him outside as well. He scanned the area, his dark eyes falling on me. His shoulders slumped in relief as he approached.

Maybe he'd suspected that I'd try to run rather than face the fallout from my feral outburst. I *wanted* to run… it was agonizing standing here while he stared at me as though he'd never seen me before. I looked away. Not showing my throat to him—never that. But hiding my face, which I could tell was flushed beet-red with humiliation.

He stopped several paces away. It still wasn't far enough to keep his cedar-campfire scent from tickling my nose. The deep alpha pheromones were twisted up with uncertainty and half a dozen conflicted emotions that I couldn't read.

Belatedly, it occurred to me that if I tried to run, Heath would just track me down through the bond. I slumped in defeat, still not meeting Knox's gaze.

"I'm so sorry," I mumbled, relying on alpha hearing to make out the words past the background noise of the city around us. "I didn't... I don't know why I..."

Great. I still couldn't put a sentence together.

The phone in my pocket buzzed again.

Knox let me trail into silence before he spoke.

"That woman was being incredibly rude to you," he said. "You were well within your rights to call her on it. There are plenty of other driving schools in Chicago — or I can just as easily hire someone to give you private lessons. Seriously, don't give it another thought."

The words were calm, but I could sense the underlying tension in him. Could he tell what I was feeling by my scent? Because if he could, that was bad, bad, *bad*. Even now, half-panicked and with my face red from embarrassment, I was fighting an insane urge to run into Knox's arms and climb him like a tree.

I wanted to rub my body all over his expensive suit until anyone with a nose would be able to tell that he belonged to me. I wanted to bite bloody marks into the skin of his throat, visibly claiming him as mine.

This time, my phone rang instead of buzzing; the notification of an incoming voice call rather than a text.

I took a step backward, and then another.

Knox eyed me nervously. "I'll, um… I'll just let Bud know to bring the car around."

He drew out his phone and thumb-typed rapidly. The cell phone rang before he could put it away. Frowning, he lifted it to his ear.

"Gage," he said. "No, she's here. We're fine. Just a… well, a misunderstanding, I guess you'd call it. Here, you can talk to her directly."

He stepped forward and thrust the phone at me, looking more out of his depth than I'd ever seen him before. I took it gingerly, because refusing would only cause more of a scene.

"Hello?" I said in a tiny voice.

"*Kitten!*" Gage sounded almost frantic. "*What happened? Why wouldn't you answer your phone? Heath and I were worried that something happened to you!*"

Something did, I thought, a bit hysterically.

"No, it's—" Words tangled up in my throat again. "It was stupid. I'm being stupid. I just want to go home." My voice broke on the final words.

There was a brief pause.

"Okay, hand me back to Knox, sweetheart. We'll be waiting when you get here. I love you."

I would not burst into tears on a busy sidewalk. I would *not*. I held the phone out to Knox. "He wants to talk to you again."

"Okay." Knox took it. "Here's the car. Why don't you get in, and I'll be with you in a minute."

The black limo rolled to a silent stop next to us. Bud got out, striding around to our side and opening the door for me. Defeated, I got in and scooted to the farthest corner of the leather-upholstered seat, curling against the window in a miserable slouch. My pussy ached and throbbed accusingly, uncaring of how badly I'd humiliated myself.

Had Knox relayed a blow-by-blow account of my meltdown to Gage? If so, he'd been quick about it. His phone was once more hidden in a pocket when he sank into the back seat, the door closing behind him.

"We'll be back at the house in about thirty-five minutes," he said, as though nothing at all was wrong.

It was the longest thirty-five minutes of my life—and with my history, that was really saying something. My pheromones swirled together with Knox's in the enclosed space, a cocktail of conflicting emotions that included, but wasn't limited to, guilt, worry, frustration, and unfiltered lust.

The entire time, my instincts screamed that the way to fix this situation was to fling myself across the seat and wrap my arms and legs around Knox like an emotionally stunted barnacle. I was getting increasingly freaked out by how difficult it was to ignore that impulse in favor of my higher brain functions.

Knox didn't speak a word. Neither did I. Instead, we sat on opposite sides of the car, not looking at each other and trying not to breathe in each other's scents. Or maybe that was just me. I wasn't about to look at him to find out.

When the car pulled up to the gigantic fucking mansion that I'd unthinkingly called home—after only staying there for a little more than a *day*—I bolted from the car, not waiting for Bud to open the door for me. Heath was waiting outside the main door, his presence in my mind twitchy and on-edge.

I rushed past him, not meeting his eyes, either.

"Jez—"

My name chased after me as I ran into the house and charged downstairs, taking the steps two at a time. My nest was a dark sanctuary at the end of the hall. I rushed inside and closed the door, leaning my weight against it and shaking.

Gage and Heath were worried shadows hovering on the edges of my awareness. As my adrenaline gradually wore off, I realized how badly I wanted them to be here with me. But if they were here, I'd have to talk about why I was battling the urge to thrust my hand into my jeans and frig myself to orgasm while imagining Knox slamming into me from behind.

With a frustrated groan, I crossed to the piles of pillows and blankets on the sofa, where Gage, Heath, Tony, and I had piled together to sleep. I faceplanted onto the soft, upholstered surface, breathing in.

It didn't smell like Knox.

Another groan tore free from my throat, this one sounding more like a growl. I lay face-down, trying to remember what sanity felt like. Here I was—a broken and discarded gutter rat living in a fairytale castle with two amazing mates—and I was hiding away in the dark, plotting how to steal dirty laundry from the guy I'd tried to kill so I could use it to line my nest.

Fuck my *life*.

A hesitant knock sounded at the door. I lifted my head far enough to gently beat my forehead against the couch cushion. Which was, of course, completely ineffective, because it was so soft.

I knew without having to call out that Gage and Heath were on the other side of the door. And, in the end, trying to put this off any longer was pointless. Dragging myself upright, I crossed the room to open it.

"Can we come in, kitten?" Gage asked from his wheelchair.

I'd been wrong; it wasn't just him and Heath. They'd brought Tony, too.

"Okay," I said in a whisper, and stood back to let them in.

"Do you want me here?" Tony said, uncertainty lacing the words.

I hesitated, and then nodded. I'd told Heath the absolute truth when I'd said I needed Tony in the pack as a buffer against my own fuck-ups. And now, here we were.

Heath wheeled Gage inside, following Tony to the sofa where I'd been trying to suffocate myself a minute ago. Tony and I sat down facing Gage, while Heath hovered nearby.

"So…" Tony began. "Do you, um, want to talk about it?" He looked as out of his element as I felt.

"No," I said. "But you all need to know what happened, assuming Knox didn't already tell you over the phone." I gnawed on the inside of my cheek and looked up at Heath. "You know how I told you that I fantasized about clawing Paolo's eyeballs out when he called Knox 'Matthew' to my face?"

Silence settled over the room.

"To be fair," Tony said. "I kind of fantasized about ripping his throat out, just because he's generally an asshole."

"Omega instincts, kitten," Gage said, although there was a speculative light in his eye. "Knox is your scent match, too. No surprise that you've got some feelings around that."

I covered my face with one hand. "Some beta bitch at the driving school tried to come onto him while I was sitting right there," I muttered. "And I might've… um… lost it, a bit. In public. In front of him."

"Oh," Gage said. "Shit. What'd he say afterward?"

I sighed and let my hand drop. "You know. A bunch of Knox stuff. *'She was rude, don't give it another thought, I'll get you private driving lessons, blah, blah, blah.'* I nearly swan-dived into a manhole and disappeared into the sewers to get away, so I could go and live with the rest of the city's trash."

Gage scoffed. "Then I would've had to send Heath into the sewers after you, and he'd get all irritated when his nice shoes got dirty."

"Gage, I wanted to *hurl myself at him in the back of the limo*," I said, with more than a little desperation. "I already tried to kill him! Am I supposed to add sexual assault to the rap sheet now?"

Tony looked deeply uncomfortable, but he cleared his throat and asked, "How sure are you that it would have been assault?"

"Isn't *that* an interesting question," Gage said.

"He told me ages ago that he couldn't mate me after what I did to him," I replied miserably. "And, I mean... *no kidding*. You don't mate your attempted murderer."

Heath had been uncharacteristically silent throughout the exchange. Now, he shifted uncomfortably in place.

"You don't mate your prisoner either," he said. "And yet, here we are. I want to talk to him about this, if you'll let me. Let's just say that I've got a bit of a different perspective on things, these days."

I ought to protest. Tell him that if anyone should be talking to Knox about this, it should be me. Letting Heath fight my battles just because I was an omega was a coward's way out.

"Okay," I said weakly, crashing head-first into my coward era.

"Good," Gage said. "Now, let Heath hold you for a bit. You look like you're about to collapse. I'd do it myself, but..." He gestured one-handed at his cast and sling.

I got up, zombie-walked into Heath's arms, hiding my face against his chest. His long arms closed around me, his scent enveloping me as I breathed in deeply. I hated myself just a little for the fact that my pussy still throbbed with need. The rest of me only wanted to turn everything off for a bit, though.

"Help me onto the couch, Tony," Gage said. "Sleeping together like that was really good yesterday, so let's do it again."

"It's, like, three-thirty in the afternoon," Tony protested.

"And?" Gage asked. "I'm an invalid. The docs said to get lots of rest. And Jez is tired. Look at her."

"And you had a concussion," Heath said pointedly, the words rumbling against my cheek.

"Fine," Tony said, not sounding too upset about it. "I swear, the things I do for this pack."

506

"That's why we love you," Gage said. "Right, Jez?"

Wait—Gage was sweet-talking Tony now? I lifted my head so I could meet his eyes as Tony helped him slide out of the wheelchair and onto the couch. Had he asked Tony about the two of them having a relationship? My eyes slid to Tony, whose burning cheeks and shy gaze said that he had.

"Are you two together now?" I blurted, since apparently my brain-to-mouth filter was still missing in action. "Oh my god—that's *fantastic*."

Tony's blush deepened. "He and Heath said you were okay with it?"

"Tony, you're my best friend! Of *course* I'm okay with it," I told him, breaking free of Heath's embrace to hug him instead.

"I'll make a point of not flashing my cleavage at Knox anytime soon," Tony joked weakly, wrapping an arm around me in return.

I smacked Tony lightly in the kidney for that, and Gage let out a bark of laughter—the bastard. Instant karma hit him immediately afterward, when he winced and lifted a hand to his busted ribs.

"Ow."

"Serves you right," I mumbled, and let Tony go.

"Everyone get down here with me," Gage said. "We're napping until dinnertime. No arguments."

I had no desire to argue. I gently shoved Tony onto the couch with Gage, then plopped down in the mass of pillows on the floor and held out a hand to Heath, drawing him down with me. The door to the nest was still partway open, but I couldn't bring myself to do anything about it.

I was safe here; I didn't need a locked door between me and the rest of the world. Not while I was in this house, surrounded by these men. Smiling, I curled into Heath's body and tried not to think too much about the nagging thrum of leftover sexual desire still singing along my nerves.

It didn't take long for sleep to pull me under. In my dreams, at least, no one could judge me for what happened inside my subconscious mind. Soft hands caressed my body, the smell of smoke and evergreen needles joining whiskey and orange peel, with a hint of Tony's beta musk woven into the tapestry.

Bodies moved, pale skin twining with tanned gold and tawny brown. Moans pierced the silence, growing sharper and more desperate before being deliciously muffled. I writhed against the warm body cradling me, rubbing my cheek against a broad chest to scent-mark it, and receiving a rumbling purr in return.

Thick fingers stroked through my hair, my awareness surfacing by degrees. The muffled moans continued in the background as I blinked my eyes open in the dim light.

"Jez?" Heath asked. "You said something about wanting to see Gage and Tony together. Wake up, because I don't think you'll want to miss this."

FIFTY-FIVE

Jez

THE STRINGS OF HANGING fairy lights illuminated Gage and Tony on the couch, outlining them in a warm glow. Gage had the hand on his uninjured side shoved inside Tony's waistband, while Tony had his fist crammed into his own mouth, muffling his needy moans.

Gage's gaze met mine, and his movements beneath Tony's clothing stilled.

"Hey, cub," he said, drawing another stifled groan from Tony. "You know how we talked about Jez saying she wanted to watch us together, and you said that sounded hot? She's watching us now. Is that still okay with you? And you, kitten?"

Tony tugged his hand out of his mouth. Even in the dim light, I could see that dents from his teeth where he'd bitten down to keep himself quiet. His eyes were huge and liquid in his flushed face—pupils blown wide with desire.

We looked at each other with deep vulnerability. It was one thing to fantasize about watching, or being watched. But now, it was actually happening.

"Yes," Tony whispered.

"Yes," I agreed.

"Good boy," Gage said, and started pumping again. Tony let out a startled cry, his hips rising off the couch cushion.

Heath made a low noise in his throat. "You know Knox is right upstairs." His voice was nearly a growl. "Better keep it quiet if you don't want him to hear exactly what's going on down here."

Tony's breath stuttered, and he quickly shoved his fist back in his mouth. I couldn't say a word, because I was no better off than he was. This whole situation was close enough to the dream I'd been having that I didn't manage to swallow my needy whine.

Heath pulled me onto his lap, my legs straddling his and my back pressed against his front. I was still wearing the baggy jeans I'd dressed in this morning. Heath popped the button at the waistband and tugged the zipper down, leaving enough space for his hand to delve inside both jeans and panties.

I was already slick from my dream, and watching Tony squirm was only making it worse. Cool fingers teased my flesh, sliding up and down the length of my folds. Pleasure rushed outward from the point of contact, and I cried out mindlessly.

Heath snorted. "I think you and I have very different definitions of the word *quiet*."

I writhed in his lap, because he hadn't stopped playing with my clit, even as he said it. A half-formed memory from my heat brought another choked noise of lust to my throat, and I grabbed his free hand that had been wrapped around my stomach to steady me. Tugging it up, I brought his palm to cover my mouth and held it there.

Now it was Heath's turn to groan. His cock twitched hard against my ass, and he immediately pressed his hand hard to the lower part of my face, silencing me. I let go of his wrist, slumping back against him as he stroked me toward an orgasm—my breath whistling in and out through the tiny gap between his fingers and my nostrils.

"That's a hell of a pretty picture," Gage rumbled from the couch. "*Fuck*, I need both hands. We could make 'em stare at each other while we forced them to come, neither of them able to do more than whimper."

"Oh, *f-fuck*," Tony groaned, pulling his fist out of his mouth again.

"You could always gag him with something else," Heath suggested, two of his fingers circling my clit in an achingly slow slide.

Gage paused. "Hmm. That might work. What do you think, Tony? I won't be able to reach your pretty cock if you're on your knees, sucking me... but you can touch yourself, and I'll tell you how fast and how hard."

Tony nodded like a bobblehead doll left on a shelf during an earthquake. "Y-yes, please..." He was already sliding off the couch to kneel before it.

Gage's broken leg was stretched out in front of him. He angled his good leg to the side, wide enough to give Tony space to squeeze in close.

Gage had been wearing a thoroughly disreputable pair of gray sweatpants that someone had sliced the left leg off of, to accommodate his thick plaster cast. Tony hesitated for a moment before dragging the worn elastic waistband down just far enough that he could pull Gage's huge cock out.

Heath's fingers drew more shudders from me as Tony looked up at Gage and said, "Stop me if anything hurts, okay?"

Gage ran his fingers through Tony's messy hair. "Don't make me come, and we'll be fine. Get a hand around yourself and stroke your cock, now. Nice and slow—you don't get to come yet, either."

Maybe Tony wasn't going to come anytime soon, but if Heath didn't stop what he was doing, *I* sure as hell was. My nerves buzzed beneath my skin, from the tips of my toes all the way up to my scalp.

Tony lowered his head, making a humming noise of satisfaction as Gage guided him down the length of his impressive hard-on with the hand still tangled in his hair. My eyelids fluttered as my awareness ricocheted back and forth between what Heath was doing to my body, and the sight of Gage sliding Tony's mouth up and down his cock in a leisurely rhythm.

Past the scent of Heath's palm wrapped across my face, I pretended I could smell cedar and smoke as well as Gage's spicy orange Christmas bread. The four of us, our fate-matched scents twining together with the odor of sex and sweat.

That fantasy, combined with the wet sound of Tony choking on Gage's cock and immediately begging for more, sent me over the edge. My muscles locked, trembling and jerking. The strong hand clamped over my mouth only partially managed to muffle my startled shriek of ecstasy.

"So much for being quiet," Gage said, sounding a bit breathless.

Heath chuckled, low and dark. "It was worth a try."

I shuddered as he continued to tease my oversensitive nub, ignoring my muffled keening. His hard dick rubbed against me through two sets of clothes, teasing me with what I really needed. Having our matched scents mixing together like this was making me feral with lust, even if Knox's pheromones only existed in my imagination.

Wriggling, I tried in vain to get my jeans down around my thighs. With Heath holding me in place like this, straddling his lap, it was impossible. He growled and thrust his hips beneath me, rubbing against me harder. The imaginary scent of cedar and woodsmoke grew stronger in the nest. I pressed back in wanton counterpoint, feeling drunk on it.

Heath froze abruptly, his fingers stilling on my clit as he sucked in a startled breath. I made a noise of protest and nipped at his warm palm, trying to crane around so I could see his face. Had I done something wrong?

Then Gage's voice cut through the room, hoarse with what Tony had been doing to him, but underscored with wry amusement.

"You gonna come inside, Knox… or just skulk in the doorway? Because I get the impression Jez is happy to invite you into her nest. We probably ought to have a quick word about some other things, though."

FIFTY-SIX

Knox

THIS WAS HELL. I was living in hell. And the worst part was, I knew there were damn good reasons why I'd decided to pack my bags and move into the burning lake of fire... but at the moment, I couldn't have articulated a single one.

I'd managed to survive the limo ride to the house with Jez—*somehow*. Sitting in the back seat, mirroring Jez's position, pressed into opposite corners while both our scents screamed the truth at us. Then we'd arrived, and she'd fled to her nest before I could say a single word.

But what could I have said to her, anyway?

Heath's accusing gaze pinned me, as though he suspected me of being responsible for her distress. *Was* I responsible for her distress?

"Knox," Heath said. "What the hell?"

I had to keep my shit together.

"Like I told Gage over the phone, there was a misunderstanding." I swallowed, not sure when my throat had gotten so dry. "I think Jez feels embarrassed about it, although she shouldn't."

Gray eyes blazing with territorial jealousy. Ragged fingernails digging into the edge of a cheap desk, to keep from digging into her perceived rival's throat instead.

My dick twitched.

I prayed Heath wouldn't notice.

"A misunderstanding," he echoed, his tone deep with veiled skepticism.

"Yes," I told him firmly. "A misunderstanding. Nothing to worry about."

"Right…" He trailed off. "So, you're sure you're okay, then?"

"Of course I'm okay," I said. "I'm *fine*. But… erm… it might be best if we get a private driving tutor to come out here for her. Less complicated."

He stared at me, his hard green eyes unblinking. "You know I'll get the full story one way or another."

I suspected he would, and I wasn't at all sure why the thought bothered me as much as it did.

"It would probably do her good to talk about things," I replied, because that sounded like the sort of thing a rational person would say.

Heath's wordless noise of incredulity in response to that platitude neatly summed up the entire exchange.

I shifted from foot to foot. "If you'll excuse me, I have quite a bit more work to finish this afternoon. I'll see you later, Heath." And then, I fled with only marginally more dignity than Jez had managed.

I'd chosen the airy, open-plan space adjacent to the main floor library as my office shortly after purchasing this property. At the time, it had seemed like a serene place to get work done—not that I'd spent much time in this house since buying it a couple of years ago.

Now, I cursed myself for not choosing some cramped, remote closet space in far corner of the attic, and having it soundproofed to professional music studio standards.

First, I heard Heath conferring in low tones with Gage and Tony. Then the elevator doors opened and closed, after which I could make out the sound of cables and pulleys as the car descended to the basement level. Shortly afterward, the sound of a tentative door-knock filtered up from almost directly below me.

More voices, the exchange indistinct. The conversation rose and fell, Jez's voice gaining volume until I clearly made out the words, "*I already tried to kill him! Am I supposed to add sexual assault to the rap sheet now?*" before growing too quiet to be intelligible.

I ground my teeth together and cursed alpha hearing... alpha smell... alpha possessiveness—

Basically, all things related to being an alpha.

Everything had seemed so simple before Jez came along. It wasn't so much that I didn't desire things that I couldn't have. I wanted my sister back... but she was gone. I wanted to take down the Vozzina gang, and all the other people like them… but I couldn't do that without legal proof that seemed impossible to obtain. I wanted to save as many omegas as I could from the same fate that had claimed Maria… but no matter how many we rescued, there were always more that we couldn't help.

Now, though, the object of my desire was in a room directly below my feet, surrounded by the rest of my pack. Unattainable only because I'd decided she should be.

The conversation downstairs trailed off to silence. With a sigh of relief, I turned my focus to the very real pile of work that genuinely did need to get done. I opened the first email…

… and I was still staring blankly at it ten minutes later. I hadn't even made it past the first sentence. It was so *quiet* downstairs. What were they doing?

I returned my fractured attention to the urgent message from my customs contact in Canada, trying not to picture Jez wrapped up in the others' arms, seeking comfort from them inside her cozy nest.

An hour passed, as I doggedly worked my way through the backlog of important communications piling up in my inbox. The silence in the house stretched. Had they fallen asleep? It was still afternoon—but Gage and Tony were recovering from serious injuries, and Jez might have crashed pretty hard after her earlier adrenaline dump.

"Nngh…"

The wordless moan teased the edges of my hearing, and my fingers stilled on my keyboard. Was someone having a nightmare?

"*Ah… ah… ah!*"

More moaning. Not Jez. Tony? The anguished sounds grew louder, before being promptly muffled. Silence fell again, only to be broken by more low conversation that I couldn't make out.

A louder cry punctuated the indistinct muttering—sharp and startled. That was *definitely* Tony, and if I was working on the assumption that no one here would actually torture our resident beta, that really only left one other possibility.

My cock, which had spent my entire adult life not giving a flying fuck that other people around me were having sex, jumped to full hardness so fast that it left me lightheaded.

A second, different cry pierced the walls—this one in a higher register. It, too, was quickly cut off; but the damage had been done.

MATE.

The word echoed through my body like a clarion call, dragging me up and out of my chair without prior approval from my brain. I didn't remember deciding to leave the office. I didn't remember choosing to walk down the winding central staircase to the basement level.

I *did* remember the feeling of slamming face first into the invisible wall of Jez's sex-soaked pheromones. Except this time, there was no convenient dampener shot waiting for me. Only espresso and burnt sugar, the odor of a desperate omega silently begging for a knot.

My dick throbbed painfully against my trousers; the sensation multiplied a hundredfold compared to how bad things had been in the back of the limo. My feet carried me down the darkened hallway to the half-open door that was the source of both the sounds and the pheromone cocktail.

Wet, gagging noises came from inside, interspersed with Tony mumbling things like, *"More!"* and *"Please!"* while sounding like he had marbles in his mouth. Then came Jez's muffled scream, and I was in the doorway, staring shamelessly at the sight of Jez convulsing in ecstasy on Heath's lap while Tony jerked his own cock with frantic movements as Gage fucked his face.

Heath froze abruptly. Gage looked up, meeting my gaze without surprise.

"You gonna come inside, Knox... or just skulk in the doorway?" he asked. "Because I get the impression Jez is happy to invite you into her nest. We probably ought to have a quick word about some other things, though."

Abruptly, every eye in the room was on me. Or, rather, every eye except Tony's, since Gage was still holding his head down, choking Tony on his cock. The sound of Tony coming broke the sudden silence. He sobbed, his hips jerking as he spurted jizz onto the cushions below him as though he might never stop.

"Looks like you've got Tony's seal of approval to be here, too." Gage's voice had gone hoarse. He eased Tony's mouth off his jutting erection with a murmured apology. Tony collapsed against the edge of the couch, panting hard and looking like all his bones had dissolved. Gage murmured soothing nonsense and stroked his thick, dark hair.

"Jez," Heath said, sounding cautious. "Would you like Knox to come inside and join us?"

"Yes," Jez whispered, her eyes huge and dark with the same lust that spiked her scent. She slid off of Heth's lap and crawled toward me.

A feral growl ripped free of my chest. In three strides, I was in front of her, dropping to my knees and rolling her unresisting form into the piles of pillows surrounding us. She whimpered and settled on her back, her shirt riding up to show the pale skin of her vulnerable belly. Her jeans were undone, the waistband low on her hips. A hint of pale-blond curly hair was visible in the V of the open zipper.

Instinct drew my hand down to frame the graceful line of her throat, and her entire body went soft and pliant as she arched her neck, baring her most vulnerable places to me. Her intoxicating perfume rose around me like a cloud, promising all sorts of delicious and forbidden things.

"Knox," Gage said. "We should—"

I straightened from my crouch, snarling at him. His jaw snapped shut, his eyes going wide with shock. Jez shuddered, her scent growing even sharper. She scrambled onto her hands and knees, practically shoving her gorgeous ass at me.

And that was it. I was done.

I ripped my fly open and shoved my trousers down to my hips. Then I dragged Jez's jeans and panties down until they caught around her thighs. Grabbing her by the hips, I slammed home.

It was like sinking into hot molasses. She took me and took me and *took me*, sucking me into her body until I was completely buried in her scalding heat. The noise she made was strangled and desperate, as though she was biting her lip in a doomed attempt to stay silent.

"*No*," I growled, sliding one hand up the length of her spine and using it to press her upper body flat to the floor. I pinned her there, my fingers tight around her nape, gasping as the new angle squeezed her walls tighter around me. "I want to hear you scream like you *mean it.*"

Still pinning her, I pulled almost all the way out and shoved back in, harder than before. She rewarded me with a high-pitched cry, and the fluttering of her inner muscles as they tried to keep me from pulling out.

"That's it," I hissed. "You're *mine* now. Sing for me, my little murderer."

I pulled back again, and this time she slammed backward, meeting me halfway with a wavering wail that sounded like it was half rage, half rapture. All control lost, we descended into a frenzy of wild fucking.

I was only vaguely aware of Heath and Gage groaning... of Heath growling, "Fuck... Tony... I can feel them. Can I—?"

Time was meaningless. Beyond the red haze across my vision, I caught glimpses of Tony once more on the floor with his head over Gage's lap, Heath fucking between his thighs and shoving Gage's cock into his throat with every thrust.

Jez went wild, clawing and biting at the pillows beneath her as her body shuddered under me. My entire world narrowed down to the sensation of her passage clamping around my length, sending white-hot streamers of pleasure careening up and down my spine.

She screamed. I roared. The heat flooding through me circled tighter and tighter, gathering at the base of my spine and exploding outward as I spurted into her welcoming depths.

Mine... mine... mine, I chanted silently, shoving deeper just to feel my release jetting as far into her body as I could get it.

Heath cried out as well, followed a moment later by Gage's, "Fuck, yes! *Fuck*! Ow, yes, no, don't stop... goddamn broken ribs, *fuck*!"

The base of my cock swelled, caught fast in Jez's unforgiving embrace. What felt like twenty years' worth of stress drained out of my muscles like water, leaving me weak and shaky in its wake. Gracelessly, I dragged Jez into a barely controlled sideways roll; more of a collapse, really. We ended up spooned together on our sides, breathing hard.

A few feet away, Heath and Tony had collapsed in a similar manner, with their legs tangled together. Only Gage was still upright, and that was just because he was sitting on the couch.

The sharp neediness of Jez's scent mellowed into sweet, drugged satisfaction. My nose was buried in her hair, but I sniffed down the side of her neck to where it was strongest. Her gland was right there, beneath my lips. I ran my tongue over it, drawing a shudder from her as I traced the indents from two sets of teeth.

Two sets of teeth that *weren't mine*. My incisors scraped temptingly over the scars.

"Knox." Gage's voice was soft. "Not like this."

Saliva flooded my mouth. I wavered… but then I remembered the shock of finding out that Heath had bitten her when they were both out of their minds with heat drugs. I pressed my lips tightly together and rested my forehead against her soft hair instead.

"Not like this," I agreed, my voice a dry rasp.

"Good." Relief colored Gage's voice. "Tony, you okay down there, cub?"

"Uh-huh," Tony mumbled blearily, sounding like he was phoning it in from somewhere beyond Pluto's orbit.

"Kitten, how about you?"

Jez stretched like a cat, humming as the movement sent shockwaves through us both. "Mm-hmm. Could've bitten me, though. I wouldn't mind."

My mouth started watering again. I swallowed rapidly.

"Not till we've talked," Gage said. "But at this point, I think you're gonna get your wish one way or another. Ain't that right, Knox?"

I licked my lips, trying once more to remember all the reasons this couldn't work.

"Maybe so," I said.

FIFTY-SEVEN

Jez

SOMEHOW, WE ENDED UP in a messy sprawl on top of and next to the sofa. I'd lost my jeans and panties along the way; Tony was naked except for a worn pair of boxer briefs. The alphas were in a bit better shape when it came to clothing, but Knox had at least taken off his button-down shirt and his polished leather loafers.

I sat curled in Knox's arms on the floor. His low purr rumbled through my chest, soothing parts of me I hadn't even known existed before I met this pack. Heath lay on his back on the couch with Tony draped over his chest. One of Heath's arms looped around Tony's shoulders to steady him in place. His other arm flopped over the edge of the sofa cushion. His hand rested on my head, and his fingernails scratched idly at my scalp, spreading warmth down the length of my spine.

At some point, I would need to get up and take a shower. I could feel Knox's release dripping out of me, mixed with my own leftover slick. On the streets, I'd been used to being filthy during stretches of time when I couldn't afford a gym membership with locker room shower privileges. But after only a few weeks with regular access to bathing, I'd already started to go soft.

Besides, this was a different kind of filthy. If I wasn't careful, thinking about Knox's seed inside me would have me trying to start a new round of sex with the alphas. And Gage was right. We did need to talk first.

As if he'd heard my thoughts, Knox drew in a breath, his purr trailing off.

"I… shouldn't have lost control like that," he began. "It sounds like a cliché to say that this kind of behavior isn't like me, but… it *really* isn't. I owe you an apology, Jez—"

"No, you don't," I mumbled, still floating in my post-sex haze.

"I do, though. I didn't even *think* about using protection." He sounded appalled at himself.

Gage had been lounging back against the couch as much as his injuries allowed, with his good hand wrapped around his swollen knot to ease the ache. At that, he lifted his head to look down at us.

"Jez had a full panel of tests after her heat, along with her pregnancy test," he said. "She's clear. And it's not like you've got a laundry list of high-risk sexual encounters in your past, Knox." He paused, his heavy brows furrowing. "In fact—and maybe I shouldn't ask this, since it's none of my business…"

"We all know you're going to ask anyway," Heath said. "Was Jez your first, Knox?"

I craned around to catch a glimpse of Knox's expression, surprise threading through me.

"Not quite," Knox said, sounding uncomfortable. "Some friends in college dragged me to a brothel outside of Las Vegas. I went along with it so they'd stop harping at me, but it was, erm... fairly awful, if I'm being honest."

Gage nodded. "I had you pegged as asexual, and probably aromantic, too. Might need to change that to demi, on both counts."

Knox sighed. "It seems so." His dark eyes met mine. "I know the scent match plays into this, Jez—and all the complications that come along with it. But it's only since I really got to know you as a person, that I can't seem to get you out of my head. I hope that's all right, after all the things I said to you before."

I can't forget that you're my scent match, any more than you can forget I'm yours. But I don't think trying to act on that would be fair to either of us. Not after everything that's happened.

The words had lived inside my memory in vivid detail, ever since he'd said them. I thought I'd been fine with what he'd told me. I *had* been fine with it.

Knox wasn't finished, though. "You're brave. Loyal. Fierce, even when people hurt you. If it wasn't for you, Gage and Tony wouldn't be here. I can never repay you for that. But this feeling is something different. It's more than gratitude. I've never felt like this about another person before, Jez."

I couldn't breathe. On the couch, Heath, Tony, and Gage were also staring at Knox like they didn't recognize him.

Knox swallowed hard, his Adam's apple bobbing. "If you'll have me, it would be my honor to mate you, once we've both agreed to it while in our right minds. But not right away. I want you to think about it first."

I opened my mouth to say that I didn't have to think about it, but Knox shook his head, stopping me.

"And if you agree, I'd like it to happen during your next heat," he finished.

I paused to make sure he was actually done this time.

"The answer is yes," I told him.

His shoulders slumped in relief. "Oh. All right then."

Tony was staring at us, looking so much like a live-action heart-eye emoji that it almost made me laugh past the burn of my unshed tears. Then Knox turned to him, and he froze.

"Tony," Knox said. "I'm still figuring this out… but if everyone else is amenable, and, I mean, if *you're* amenable, obviously — then I'd like permission to also court you. Romantically, that is. I can't promise anything sexual, but I'm not ruling it out, either." He cleared his throat, looking awkward. "As you can probably tell, I'm still figuring myself out at the age of thirty-two. Which is fairly embarrassing."

Tony looked shocked, but he recovered way faster than I had. He lounged on Heath's chest with an exaggerated look of thoughtfulness.

"Hmm. Would it involve you buying me more nice clothes and taking me to fancy restaurants?" he asked.

"Whatever you like," Knox said.

"What about movie nights with popcorn and cuddling?" Tony leaned on his elbows and shot me a wink so fast I barely caught it.

Knox squirmed. "Yes, but I might be really bad at it."

"You're not bad at it," I assured him, wriggling in a bit more snugly against his toned body.

"Congrats—you got the Jez *Seal of Cuddling Approval*, boss," Gage said, amusement clear in his voice. "Holy shit. We're gonna be a proper pack? For real? This is *fucking awesome*."

"Who would have guessed we'd end up here?" Heath added dryly... but I could feel how pleased he was through the bond.

"Who indeed?" Knox echoed wryly, his strong arms squeezing tighter around me.

<hr>

After the growing stickiness finally drew me to the luxury six-jet shower in the nest's attached bathroom, the others wandered off to get cleaned up and arrange for a meal to be delivered. Clean and sated, I lay on my back on one of the nest's scattered beanbag chairs, staring at the twinkling fairy lights above me with unfocused eyes.

Was this real?

Idly, I slipped a hand inside my fuzzy robe and pressed my fingers to one of the matching sets of bruises on my hips. The imprint of Knox's grip gave a low, achy throb in response—physical proof that the stoic pack leader had, in fact, been balls-deep in me less than an hour ago.

A light knock tapped at the door, followed by a muffled voice. *"It's Tony. Can I come in?"*

I retied my robe and went to let him in. "Hi."

"Hi." He crossed to the couch and flopped down on it, staring at the ceiling much as I had been doing a minute ago. "So. Um. That was a thing that happened. Apparently."

I went back to my beanbag, but this time I perched on it and hugged my knees to my chest as I contemplated the last few hours. "… Yeah."

Tony ran a hand roughly through his damp hair before letting it fall. "Yeah. Except, this kind of stuff *doesn't* happen, Jez. Not to people like us."

I knew exactly what he meant. *People like us. The broken ones. Society's discards.*

"But what if it did?" I asked.

He threw his hands up in the air. "I mean— I don't know? Are we supposed to just… what? Live happily ever after like a pair of really fucked-up fairytale princesses?"

We stared at each other for long moments.

"I will if you will," I said, before smirking at him and adding, *"Princess."*

He flipped me the bird. I laughed, and a second later, so did he.

"Oh, my god," he groaned. "This is seriously happening. No, listen, Jez… *it's really happening.*"

I wasn't quite ready to say that part out loud, so I pivoted.

"You know, you're kind of hot when you're getting fucked from both ends," I told him. "Is it okay that I liked that?"

His cheeks flamed scarlet. "It's okay. You already know how gay I am—"

"So gay," I assured him. "The gayest."

He choked on another laugh. "Yup. And… I thought it might be weird, you know? Seeing you like that. But when Gage started teasing me about forcing us to watch each other while they made both of us come…"

"Oh, god." I buried my face in my knees. "Yes. That part."

"I nearly shot my load, right there and then," Tony said.

"I came like a freight train when Gage shoved your face down on his cock and you choked," I told my knees. Then I lifted my head. "Maybe there are, like, gay 'get-out-of-jail-free' cards because there's three of them, and they're all super-hot?"

Tony nodded solemnly. "I will accept the gay 'get-out-of-jail-free' card. Thanks."

"I guess if you think it's hot, and I think it's hot, and they think it's hot—then, maybe it's just hot?" I suggested.

"Yeah, I'm pretty sure it was hot," he agreed.

"We're really going to do this, aren't we," I said, feeling wonder spread through me like warm sparkles. "We're going to live with a fucking rich-as-fuck alpha pack."

"And we are going to screw them incessantly," Tony replied. "Jez, there is going to be *so much screwing* in this house."

"*Jesus*," I said unthinkingly, unable to believe that lust had started tightening in my belly again, so soon after having my insides rearranged by Knox's giant dick. Twin prickles of interest reflected back along the bond.

"I need to go shopping for lube," Tony muttered, as though to himself. "Lube and butt plugs. Because *Christ*, these guys are big."

I pursed my lips, trying to hide my stupid grin.

"I will clean your bathroom for a month if you make Knox take you butt-plug shopping as part of his *romantic courtship*," I told him.

Tony rolled his head to the side to meet my gaze, wide-eyed. We stared at each other for a beat, and then we both descended into undignified, hiccupping peals of laughter.

FIFTY-EIGHT

Tony

I DIDN'T MAKE Knox take me butt-plug shopping. I wasn't a *monster*, and that would have been cruel and unusual punishment for a guy who still seemed vaguely grossed out by the memory of having been dragged to a brothel more than a decade ago.

Even without the butt plugs, it was pretty clear that any ideas Knox had about 'courting,' as he insisted on calling it, had been taken directly from Victorian romance novels. Or… possibly not, since try as I might, I couldn't picture Knox actually *reading* a Victorian romance novel.

And so, I hung out with a faintly perplexed bazillionaire a couple of nights per week, had doors opened for me, chairs pulled out for me, ate the most amazing food I'd ever had in my life, and went on truly epic, paid-for shopping sprees, often with Jez joining us as well.

I probably shouldn't have been surprised that a pack who ran a sprawling import/export empire was good at organizing things and using their time wisely. At no point did either Jez or I feel like we were taking a back seat to the other. We got alone-time with each alpha on a regular basis, and also group time in various combinations.

I'd been wrong about one thing, though. It wasn't a constant sex-fest. That might have been disappointing, if it weren't for the reason behind our near-celibacy.

With the mating bond, Gage could feel it whenever either Heath or Jez got frisky, whether it was happening right in front of him or a thousand miles away. And despite his protestations, it was miserable for him while he couldn't knot a partner because of his injuries.

Yes, there were knotting sleeves available, designed to make busting a nut outside of a willing body more comfortable for an alpha—but a knotting sleeve wouldn't do a damn thing to dull the pain of climaxing with three broken ribs.

Of course, Gage being Gage, he'd been adamant that just because he was out of action, it didn't mean the rest of us had to be. Jez had immediately vetoed that, and I didn't blame her one bit. Unfortunately, that left only two people outside of the mating bond—me and Knox. And I was pretty sure Knox and I weren't going to be together sexually. He simply wasn't wired that way.

At the end of the day, maybe it was just as well. I had an industrial-sized bottle of the best lube money could buy, a set of brand-new, graduated anal dilators, and an increasingly large mental vault of wank material, because *damn*.

Plus, I was good at staying quiet… mostly.

Let's just say, it was easier when it was just me by myself, instead of me in a room with one or more growly and dominant fantasy men with huge dicks. My goal was to be ready for Jez's upcoming heat, when the growly, dominant fantasy men with huge dicks might not be under careful control, like they usually were with me.

Which, yeah… that prospect was a big part of my previously mentioned mental wank bank material these days.

But other parts of pack life were good, too. Very, *very* good, in fact.

I had no worries about money, no worries about loneliness, no worries about physical safety as long as we were holed up in the mega-mansion, safely out of reach of the Vozzinas or anyone else who might wish us harm.

Plus, there was my new favorite hobby of making Knox watch the most ridiculous movies Jez and I could come up with. He'd admitted to having seen *Airplane!*, but he hadn't seen the sequel. He made it to the periscope scene with William Shatner before silently cracking up over the line about irony being pretty ironic sometimes; his chest shaking beneath Jez and me as we curled up against his sides.

From that, we graduated to *Killer Klowns from Outer Space* and *Attack of the Killer Tomatoes*. After which, he countered with *Monty Python and the Holy Grail*, which I'd already seen, and *Life of Brian*, which I hadn't.

We'd just finished that last one earlier to-night. I was pretty sure everyone else had headed to bed, but an odd restlessness had me pulling out my laptop. There was something I'd been putting off. For some reason, this finally felt like the right time.

I brought up my group chat with Byron's pack in St. Louis on Messenger. It had been quiet lately, mostly because everyone else in the chat saw each other on a daily basis, while I'd been a bit distracted by the whole 'nearly getting blown up' thing and hadn't wanted to worry them.

Hey, I typed. *Anyone awake and online?*

I'd figured no one would be, so I'd have plenty of time to mentally compose and edit what I wanted to tell them. The Price pack wasn't my family. But they were the only people who'd looked out for me when my own flesh and blood couldn't be bothered to give a shit. I figured they deserved to know about the recent changes in my life.

Dots marched across the screen.

Whoops. So much for mental editing.

A message from Nat—the pack's beta—popped up.

Heya. Yeah, couldn't sleep. It's been a while, hasn't it? How are you doing?

I'd had less interaction with Nat than I had with Byron, or the pack's leader, Zalen. I knew he'd been married to the pack's female omega before they met the others, and that their introduction had been messy... but I'd never gone prying for details.

Maybe I should have talked to him more, because right now, getting wisdom from a male beta who was part of a pack sounded like a really smart idea.

I'm good, I sent back. *Really good. I'm pretty sure I found a pack, here in Chicago.*

An incoming video call window popped up barely two seconds later.

Sheepishly, I clicked the green icon. The screen pixelated for a moment, and then cleared to show an Asian man in his late thirties with messy dark hair and deep-set brown eyes.

"You're joining a pack?" Nat demanded. *"Turn your camera on; I need details. Actually, no. Wait. Hold that thought."*

He was on his phone, based on the narrow portrait image. The room behind him spun crazily, the picture catching and freezing again for a second. The sound of loud knocking came through the speaker as the view swung again to show a random patch of ceiling.

"Hey, wake up, you guys! I've got Tony on a video call. He says he's joining a pack!" The video swooped again, settling on Nat's face. *"Okay, now give me those details. The others will be here in a minute."*

I swallowed hard. This was why I'd needed time to edit the story. Somehow, blurting out that my ex-best friend, who'd secretly murdered my stepdad, had also tried to murder the head of the pack I'd been doing odd jobs for, didn't sound like a good way to open.

"Um…" I said. "It's kind of complicated?"

Nat snorted. *"You think so? I hate to say it, but you're talking to the king of 'it's complicated,' when it comes to relationships."*

"Well, he's not lying about that," said a familiar voice, rough with sleep. Byron shoved into the camera frame.

"Hi, Byron," I said weakly.

"What's this about a pack?" Zalen said, squeezing in as well.

Maybe I could just fast-forward past the awkward parts. "Well… uh… there's this pack who runs a business here in Chicago. I started taking odd jobs for them to make extra money, and…"

I ran through a heavily sanitized version of reuniting with a close friend after losing touch with her for more than a year, only to discover that she was scent-matched to the pack I was working for, after I'd already fallen into bed with one of the alphas.

"I thought he only wanted a one-night stand," I finished. "And I would have been okay with that! I mean, mostly okay? But it turns out, he wanted more, and one of the other alphas was also interested, and Jez is okay with it, so…"

I trailed off.

Emiel, the hulking alpha who fought in cage matches for fun, tilted the phone until I could see him.

"*Are they good people? They treating you right?*" he demanded.

The first part was a loaded question, especially when it came to Jez and her murderous tendencies… not to mention Heath and his familiarity with scrubbing the evidence from homicide scenes. But the second part was easy.

"I've never felt as safe and cared for as I do with these people," I said honestly.

After a moment, Emiel nodded. "*Okay. That's good. But you know if that ever changes, you gotta tell us right away.*"

I smiled a watery smile. "I don't think that's going to happen… but thanks."

Byron tilted the phone back toward himself. "*When do we get to meet this pack of yours?*" he asked.

Mia, the pack's female omega, ducked under his arm to get in the frame. "*Can you bring them to St. Louis one of these days? You could bring them to the restaurant. I'll have a word with Shaniqua.*"

Mia and Nat had owned an award-winning restaurant together before they'd met Zalen's pack. They'd since stepped back to focus on running a culinary arts program through Zalen's youth center, but they were still close friends with the family that had bought the restaurant from them.

"I'll ask," I said. "I'd really like that, actually. It would be great to see you all in person."

A knock sounded at my bedroom door, nearly making me jump out of my skin.

"Tony?" Heath's muffled voice filtered through to me. *"You up? You're going to want to see what's on the news!"*

"Is everything okay there?" Zalen asked.

I blinked my attention back to the video call. "Yeah, I think so. Apparently, there's something on the news I'm supposed to see." I leaned away from the screen and raised my voice. "Just a second! I'm on a call to St. Louis!" I turned back to the screen. "Seriously, I'll ask if there's a way we can all come down and see you. Take care, you guys. And thanks for being there. Give the kiddos my love."

"Don't be a stranger," Zalen said. *"We're really happy for you, by the way. Congratulations."*

"Thanks," I told them again, unable to hold back my sappy smile this time. "Talk soon, okay?"

After closing the call, I set the laptop aside and went to the door. Outside, Heath was pacing restlessly in the hall.

"Hi," I said. "What's on the news?"

He came to an abrupt halt and gestured me to head toward the TV room. "Oh, just the little matter of the FBI descending on the Vozzina pack house and arresting everyone they found inside."

I stumbled, nearly falling over my own feet as I whirled to face him. "What?"

He nodded, his bushy red eyebrows lifting for emphasis. "Yep. The clip of Lorenzo Vozzina getting handcuffed and perp-walked to a black SUV is all over the news channels. Come on—Gage is recording it for us."

FIFTY-NINE

Jez

I WAS HALF-ASLEEP when the others dragged me into the entertainment room, but that wasn't the reason my brain kept stuttering over the image of a tall, square-jawed alpha in silk pajamas and a bathrobe getting dragged past a group of chattering reporters and shoved into the back of an official-looking black vehicle with his hands securely bound behind him.

"You're *sure* that's him?" I asked Knox.

Our pack leader looked similarly groggy after having been roused from a sound sleep. However, that didn't dull the sharp edges of the smile he was wearing. "Oh, that's definitely him."

Gage was scrolling his phone one-handed, having passed the TV remote to Heath. This was the third time Heath had rewound the footage to show the perp-walk to the SUV, and I was pretty sure I could have watched it another dozen times without getting bored.

"Says here they scooped up everyone in the house," Gage said, not looking away from his phone. "Thirteen people arrested, with more expected in the next few days as they follow up with other *'people of interest'*."

"Anything yet about the charges?" Knox asked.

Gage scrolled some more. "Suspicion of interstate sex-trafficking of minors… solicitation of prostitution with a minor under the age of fifteen… conspiracy to commit sex-trafficking… conspiracy to murder. *Shit*. They're really throwing the book at him. Paolo must be singing like a canary."

"He is if he knows what's good for him," Knox said grimly.

Once again, I felt a little shiver travel down my spine at the cold calculation in the pack alpha's voice—confirming what I already knew, that I was just bent enough in the head to find Knox's icy manipulation of Paolo a turn-on.

Gage's eyes flicked to me, and he snorted. "Hey, Knox? You smell the way Jez's scent changed just now? That's how she smells when she wants to jump your bones."

Knox cleared his throat awkwardly. I was pretty sure that if his skin was any lighter, I'd have seen his cheeks redden. Mine were certainly flaming.

"Sorry," I said in a small voice.

"Don't worry, it's not just you," Tony muttered.

"I can't believe you pulled this off," Heath put in. "Do you think the feds will be able to get any of those charges to stick?"

Knox looked relieved at the change of subject. "Let's just say I've got deep pockets, and I intend to use those deep pockets to ensure that the Vozzina pack gets nailed to the fucking *wall*."

I swallowed the helpless whimper of arousal that tried to escape, even if I couldn't do anything about my scent. It would be bad and wrong of me to ask Knox if he'd be willing to talk like that while he was fucking me in the heat nest, right?

… right?

Gage looked at me with a furrow forming between his heavy brows. "This is really affecting you, kitten. You too, Tony. Knox was always gonna do whatever it took to make sure these assholes pay for what they did."

I exchanged a helpless glance with Tony.

He found his words first.

"That's the thing, though. People like Lorenzo Vozzina don't ever pay for the stuff they do. Not as long as they only hurt the victims that no one in power cares about."

That was exactly it.

I licked my lips. "I learned way too young that what happens to people like me doesn't matter."

"It fucking *does*," Heath said. His presence snapped angrily inside the bond, like flames licking at dry wood.

"It does to *you*," I shot back. "But you are literally the first people I've ever met who were actually *doing* something about it, even though it put you at risk."

Tony huffed out a breath. "They're the third people I've met. The first was a pack in St. Louis who helped me get out from under my stepfather's boot. *You* were the second, Jez."

I paused, my jaw clicking shut as I remembered the resounding *crack* of a heavy lamp base slamming into bone.

"And this pack was the third," Tony added. "But it's different, seeing society forced to deal with someone like Vozzina publicly. *That's* the part that doesn't seem real."

Knox's voice and expression softened. "The Vozzinas are about to experience just how *real* things can get. It's wrong that neither of you got the help you needed, back when you really needed it. It's *wrong*, and to the extent that it's within my power, I'm not going to let it stand."

"We've been chipping away at the edges of this shit," Gage said. "Doing damage control… sticking our thumbs in the dike, trying to plug up the holes. Maybe it's time to drain the floodwaters instead."

Knox raised an eyebrow. "Tortured metaphors aside, you should both know up front that the court cases are likely to drag on for ages. Dockets, appeals, more appeals… there won't be instant justice. But with everything I've put in motion, there isn't going to be any bond set for these assholes. The Vozzina pack is behind bars, and they'll stay that way while the wheels of justice grind onward."

"So, we're safe now?" I hadn't meant to ask the question aloud. But I'd *never* been safe. Not being safe was, quite possibly, the defining characteristic of my entire life to date.

Heath and Gage exchanged a glance, twin waves of protectiveness washing across our connection. Heath crossed the room and wrapped me in his arms. Then he gestured with one for Tony to join us in a three-way hug.

Gage grumbled, "Argh. These fucking bones can't knit fast enough. Give 'em an extra squeeze for me, Heath."

"Jez—you and Tony are members of my pack," Knox said, from his perch against a heavy side table. "Any danger that comes for you has to go through all three of us first."

I felt Tony tremble in reaction to the words… or maybe that was me.

"And there's a lot fewer dangers for us now, with these sadistic shitheads locked up in the slammer," Gage said with finality.

Tony let out an unsteady breath and eased away from Heath's hold.

"In that case, do you think we could arrange an overnight trip to St. Louis, one of these days?" he asked. "There are some people back home that I'd really like you all to meet."

❖

I'd heard a lot from Tony about the pack in St. Louis that had helped him when he was a kid. I wanted to meet them, but I was also super-nervous about it. Not a surprise to anyone, since I didn't exactly have a lot of experience being invited to nice places where I was expected to make polite small talk with respectable people that I was trying to impress.

For better or worse, it ended up taking several more weeks before Knox was willing to consider traveling away from the safety of the gated community where we were staying. This was good in one way, because it meant that Gage was out of his leg cast and sling, although he was still using a cane and doing PT exercises several times a day.

However, it was also nerve-wracking, because the main reason Knox kept putting off the trip was because the police and FBI were still tracking down more people connected with Lorenzo Vozzina's operation.

An abundance of caution, he called it.

Even Knox seemed taken aback by how *huge* the investigation had grown.

"I thought we were tackling one asshole and his minions, trafficking omegas through Chicago as a side hustle," he muttered, after yet another call with his team of high-paid lawyers. "But this fucker has been running the largest operation in the Midwest, with ties to Mexico and Canada as well."

My heart skipped a beat.

"Canada?" I asked in a choked voice.

He put his phone down, giving me his full attention. The two of us were alone in the kitchen—him with a cup of coffee, me with a late breakfast since I'd overslept for the third day in a row. I'd been exhausted and cranky for the past few days, and this new revelation wasn't helping.

"Yes," Knox confirmed. "I'm not sure that we'll ever be able to prove it legally, this far after the fact. But it's possible—even probable—that the people your father sold you to were part of his operation."

I tried to process that for a few moments, and failed utterly.

"Oh," I said, after a long pause.

Knox looked as though he was debating his next words. "Jez... I've been meaning to ask you something, but I'm not sure how to do it."

"Just ask," I said.

At this point, how bad could it be?

He gave a slow nod. "Would you be willing to give me your father's last name, so I can try to track him down? Whether you were trafficked through the Vozzina syndicate or some other group, he should be held to account."

I sat very still. For several moments, I didn't even breathe.

Omega freeze instinct, hard at work.

"Jez?" Worry laced Knox's voice.

Heavy footsteps beat rapidly toward the kitchen. Heath appeared in the doorway.

"What's going on?" he demanded.

"I asked Jez if she'd like me to try and track down her father," Knox said quietly. "For justice."

The clack of a cane on tile announced Gage's arrival a few moments later. He raised his free hand when Heath glanced at him and drew breath to speak. "I heard him. Jez? You okay?"

"Yeah," I managed.

"What do you think about what Knox said?" he asked gently.

"Levine," I said.

"What?" Heath asked.

"My father's name is Levine. Michael Levine. We lived in Thunder Bay, Ontario." I met Knox's dark eyes and held them, unblinking. "Do it. Find him and bury him so deep in the legal system that he never sees the light of *day*."

"I'll do everything in my power to make that happen," he vowed. "But I also have to ask about your mother. Was she involved at all?"

I shook my head so fast that my neck hurt. "No! She tried to stop him. He hit her. Knocked her down. I didn't see her get up afterward. I don't know if she—"

My throat closed up, cutting off the words. Gage limped forward, his big hand closing on my shoulder and squeezing.

"If I can find her as well, would you want to have contact with her?" Knox asked, still in that painfully gentle tone.

Would I want to see my mother again, if I could? I closed my eyes, memories of toasted marshmallows over a campfire, and Christmas baking, and warm hugs piling on top of each other in my head. Was she even still alive? I hadn't thought about her in so long; her ghost was locked away with all the other parts of my past that I couldn't risk remembering.

"Yes," I whispered, not daring to believe it might happen.

"I'll see what I can do." Another warm hand closed on my upper arm, Knox's woodsy scent filling my nostrils in the instant before his dry lips brushed my hairline. "In fact, I'll get started on that right now. Oh, and Tony's arranged for us to meet his St. Louis pack this coming Saturday. I think it's safe enough, now. Bud's arranging the travel details."

After a final, reassuring squeeze of my arm, he turned and left the kitchen. I twisted to press my face against Gage's chest, letting myself be sandwiched between my two mates as Heath wrapped himself around my vulnerable back, covering me.

◆

The plan was for us to fly down to St. Louis on Friday night and make a weekend of it. On… get this. A private. Fucking. Jet.

"You have a *private jet*?" Tony had squeaked, when Knox relayed the details.

Knox looked at him in evident surprise. "No, of course not. That would be wasteful. I charter one whenever I need it."

So, that was… a thing that rich people did, apparently. And me? Yeah, I'd never even been on a plane before. It was probably bad that flying to St. Louis and back was the part of the trip I was most excited about.

I was also feeling increasingly nervous and out of sorts. I still couldn't seem to sleep when I was supposed to. Instead, I slept late into the morning and dragged for during the rest of the day, feeling itchy and uncomfortable in my own skin.

It got worse and worse until finally coming to a head on Thursday morning, when Gage and Heath cornered me in my nest to ask me what was wrong. My temper snapped, and I yelled at them, snarling in their faces until they both beat a hasty retreat. After which, I ran into the bathroom and burst into hysterical tears, curled up in the tiny space between the toilet and the wall.

My head ached. My sinuses hurt. I felt feverish and twitchy. But most of all, I was overcome by the sudden obsessive belief that everything about my nest was *wrong*.

When a tentative knock came, maybe an hour later, I was halfway through piling every single cushion and blanket in the room into a messy mountain of soft furnishings. I froze, realizing abruptly how insane I probably looked. It wasn't Gage or Heath, though—they'd both slunk off to the far end of the massive house. Knox wouldn't have tapped on the door like that. He'd have knocked properly a couple of times and announced himself.

That left Tony. And for some reason, the idea of Tony being here didn't make me want to scratch furrows into my own skin. I stilled, a blanket clasped in one hand and a fur-covered cushion in the other.

"Can I come in, Jez?" Tony called softly, his voice muffled by wood.

I hesitated… but I knew something was wrong—*badly wrong*—and maybe Tony could help.

"Yes," I said.

The door opened slowly, revealing Tony standing in the opening, holding a bundle of cloth.

"Gage and Heath said you wouldn't let them come in, or talk to them," he said, not moving.

I looked up helplessly. "They can't be here right now. The nest isn't right!"

The nest was so, so wrong. Everything was *wrong*.

Tony looked around at the carnage, his eyes falling on Soft Mountain in the center of the room. His breath whistled out in a slow exhale.

"*Hoo-boy*," he mumbled. Then he stepped forward and held out the bundle. "Here, take these. See if it helps."

"What?" I asked, bewildered… but I accepted the mass of crumpled cloth.

Immediately, the smell of sweat mixed with cedar, woodsmoke, oak, whiskey, orange peel, and baking bread wafted upward like a cloud of bliss, enveloping me. I shoved the handful of clothing against my face and breathed in like an addict taking a hit—not giving a second thought to how I must look.

"Um…" Tony said.

I flushed in embarrassment and yanked the fabric away from my nose.

"Jez," Tony went on. "I think we're going to need to postpone the trip this weekend. You're coming into heat."

Every thought in my brain froze and clattered to the ground like icicles falling from the edge of a roof. "*What?*"

Tony shrugged, shooting me a helpless expression.

"No," I said slowly. "But that's not right. It won't be three months since the silos for another… two-and-a-half weeks?"

I'd always used suppressants during my heats, even if it took my last dollar to buy them on the streets. But my heats came like clockwork—every ninety days. No surprises.

"That wasn't a natural heat," Tony pointed out. "You were drugged. Who knows what that did to your cycle."

I looked down at the dirty laundry in my hands… then at the huge pile of disassembled nesting materials.

"Shit," I said brilliantly.

Tony gave me a sympathetic smile. "I'll just go and let the others know, shall I?"

SIXTY

Jez

APPARENTLY, I WASN'T the only one panicking. Fifteen minutes after Tony left to share the news, he was back at my door, fidgeting awkwardly.

"They want to know if you feel well enough to come upstairs and talk about some things," he said. "And it's okay if you don't! It's only that—"

"I'll come," I said, even though the thought of leaving my nest looking like a tornado had torn through it spiked my anxiety to new heights.

"All right," Tony said, sounding relieved.

I excused myself for a minute, heading back to the bathroom to splash cold water on my face. Straightening, I stared at my reflection in the mirror for a long moment, trying to convince myself that this wouldn't be like last time. Or, god forbid, like the *first* time, way back when I was thirteen.

My pack was here. My mates were here. My closest friend was here… even if I'd just ruined the weekend trip to St. Louis that he'd been so excited about.

I'd known my heat would be coming. I'd even been excited about it. I just hadn't known it was coming so *soon*.

Pushing away from the marble vanity, I took a deep breath, let it out slowly, and went to rejoin Tony. As we headed upstairs, I fiddled with the hem of my turtleneck, not looking at him.

"I'm really sorry about messing everything up for you," I said, and then added, "*Again*," under my breath.

He cut a sideways glance at me. "Didn't realize you were a magic omega with special powers who gets to choose when you come into heat. In which case, yeah—total asshole move on your part. And here I thought we were friends."

I shot him a glare, only to find him smirking at me.

"*Dick*," I told him.

"It's not like the restaurant won't still be there a couple of weeks from now," he said. "And there's always a line out the door, so Shaniqua won't have a problem finding someone else to take our table."

"But your friends—" I began.

"My friends have two omegas in their pack, and they're well aware of what an unexpected heat means," he finished.

I deflated. "Okay. Well, I'm glad you're not angry."

"Angry? I'm about to get more smokin' hot sex in the next few days than I've had collectively in the past several years." He rolled his eyes. "Oh, no... poor me. How ever will I survive?"

Then he looked me up and down as we reached the top of the staircase. "What about you? Are *you* okay?"

"No," I said. "Maybe? I don't know!"

He hesitated. "Do you want a hug? Or would that make things worse??"

I wrapped my arms around my torso, rubbing my biceps as though I was chilled. I felt twitchy and wired; still feverish. "After we talk to the alphas, maybe?"

Tony nodded easily. "Only if you want me to. Come on, they're in the library."

Neutral territory. Much better than having them come to my nest before it—before *I*—was ready.

We walked through the east wing of the giant house. I timed my breathing, trying to quiet my racing heart. Gage and Heath looked up sharply as we entered the elegant, wood-paneled library. Knox, who'd been pacing, turned around to look at us so fast he nearly tripped over his own feet.

The scent of the alphas I was fated to mate hit me like a wall, nearly choking me.

"Jez!" Knox said. "I'm so sorry. I wasn't prepared for this possibility. We don't have a birth control shot on hand yet, but I can tell Bud to get us one; it shouldn't take long."

A strange sense of certainty settled over me, in direct opposition to Knox's barely concealed panic. My right hand crept up to settle over my belly.

"Are you still going to mate me?" I asked, cutting off his torrent of words.

His jaw clicked shut in surprise. "Of course I am," he said, after a slight pause.

I rubbed slow circles over my womb, which had already started to throb with a dull sort of ache.

"Then I don't need birth control," I said… imagining my belly swelling with new life that would actually be loved and protected. Children—*pups*—who would grow up knowing nothing but adoration from five adults. I knew without having to ask that each of us would give up our own life without a second's hesitation to stand between our babies and danger.

Four pairs of shocked eyeballs landed on me. That same shock echoed through the mate bond, blowing past the walls I'd put up after my meltdown this morning. Worry flooded me, chasing away my brief flash of confidence.

"I mean," I stuttered, "maybe you don't want pups? I'm sorry, I should have asked first… I didn't mean to assume—"

"Stop," Gage said, recovering first. "Jez, just hold up for a minute. We're surprised is all. Yes, I want pups. Can't speak for the others."

"We're going to have pups?" Tony asked in a young-sounding voice. I could practically see the same thoughts speeding through his brain that had rushed through mine a minute ago.

Family.

Safety.

Nurture.

All the things we never got from our own families.

"We should have pups," Heath said with certainty, surprising me.

A sense of wonder filtered through my connection with him and Gage, blossoming into giddy happiness.

I looked to Knox, who'd been very quiet during the exchange.

"I am… not against making a family — even though I never expected to have one. At least, not in the sense of having children," he said carefully. "But I want to make very sure that this is *you* talking, Jez, and not your heat hormones talking."

I frowned at him, irrationally incensed even though the rest of me understood that it was a reasonable question. We hadn't talked about children at all before now. I'd pulled this bombshell out of nowhere, and it made sense that Knox would have concerns.

Tony ducked in before I could put words to what I was feeling.

"Knox, she's not in heat *yet*. It's considered patronizing to assume that omegas can't make decisions for themselves, simply on the basis of being hormonal."

I blinked at Tony. Had I *ever* heard him directly chastise Knox like that before? He'd even stepped slightly in front of me, placing me behind his shoulder as though to shield me from Knox's words.

I ducked past him—avoiding touch as I did so, because my nerves still itched and buzzed as though ants were marching over my skin.

"It's okay, Tony," I said. "He's right to ask. Knox, I got angry just now, when you said that. But I can tell that the anger was caused by my hormones. I'm on edge because my heat is close; yet I can still think for myself. I can tell the difference between irrational feelings and rational thoughts. If we're all mated… if we're a pack… then I want to bring our pups into the world, so they can experience all the love we have to give them."

Knox's breath caught. His hand lifted almost convulsively to his chest, and I had the briefest flash of worry that he was having some kind of heart issue that the doctors hadn't caught when he was in the hospital. But a moment later, he seemed to realize what he was doing and let his hand fall.

"I…" He hesitated and swallowed hard. "You should all know something about me that I've kept quiet over the years. My twin sister was taken by omega traffickers when she was twelve."

Several intakes of breath broke the silence. Puzzle pieces quietly clicked into place in my mind, revealing a clearer picture of the alpha in front of me. My heart ached in sympathy with his.

"Losing Maria when we were both so young has shaped my life in a number of different ways," he went on quietly.

"That's why you started hunting traffickers and saving omegas, isn't it," Gage said, not phrasing it as a question.

"It is, yes," Knox confirmed. "But… if we bring pups into the world, I'm going to be *feral* about protecting them. And I do mean, *completely batshit* about it."

"Join the club," Heath said.

Knox shook his head in frustration. "No, I'm serious—if we're going to do this, I'm chucking it all in. The business, the omega rescues, Chicago… *all of it*. We're taking my money, and we're moving somewhere *safe*. Somewhere no one's ever heard of me, or of this pack."

Heath and Gage exchanged a look.

"Might be safer that way for Jez, too," Gage said. "I know you got her a shiny new identity an' all. But she's still someone with a body count. Not that they didn't all deserve it," he added quickly.

God, I *hoped* they'd all deserved it. The idea that I might have been wrong about any of my other targets the way I'd been wrong about Knox still haunted my nightmares.

Knox ran a hand over his scalp, rubbing at it. "We seem to be making all the life-changing decisions at once, today. So, is anyone *against* uprooting the pack and living quietly somewhere off the radar?"

"I've got no blood relatives that are worth a damn," Tony said. "As long as I could still visit the Price pack in St. Louis occasionally, I'm okay with it."

"I'd miss the hot dogs here," Gage said. "That's about it."

"As long as it's warm, I'm in," Heath said. "The winters in Chicago fucking *suck*."

Knox met my eyes, his whole face a question.

"There's nothing to keep me here," I said. "I've been a ghost since I was thirteen years old."

Knox let out a huge breath, his shoulders dropping. "We're doing this, then?"

Tony looked a bit shell-shocked, and I couldn't really blame him.

"I think we're doing this," he said.

<hr>

Unfortunately, even life-altering decisions didn't do much to make the run-up to heat any less awful. By that evening, I'd reassembled my nest in a way that felt a little less wrong than before, although I was still fretfully moving cushions and beanbags around every few minutes.

I wavered back and forth wildly between wanting the alphas here and wanting to be *left the fuck alone*. Tony came and went to suit my mood, giving platonic hugs when I wanted them, and avoiding physical contact when my nerves were too badly shot to handle it. He also pushed food and sports drinks on me until I felt like I might burst, since I wouldn't be eating or drinking for several days once things started.

"What if he changes his mind?" I bleated out of nowhere, shoving the latest plate of toasted cheese sandwiches aside.

"What if who changes his mind about what?" Tony asked patiently.

"What if Knox realizes that he'd have to be nuts to mate me after I tried to kill him?" I nearly wailed.

Tony calmly picked up the plate and nudged the bottle of blue sports drink closer to me. "I think we're pretty far past that point, to be honest. He nearly put toothmarks in your neck that night we all had sex together, and you weren't even in heat then."

I pushed the blue drink back toward him. "I guess."

"If you can't eat or drink anything more, maybe you should try taking a warm bath," he suggested. "I read that can help sometimes."

"Help with what?" I asked sourly. "I already feel like I'm in a sauna."

It was true. I knew, logically, that the nest was the same cozy, comfortable temperature as always. But my scalp was sticky with sweat, my stomach felt like someone had dropped hot coals in it, and my heart was beating double-time against my ribs.

Tony's expression turned sheepish. "Right. Maybe a lukewarm bath, then?"

I drew breath to agree, figuring it couldn't possibly be worse than sitting here in a puddle of my own sweat. Before I could, though, a vicious cramp nearly doubled me over.

I whimpered, clutching at my belly with clawed hands.

Tony shot bolt upright. "Was that a cramp? Is it time? Should I go get—"

Footsteps thundered toward the room—several pairs. The most amazing mix of scents ever created teased my sense of smell, promising relief from the pain and delights beyond anything I'd ever imagined before. Possessive lust slammed across the mating bond from all three directions—my own every bit as strong as Heath and Gage's.

Three alphas skidded to a stop outside the door, poised there as if held back by the thinnest of fraying threads.

"You have to invite them in," Tony whispered, hurrying to set the abandoned plate and bottle out of the way.

The soft, oversized T-shirt I'd been wearing abruptly felt like scratchy burlap pierced through with cactus spines. I tugged at it fitfully, trying to wriggle free without taking my eyes off the display of male flesh hovering outside my door.

"*Please*," I begged, rubbing my thighs together to ease the ache... and three alphas descended on me like iron filings drawn to a magnet.

SIXTY-ONE

Jez

I WAS GOING TO burst into flames, right here in the middle of my nest. Three hot male bodies converged on me, wrapping me up between them in the instant before my knees would have given out.

Heath's soft beard, Gage's prickly stubble, and Knox's fresh-shaven cheek all rubbed against my head and neck, warm breath whuffling over sensitive skin as they scented and marked me. I moaned, and Gage did, too.

"Oh, kitten," he said on the heels of a deep groan. "You smell like every Christmas ever."

I turned my head far enough to catch his earlobe between my teeth, licking his addictive taste from the small bit of skin before letting it slide free.

"No, that's you," I managed, only to gasp as Knox tugged me free of the others' grasp and hauled my stolen T-shirt over my head. I lifted my arms to help—desperate to have it gone, now that I had the real source of those alpha pheromones in my nest.

Mine, to scent and mark and claim.

Gage cupped my face between his big palms, his hazel eyes flicking down to take in my nakedness before dragging back up to my face.

"I took a dampener shot before I came down here, sweetheart," he said.

I struggled to focus on his words as Heath and Knox sniffed their way down my back.

"My body's still too beat up for a full rut," Gage went on, still holding my gaze. "Now, don't get me wrong—I want my dick buried in that pussy of yours as often as you'll let me. But this way, I can keep also an eye on things and make sure Tony doesn't get overwhelmed."

"Too late," Tony said, sounding choked. "I'm already overwhelmed. Jesus *Christ*, you guys are hot."

On either side of me, alphas were stripping out of clothing, revealing sleek muscles under skin. I stared at the contrasting shades of pale and dark, my mouth watering with desire.

I'd more or less lost the thread, after the part where Gage said he wanted to fuck me. But I trusted that whatever the others were talking about, Gage would take care of me—just like he'd always taken care of me. Right now, I was more worried about the way my womb seemed to be spontaneously combusting.

"I need a *cock*," I whined, because my body was *empty*, and being empty *hurt*.

Knox snarled and snapped at Heath, who snarled and snapped back. Possessiveness spiked through the bond; I was just aware enough to understand that Heath should have backed down from his pack leader's claim, and he hadn't. An instant later, the pair sprung at each other, Knox dragging Heath to the cushion-covered floor as the naked pair wrestled for dominance.

"Oh, shit..." Gage huffed a breathless laugh and tugged me away from the writhing male bodies. He flopped down on his back, taking me with him.

"Quick, kitten—hop on my dick before they get their dominance issues sorted out," he said, yanking his loose track pants down to free his erection. "Oy, Tony—you're wearing too many clothes. I want you naked, lubed, and ready to go... because when these knot-brains figure out that you've got an unoccupied hole, they ain't gonna be gentle with you."

"Jesus, are you *trying* to make me come right now?" Tony grumbled. "And for your information, my hole is not unoccupied. I'm using my biggest plug to get loosened up."

"Time to take it out, in that case," Gage shot back.

As far as my brain was concerned, it was all *blah-blah-blah* background noise. Someone was waving a huge dick in front of me, and I was going to ride that motherfucker into the sunset. Gage helped me get my uncooperative body in position, straddling his hips.

"*Oh fuck yes*," I breathed, as I lined him up and impaled myself, shuddering in delicious agony as he stretched and filled the empty, cramping spaces within me. Gage's pleasure roared through the bond, crashing into mine. I felt his smug amusement at having outsmarted the others, who abruptly froze in mid-fight, staring at us with identical expressions of outrage.

From my position riding Gage, I could see most of the room if I turned my head. Tony was naked and looking a bit self-conscious, based on his pink cheeks. He sank down on a handy beanbag and lifted his chin defiantly.

"Hey, why'd you two stop wrestling?" he asked Heath and Knox. Then he deliberately held eye contact with them as he wrapped a hand around his dick and stroked it slowly up and down. "I was enjoying the view."

Heath let out a feral growl and twisted free of Knox's grasp, covering the distance to Tony in three long strides. I ground down on Gage's hard length, letting lust swamp me as Heath grabbed Tony by the ankles and tipped him backward. Tony yelped as his upper body disappeared into the sea of cushions behind him, his hips still balanced on the beanbag even as his arms flailed.

I rolled my hips, purring in delight when Gage wormed a hand between us and started playing with my clit. Heath, still holding Tony by the ankles, bent his legs nearly double before kneeling in front of him and shoving his thick cock into Tony's hole.

Tony bucked and yelled, his head and shoulders still hidden from view by cushions. Heath snarled and pulled back, slamming in again. Tony yelled louder.

"All good over there, cub?" Gage called.

"Oh, f-fuck," Tony moaned, as another brutal thrust rocked him. One of his flailing arms settled between his legs, and he started fisting his bobbing erection with fast, almost frantic movements. "Fuck! *Fuck* yes! S-so good! Harder, goddamn it! *Give it to me harder!*"

My first orgasm rose up, teasing me with its promise of relief as Heath folded Tony in half and pounded into his unresisting body with abandon. Tony's cries rose up, increasingly desperate, just as another warning growl wrenched my attention back to Knox.

The pack leader crawled toward me on hands and knees, an expression of such intensity on his face that my body clenched convulsively in reaction. His brown eyes were all pupil—blown wide. Dark and mindless with desire.

I rose and fell, sliding up and down the slick, heavy length buried inside me—flaunting what my mate and I were doing together. Knox approached us like a hunting cat, his movements smooth and deadly. Gooseflesh erupted up and down my body as he knelt next to us, staring down at Gage lying helplessly on his back.

Quick as a snake, Knox's hand darted out and closed around Gage's throat, pinning him in place as alpha power washed over us. Gage let out a choked noise of shock and climaxed so hard that his jerking hips lifted my entire body off the ground.

His cock jumped and throbbed inside me — the last push I needed to follow him into a crashing orgasm. My vision whited out, every sense focused on the perfect pressure of my mate's knot swelling to fill me.

"Fuckin' *hell*, Knox," Gage said, sounding wrecked.

I flopped down on Gage's broad chest as my muscles abruptly decided to stop working. A miasma of cedar and woodsmoke settled around us in a suffocating haze of unspent lust. Knox nuzzled at my mating gland, sending a shudder through me. But rather than bite, he nibbled down the length of my spine, not stopping until his nose was pressed between my ass cheeks.

I moaned with delight as his tongue delved, lapping at the place Gage and I were joined. My body melted into a puddle as he licked deeply, sliding his tongue forward to tease my stretched passage, then back to circle my hole. He repeated the path for slightly more than an eternity before finally pressing the tip of his tongue inside my body.

Tingles shot up my spine. My clit throbbed and my hips twitched, moving Gage's knot around inside me. Knox shoved his tongue deeper, just as Tony's rhythmic cries rose into a full-throated scream.

As though in sympathy, a second orgasm washed over me. I clamped hard around Gage's knot as the wave took my breath away, drawing a shudder from him. Knox, who hadn't slowed down, seemed prepared to eat out my ass until the sun burned down to a cinder.

Inside, I was flying, even though my body was very much tethered in place by Gage's knot. Giving in to the inevitable, I lay limp and spent on top of him, letting my low, keening cries join Tony's harsh panting and occasional strangled curses as Knox continued to lick into me. A whimper lodged in my throat as blunt fingers dragged through my leaking slick. They replaced Knox's tongue, probing inside and teasing the thin barrier of flesh stretched around Gage's knot.

"*Fuck...*" Gage craned his head up far enough to get a glimpse of what Knox was doing; then he let it fall back in the pillows. "Jesus Christ, kitten. You think this is bad? Just you wait until Mr. OCD here discovers all the ways he can make you scream by playing with your clit for twenty-four hours straight."

Slick pulsed around his cock as my hazy mind painted a picture of that. I gulped hard when the fingers buried in my ass scissored, stretching me open for the return of Knox's tongue.

With no other option than to take those slow, deep licks and let my climax come and go in lazy waves, I lay on top of Gage like a beached jellyfish. As time stretched out like warm taffy, his deep, alpha purring combined with the scent of sex and the feel of a rough tongue inside me—all of it conspiring to send

me into the serene fugue state that signaled the
end of my first peak.

SIXTY-TWO

Tony

I'D PREPPED FOR Jez's heat in several ways, not all of which had involved a butt plug and copious amounts of lube. That didn't mean I'd truly understood what I was getting into.

At least I'd been right about one thing—seeing a pack of alphas completely off the leash was hot as hell. It was so different now than it had been when Gage and I rescued Heath and Jez from the silos.

Even at his worst, I hadn't exactly been *scared* of Heath when he was in that awful, chemically induced rut. But I'd been scared shit-less of *other* things. Like, y'know, vengeful mob goons with guns.

Worse, seeing Heath mated to Jez—seeing how wrapped up they were in each other, and how possessive they were acting—had convinced me that there was no future for me and Heath.

I sort of wished I could go back in time and reassure Past Tony that things would work out way better than I could have dreamed. I could also have used the chance to warn myself that letting an alpha force prostate orgasms out of me until I fainted from exhaustion—while super-hot at the time—did result in a killer headache afterward.

And, erm… some other interesting aches, as well.

That part had happened on day two, after which I'd woken up naked in my own bedroom to find Gage camped out nearby in a chair.

"Good morning. Did you have fun?" he asked wryly.

Despite my best efforts, I immediately flashed back to the feeling of choking on his cock while helplessly pumping out what had felt like gallons of jizz, my ass stretched around an alpha knot that was probably classified as a dangerous weapon in several jurisdictions. My dick gave an exhausted twitch of interest, only to remember how hard it had been working for the past two days and give up in defeat a moment later.

"Yes," I said meekly.

Gage sighed, and pressed electrolytes and a ham sandwich on me, pinning me with a meaningful gaze until I finished them.

"Good boy," he told me when I was done. "Now, take a hot shower, pop some aspirin, and get at least eight hours of sleep before you come back to the nest. Oh, and maybe hold off on the butt sex for a while.'

"But I *like* butt sex," I protested.

"Yeah, we noticed," he said. "Shower. Drugs. Sleep. See you in a few hours, cub."

Before I could whine about it anymore, he leaned over and tongue-kissed me like he was attempting to diagnose tonsilitis by feel alone. A large hand wrapped around my overworked cock, squeezing and milking it until I whimpered into the mouth covering mine.

Then he was gone, leaving me lying on my oversized bed with the ceiling spinning lazy circles overhead.

"Fuck," I said hoarsely, and promptly fell asleep for ten hours straight.

After a belated shower and some belated pain relievers, I shrugged into a bathrobe and stumbled down to the kitchen, where I made whatever you called a meal that felt like breakfast but was happening at four-thirty p.m.

Fed, bathed, and rested, I grabbed a couple of poppers and a fresh bottle of lube from my stash, stuffing everything into the robe's oversized pockets. Nat might have been blushing beet-red during the conversation we'd had over video a few days previously, but his suggestions for how to cope as a beta male in a heat nest with a pack of horny alphas had been spot-on so far.

Well... except for the 'passing out from coming too much' thing. He hadn't mentioned that possibility.

The sound of Jez's rhythmic, high-pitched cries greeted me as I approached the nest. The door was open, which was just as well since she didn't sound like she was in any condition to open it and invite me in.

Working on the assumption that I had a standing invitation as long as her heat lasted, I sidled inside and found her on hands and knees, getting plowed into the cushions by

Heath while Knox held her by the hair and rubbed the tip of his dripping dick over her face and lips.

It was still… *weird,* watching a woman getting fucked right in front of me. And that was before you factored in the part where the woman in question was Jez, and one of the guys doing to fucking was my boyfriend as well as hers.

But it was also affecting, in a way that heterosexual porn hadn't been when I was a kid and still figuring myself out.

"You doin' okay, cub?" Gage asked. "Did you have a good sleep?"

He was sprawled in his customary spot at one end of the couch, lazily stroking his big cock with one hand as he watched the show. My dick immediately started to swell and throb as I thought of all the other things he could be doing with that impressive erection.

"Yeah, I'm good," I said past a dry throat. "I could help you out with that, you know."

From the other side of the room, Heath let out a feral roar; joined a moment later by Jez's ear-piercing shriek of release. Knox started to purr, still teasing her lips with his tip, even as her eyelids grew heavy.

Gage let go of himself, his heavy cock settling on his stomach. "Nah, I'm good for now. C'mere."

He patted the sofa and urged me to lie down on my side. I let him position me the way he wanted, and lay pliant as he untied the loose knot holding my robe closed. Once he'd flicked it open, exposing me, he settled onto the floor with a grunt of effort.

I wondered if Gage had carried me to my room this morning. It was easy to forget that a team of surgeons had pieced his body back together like a jigsaw puzzle only a few weeks ago. He wasn't using his cane much anymore, but he still walked with a limp, and he still had to be careful getting up and down from the floor.

All worries about Gage's health vanished from my head when he shuffled around to face my hips and took me in hand again. Following his commanding tug, I wriggled forward until my dick jutted in his face. Warm heat engulfed my length as he wrapped his lips around me and sucked.

My toes curled. An undignified noise of desperation choked its way free of my throat. Heat pooled in my gut, pulsing in time with the gentle suction on my cock. Gage worked me steadily until my muscles began to shake with warning… and then he stopped.

I groaned in disappointment, but managed to swallow the pathetic complaints that tried to escape. I knew Gage, and we were way too early on the game for me to show that kind of weakness. Doing my best to pretend that I wasn't hanging by a thread, I casually pillowed my head on one bent arm.

"So, has Knox bitten Jez yet?" I asked, striving to keep my tone conversational.

"Not yet," Gage said, giving my cock the lightest stroke with a circled thumb and forefinger.

Gooseflesh erupted down my back.

"Really?" I managed. "I figured he wouldn't be able to keep his teeth away from her neck."

Gage shrugged and swiped a thumb over the head of my cock, smearing pre-come around. "They fucked earlier today, while you were sleeping. Dunno what he's waiting for, but whatever it is, it probably makes perfect sense inside his head."

As though we'd summoned him by talking about him, Knox appeared and crawled onto the sofa behind me. A moment later, I was wrapped up in strong arms and legs, barely able to move an inch.

"She hasn't begged for it yet," he mumbled against the nape of my neck, drawing a shiver from me.

I'd learned yesterday that Knox was what you might call an *aggressive snuggler*. His hard cock rested between my ass cheeks, our skin separated only by the fabric of my bathrobe. It was no surprise when he began to go limp a few moments later, though—and I didn't take it personally.

Even when he was more than halfway consumed by a rut, it didn't magically make him less asexual. His connection with Jez was something different—and maybe it wasn't one-hundred-percent caused by their scent match, but the scent match was definitely a contributing factor now that they actually liked each other.

Jez got the benefit of Knox's newly discovered sexual side, but I got his demi-romantic side. Which included, at the moment, cuddling that was less like spooning and more like organic bondage. Or like being the loser in an Olympic wrestling match.

That was fine. Better than fine, really—since Heath was more than capable of destroying my ass without any help from the others.

It was even more awesome when Gage took advantage of my restraint to start edging me again. Beads of sweat popped into existence on my forehead as the pleasure he was administering crested and ebbed, higher each time.

Any attempt to wriggle or buck my hips only resulted in Knox wrapping me up tighter and growling a playful warning in my ear. I knew for a fact that the man only had two arms and two legs, but the overall effect felt like being sensually restrained by an overly friendly octopus.

I'd just decided that maybe the hentai freaks were onto something when Knox's teeth closed over my left trapezius muscle. He bit down lightly, sending lightning bolts up and down my spine. I yelped and came hard, spurting come all over Gage's face since he'd just pulled away from sucking me.

The alpha laughed and wiped spunk off his cheek. "Damnit, Knox, why'd you have to go and do that? I coulda kept him riding the edge for another hour, at least."

Knox let out another low growl, the sound vibrating against the skin he still held between his teeth. After a moment, the sound modulated to a contented purr, and the iron grip of his arms and legs loosened into something tender.

I was still seeing stars after blowing my load so hard that I was pretty sure it had taken a few brain cells with it. But there was no mistaking the stickiness on Gage's fingers as he brushed them against my lips. Floating on a cloud of endorphins, I opened for him and dutifully licked away my own mess. The salty-bitter taste clung to my tastebuds.

Gage leaned forward and kissed my forehead.

"You look gorgeous like that, cub," he said. "I'm going to go wash up, and then cuddle Jez for a bit, okay?"

"Kay," I said dreamily, Knox's purr combining with post-orgasmic sleepiness to close my heavy eyelids. Safe in the pack leader's embrace, I let the warmth of the nest draw me down into darkness.

———◆———

When I woke up, the scent of whiskey and oak proclaimed that Heath had replaced Knox on the couch behind me. His chapped lips teased the side of my neck, and then he licked over the bruise Knox had left. From across the room, soft cries and garbled words rose and fell in my ears. I opened my eyes to find Gage using the front of the couch as a backrest.

"Oh, god!" Jez sobbed, clawing at the cushions beneath her as Knox rode her hard from behind. "I need… I need… oh, *god*! P-please… please bite me! *Please*!"

Gage craned around as I stirred, meeting my eyes in the nest's warm light. "Good, you're awake. Sounds like we've reached the begging part of the program. I'm guessing a mating bite isn't going to be far behind."

As though to second the sentiment, Heath nipped the same spot Knox had bitten earlier. His big cock rubbed insistently against my ass. I moaned, my dick twitching to life, even as Knox leaned forward, covering Jez's body with his much larger one.

SIXTY-THREE

Jez

EVERYTHING HAD BEEN a hazy swirl of orgasms, darkness, and sweltering heat for what felt like days now. Had it been days? My body ached enough for it to have been days.

I'd received more than I ever could have asked for. My pleasure, without limits. My mates' pleasure. Safety and comfort. Yet, none of it scratched the final itch that had been festering steadily beneath my skin.

Some tiny, lingering fragment of my past whispered that I shouldn't ask for the one thing I still needed. It murmured in my ear that I didn't deserve my final mate... the mate I'd tried to kill. It snickered and sneered at my desire for Knox's bite, trying to tell me that if I begged him to mate me, he'd get up and leave the nest in disgust.

For days, I'd resisted asking, even as my need for him grew. Instead, I let myself melt beneath the thrust of his cock and the sound of his growl. If I was allowed that much of him, I would soak it up without risking the rejection that part of me believed would come as soon as I dared to demand more.

That had worked, for a while.

Inside my mind, Heath was heat and passion. Gage was protective care, insulated from my madness by the dampener shot he'd taken.

Tony wasn't part of my bond, but I imagined him as a bright spot of sunshine, making my mates feel good when I couldn't.

Now, something inside me sensed that time was growing short. The idea that my heat might end without experiencing the feeling of Knox's teeth piercing my flesh brought on increasing panic, and I couldn't hold back the words that had wanted to escape all along.

"Oh, god!" I sobbed, clawing at the cushions beneath me as Knox pounded into me from behind. "I need… I need… oh, *god!* P-please… please bite me! *Please!*"

My panic crested, dreading the prospect that he might pull out of my body altogether. But instead, the pack alpha leaned forward, draping his heavy frame over mine like a blanket. His growl settled into a contented purr, and my fears eased.

"About time," he rumbled.

A strong arm wrapped around my chest, preventing me from collapsing into a heap beneath the combined weight of his body and my relief. I sagged in his grip, rolling my head to the side since I couldn't exactly tape a sign to my neck saying *'Bite Here Now.'*

Lips played over the scarred marks left by Heath and Gage's teeth in my mating gland. I shuddered and moaned, my internal muscles milking Knox's cock with all the strength my exhausted body possessed. Hot breath exploded against my sensitive skin, and a rough thrust sent sparks exploding across my nerves.

Knox took the juncture of my neck and shoulder between his teeth, teasing my gland with enough pressure to drive me crazy, but not enough to break the skin as his hips pistoned into me. My wavering cry grew into a hoarse scream as my body short-circuited, ricocheting back and forth between one sensation and the other.

The stretch and friction of Knox's big cock slapping into me won out momentarily, drawing an out-of-control, jerking climax from me. And *that* was when Knox bit down, the bastard. His teeth plunged through the thin barrier of my skin; the pain of the bite lost beneath my orgasm.

My blood flowed into his mouth. His saliva flowed into my wound. He'd been *salivating* for the taste of my flesh, and the realization drew a second shuddering peak from me. My mouth was still open to scream, but there was no sound in my ears beyond a distant, high-pitched buzzing. Had I screamed myself hoarse? Or had my hearing fled along with the rest of my senses that weren't devoted to experiencing pleasure?

The two of us collapsed to the cushion-covered floor. I was aware of my passage clamping around the growing swell of his knot, just like I was aware that his weight on me should have been suffocating, but wasn't. Both sensations were lost beneath the feel of a third presence opening up in my mind.

Heath had always been sharp edges, harsh angles, and fiery passion. Gage was like a golden retriever most of the time, only becoming a werewolf when danger threatened. By contrast, Knox was quicksilver suspended in liquid nitrogen.

His presence burned with intensity in a way that I would never have guessed from his usual calm demeanor. A thousand thoughts flitted through his mind like a school of gleaming fish, but his cool focus made sure every single one of them was directed in service to whatever he was doing at the time. Whether he was taking me apart in the heat nest or playing three-dimensional chess with an organized crime kingpin, no part of him was distracted.

As his presence wove through the bond like shiny silver thread, I felt the rest of us slide together into a smooth, cohesive whole. Passion, loyalty, and stubbornness—all of it bound into a single, functional unit by the smooth embrace of Knox's cool logic.

"I love you," I sobbed, not directing it at any one person... just the room as a whole.

Instantly, that love was reflected back to me, multiplied a hundredfold. I was swimming in it, drowning in it, breathing it in until my body stopped relying on air and started living on adoration.

"We love you, too," Tony said unsteadily, his steadfast friendship weaving seamlessly into the new tapestry of my life, even if he didn't live inside my consciousness like the others.

"I don't deserve this," I whimpered, my voice wavering dangerously.

"Kitten, *everyone* deserves love," Gage said, his warmth swelling to the forefront of the bond.

"Goddamn it, Gage," Tony said, not sounding any better off than I felt. "Don't make me cry while I've got Heath's knot up my ass. It's undignified."

Knox's quicksilver presence shimmered, amusement breaking through the cool façade. A moment later, he was chuckling — his forehead pressed to my nape as laughter rippled outward through the bond. Gage was the next to break, leaning his head back and guffawing. Heath followed, his stifled snorts muffled in Tony's hair.

The bubbly feeling of joy flowed over me until I was half-laughing, half-crying.

Tony made a disgruntled noise as merriment echoed through the nest.

"Glad *someone's* getting amusement value out of this," he muttered in a sour tone.

The laughter rose higher, echoing through the bond like bells ringing.

SIXTY-FOUR

Tony

TWO WEEKS AFTER Knox finally mated Jez, my new pack sat at a giant table in a trendy Michelin-star restaurant in St. Louis, breaking bread with my old pack.

Not that I had any real claim on the Price pack. They'd taken me in and sheltered me five years ago, back when I'd been a desperate, emotionally damaged teenager. For them, it had probably been a normal Tuesday. For me, it was the first time I'd seen people treating other people like a real family.

Zalen Price, Byron Harper, Emiel Hamilton, Luca Doyle, Nat Bell, and Mia Dimitriadis had welcomed me back to the city of my birth with open arms. The owners of Nat and Mia's former restaurant had closed the place down for the evening, turning St. Louis's hottest eatery into a one-night-only private venue for us.

In addition to the main pack, Byron's nononsense adoptive grandmother Bea had showed up, and nearly made me start bawling on the spot by telling me how proud she was of me. It was Bea who'd hidden me away from my abusive stepfather—and the juvenile authorities—when staying at my house had become too horrible to bear. The old alpha matriarch looked the same as she had back then—stoop-shouldered and indomitable, with frown lines and smile lines etched into her craggy face in equal measure.

She pointed a forkful of pasta at Jez, who was sitting across from her and looking generally overwhelmed by the sheer number of people talking and laughing.

"You're carrying pups," Bea said, completely unfiltered as always. "I can smell it on you. Have you taken a pregnancy test yet?"

"Bea!" Byron yelped, his gray eyes going wide.

The table went abruptly quiet. Jez lifted a hand to her belly — a subconscious gesture she'd been making more and more often over the past few days.

"Not yet," she said softly. "It's too soon for a test to work. Do you really think I am, though?"

Bea gave a decisive nod. "Oh, yes. It'll be twins, I expect."

Jez's cheeks pinked, but her expression was pleased as her eyes darted first to Gage, then Heath, and finally Knox.

As though the mention of kids had summoned them, three of Mia and Luca's brood came flying into the dining room from the back, where the owner Shaniqua and some of her staff had been keeping them entertained.

"I may have to pick your brains when it comes to childcare," I said wryly, grabbing the little girl who launched herself into my lap and steadying her in place.

"Hide and seek," Emiel said, nodding wisely. "Lots of it. Except instead of hiding in the house, you slip outside and take a walk for twenty minutes while they run around looking for you."

All three children glared at him in outrage.

"I knew it!" crowed one of the older boys.

"Snitch," Luca said. "Now we're going to have to find an entirely new way to cheat."

Three childish voices rose in outrage, as I tried not to give in to laughter.

"Have you decided on a place to move yet?" Zalen asked, addressing Knox—pack leader to pack leader.

Knox made an affirmative noise and set down his cutlery. "We're leaning toward an area outside of Lisbon. I have an acquaintance who keeps a villa there in addition to his pack's main home in New York, and he speaks highly of the place."

"Lisbon," Byron echoed. "That's Portugal, right?"

"It is," Knox confirmed.

Byron met my gaze. "That's quite a move."

I shrugged. "Yeah. New language; new customs. But I think we can all use a change after everything that's happened. Besides, we'll visit the States at least a couple times a year, if not more. And video calls still work from Europe—I checked."

Mia chimed in. "If it's anything like Spain, I bet it's gorgeous. I did a two-week exchange program to Madrid when I was in high school, and I loved it there."

"It's a slower pace of life than what I'm used to," Knox admitted. "That's for sure."

"You say it like that's a bad thing," Gage muttered around a mouthful of lobster.

Heath snorted and tipped his head in Knox's direction. "We're taking bets on how long he holds out before he's starting a new business empire on the Iberian Peninsula."

"Ha, ha," Knox said. "Very funny."

<hr>

After the meal, Nat joined me outside for some air while the others were busy exchanging contact information in the dining room.

"How are you doing, Tony?" he asked. "How are you *really* doing, I mean?"

I paused and blew out a slow breath, letting the question settle over me for a moment.

"I'm… good. Really good. It's been a lot, though."

Nat settled back against the brick wall of the restaurant, crossing his arms as he regarded me. "You're okay with the others having a mating bond, when you're not a part of it?"

And that was… *direct*. Apparently, he'd been spending too much time around Bea lately.

"Yeah," I told him truthfully. "I am. Though I won't deny that it can be a bit freaky sometimes."

"Oh, yeah. The silent conversations, am I right?" Nat agreed, nodding his head in understanding. "Anyway, the reason I ask is to make sure you know about the hormone thing. For heats."

I blinked at him. "The… what?"

"The *hormone* thing," he repeated unhelpfully. "You have to get them through, erm… creative means. But betas can get in on the edges of a mating bond by taking omega hormones in the run-up to a heat, and then being bitten in by the alphas. I've done it a couple of times, and it can be… well… pretty intense, actually. But it fades after a few days, since betas don't have a mating gland to regulate the connection."

I blinked at him some more.

"Oh," I said eventually.

"I figured you should at least know about it," Nat said with a shrug. "I don't get the impression that it's widely discussed."

"I'd have to think about it," I said, after another long pause. "I'm not sure I've got room inside my skull for any additional layers of crazy, beyond what's already baked in."

Nat snorted, ducking his face to hide his smile. "Fair. If you ever want more info, I can link you to some forums and other resources. Nothing scientifically published, unfortunately—but for what it's worth, it doesn't seem to have done me any harm so far."

"Good to know," I replied, filing that away as something to think about later. Possibly *much* later.

I loved my new pack with every fiber of my being—but they were also a bunch of psychologically twisted-up bastards. For now, I was more comfortable having them inside me in a physical way, as opposed to a psychic way.

Still, it was nice to have options. Maybe someday, I'd feel differently about the idea.

———◆———

It was getting late by the time all the goodbyes had been said, and the high-end leftovers boxed up for storage in our hotel suite's refrigerator.

The stretch limo Knox had hired for the night was beyond ostentatious, but I was tired enough and stuffed enough that it didn't even bother me anymore. Once we'd all piled inside and left Soulard, bound for the Ritz-Carlton in Clayton, Knox leaned forward and took Jez's hands in his.

"I've arranged a surprise for you, back at the hotel," he said, looking into her eyes.

A furrow appeared between her eyebrows. "A surprise? Is that why you were texting back and forth like crazy while we were waiting for the car to pull around?"

"It was," he admitted. "Do you trust me?"

I watched with interest as all four of my packmates did the silent telepathy thing for several seconds.

"You know I do," Jez said softly.

Knox nodded. "Thank you. In that case, your surprise will be waiting for us in the hotel suite."

Despite my best efforts, I ended up fidgeting almost as much as Jez for the remainder of the trip. Meanwhile, the alphas looked positively smug. Once we arrived, we carried our plastic bags full of Styrofoam food containers to the elevator bank, and took a car up to the insanely expensive set of rooms, which I'd been informed wasn't technically a penthouse suite.

Knox led the way down the hall to the end, swiping his keycard and opening the door. Gage took Jez's leftover food and ushered her forward, while Knox stood to one side to let her pass. Consumed with curiosity, I hovered behind Jez's shoulder with Heath standing next to me, both of us peering past her into the room.

Inside, a careworn middle-aged woman with dark blond hair going gray leapt up from the comfortable sofa in the sitting area as though she'd been propelled from a Jack-in-the-box.

Jez gasped and froze in place. I was sure that if Gage hadn't taken the plastic bag of food from her hands earlier, she would have dropped it on the floor in shock.

"Jezzie?" the woman asked in a wavering voice. "Baby? Is it really you?"

Jez's breath hitched — almost a sob.

"*Mom*?" she said, her voice shedding a decade or more in the space of a single breath.

SIXTY-FIVE

Jez

THIS… COULDN'T BE. I was looking at my mother, but through the frosted glass of eight years' passage of time. Her lank, dark blond hair, always swept back in a bun or a braid, was now cut to bob length and peppered with silver. She was thinner than I remembered, deep lines of stress and worry cutting across her brow and cheeks.

"*Mom?*" My voice sounded high-pitched and unsteady, like a child's.

Like a thirteen-year-old girl's.

"Oh, Jezzie," she said, the words riding on the back of a jagged breath. "You're here. You're actually *here.*"

We both moved at the same time, staggering toward each other like two people caught in an earthquake. Then we crashed into each other, and bony arms wrapped around me with the strength of a mother's love.

I wrapped her up in turn, hating how hollow and birdlike her jutting bones felt.

"*Mom…*" I choked, since that was apparently the only word I still knew.

Her fingers combed through my hair, the movements nearly frantic. Through the bond, three presences hovered as though trying not to intrude; alpha protective emotions held tightly in check.

"I never stopped looking for you, baby. I swear I didn't!" My mom buried her face in my neck. "But there were no leads... it was like you'd disappeared from the face of the earth! I talked to the police... tried to hire a private investigator —"

"It's all right, Mom," I interrupted, but she shook her head sharply. The tears on her cheeks matched the tears on my own.

"No," she said. "It's *not* all right. *He* found out what I was doing. Kept me trapped in the house for weeks; wouldn't let me near a phone or a computer. He even smashed the TV so I couldn't watch the news."

There was no need to ask who 'he' was. I squeezed her tighter.

"I would have come back home," I whispered. "I wanted to, but I couldn't." *Not while my father was there.* The final part went unsaid, but it echoed still between us, deafening.

How had she gotten away from him, even so many years later? Had she managed to run? To get a divorce?

"Are you and he still —" I began, hesitant.

"He's dead," she said, the words dropping like boulders. "An accident. He was drunk. He fell down the stairs."

I jerked backwards, my hands on her shoulders to steady both of us. The sudden suspicion in my own mind echoed back and forth with a similar suspicion from my bondmates.

"He... fell?" I echoed cautiously, scanning my mother's face.

Her expression hardened in a way that was completely foreign to my memories of her—the righteous, unyielding planes and angles of a monument to Lady Justice.

"Yes," she said, her tone absolutely flat. "An accident. He fell down the stairs."

Inside the doorway, Gage let out a low whistle.

"Guess the apple don't fall far from the tree," he said under his breath.

"I got his money, eventually," my mother went on, still stony-faced. "I've been searching for you ever since. For seven years and four months, I looked everywhere I could think of. Hired people, tried to get the news channels interested, lobbied every politician I could find."

Her shoulders slumped beneath my hands.

"And I got nowhere, until a lawyer contacted me a few days ago and gave me Mr. Knockley's number."

My eyes flew to Knox.

"I've had people searching since we discussed the matter, before your last heat," he said. "It took a little longer than I would have liked—sorry about that."

"I changed back to my maiden name," my mother said. "That probably made it harder."

It was so much to take in—but there were other questions I needed to ask. "What about Jackson and Jonathan?"

My older brothers, who'd been away when the whole thing kicked off. Jackson, in the army, and Jonathan at college.

My mother nodded quickly, wiping at the tear tracks on her cheeks. "They're both fine. Our relationship has been… strained… since you were taken. But they'll want to see you. I held off on telling them about this trip, because I had to make sure first." A look of exhaustion swept over her. "There have been, well, some false alarms over the years. I'd see someone from behind, or from a distance, and for a moment I'd be so sure it was you."

My heart ached at the idea of my mom rushing toward a stranger in the middle of a crowd, only to find out it wasn't me. I'd spent so much time trying to survive, trying to manufacture some kind of meaning for my own life, that I hadn't thought much about what the last eight years must have been like for the rest of my family.

"I want to see them, too," I assured her.

I hadn't even begun to truly wrap my brain around the idea of my father being gone. Much less the idea of seeing my brothers after so long. But I also had news to share, after eight years apart.

"I don't know how much Knox told you about us," I began.

"Nothing about the pack," he said. "Just that you were with us and safe."

I nodded, taking a deep breath and stepping back to include the others. "I'm mated now, Mom. You already know Knox, or at least, you've spoken with him. This is Heath. This is

Gage. And this is Tony, my best friend in the entire world, who is also in our pack."

The others approached. Heath stuck his hand out as though he wasn't sure what the proper greeting was for a long-lost mother-in-law, but my mom scoffed at him and drew him into a hug instead. From him, she went on to Gage, who wrapped her up until she practically disappeared beneath his bulk—and then to Tony, who was doing a bad job of hiding tears.

"Hi," he told her unsteadily, "Nice to meet you. And if you're willing to take on an honorary kid, I'm very much in the market for a parent who doesn't suck."

My mother let out a little noise that was half-laugh, half-sob. "Hi, Tony. I'm not so sure how well I qualify for that. But if you're part of Jezzie's family, you're stuck with me now, too."

Tony pulled back and gave her a watery smile. "Trust me on this part—you qualify. Welcome to the pack."

She smiled back, before turning to Knox. "*You*. Come here."

Knox submitted to a hug, and then to letting my mom take his face in her hands and tug him down until she could press a kiss to his forehead.

"Thank you," she said simply.

He gathered her hands in his and straightened, smiling down at her from his ten-inch advantage in height. "You're welcome."

The six of us talked long into the night, while Gage plied my mom with Michelin-star leftovers.

Our plans, our hopes, our dreams… talk of the future, now that the darkness of the past no longer ruled our lives. There were still aspects of that past I wasn't willing to tell her about—like how I'd first met Knox, for one thing. Maybe one day, I'd be ready to share that.

For now, though, it didn't matter.

We were together.

Safe.

Loved.

"How would you feel about the idea of living overseas?" Gage asked, his elbows resting loosely on his knees as he leaned toward my mother. "Someplace like, for instance, Portugal?"

Mom blinked. "I… don't speak Portuguese."

"Neither do we," Heath muttered wryly.

The conversation continued on a hundred different subjects—years' worth of pent-up words, finally freed. Eventually, exhaustion set in—for Mom and me, at least.

"You could stay here with us tonight," I said. "Right, Knox?"

He smiled. "She has the suite next door. If you two would rather have some privacy, that is."

Mom raised an eyebrow. "Your new pack is *rich*-rich, baby. I'm pretty sure the nightly rates at this hotel are about the same as our mortgage used to be."

"Only the best for our mother-in-law," Gage said magnanimously.

My mother smiled at him, before turning the expression on me. "I can't say I'm in a hurry to let you out of my sight, now that I've finally got you back, baby. Want to come camp out with me for the night? It'll be like old times—there's even a fireplace in the room."

Immediately, I was swept back to memories of campfires in the forest—wrapping up with blankets and singing at the top of our voices.

"Does room service do hot cocoa?" I asked.

"Almost certainly," Knox said.

Mom shot me a conspiratorial look. "How about s'mores?"

"That, I'm less sure of," Knox replied, visibly amused.

"There's a bit of chocolate lava cake left in one of the restaurant bags," Gage offered.

My mother and I shared a look.

"Close enough," I said.

✦

Later, we sat leaning together on the rug in front of the crackling fireplace with full bellies and overflowing hearts. Mom had dragged the expensive comforter off of the queen-sized bed and wrapped it around both our shoulders, even though the room was a comfortable seventy-two degrees.

I found my hand wandering once more to my belly, as it had been doing often over the past couple of weeks. My mother glanced down and nudged my shoulder with hers.

"Too much cake?" she asked gently.

I shook my head. "No, it's..." I trailed off, unable to stop a wistful smile from curving my lips. "My heat was two weeks ago. I haven't taken a test yet, but... I think I'm pregnant. An old alpha grandma told me tonight that it would be twins."

My mom's breath caught. "You're going to have twins?" Her voice sounded faint, but she pulled me tight against her side. "Oh, *Jezzie*...!"

"I'm terrified," I admitted. "And also so excited that I can barely think about anything else. What business have I got raising kids? But, this pack—"

"Your pack," my mother said, taking my face gently in her hands, "is *amazing*." She paused, a smile like the sun coming up sliding over her careworn features. "And, you know—I did pretty well in Spanish class, back when I was in high school."

"Is that right?" I asked, an answering grin tugging at my lips.

"Mm-hmm," she confirmed. "So, I bet I could learn Portuguese, too... if I put my mind to it."

EPILOGUE

Jez

ELEVEN MONTHS AFTER Knox arranged the reunion with my mother in St. Louis, we were on the other side of an ocean—wandering along a beautiful walking trail in a quaint southern European town outside of Lisbon.

Late afternoon sun painted everything gold. To my right, Tony kept pace while wheeling our baby girls in a double stroller. To my left, Emma Hope—one of our neighbors—strode effortlessly along the paved path in a pair of stylish four-inch heels. Her designer sunglasses glinted in the slanting light.

Emma, a former fashion model, was one of two omegas mated to the Rosencranz pack, who lived part-time in a mansion down the road from ours. Gabriel Rosencranz—Knox's acquaintance who had originally suggested Portugal as a good place to retire—was allegedly even richer than Knox himself. His pack jet-setted back and forth between New York and the village of Reguengo Grande several times a year with their three children. The triplets, two girls and a boy, ran in and out of the trees ahead of us, shouting excitedly.

"I d-dread to think how difficult it's going to be keeping those three corralled during their teenage years," Emma said wryly, a faint stutter marring her fancy English accent.

I chuckled, my gaze darting to my two beautiful babies as they cooed and waved their tiny fists in the stroller. "Believe me, I'm not taking things for granted. We may not be getting much sleep these days, but I have no doubt that changing diapers and filling bottles is a lot easier than navigating adolescent dating drama and social media restrictions."

Emma let out an amused snort at odds with her polished appearance. "Oh, you have no idea."

Behind us, my mother laughed loudly at something her companion, an androgynous, dark-skinned alpha named Onyx, had said to her. I couldn't help smiling as I glanced back at the pair trailing us. Not only had Mom moved here with us; she'd also made good on her promise to learn Portuguese faster than any of us. Having her here had been invaluable when it came to making me feel less overwhelmed and incompetent as a parent.

She looked so much better now than when I'd first seen her again, waiting for us in our St. Louis hotel room. Not only physically healthier, with her gaunt face and body filled out thanks to plenty of good food, sunshine, and gentle exercise — but also happier.

We all were.

She saw me looking and winked at me before turning back to her conversational partner. Emma, who'd followed my gaze, smiled at the pair as well.

"Have you decided to stay here permanently, then?" Emma asked. "It's such a beautiful place… I just can't quite seem to let go of New York. Not yet, anyway."

"We're planning on staying for the next few years, at least," I said. "It might not be forever, but I do like the idea of putting down roots in a place that doesn't have a bunch of baggage attached."

Emma gave a thoughtful nod. "Oh, I understand completely. That's exactly how Gabriel and I feel about London."

"I think it helps that we don't own a successful modelling agency back in the States, like you do," Tony joked.

"There is something to be said for that." Emma adjusted the rolled cuffs of her fashionable chiffon blouse. "I'm not ready to give up the rat race quite yet, but I c-could see myself changing my mind in a few more years."

It had taken me the better part of a year to make the transition from scrabbling for every crumb of food and constantly scanning for danger, to living with no worries beyond interior decorating choices and the occasional bout of baby colic. I wasn't sure if that meant I could relate to what she was saying, or if it just meant I needed more therapy.

"I'm becoming a big fan of being a rich man's kept omega," I told her, because that much was certainly true.

"Seconded," Tony said. "I mean, except for not being an omega, obviously."

The sound of heavy footsteps closing fast from behind us had me turning sharply as old instincts surged to the fore. Onyx had whirled as well, placing their body protectively between our group and the person approaching.

"It's okay," I said quickly, feeling a familiar presence through the mating bond. "It's Heath."

Onyx relaxed as a tall, red-haired figure jogged up to us.

"Out for an afternoon jog, mate?" they asked dryly, their Australian accent broadening the vowels. "Sounds like you could use a bit more cardio than you're getting these days."

Heath leaned over and waved a hand, getting his breath back. "Yeah, yeah. Very funny, Crocodile Dundee." He straightened, turning his attention to Tony and me. "Come back to the house. There's news about the sentencing."

———————◆———————

After some quick goodbyes to Emma and Onyx, the four of us returned home as fast as a group of people wheeling a pair of two-month-olds could manage.

"How long are they going to prison for?" Tony asked, power-walking behind the stroller. "Did they say yet?"

"Dunno," Heath replied grimly. "Gage is recording the news feed. I came to get you as soon as we heard they were about to hand down the sentences. I expect Knox is on the phone with his lawyers as we speak."

We'd been waiting on federal sentencing in the Vozzina case for what felt like ages. The case itself dragged on for months. But Paolo testifying against them, combined with all the evidence Knox's lawyers had dug up, meant that a guilty verdict had been more or less a foregone conclusion.

The sentencing… not so much.

Tony and I went back and forth between following the trial obsessively and trying to pretend it didn't exist. Even Knox had been taken aback by the sheer *scope* of what Lorenzo Vozzina had been doing.

There was no real way to find out if I'd been in Vozzina's pipeline or someone else's when I'd been trafficked as a kid. Knox hadn't let any of our names get dragged into the trial, which meant I would probably never know for sure. But as more and more information came out, it seemed increasingly likely. The Vozzina pack's victims didn't number in the dozens, or even the hundreds.

They numbered in the *thousands*.

Canada… Mexico… Central and South America… Africa… kidnapped omegas came into the country by boat, by semi, and by train. Some were sold locally. Some were sold to rich perverts overseas, in Asia and the Middle East. Many simply seemed to disappear without a trace.

The numbers—the unbelievable *scale* of suffering—was mind-boggling.

As predicted, Knox was talking on his cell phone when we piled into the entryway. He gestured us toward the media room with a serious expression, but added a reassuring thumbs-up as we passed.

In the stroller, Julia began to cry fitfully. Heath scooped her up and cradled her against his broad shoulder, patting her back soothingly. My mother lifted her sister Mariah into her arms, shushing her as she, too, began to fuss.

Gage was waiting for us inside the dark-panelled room with one wall taken up by a massive flat-screen TV. A frozen scene of a reporter standing outside an official-looking building stared out at us.

"Oh, you guys are gonna *love* this," he greeted. "Settle in and enjoy the show."

He leaned over and took Mariah from my mother, bouncing gently on his toes to quiet her. With his free hand, he tapped the trackpad on his laptop, and the scene on the TV began to play.

The reporter lifted a hand to her earpiece. *"We're outside the US Court for the Northern District of Illinois, and I've just received word that the sentencing for the co-conspirators in the high-profile Vozzina omega trafficking case is about to be handed down."*

She paused, listening through her earpiece. I bit my lower lip hard enough to hurt, my hand creeping toward Tony, who took it in his and squeezed. My mother grabbed my other hand, standing close enough that our shoulders brushed.

"On count one, trafficking of minors across state lines for the purposes of prostitution, the sentence is life in prison without parole."

My breath caught in my lungs for a second before escaping explosively.

"One count two, conspiracy to commit human trafficking, the sentence is life in prison without parole." Another pause. *"On count three, conspiracy to commit money laundering in an amount above one hundred million dollars, the sentence is fifteen years and a fine of one hundred fifty million dollars. On count four…"*

We listened, rapt, as the sentences piled up, one on top of the other. After several minutes, the reporter gave a decisive nod and lowered her hand from her ear.

"Sentences to be served consecutively, not concurrently," she finished. *"Back to you in the newsroom, Todd."*

Gage lowered the volume as the camera cut back to a man seated behind a desk, who started talking about the historic nature of the trial and the severity of the sentencing. I let go of Tony's hand and felt behind me for the couch before sinking onto it heavily. Mom followed me down, still holding my other hand.

"Well," Tony said faintly. "I guess that's that."

Movement in the doorway caught my attention. Knox braced a hand against the doorframe, a grim smile on his face.

"So it is," he agreed. A look of deep satisfaction glinted in his gaze. "I suppose someone should have warned Paolo up front that there's no federal death penalty for human trafficking."

Gage grunted. "Guess he's going to need that glandectomy after all. At least, he will if he doesn't want to be bonded to a jailbird for the next several decades."

I tried not to take satisfaction in the idea of Paolo listening in horror to the sentencing, realizing that he was about to be stuck with a miserable asshole inside his head after all.

"Maybe one of the state trials will involve a gas chamber or an electric chair," Heath said. "There are still a few other jurisdictions going after him, aren't there?"

"There are," Knox confirmed. "But as of today, the Vozzina pack is officially someone else's problem. Lorenzo and his lackeys are out of our lives forever."

A tremor shuddered through me as an invisible, crushing weight lifted from my shoulders, leaving me lightheaded. Three presences inside my head crowded closer, humming with comfort and satisfaction.

"Are you okay, baby?" my mother asked, her fingers giving mine a grounding squeeze.

I licked my lips and swallowed a couple of times, not sure if my voice was going to cooperate or not.

"I think…" I began. "I think I'm more okay than I've been in a very long time."

"I think maybe we all are," Tony agreed.

Knox's smile widened as he picked up the remote and powered the TV screen off. He moved in front of me and leaned down, pressing a kiss to the top of my head. Then he reached out to clasp Tony's shoulder, giving it a gentle shake.

"The good news is," he said, "this is just baseline levels of 'okay.' From here. it only gets better."

"Right?" Gage said, stroking Mariah's wisp of red hair with a fingertip. "I bet if we try, the eight of us can do *way* better than just being *okay*."

Mom bumped my shoulder with hers. "I'm game if you all are."

"Seconded," Tony agreed.

"Hear, hear," Heath agreed. He smiled down at Julia, rocking her in his arms. She reached up, wrapping a chubby fist in his beard.

I closed my eyes as her happy burble joined her sister's, filling the room with all the beautiful possibilities of a future filled with love, safety, and family.

SECOND EPILOGUE

Ruby — Subject 8008

THE EXERCISE AUDITORIUM in the lower levels of the Vault was as gray and depressing as always. I trudged around the perimeter in slow circles—blending in with the other hundred and fifty or so omegas in my shift, while trying not to let on how terrible I was feeling today.

The guards were always watching. A dozen or so stood in a loose circle at the center of the echoing space, staring at us impassively with tasers and truncheons at the ready. Another dozen looked down on us from the level above, armed with tranquilizer guns. Acting in a way that attracted their attention rarely ended well for anyone involved.

Once upon a time, I'd appreciated the brightness of our orange jumpsuits is such a dull and cheerless place. Now, they just hurt my eyes. Orange stood out from the background. It made us easy to see. Easy to catch if we tried to run.

Not many people tried to run.

At least, not more than once. Where would we even go?

A hand brushed mine. I flinched hard, barely able to stop myself from jerking back and whirling around to see who had touched me. *Making a scene.* Then I caught a whiff of crisp lemon and rosemary omega perfume. It was soured by loneliness and confinement, but still as familiar as my own papaya and ginger.

Del.

My sister, Delilah; kidnapped at the same time as me and brought here from our home, to be poked and prodded and experimented on by the white-coated doctors who seemed to run this place.

I risked a sideways glance, keeping my head facing straight forward. Del's curly, short-cropped brown-black hair and umber skin greeted me—a mirror of my own, even if she was several inches shorter and a couple years younger than me.

My jaw ached with the need to speak to her… to ask how she was doing and if they'd hurt her yet. But speaking during the exercise hour brought swift and certain punishment.

We walked side by side, both facing forward and not changing speed. Her hand brushed mine again, and this time, a wad of something was pressed into the loose cage of my fingers.

I didn't look. Didn't react. Just twisted and wriggled my arm, poking and shoving the wad as far up my orange sleeve as I could get it, since pockets weren't a luxury we were allowed.

With a final brush of her pinky against my skin, Del increased her pace just enough to draw away from me, disappearing into the crowd. The soft bundle of mystery burned against my forearm, as though desperate curiosity could somehow generate its own heat.

I had no idea how much of the exercise hour was left. The muscles in my legs ached, but that didn't mean much. Every other part of my body ached, too, after the last round of bone marrow injections the doctors had given me.

Eventually, we were herded back to our cells. I sent a covert glance toward the door of the cell just beyond mine, watching Del's back as she disappeared inside. The heavy door clanged closed behind her.

"Move." A hand shoved me between the shoulder blades, drawing a startled gasp from me as I stumbled forward, my own door slamming behind me. The noise echoed in my ears for a long moment before my heart rate slowed from its startled jump.

The narrow cot in the corner beckoned me like a lighthouse in stormy seas.

Lie down, it whispered. *You'll feel better if you sleep.*

It probably had a point, but there were more important things to focus on right now. Instead of giving in to the lure of the one-inch-thick plastic mattress, I limped over to the wall separating my cell from my sister's and slid down it to sit on the cold floor.

The wall was too thick to hear anything from the other side. Or, more accurately, any sound loud enough to penetrate the insulated concrete would also bring guards running. I still liked to sit here and pretend Del was doing the same on the other side. I liked the idea that we could whisper secrets to each other, even if it was a fantasy.

Angling my body away from the camera mounted at ceiling height in the corner, I pulled the mystery wad out of my sleeve and examined it.

It was a bunched-up mass of toilet paper, but the white single-ply tissue was covered in squiggles of black and gray. I straightened it out and squinted, taking in the small, messy writing crammed onto the long strip.

Paper is paper, it said. *Right? So, I managed to steal a sharpie, but I think it's about to die. Anyway…*

I settled in, still keeping the message hidden from the red eye of the camera gazing down at me.

It was typical Del—reminiscing about our childhood before we were taken, wishing we could escape. Writing things that would get her thrown in the Pit for a week if she got caught. Of course, the same thing would happen to me if I got caught reading what she'd written.

The ending felt different, though. Heavier… more immediate, somehow.

I heard some guards talking about their supply of omegas getting cut off, and how the people in charge were freaking out. What do you think it means?

By the last sentence, the sharpie had grown so faint that I could barely make out the words.

The lock on the door clanked, and I shot to my feet so fast that my muscles screamed in protest. Rushing over to the toilet, I tossed the note into the bowl and flushed—turning around just in time to look at least vaguely casual as two guards entered.

"Time for another session with Dr. Sakarov," said the one on the right. "Get a move on, Boobs."

I ignored the rude nickname, but I winced internally at the prospect of another session so soon. It had only been three days, and since yesterday, the nausea had been so bad I could barely keep water down.

Knowing there was no point in trying to resist. I walked out of the cell on shaking legs. The second guard—one I didn't recognize—made no attempt to hide the way he stared at my chest as I passed.

"Why d'you call her Boobs?" he asked, as they fell in on either side of me. "They ain't *that* big."

The first guard grunted. "It's her number. She's Subject 8008."

I could imagine the second guard's heavy brow knitting as the silence stretched.

"I don't get it," he said eventually.

"That's cuz you're an idiot," replied the first guard.

The walk to the labs felt nearly as long as the exercise hour. When we finally arrived, Dr. Sakarov was waiting, along with Dr. Hwan.

Both men were gray-haired and pudgy, smelling of soap, disinfectant, and beta-male sweat. Dr. Sakarov was several inches taller than Dr. Hwan, with a shiny bald spot on the back of his head and a mask covering his sagging jowls. All the doctors here were bad news, but being in Sakarov's vicinity always gave me a special level of cringe.

It was something about the proprietary way he handled my body, as though he'd claimed ownership, with plans to move in and redecorate.

"Put her on the table," he ordered the guards, with his raspy Russian accent.

The guards manhandled me onto the metal table and strapped my arms and legs down before retreating to the area just inside the doorway. I closed my eyes, hoping to go away inside my head before the needles came out. Sometimes that worked. Sometimes it didn't.

Today, I thought about the things Del had written. Our childhood… our home in the windy desert of southern New Mexico, with mountains looming on the horizon, clad in shades of purple and orange.

It… sort of worked.

I was aware of my blood being drawn, but it felt distant. When the bigger needles came out, it was worse—but then, Dr. Hwan said, "This Vozzina case. Are you following it?"

"Obviously," Dr. Sakarov replied in a dry tone, not stopping what he was doing to my arm.

"The sentencing came down today," Dr. Hwan went on. "The organization isn't going to recover from that. Our supply has already dried up."

My eyes flew open, landing on the readout screen where green digital readouts against a black background tracked my heart rate and blood pressure. '8008' flashed in the upper right corner, the numbers chunky and square. B-O-O-B.

I heard some guards talking about the supply of omegas getting cut off, Del had written. *And how the people in charge were freaking out.*

Dr. Sakarov grunted. "Don't talk so openly in front of the subjects."

I gritted my teeth as the needle withdrew, scraping against bone as it went.

Sakarov held up the vial of collected fluids, tilting his head as he regarded it. "Besides," he said, removing the vial from the needle and placing it inside a machine set next to my metal gurney. "I have a feeling we won't be needing any more test subjects."

He turned back to me, looming over me with his thick glasses and masked face. A gloved hand stretched out, and he rubbed a thumb over my lower lip. The latex caught on my chapped skin, dragging at it. I froze, wanting desperately to jerk away from the touch.

Knowing there was no place to go.

His head moved sideways, regarding me the same way he'd regarded the vial of my blood and bone marrow a moment before.

"You, my dear, are poised to make the members of this project very rich indeed."

I tried to stiffen my lips, pursing them together to prevent his finger from moving them. A moment later, the thumb moved away.

"Take her back to her cell," Sakarov ordered the guards. "I have what I need."

My legs didn't want to work properly as the guards unstrapped me and herded me back down the long, lonely corridors. I kept stumbling over my own feet, the hallway tilting sideways at unexpected moments.

When I finally sank down next to Del's wall in my cell, the door shutting and the lock clanking behind me, I wanted nothing more than to see my sister's face and wrap my arms around her. Instead, I pressed my forehead to the cold concrete.

I wasn't as clever as Del. I didn't have a stolen sharpie hidden in my cell, or a pencil, or anything else I could use to write. Even though I knew it was pointless, I rolled my head to the side until my ear was pressed to the wall, hoping to catch a hint of her presence.

Anything.

Was she sitting on the other side, separated from me by inches that might as well be miles?

My eyes began to burn as I drew in a shaky breath

"I don't know how, but we're going to get out of here, sis," I whispered. "We'll go someplace far away, with trees and mountains and a river, and it will just be us and a bunch of dogs and cats and chickens. Maybe horses, too. You'd like that, wouldn't you?"

I paused. A tear spilled over, rolling down my cheek.

"Wouldn't you?" My voice broke.

There was no reply.

The End

Discover Ruby's story in *Knot Your Weapon.*